Praise for THE END OF THE DAY

"Clegg delivers a thoughtful, well-observed story . . . The splendid prose and orchestrated maneuvering will keep readers turning the pages and send them back to the beginning, to read it all over again."

—*Publishers Weekly* (starred review)

"Written in lyrical, beautiful prose that makes even waking up seem like a poetic event, *The End of the Day* makes sense of the events of a single day in a compelling work of fiction."

—*Good Morning America*

"Remarkable . . . For the beautifully complex characters who populate *The End of the Day*, whom or what the truth actually sets free is richly called into question. With detail and empathy, Clegg is particularly effective at describing the subtleties of relationships. His work is political without being didactic or dogmatic . . . he illustrates the elusiveness of the American dream."

—*New York Times Book Review*

"As usual, Clegg's prose is simple and graceful, his third-person character portraits precise, but his plotting, with its intricate, keen-minded twists give his writing the cumulative effect of poetic ambiguity and mystery. Clegg's first novel was a novel of grief; this is a masterly story of an attempt at righting the misunderstandings of the past that is resonant and true to life's inherent uncertainty."

—*Boston Globe*

"A declining heiress returns home for the first time in decades, but can't remember why. Her former maid's daughter runs a taxi company in Hawaii. Her aunt is left with a baby whose parents have vanished. Leave it to Clegg to brilliantly bind these threads."
—*Entertainment Weekly*

"A mesmerizing book about family and memory and friendship and the long arc of life. I've loved every book by Bill Clegg, but *The End of the Day* might be my favorite because these characters, these quietly remarkable women, remind me of the epic lives hidden within all of us. Reading it is like studying a stained-glass window up close, each piece bright and sharply cut, but when you step back and see it as a whole you discover a large, beautiful, mysterious work of art."
—David Ebershoff, *New York Times* bestselling author of *The Danish Girl* and *The 19th Wife*

"Ambitious in scope, tender in detail, Bill Clegg's *The End of the Day* is a story that crosses boundaries of age, class, gender. Anyone who has a beating heart will find some part of themselves in this story."
—Mary Beth Keane, *New York Times* bestselling author of *Ask Again, Yes*

"Delicate, deeply observed, and deftly crafted, *The End of the Day* is a beautiful mosaic of memory, regret, and loss. A triumphant and noble novel."
—Nickolas Butler, author of *Shotgun Lovesongs* and *Little Faith*

"An exquisitely structured book of reckonings. Clegg is a fearless investigator of the past and how it, no matter how buried we believe it to be, will always rise. *The End of the Day* left me shaken."
—Peter Orner, author of *Maggie Brown & Others*

"In his utterly absorbing and socially trenchant novel, Bill Clegg's vision is both intimate and grand. He paints precise and unerring portraits of his characters and the dynamics of class that inform their lives while at the same time asking sweeping and urgent questions: What is fate? What responsibilities do we bear for the way in which our actions and our passions alter the course of one another's lives? The novel's shattering resonance emerges from its masterful construction. Clegg leads us, and his characters, toward the discovery of long-buried secrets at the same time that he shows us that the facts of a life do not always add up to the truth."

—Marisa Silver, *New York Times* bestselling author
of *Little Nothing* and *Mary Coin*

"Intricately plotted . . . measured pace, slipping smoothly from the life of one character to another and from present to past, revealing how entire lives have been marked indelibly by teenage impulses and mistakes. Though Lupita believes at one point that she is 'safe from the truth,' *The End of the Day* explains with painful clarity why, in some lives, that can never be."

—*BookPage*

"Magnetically insightful storytelling. Clegg grasps what is deeply human, from a subtle movement to the spirit in a laugh shared between friends. His diction mirrors the emotional gravity in each scene, which, combined with raw honesty, is what makes his writing so relatable. . . . Enriching and engrossing, *The End of the Day* traces the complicated web of connection in a person's life that exposes the deepest, and occasionally darkest, sense of what it means to be human. Love, friendship and the connections that bring us together are the fabric of Clegg's masterful framework of a novel with an impeccable scope and unforgettable characters."

—*USA Today*

THE END
OF THE
DAY

THE END OF THE DAY

Bill Clegg

SCOUT PRESS

New York   London   Toronto   Sydney   New Delhi

Scout Press
An Imprint of Simon & Schuster, Inc.
1230 Avenue of the Americas
New York, NY 10020

First Scout Press trade paperback edition May 2021

SCOUT PRESS and colophon are registered trademarks of Simon & Schuster, Inc.

For information about special discounts for bulk purchases, please contact Simon & Schuster Special Sales at 1-866-506-1949 or business@simonandschuster.com

The Simon & Schuster Speakers Bureau can bring authors to your live event. For more information or to book an event, contact the Simon & Schuster Speakers Bureau at 1-866-248-3049 or visit our website at www.simonspeakers.com.

Manufactured in the United States of America

10 9 8 7 6 5 4 3 2 1

Library of Congress Cataloging-in-Publication Data

Names: Clegg, Bill, author.
Title: The end of the day / Bill Clegg.
Description: First Scout Press hardcover edition. | New York : Scout Press,2020
Identifiers: LCCN 2019022567 (print) | LCCN 2019022568 (ebook) | ISBN 9781476798219 (paperback) | ISBN 9781476798226 (ebook)
Classification: LCC PS3603.L455447 | DDC 813/.6—dc23
LC record available at https://lccn.loc.gov/2019022567

ISBN 978-1-4767-9820-2
ISBN 978-1-4767-9821-9
ISBN 978-1-4767-9822-6 (ebook)

For Ivy

but what could we
do to prevent a day from ending
or a winter from finding
us how could we stop a wind
with no home

—"Fulfillment" by W.S. Merwin, from *Travels*

Part One

Dana

The tapping at the door is so faint and tentative it's easy to pretend it's not happening. The words that follow are whispered just as softly, but too audibly to ignore. *Mrs. Dana, good morning. It's after seven o'clock. The car is downstairs. Hello?*

Brisk footfalls pad away. Dana has been dressed and ready to leave for more than an hour but is not yet prepared to face Marcella who begins flipping on light switches and emptying the dishwasher every morning at six-thirty. Marcella is an excellent cook and keeps the house in order, but it galls Dana how patronizing she can be, often speaking to her like she imagines someone addressing an imbecile—crossed arms, tilted head, exaggerated care—with words that to a stranger might sound respectful, even kind, but Dana hears disdain behind every syllable.

It's time, Mrs. Dana, Marcella singsongs from behind the door, as if coaxing a child to eat vegetables. *Time to go.*

Another voice, higher-pitched and less sure, follows. *Yes, hello? Miss Goss, are you awake? Marcella's right. It is time.*

Cristina. Marcella has brought her as back-up, Dana thinks, eyeing the door as a chess player anticipates her opponent's next move.

The driver called to say he's parked outside. It's Philip. The one you like . . . not one of the old ones.

Cristina is less annoying, but she can be manipulative, too, when Marcella puts enough pressure on her. She's younger than Marcella, who's in her early sixties, though to Dana hardly looks fifty. The olive skin, she thinks. And the extra weight. Dana remembers something her grandmother told her when she was in high school: *When you get older you choose your fanny or your face—one or the other, but never both. Just look at your Aunt Lee, she looks young and adorable, for her age, but she absolutely can't wear clothes. She looks like an Irish nanny with good jewelry.*

Looking in the mirror across the room from where she sits on the bed, Dana reports joylessly, *Grandmother, today I choose my fanny.* She runs her hands across her flat stomach to remind herself why she has allowed her face to thin the way it has. She loved her Aunt Lee when she was alive, but agreed with her grandmother: size two and scary was better than size ten and adorable.

Good morning. Hello? Are you awake?

Cristina again. What Dana appreciates most about Cristina is that she doesn't exude disapproval the way Marcella does; does not presume to know what is best, nor register impatience when she refuses to finish the meals Marcella has prepared, or when she does not respond right away when called to wake up. Unlike Marcella, who lives in Washington Heights with her husband, daughter and granddaughter, Cristina has no children, no husband, and lives in a room behind the gym in the basement of Dana's townhouse. She is nearby, and more useful, though lately has frequently been called away to tend to her mother's ill health.

Cristina's mother was one of the maids in the apartment Dana grew up in on the Upper East Side. Her name was Ada and she'd come with her parents from Florida, and Mexico before that, to work for Dana's family when she was a girl. Ada had already dropped out of high school by then, but her younger sister, Lupita, was only nine, one year younger than Dana. Their mother, Maria, had been in charge of everything inside the apartment in the city as well as at Edgeweather, the estate in Connecticut that had been in her father's family since the Civil War. Maria's husband, Joe, took care of the house and grounds, and lived there year-round with Lupita, while Maria and Ada stayed in the city during the week and came up to Edgeweather with Dana's family most weekends.

Dana can still remember how ecstatic her mother was when the arrangement had been made to have the Lopez family come from Florida to work for them. She'd overheard her parents discussing it and her father finally agreeing to some kind of legal responsibility having to do with green cards that her mother had been pressing him to commit to. There hadn't been a full-time staff at Edgeweather since the Deckers, a couple who'd taken care of the place for many years, had to leave because they'd gotten too old. Dana's mother was also having a bad run with housekeepers and maids in the city at the time and the only person she trusted was Maria Lopez, the part-time maid in their house in Palm Beach. For a while it seemed that Dana's mother's entire well-being hinged on whether Dana's father could manage to deliver Maria and her family to New York. Once he had, Dana remembers hearing him tell a colleague who'd come to their apartment for drinks that not since the days when staff was shipped from Africa had anyone gone to the lengths he'd had to go to in order to employ the Mexican family his wife had become fixated on.

Miss Goss, Cristina pleads from behind the door. *You said to make sure you were out the door by seven and it's already seven-fifteen.*

Cristina is on her own now. Smart, Dana thinks with a rival's respect, imagining Marcella ten steps down the hall, motioning with her fist for Cristina to knock again.

I'm so sorry, she says, beginning to sound defeated, *but . . .*

Fine, Dana exhales, shrugging her shoulders like a teenager, as if leaving the apartment on time wasn't precisely what she'd insisted on the night before. Groaning, she pulls an old briefcase from her bed to her lap. It was a gift her father had given her the summer between her freshman and sophomore years at Bryn Mawr, the summer he'd arranged for her to work at the bank with him. The case is the darkest brown, nearly black, made by the same company in England that made her father's. The brass hardware was now dulled, but in gold her embossed initials, *D.I.G.*, marched crisp and clear and still embarrassing beneath the handle. Dana Isabel Goss. The case was ridiculous. It always had been. Boxy and manly and expensive, and save for her father's far more preferable initials, *G.R.G.*, an exact copy of the one he carried most days of his life. Dana had held hers only a few times.

As her mother had predicted, Dana didn't last long at the bank. After two and a half days on the job she withdrew three hundred dollars in cash from the trust her grandmother created, something her nineteenth birthday in March had finally allowed, walked out onto Park Avenue, and with briefcase in hand, hailed a taxi. She remembers feeling simultaneously rebellious and professional, a soon-to-be-fugitive in a tasteful blue blazer and skirt, clothing her mother had insisted on. *Wells, Connecticut*, she commanded after closing the taxi door, sounding as much like her father as she could. When the driver began to say, *Miss, I don't know* . . . she clicked open the briefcase, pulled out a handful of cash and fanned it in front of her so that he was sure to see it in the rearview mirror. This was something she was sure her father would never, ever, do. *Okay, okay, just tell me how to get there*, the driver said. Already mortified by her own theatrics, she slumped back in the seat and tried her best to explain how to drive from the city to Litchfield County.

The day was July 3, 1969, a Thursday, one of the only dates Dana remembers. Not because she'd left the bank that morning without telling her father, or even because she'd spent the first money from her trust on a ridiculously expensive taxi ride. She remembers the date because it's the one that marked the last day of what she would imprecisely call her youth, a period where her actions didn't yet have consequences, or if they had, they hadn't mattered very much. At least not to her.

Do you need my help? Cristina calls again from behind the door, louder than before, her tapping escalating to a full-blown knock. *I can help*, she offers, the manipulation creeping in, Marcella no doubt looming nearby.

Coat on, briefcase held in front of her with both hands at the bottom corners, she gets up from her bed and walks to the door. When Cristina's knocking finally stops, Dana speaks—just above a whisper, with a trace of acquiescence, as if selflessly agreeing to perform a very difficult task being asked of her. *I'm ready*, she says, and waits for the door to be opened.

Jackie

A vinyl shade slaps the window near the foot of her bed. From the basement, a slow ticking, the bang and shudder of the propane furnace. Outside, old tree limbs creak and pop above the single-story house. Robins and finches deliver the news of morning, but more loudly than usual, as if they are greeting sunlight for the very first time.

Eyes closed, cheek pressed into the foam pillow she's slept on for decades, Jackie curls onto her side toward the middle of the mattress. She rubs her feet together, circles the pillow with both arms, and burrows deeper into the familiar softness. The lingering fragrance of dryer sheets tugs her gently back across the gap between awake and asleep, where ghost sounds of crowded mornings fill her ears—cabinet doors slamming shut, young voices tangling from the kitchen, a chair squeaking along the linoleum floor. An old, low flame of duty flickers to life. Lunches to pack, report cards to sign, laundry to graduate from the washing machine to the dryer, hamburger meat to move from the freezer to the refrigerator to thaw, a blouse to iron for work. A rapid-fire volley of shouts, *Give it back! Leave me alone! I'm telling Mom!*

A crow's mad caw fouls the air. *Nawwwh! Nawwwh!* The shrill holler repeating, repeating. Jackie refuses to open her eyes, though the half-dream of facing a day busy with errands and work and children has gone. *Nawwwh! Nawwwh!* The almost-words feel like rocks thrown at her. She winces and pulls the bedding around her shoulders. The crow continues, its call bossier, more human. *Now!*, it insists. *Now! Now!*

When it finally stops, Jackie listens for the noise of her squabbling children, both of whom have long since grown up and moved out. She tries to will the old feeling of too many demands on her time to return, but she only becomes more awake and aware of the morning as it actually is. The slapping shade. The tick and moan of the furnace. The straining hum of the refrigerator in the empty kitchen. And on the other side of her bedroom door, what is always there: lifeless rooms and a day that does not need her.

Jackie opens her eyes, but remains still. Something flashes in her peripheral vision and she tilts her face to the wall next to the bed. On the scuffed pine floor, blades of light expand and thin as the shade gapes out and up, then down. She remembers how her son, Rick, would taunt the family's cat, a skittish calico named Maude, with the beam of a flashlight along any surface. Watching Maude scramble and rush after the bright spot was one of his favorite mischiefs. No matter how forcefully Amy would marshal her older-sister authority and insist he stop, Rick was unmoved. The cat would go berserk and hurl itself at the elusive glow until it slammed into the wall or a piece of furniture, shaking its whiskered head, stumbling to regain equilibrium. Amy would eventually put a stop to it, scoop Maude in her arms. *You're going to kill her*, she'd hiss. *Look at her shaking!* Rick's pleased grin made clear that his sister's fury had been the goal all along.

The window shade calms and the light show ends. What's left is a bedroom wall with cracked paint and brown silhouettes of small fist-shaped clouds—water stains from a roof leak in the '90s. Jackie hears the dull sizzle of a bumblebee buzzing and bumping against the screen. She's seen the bee only once, less than a week ago, when it came around for the first time. It was enormous, and appeared drunk or ancient or both and seemed barely able to stay aloft as it knocked softly against the wire mesh. It has returned every morning since but only as a sound.

She remembers Rick mowing the lawn at fourteen, upsetting a nest of yellow jackets. When Jackie first heard his shouts she'd reflexively reached for a dish towel and ran it under water. Swatting and howling, ripping off his shorts, T-shirt and underwear as he made his way down the hall, Rick exploded into the kitchen like he was on fire. But before she went to him, she noticed small, blond-brown hairs curling at the center of his chest, under his arms, above his privates. She could also see the beginnings of muscles along his shoulders and arms, nudging from beneath his still-perfect boy's skin. For the first time approaching her son's body, she paused. In that split second Jackie felt simultaneously startled, shy, and betrayed. It was as if he'd deliberately grown up behind her back, and was only now, by accident, getting caught. A sharp pinch of fear tightened in her chest with every other complicated and all-at-once feeling. She rushed to her son and began swatting the yellow jackets from his neck and legs, stomping them under her rubber-bottomed slippers as they fell to the kitchen floor. *Get them! Hurry, Mom!*, he'd shouted as he danced naked and desperate, a little boy again, between the butcher block and the kitchen sink.

Outside the bedroom window, the bee's drone fades, and as Jackie's eyelids close again slowly an older memory overwhelms the one of her son. Floyd, the summer between her junior and senior years in high school, standing alongside a green barn, looking intently at something, or someone, behind the building. There is no break from his focus and Jackie cannot tell if he's upset or curious. She's pulled into the dirt driveway at Howland's Farm to pick up eggs for her mother. A quarter for a dozen, which everyone who knew to do so left in a rusty blue coffee can that sat on the plastic crate by the door. Of course she'd hoped to run into Floyd. Why else would she have driven her mother's Mercury wagon twenty minutes to get eggs when the grocery store in Cornwall was less than five minutes from her house? Seeing him right away feels like a too-good-to-be-chance stroke of luck, like a shooting star at the first glimpse of the night sky. And here he is. The second tallest boy in the senior class, the one who kissed her two Saturdays ago on the dock at Hatch Pond. It hadn't been a long kiss, and it started more on her right cheek than on her lips, but it was her first. He'd kissed her again last night, too, briefly, in his truck, after driving her home from the Fourth of July picnic. Now, appearing in almost perfect profile to her, so transfixed by whatever lay just beyond the barn's edge that he hadn't heard the station wagon crunch dirt and rock as it rolled to a stop, she wonders if these had been his first kisses, too.

A pipe rattles in the bathroom wall. Jackie opens her eyes, but it's not the edge of her pillowcase bunched against the fitted sheet that she sees, it's Floyd's blue shirt. It must be new, she decides, as it starts to fade from view, because the collar is stiff, like a dress shirt, and the color—some shade between denim and cobalt—is flawless in the way that's only possible before a garment has had its first wash. Against the brilliant green of the barn, the blue is striking, even strange. Has she seen these two colors, on their own or together, since? Not likely, she thinks, squinting her eyes shut—tight, quick—and opening them with purpose to switch off the memory as she would an annoying television commercial.

Jackie jerks from her side to her back and begins to sit up. She grabs the cool, unused pillow and places it behind her on top of the warm, wrinkled one she's clung to all night. She scooches her back against it and straightens her spine, the noise of mattress coils ceasing as she stills. How many times has she completed these precise movements, drifted into these same half-dreams and considered how often this exact morning has happened before? She ignores the old questions and breathes in deliberately, deeply, as if bracing for an attack, or preparing for an action that demanded great courage. Fully awake, she exhales, and in the silence that follows feels the present gather as a dull weight on her chest and shoulders.

The window shade floats up and light dazzles the room. Cool air chills her hands. Through the exposed gap she sees the spotty April lawn, the cracked asphalt driveway, the budding and newly leafed trees. She scans for the scolding crow and the bumblebee but sees neither. The shade glides down, settles again. Jackie's right hand covers her left and her fingers find the surface of her wedding ring. She presses her thumb into the small round diamond there, her pointer and middle fingers taking their positions along the thin gold band to commence their old habit of twisting back and forth, tugging the ring gently and then occasionally with force, against her knuckle.

From outside, she hears the low crumble of tires on asphalt, the smooth growl of an engine whining momentarily as it shifts to a high, soft, idling hum. At first Jackie thinks it must be the UPS truck, or Amy, but minutes pass without the expected sounds of cut engine and slammed door.

Eventually, the shade lifts again, slowly, as if by a reluctant hand. She sees only for a second what is there, parked at an odd angle as if to further emphasize how temporary and unlikely its visit. A black car, dark-windowed and new, with New York plates and plumes of exhaust billowing extravagantly into the cold morning air like cream clouding into tea, or the special effect Jackie had seen in movies when she was young, the one that signaled the presence of a diabolical ghost, or the arrival of a witch.

Lupita

Not a word in all these years, and now so many. *I found your number in a photograph, it was on the side of your van. I'm sorry, I know that sounds strange. I thought . . . Can you please call me. It's important.* She'd never heard the sounds of her first coos and mangled words, and now, in her ear, complete sentences, hurried and adult. The woman speaking in the voicemail message is so upset she forgets to say who she is, where she's calling from. But Lupita knows. She's listened to the message twice since dropping off a family from Ann Arbor at their hotel in Princeville. Her phone had rung an hour before from an unidentified number. A pale, blonde woman with her bald husband and teenaged son were still in the minivan, telling her about the harsh Michigan winter they'd just escaped. She'd clicked the button on the side of her phone to silence the ring and let it go to voicemail as she half-heard the family's stories of frozen pipes, canceled basketball games, and fender benders on ice-slicked roads—the same calamities of winter Lupita had grown up with but left behind when she moved to Hawaii half a century ago.

As she's heading back to the airport in Lihue to pick up another weary family antsy for Kauai's wild beaches and misty cliffs, her phone rings again, vibrating in the dashboard mount, *Unknown Caller* flashing from the screen for several seconds before it vanishes. She exhales when the call drops and only then realizes she's been holding her breath.

Traffic on Route 56 slows to a stop. Brake lights on cars and buses and vans blink a long, erratic line of agitated red ahead of her. A local girl without a helmet speeds past on a mini-bike, the ragged growl of her wrecked muffler for a moment the only sound; she shoots ahead in the narrow space between the traffic and the road's shoulder, her long brown hair whipping behind. Lupita watches until she disappears over the first hill. The phone rings again. Distracted, she pushes the green "Accept" button on her phone screen.

Hello?, the voice is timid, no trace of Mexico but why would there be. *Is this Lupita Lopez?* Harsh, crackling static suggesting a very long distance fills the van. Before she hears another word, Lupita stabs the phone with her finger and ends the call.

Dana

She'd planned to stay in the car for as long as it took. She had no strategy other than to wear Jackie down, as she had when they were kids—wait in the driveway, all day if necessary, until she opened the front door. But it was now after eleven o'clock and Dana hadn't counted on needing to use the bathroom; nor had she considered that Philip, her driver, would need the same. This was just the sort of thing she tended to overlook, the kind of mistake that tripped her up more and more lately. Like leaving the briefcase in the house this morning. She'd put it down for just long enough to look in the small mirror that hangs in the elevator, pinch a rogue eyelash that had landed on her cheek between her fingers and blow it away. But reckoning with her reflection flatlined all other thoughts, so by the time the small elevator finished making its way down four floors of her townhouse and grumbled to a stop, she'd forgotten she had something important to carry to the car.

It wasn't until they were reaching the speed limit on the West Side Highway that she'd noticed the case missing, and when she did she balled her fist and punched the back of the passenger seat in front of her. After a few desperate seconds scouring her memory, lurching from Cristina to Marcella and even to Philip, hoping to hold anyone but herself accountable, she gave the directive to return home. Without asking why, Philip calmly exited on Thirty-Fourth Street and made his way back to Eleventh, where Marcella was waiting at the top of the stoop, briefcase pulled to her bosom.

Marcella's face, at precisely that moment of victory, reminded

Dana of a very briefly employed nanny she'd had when she was young. She'd long forgotten her name but recalls clearly how the woman held a bowl with three dead goldfish spinning lifeless on the water's surface, damning proof that she'd been correct when she'd warned Dana that not feeding the fish would result in their death. Dana remembers her perfume, which she would later recognize as gardenia and forever after despise.

Once he'd stopped the car and flipped on the hazard lights, Philip fetched the case while Dana scanned Marcella's features for signs of betrayal—a rolled eye, her head shaken in disgust, an eyebrow arched in mock surprise. Dana pressed her forehead into the car window as Philip climbed the stoop and with one hand grabbed the case's handle, and without stopping descended back toward the car. She would consider anything more than apparent indifference between Marcella and Philip insubordination, and upon sighting would pounce to reassert her authority. Her heart sped at the prospect, thrilled by the opportunity to put Marcella in her place and impose order on the morning which was off to a sloppy start.

But Marcella never lapsed, never crossed the line to expose what Dana knew was seething behind her creaseless and chubby face. Nor did Marcella ever register an opinion about any of the men and women Dana had been involved with, most of them not appropriate for anything longer than a fling. The married diplomat from Portugal, the forty-something cater waiter she met at a dinner party, the former helicopter pilot in early recovery from heroin addiction, the Pilates instructor who came twice a week until the month-long affair was over. Marcella referred to all of them as Dana's friends—*Will your friend be staying for dinner? Will your friend need anything washed or dry cleaned? Will we need to messenger your friend's cuff links to his office or hotel?* The last *friend* was the younger sister of a college acquaintance from Bryn Mawr who'd recognized Dana browsing the front table at Three Lives, the neighborhood bookstore. Dana hadn't remembered her from the few weekends she'd spent at her college friend's country house in Michigan, but was flattered to be remembered after so many years. Samantha was a successful chef and restaurant owner who had recently opened a small, very crowded pizza place a few blocks away. She was younger by eleven years, bossy, and drank more than anyone Dana knew. Every aspect of the relationship was foreign territory to Dana. Samantha's boozy volatility, her possessiveness, her local celebrity which resulted in dozens of afternoon walks and dinners out in restaurants interrupted by admirers. But Samantha's ardent pursuit, particularly given her status, was flattering and it had been a long time since Dana had been involved with a woman.

The relationship lasted almost a year, longer than any that had preceded it, and was the first to end by someone else's choice. One morning after they'd showered and dressed and were preparing to leave for a walk on the High Line, Samantha mentioned that she'd been asked to collaborate with a boutique hotel chain opening properties in England and it would require her to be in London often. When Dana offered to help look for a place to rent there, Samantha declined. *This seems like a good moment to make a change, no? A natural break*, she'd said, as if a break had been something they'd discussed and agreed on. Dana didn't know if it was mortification at being blindsided or genuine heartbreak, but in the three years since, she'd avoided the possibility of either again. When Samantha stopped turning up after midnight, and no longer jammed the refrigerator with vegetables and herbs she'd carefully selected at the farmer's market in Union Square, Marcella never said a word. It was Cristina whom Dana asked to gather the clothing, books and jewelry Samantha had left all over the house. As Cristina progressed from floor to floor, scouring coffee tables and closets and filling shopping bags, Marcella went about her business and withheld questions or comment. A week later, Dana found a pair of

Samantha's leather sandals in her closet and exploded at Cristina for being so careless and ordered her to get them out of the house right away. Even then, Marcella remained stone-faced.

This morning was no different. She stood like a woman-sized trophy at the top of the stoop, arms crossed, motionless. After Philip had returned with the briefcase and the car began to inch west in traffic down the block, Dana watched her housekeeper get smaller and smaller until she was reduced to a smudge. It was only when Philip turned up Sixth Avenue and Marcella had completely disappeared from view that Dana settled back in her seat and exhaled. It wasn't yet eight in the morning and she was already exhausted and resentful on a day she needed to be neither. She'd considered for a moment not going any further and telling Philip to take her home. But then when would she make this trip? The next day? The day after? Soon it would be too late. She looked warily at the briefcase in the seat next to her. She touched its surface with her pinky finger and dragged a slow, wide careful circle against the dry grain. She traced the same path again and again, round and round, in one direction and then the other, until she stopped, fingertip at a perfect ninety degrees with the flat surface, less than an inch from the handle edge of the case. She closed her eyes and held perfectly still for several seconds before gliding her hand away, folding it softly into the other and resting both in her lap. Philip accelerated on the Saw Mill River Parkway and Dana drifted to sleep, exactly as she'd done the last time she rode from the city in the back seat of a car with this briefcase beside her.

Miss Goss, I'm afraid I'll need to find a restroom somewhere. Very sorry for the inconvenience.

Philip, from the driver's seat, is speaking softly and without turning around.

Dana, her eyes on Jackie's house, pretends not to hear.

Ma'am?

In addition to her own pressing bladder, it irritates her to imagine Jackie, bent at her window, smug and victorious, watching the car retreat from her driveway. Though she hasn't seen it in a very long time, it's a look Dana remembers. She saw it the first time they met, when they were both eight years old and Jackie came to see the horses at Edgeweather's stables. Dana's father had reported at supper the night before that on his afternoon walk he'd met a mother and daughter, neighbors, who had been unloading groceries from their car. No one in the Goss family had ever met them. He explained that he was charmed by the girl and thought she'd enjoy seeing the horses, so he'd invited them to come to the stables the next day for a visit. Dana remembers her mother being confused and distressed, which was how she remembered her in general, but on that night especially so. *Why on earth would you do that? I can't understand why you'd complicate things here*, she worried from her seat. Her father didn't usually pay much attention to her, but he slammed his hand against the table, once, and hard enough to rattle the glasses and silver. In the silence that followed no one spoke. Jackie and her father came the next morning.

Dana remembers pointing to one of the stallions in the barn and insisting the animal was a pony named Cindy, which no one questioned until Jackie said, *What's wrong with you? Look at his privates.*

On her face and in her voice, Dana recognized in Jackie a kind of person she had not met before, certainly not her own age. Someone who was formidable, and blunt, but not mean. It was the first time anyone had openly challenged her. After a few playdates, and one long hike in the woods that resulted in them getting lost and calling Jackie's mother from a small farm they'd stumbled upon to pick them up, Dana began calling Jackie her best friend. It would take more time for Jackie to agree, but by winter that year their dedication was mutual. Dana's father called them Laurel and Hardy; her mother called Jackie *the neighbor girl*, and Jackie's parents regarded the phenomenon of their friendship with doubt. Dana remembers Jackie saying that her mother had warned her not to become too attached to Dana or her family, and to tell her right away if anything strange happened at Edgeweather. Jackie repeated her mother's stern cautions to Dana the day after she'd made them, both mocking her mother and letting her new friend know that she understood at least some part of what she'd said was true: *Those people*, Jackie mimicked her mother's suspicious voice, *they don't treat people the way we do*.

The warning came in response to the news that Dana had convinced her parents to allow the girls to turn one of the rooms on the third floor of Edgeweather into a bedroom where they could sleep on the weekends when Dana was up from the city. Dana was given permission from her parents to pick out two beds, curtains, wallpaper, blankets, rugs, and even matching desks and chairs. Her mother would get them catalogs to browse and from these they could ask for fabric samples to be mailed. Nothing at Edgeweather seemed to appeal more to Jackie than this bedroom. In the few times Dana visited Jackie's house she was surprised that her room there looked like one that an adult would sleep in. Gray blankets on a dark wood bed, navy curtains, and a round forest-green-and-beige braided rug on the floor. When Dana asked why she didn't have any kid stuff Jackie said her parents thought it was impractical to buy things like pink curtains and bedspreads with flowers and stars which would inevitably need to be replaced, when she got older. Even as she defended her parents' theory, it was obvious to Dana that Jackie hated her bedroom. It meant that she had strong opinions about how the room at Edgeweather should look, which Dana mostly disagreed with, though she was careful never to veto anything for fear Jackie would lose interest. It was Dana's idea to have all the fabric samples sent to Jackie's house. They ordered many more than they needed in part because it became clear that Jackie loved receiving the brown parcels and having them to herself during the week. It took most of the fall of 1959 and the entire winter, spring, and summer of 1960 to transform a dreary, unused storage room on the third floor into a bright, mid-century bedroom for two girls. After narrowing down countless options, they settled on white four-poster beds, without canopies, periwinkle quilts and curtains, and a thick, bright white wall-to-wall carpet. If Jackie was leaning toward a choice that Dana felt strongly against, that choice would mysteriously be out of stock, or discontinued. This was the case with the green damask curtains and bedspreads, the mustard and burgundy carpet, and lampshades with gold tassels. In the end, they were both happy and Jackie was under the impression that most of the decisions had been hers.

Jackie was always the one who checked her watch, the one who made sure they were home on time for meals and before parent-imposed curfews. If they were exploring along the river or in the woods she kept her eye on the weather and where the sun sat in the sky so they didn't get stuck in the dark or caught in a downpour. Dana, in response, was willfully careless, would resist turning home even as thunder rumbled in the distance or rain began to sprinkle. Where Jackie insisted on the truth, Dana shaped more exciting possibilities from what was available, or refused to budge from the faulty ones she was used to or preferred. *Earth to Dana*, Jackie would say. *Come in, Dana. Reality is calling. Hello!* It still stuns Dana to remember how completely those roles would reverse, how impossible it would be for her to shout those same words to Jackie when she should have.

Ma'am, are you ok? Philip again, his distress palpable. *I'm afraid, I'm going to need to . . .*

Give me a piece of paper, she snaps. Without rushing, he opens the glove compartment. It is empty save for a flashlight which he holds up and pivots one way and then another between the front seats so Dana can get a full view. He puts it back, pats the tops of his pants, and then runs his hand along the driver's side door pocket. He leans across the gear shift to check the pocket on the passenger's side door and after a few seconds returns to an upright, seated position with both hands held up, open and empty, as if to say, *There is none*.

Dana pauses before she speaks.

That's quite a show, Philip, how about checking the trunk?

His look, in response, a mix of agony from needing to pee and genuine surprise, momentarily disarms Dana.

Wait a minute, she says with exaggerated delicacy, raising her hand—palm out, gloved fingers spread wide—as if commanding a squadron of hummingbirds to stall midair. *I might have something*. She clicks the briefcase open and begins shuffling paper, rearranging its contents. Through the rearview mirror Philip sees only Dana's head and shoulders angled intently toward whatever the case held. After a long, slow tearing sound, she briefly holds up a rectangle of yellowed paper. Philip can see on one side there is small black type and on the other a few larger words, again in black type, but in a more involved, thicker font. The only word he can make out in the rearview mirror is MORAVIAN, which means nothing to him. Seconds later, when he recognizes what he sees, he shouts, *It's the title page of a book!* Dana looks up momentarily, as if a pebble has hit the car window. She closes the case and snaps the latches shut before holding up the page again.

Here.

She thrusts the page between the seats. Reluctant to turn around, and still looking at Dana in the rearview mirror, Philip first studies her face and then what he can see of the torn page for any clue that will explain what she is asking of him. And then he just says it: *I don't know what you want.*

Dana revs with fury, the brief reprieve from the day's agitations she'd felt from hatching a plan vanishes, and swift, sharp words begin to shape a blade on her tongue; but before she wields it she remembers that it was she who needed something to write on, not Philip. And though she can remember that she needed the paper, she can't remember why. She begins to feel the dreaded, but more and more familiar, sensation that she's lost the thread—of conversation, of thought, of purpose and place. She's described it to her doctor who referred her to a neurologist but for the last year she refused to make an appointment, just as she refused to answer honestly when he asked if there was a history of dementia in her family. Her mother's forgetfulness and erratic agitations began in her early fifties, but in less than a decade had progressed to a violent and total mental decline. Despite the doctors who'd insisted at the time that early onset Alzheimer's was genetic and blameless, Dana still assumed it was the unsurprising consequences of decades of reckless pill taking, and in more than one frustrating moment with her mother before she was hospitalized, she'd told her so. That Dana would now inherit some version of what had so brutally dismantled her mother felt like both a rebuke and a punishment from the grave.

She yanks her hand back and looks out the window to avoid Philip's bewildered gaze and as she does sees the blind in Jackie's living room slowly, almost imperceptibly, lower. The blind is metal and white, the sort Dana imagines one would find in public schools or police stations. She flinches and blinks as the late morning sun glints off the institutional scales. As if awakening from a deep sleep, she quickly scans her surroundings: the interior of the car, Philip, the briefcase, the driveway, the pitiful house, and soon she remembers where she is and why, and precisely what she wants the paper for.

Philip, she asks calmly, as if nothing strange and erratic has just occurred between them, *what do you expect me to write with?*

Jackie

The car purrs outside the window. The engine's sound is simple, unmodulated, easily erased by the rush of wind over the house and through the branches of the elm tree in the front lawn. As Jackie listens to the new leaves stir, she is grateful to be reminded that there are forces greater than the one that sits in the car outside.

It was the tree that first drew Jackie to the house when she and Floyd were looking for a place to rent the October after she graduated from high school. She was pregnant with Amy and her parents were hurrying the wedding before she began to show. She didn't mind. She was getting what she wanted: Floyd, a baby, and a house in town, away from the remote dead-end road where she'd grown up.

She remembers the first time she saw the white, one-story ranch built into the small hill at the end of the short driveway. The elm in front looked like a giant's bonfire, blazing with yellow and orange foliage. Floyd's Aunt Lois owned the place and explained that the tree was one of the few to survive the bark beetles that came with Dutch elm disease in the 1930s, which had destroyed almost all the elms in the area; not just the ones that had once lined Upper and Lower Main Streets in Wells, but all over New England. The only other elm in Wells, she'd told them, was famous, one of the oldest and largest in North America. Jackie knew the tree. It was so famous locally that the estate where it stood was called Great Elm. The tree lurched from the front lawn of the cream-colored mansion and was visible from anywhere along that stretch of South Main Street. Signs of its struggle, past and present, were clear: two of its most prominent limbs had been removed, leaving black tar stains where they'd been amputated, and in season the leaves grew in spotty green patches against dead gray branches across an uneven canopy. Jackie remembers comparing the weathered wreck to the elm in front of the little house and admiring how the tree that would be hers appeared as if it had never encountered blight of any kind. She felt smug already, pleased that this modest lawn held one of the last survivors of a great plague. And the survivor was thriving. It was a clear sign to her that the property was blessed, special, and therefore a safe place to raise a family.

Jackie winces at the memory of her younger self believing that closeness to something great could protect her family, magically fortify them just by being near. She pictures Dana's house. It was not the biggest house in Wells, nor the most important. There were other houses, on South Main Street, mostly, where presidents and senators and all manner of once-upon-a-time notables had stayed or passed through. Everyone in Wells grew up on the stories of Noah Webster writing parts of the dictionary in the old Smith House and Ronald Reagan playing touch football on the front lawn of Great Elm. But for Jackie, even though there were no famous stories attached to it, Edgeweather had been grander than all of them. As a girl, she was mesmerized by its white columns and brick walls swarming with ivy. But what she'd loved most about the house was that it was a secret. It stood, as her own parents' tidy three-bedroom Cape did, a far distance from the center of Wells, at its eastern edge where the Housatonic River created a border with Cornwall. On the school bus it was almost a forty-minute ride to town. Her father liked to tell the story of how Undermountain Road was one of the earliest roads in the area but was rendered obsolete when Route 7 became the main thoroughfare. Around that time, in the 1940s, Dana's family bought a large parcel of land adjacent to their own and with it a long stretch of the road. To create more privacy, they had arranged with the town and the state to terminate the south end of Undermountain Road. Over the years, people forgot about the great house, which, as Jackie's mother would point out, was ideal for a family with no interest in anyone from Wells who didn't work for them.

When Jackie was a child, Edgeweather appeared to her as if it had existed forever—before the woods, before the river, even. She loved being one of the few people who knew about it, and one of an even smaller number of people who lived a short walk from its front door. When the Goss family was not around and when no one was on the grounds, she ran beyond the garage and across the oval driveway to the wide lawn that ended at the river. This was the place she'd liked best, between the house and the water, where the chimneys and columns cast shadows on the grass, and the canvas awnings huffed their soft thunder.

In the winter after she and Floyd moved into their house, two things happened: Jackie gave birth to their first child, a chubby baby girl named Amy; and the tree at Great Elm was finally cut down. The occasion was marked by a long cover story in the *County Journal* complete with photographs of the well-known political family who had lived there since the 1920s; the famous guests at their parties, Sylvia Plath among them. There was also a snapshot taken of the fire department in 1930, standing in front of the then-robust tree after they'd put out a fire caused by an ember that shot from an unscreened fireplace into a bookcase and nearly burned the house down. The men look sooty, like coal miners, and young. Floyd brought the paper to the maternity ward at Wells Hospital—a short walk down the hill from their house— where Jackie was recovering after Amy's uneventful birth. She remembers looking at the old black and white photo of the volunteer fire department, scanning the caption, and noticing that the names then were, for the most part, the names now. Both Floyd's family and her own were represented, along with a predictable majority of Moreys. In almost forty years, she thought, the biggest change in Wells was that a tree was cut down. Not only did the fact amuse her, but on the second day of being a mother in a town she had no plan on leaving, she found it deeply reassuring. It also occurred to her that with Great Elm's tree gone, the only one left in Wells that mattered was standing directly in front of her house. She looked again at the newspaper photo of the once magnificent tree, destroyed now, its smashed branches everywhere. There was a picture of the mayor's wife counting the rings on its stump to determine how old it had been; the caption said she'd tallied two hundred and three. Jackie can still remember the quiet triumph she felt as she snuggled into the stiff hospital bedding that morning. She recognizes that moment as the first when she felt like she'd won, that her life was enviable, one she wouldn't trade for anyone else's. It marked the beginning of a short, happy period when she only wanted what she had: her husband, Floyd; her beautiful baby girl; a clean, bright house; and in her front lawn what she allowed herself to believe was the last great elm tree in North America.

Lupita

More than half the people she picks up at the airport have kids.
How they afford to fly to Hawaii from places as far away as New
York and London, to stay for a week in hotels that cost between
five hundred and a thousand dollars a night, she has no idea.
But they do, and not just at Christmas and Easter, but year
round. For a long time, the squabbling and whining and the
incessant questioning—especially from the little boys—would
get under Lupita's skin, so much so that she did what she could
to avoid them at the loading zone at the arrivals terminal; but
over time they affected her less and less, and after decades of
ferrying them to and from the airport, the kids now amused
more than upset her.

After listening to and accidently erasing the voicemail of the
woman she'd hung up on earlier, Lupita picks up a family with
two daughters at the airport. Both girls have long black hair, like
their mother's, pulled back in thick ponytails. Their father has
black hair, too, graying at the temples just as her own father's
had. With Garcia for a last name and luggage tags from LAX,
she wonders who, if anyone—the children's grandmother? their
father?—had at some point crossed the border from Mexico into
the United States to eventually make vacations like this one possible. The oldest of the two girls must be at least thirteen and
she moves alongside the car slowly with long limbs and drooped
shoulders and falls asleep right after she reaches the far end of the
back seat. Her sister, a talkative five or six-year-old, climbs in next

to her. Once they are on the road, Lupita can see only the tops of their dark, shiny heads in the rearview mirror.

In her class of fourteen children at Wells Center School Lupita was the only one with black hair. The rest were mostly shades of blonde and brown and there was one redheaded boy. She was also the only kid with a z at the end of her last name; the only one who knew how to speak Spanish or any other language besides English; and the only one who lived above a garage with her father.

The morning bus ride took forty minutes. The first fifteen were the worst. Wanda and Kit boarded before anyone else. Both tucked their light brown hair neatly under cloth-covered head-bands, and had blue eyes, and pale, freckled skin. They lived three houses down the road from each other in the only section of Wells further away from town than where Lupita lived, so when Lupita and Jackie got on the bus in the morning they were already sitting in the back seats, one on either side of the aisle, waiting. Lupita always sat two seats behind the driver. Jackie, who rarely said more than a drowsy *hi* at the bus stop, disappeared somewhere in the middle of the bus, tucked her legs against the back of the seat in front of her, and slept most of the way to school. Lupita had a hunch Jackie's morning naps were a convenient way to avoid Wanda and Kit who wasted no time registering Lupita's arrival. Usually it began with *What's that smell?* They'd continue once Mr. Prindle closed the bus doors and slowly pulled away from the old wood post painted white with the words *Undermountain Road* stenciled in black letters that served as the unofficial bus stop. In bright voices, with mock bewilderment, they explored the possibilities. Lupita heard every word:

Bad breath?

Maaaybe . . .

Rotten eggs?
Hard to say . . .
Oh! There it is again. Gross!
Oh, hey, Lupita . . . Do you know?

A quiet boy named Peter would board the bus next and sit three or four rows behind Lupita. He never said hello, never spoke to anyone. Given how empty the bus was, and how loud Kit and Wanda were, Lupita knew it was not possible for Peter and Jackie and Mr. Prindle not to hear the taunting. After a while, it felt like the voices calling out to her were theirs, too.

After Peter, Mary Anderson got on with her two older brothers. Mary was broad shouldered and thick, with long blonde hair that was almost yellow. She would board ahead of her brothers and shoot straight to the back to sit with Kit or Wanda. From the very first time she rode the bus, Lupita recognized by the way Kit and Wanda both moved to the window-end of their seats and waited as she made her way down the aisle that Mary was their unchallenged leader. When she landed in either girl's seat they would, in unison, ask her if she smelled something disgusting. *You mean the bag of garbage disguised as a third grader?*, she would answer and the three girls would detonate with self-congratulatory laughter. As the bus filled, the teasing would stop, and the remaining ride to school was usually uneventful. After they arrived, Jackie disappeared into the fourth grade and if she saw Lupita in the cafeteria at lunch or on the playground at recess she'd smile, just as she did when she boarded the bus to go home at three-thirty. On the surface, her smiles seemed friendly, and were certainly warmer than her sleepy aloofness in the mornings, but like the *see you tomorrow*s she called over her shoulder each afternoon when she headed home from the bus stop in the opposite direction, Lupita understood that these were merely obligatory gestures that excused Jackie from further contact. Still, she was grateful to be acknowledged, and in those first few years of riding the bus to and from school with Jackie, there was never a smile or a *see you tomorrow* that didn't spark a longing for something more.

Mary had a long purple cloth coat with yellow plastic buttons that hung below her knees to the top of her pink rubber boots. It had a cinched hood with green cords that dangled on both sides with blue toggles. It was an unusually colorful piece of clothing which Mary wore from early fall to late spring. In it, Lupita thought she looked like a walking Easter egg, a version of which she drew in her notebook. She used purple crayon for the egg and covered it with large yellow dots down the front and green zigzags and pink stars everywhere else. On the top she scribbled bright yellow blonde hair and on the bottom pink boots, just like Mary's.

Lupita never told a soul what she thought Mary looked like in that coat, nor did she show anyone the drawing, but at lunch, not long after she'd made it, Kit crept up to Lupita's table from behind and stole her notebook. Frozen, Lupita watched her flip the pages, humming "La Cucaracha," which the three girls had recently discovered and sang whenever in her presence. Lupita knew they couldn't have understood the word's meaning in Spanish, otherwise by now they would have been calling her *cockroach*.

Kit stopped flipping the notebook when she reached the page where the drawing was. As she inspected what was there, her face lit with understanding. Slowly, she held the Easter egg drawing up so that Lupita could see it clearly. Kit relaxed her shoulders, squinted her eyes, and calmly reported what they both now knew to be true: *You're dead. She's going to kill you.* In that moment Lupita believed she'd never again see her mother, her sister, Ada, or her father. Kit stared at her as she squirmed. And then, propelled by a surge of unexpected adrenalin, Lupita lurched across the short distance between them, snatched the notebook from Kit's hands, and ran for the cafeteria doors. Barely a few yards into her escape, she slammed into a chair which, as she fell, made a spectacular scraping sound. Without dropping the notebook she quickly stood and shot past the other kids eating their lunch, past the row of garbage cans lined up along the floor-to-ceiling cafeteria windows, and out through the double doors. She ran across the asphalt playground, beyond the swing-sets and seesaws and onto the athletic field that fronted the school. It was February and the ground was frozen; small ridges of melted snow still streaked the brown and yellow grass. As she ran she imagined Kit behind her, legs pumping, her face a death mask, Mary and Wanda on either side.

When Lupita reached Upper Main Street, she remembered her coat on the back of the cafeteria chair. Still running, she half-turned and looked back to see how close behind her pursuers were only to see a long stretch of empty sidewalk. Kit had not rallied Mary and Wanda to destroy her. And if she had, they'd already given up. Lupita slowed her steps, the notebook still clutched to her chest. As her breathing steadied, she could feel the cold begin to seep through her thin brown wool sweater and white cotton blouse. Snot began to drip from her nose. She was now at the center of town, on Upper Main Street between the library and the Town Hall. She'd never been here on her own before, not in the summer or on a weekend, and certainly not on a school day. Instead of feeling unsure or more frightened, she felt restless, excited. This was the first time she was fully outside the bounds of other people's rules. Her father was strict about finishing meals, doing dishes, completing homework, and saying prayers before bedtime. At school every moment was spoken for and scheduled; on the bus, she barely moved in her seat behind the driver for fear of inciting further taunting. And here she was, walking in town, alone and without a single person in the world watching or knowing where she was.

She crossed the town green to Lower Main Street, squeezing her notebook and remembering the moment she grabbed it from Kit. She was sure it was the only brave thing she'd ever done. It was so far outside the bounds of how she'd interacted with those girls, she could hardly believe it had actually happened. It excited and frightened her to replay each moment. She quickened her step and decided to rip the drawing from the notebook and destroy it. Mary could never see it. Even knowing it existed, for Kit had no doubt already told her, might be reason enough for Mary to come after her.

As Lupita crossed lower Main Street and turned onto Hospital Hill Road toward the Catholic church, she tried to imagine the worst that Mary would do. Despite countless taunts and cruelties, she could not remember a single moment of violence that Mary or any of the other girls had ever inflicted—upon her, or anyone else. It was their words and their songs and their hostile glares, never more and never worse. Her father was the only person who hit her. Usually just a smack across the face or a pinched arm if she'd broken a plate or cup while doing dishes after supper, but occasionally, if he was especially upset, he used his fists. He hadn't hit her in months but his stern quiet let her know that it was always a possibility. Lupita had never thought to compare her father to her tormentors at school before now. Yes, their words felt terrible. Really terrible. And yes, she lived in fear of seeing them in the morning on the bus and at school. But compared to her father they were harmless and she'd managed to live alongside him most of her life. For the first time the girls on the bus seemed less frightening, even physically smaller, than before. Her blood quickened and without intending to she started to skip as she walked further away from school.

The wind kicked up as Lupita crossed the road to the church. Instinctively she avoided the chapel entrance and walked down the side driveway to the door to the kitchen where the women— her mother and Ada among them—made coffee and arranged Ritz crackers and hard white cheese on clear plastic trays every Sunday. Thankfully, the door was unlocked, and for the first time she did what she'd seen her mother do a million times: she made the sign of the cross with her right hand and at the end kissed her fingers.

The door opened into a small foyer, to the left was the kitchen. Directly in front was a set of stairs that at the top led through a hall to the back entrance of the chapel, the one Father Tesoro came through at mass. Instead of going into the kitchen or up to the chapel, Lupita sat on the third step and set the notebook beside her. She hugged herself as tightly as she could to get warm. The temperature inside was a world warmer than the outside she'd just left, but she felt colder than before. Her whole body shook and her teeth began to chatter.

Except for two trips to the bathroom, Lupita sat on the stairs for the rest of the day. She knew she could not return to school and she had nowhere else to go. As she'd done many times before, she prayed to the Virgin of Guadalupe, whom she'd been named after, to stop Mary, Kit, and Wanda from terrorizing her. To take her father's anger away. To somehow make it so that she could live with her mother and sister, in the city or in Wells, it didn't matter. She promised she'd be good and never run away from school again, or think bad thoughts, or make more mean drawings. She repeated her proposal, over and over, still holding her legs and shivering, clutching her knees as tightly as she could to her chest.

When Father Tesoro found her a few hours later he called Lupita's father. *She's still asleep*, she heard him say over the phone in the rectory kitchen, *perfectly fine, perfectly safe*, he reassured, though he added that he couldn't imagine how or why she was in the church on a Wednesday afternoon. In what she would later suspect was an effort to forestall Joe Lopez's wrath, Father Tesoro was careful to describe how when he first saw Lupita on the stairs he didn't want to disturb her. *She looked like an angel. Her head was resting against the white wood spindles of the banister, her hands folded tightly in prayer.*

Father Tesoro's efforts were useless. In the car, her father slapped her hard across the side of her head and squeezed her shoulder as he hollered about how much she'd embarrassed him and that it was lucky no one in the Goss family was around to see him leave work in the middle of the day. She knew not to explain why she'd run from school, that any words she spoke would result in more slaps, more hollering. She resolved to keep quiet during the car ride, through dinner, and until the weekend when her mother and sister came up from New York. Even then she would only say that she'd left her notebook at church on Sunday and thought she could retrieve it at lunch without anyone getting upset.

The older girl in the back of her minivan is still sleeping after her parents and sisters have handed their bags to the hotel porter. Her father leans in and whispers, *Wake up, Sleeping Beauty. Wake up.* He tugs her ankle and whistles a soft sound that Lupita imagines he's whistled a thousand times to his daughters. Through the rearview mirror, she can see how the girl does not stir, oblivious to the landslide of luck and love that has no doubt shaped every waking and sleeping minute of her life. Lupita taps the horn to jolt her awake and looks away when the girl begins to grumble and whine her way back to consciousness. It reminds her how Ada would shake her awake in the mornings, back when they shared a bedroom in Florida, before they moved to New York and Wells. Like their father did, but more gently, Ada would pinch Lupita's arm to get her out of bed before school. *¡Apúrate! ¡Corre!*, she'd shout. Lupita hated how Ada, once they'd moved to Florida, had started to act as an extension of her parents, her father especially. *¡Lupe!*, she'd insist, shaking her shoulders, squeezing her skin tighter between her fingers.

The hairs on Lupita's arms tingle as she taps the horn one more time, a little louder and longer than before. In the rearview mirror she catches a flash of long black hair in motion, moving toward the door. She does not watch but imagines the girl reluctantly taking her father's hand as she steps away from the minivan and into the lobby of the most expensive hotel on the island.

Her phone buzzes from the dashboard. It shimmies in its holder as *Unknown Caller* blinks from the screen just as it has the four or five times since Lupita hung up on the woman earlier. She tries to ignore the call by waving to the dark-haired family from LA before she drives back to the airport, but only the mother acknowledges her with a polite smile.

The phone stills and its screen dims as Lupita turns from the long winding hotel driveway onto the main road. A few minutes later she hears a short vibration and an electronic ping to signal that a voicemail has been left. She slows the minivan with the crawling traffic and watches the afternoon sun break through the clouds over Kealia Beach. The weak, late-day rays reach her face through the windshield and when the cars in front of her come to a complete stop she brakes to a halt and closes her eyes. She drifts to a half-sleep, and right away, Ada. She's muttering something, but too quietly to hear. One of her calloused hands lies across Lupita's forehead, the other strokes her cheek, her fingers soft on her temples. Ada's lush black hair—usually knotted into a tight bun at the back of her head or hidden behind a scarf—is now loose and falling above her, like dark curtains.

When the truck behind her honks in rapid-fire bursts, Lupita opens her eyes and sees the traffic up ahead has moved on. She waves a quick sorry with her left hand, presses the gas gently, and the minivan rolls forward. Above her, clouds float into and away from each other. The late day light breaks through and moves in beams and panels across the sky. It dazzles and vanishes, then reappears, flares bright, goes dark again—on and on, like code, as if the sun itself is speaking to her.

Jackie

Dana, Jackie whispers with a trace of wonder, watching her legs scissor in quick strides toward her front door. Her old friend is dressed like a man, tailored and lean, more handsome than pretty, looking flustered and out of her element. Her movements seem jagged. It strikes Jackie that Dana might be ill, that in fact this is the reason for her visit. She's known a few women her age who've already died from or are currently battling cancer—she herself had to have a lumpectomy and radiation a year after Floyd died—so the news of people being sick no longer shocks her. Still, the idea of Dana weakened by disease is an unexpected one. It's as if without ever being conscious of it, Jackie had all along believed she was immortal.

Dana was always thin. Even as a little girl she was at least two sizes smaller, but still taller, than Jackie. As they got older and hit puberty, her breasts never developed so much that she needed a bra. She was all angles and lines, and from childhood through high school was inclined more toward slacks and jerseys than the pastel sweaters and dresses the girls Jackie grew up with wore. More than once, after Dana cut her hair very short in the sixth grade, Jackie had witnessed strangers—a waitress at the diner in Millerton, a summer tourist asking for directions on Undermountain Road—refer to Dana as "he" or "him" or "son." It never seemed to bother Dana; in fact Jackie can still dimly remember how those incidents seemed to spark in her a quiet, sneaky pride. Like she'd pulled one over on these idiotic people and she and Jackie were the only ones in on the joke.

From the living room window, Jackie looks closer for signs of decay but Dana's torso is hidden by a dark green turtleneck sweater and gray fitted blazer. The boxy briefcase she holds to her chest like a swaddled child, albeit someone else's, looks for a moment like more than she can manage. And yet. The closer Dana comes to the house the stronger she appears. Her posture, even with the unwieldy briefcase, is long and straight and elegant. The result of personal trainers and massage therapists and the best doctors, Jackie allows herself to imagine. When they were teenagers there was a steady referencing of tutors and instructors in the city, even a dietician who told Dana never to eat a meal larger than her fist which, to Jackie, sounded like starving.

Less than thirty feet from the house now, it is clear that Dana is not sick, just much older than the last time she'd seen her. An instant resentment sparks, as if Dana had purposefully tricked her into an involuntary upset that tipped dangerously near concern, something she hadn't felt for her since high school. The little charge of anger is ridiculous, she knows this, but it doesn't budge so much as give way to an older, darker, more familiar energy. She submits to that current and with it the memory of the green barn returns—Floyd, his back to her, looking away, about to lie to her for the first time.

Jackie violently twists the cord that raises and lowers the window blinds around her hand until her right thumb and palm are crisscrossed with taut white lines, the thin flesh in between red and swollen. When Dana passes the lamppost, roughly the halfway point between her car and the house, Jackie untangles her hand and shuffles, as quickly as her slippers will allow, from the living room window to the foyer where she bolts the door. She tugs the handle on the Dutch door, once and quickly, to make sure the bolt is secure. She then rushes to her bedroom where she peeks through the gap between the shade and the window molding.

When Dana last walked down her sidewalk, it was a scorching hot, windless afternoon. Fans were blowing in every room and Jackie's halter-top clung like a second skin to her back and to her breasts, still heavy with milk for Amy and so sensitive that it was excruciating to take showers. It was the sixth of July and Floyd had come back to the house just once since the morning after their horrific July Fourth picnic at Hatch Pond and then only to get tools he needed for work and a change of clothes. Jackie had locked herself in the bedroom and refused to speak to him despite his yelling for her to come out. He'd become so frustrated that he kicked a hole in the bottom of the bedroom door. Dana showed up the next day. She was in a bright white v-neck T-shirt, cutoff jeans and leather sandals. Her attempt at a hippie look was sabotaged by her long shiny brown hair, perfectly styled under a wide green and gold silk scarf pulled across her forehead and tied to one side.

On that day, just as she'd done today, Jackie bolted the front door and hid in the bedroom. Dana had knocked, but didn't speak a word, not at first. She'd circled the house, tried to peer through the metal screens and drawn shades of every window, and eventually broke her silence with one word, repeated and pleading, spoken not shouted, and barely audible underneath the drone of fans: *Jackie*.

And here she is again, two years shy of seventy, her hair silver and short, not quite a pixie cut—something more whimsical and tussled—but Jackie has no doubt that this, as with every other detail of her appearance, had been calculated and arranged with meticulous care.

Dana slows before approaching the front step. She crosses her arms and looks up toward the top of the house and then to each side. Jackie follows her gaze and feels at the same time ashamed and proud of her one-story ranch. It's not much, she's said to her children many times, but she owns it outright and she's lived there for half a century; raised two children under its roof. Jackie can't help but retreat into her defensive litany, a version of which, in the last years, has also served as her argument to her daughter Amy against moving to Noble Horizons, the assisted living facility where most area folks end up if they live past seventy and have a house to sell to pay for it. Jackie visits there a few times a week to see friends who've made the move. Most live in apartments or freestanding houses on the property, but over time everyone ends up in a hospital-like room in the gray, five-story residence staffed with nurses and rehab specialists. Jackie never understood why anyone would make a building that was little more than a pit stop before death look so much like a tombstone. It seemed cruel. Even the flower beds that flanked each side of its entrance depressed her. The women at Noble, the ones who were still able to, planted annuals there every spring; gaudy reds and purples and blues as unconvincing in their forced cheer as the geraniums she saw planted or left in plastic pots all over Wells Cemetery when she visited Floyd's grave.

Dana continues to scan the front and sides of the house as if for some secret panel that will let her inside. Her face, so close now, looks less familiar than it did from far away. After she steps up to the door she is obscured by one of the two large forsythia bushes that grow on either side. There is no knock or pounding, no pleas this time, just the sound of the screened door squeaking open and thwacking shut followed by the scuff of footsteps. Dana reappears, heading back down the walk, and from behind, Jackie recognizes her old gait—feet splayed just slightly outward creating an almost bouncy, slightly off-kilter stride. Jackie used to tease her about it when they were girls. Less bouncy now, it still brings to mind a duck's brisk waddle. What a ridiculous woman, she thinks lazily as Dana arrives at the still idling car where her wavy-haired driver stands at the open door. Jackie notices that the briefcase is missing. She looks to see if Dana has handed it to the driver, but he doesn't seem to be holding anything. Once Dana is seated and he's shut the door behind her, the young man returns to his seat and backs the car out of the driveway onto Hospital Hill Road. As it rolls toward Lower Main Street and vanishes behind the holly that borders the front lawn, Jackie feels, for the second time in a matter of minutes, an unwanted softness toward her old friend. But as she had before, she murders that softness with memory— the green barn, a yellow car, the sound of fireworks—and before long, Dana is gone.

Dana

This is not the house she knew. While it still stands exactly where it always has—between the steep pine woods and the top of the short, wide lawn that slopes to the river's edge—there is something different about Edgeweather. Something missing or altered, something significant, but from the lowered car window it's nothing Dana can identify.

As she scans the surfaces of the house—the copper drains, the mullioned windows, the vast expanse of old brick—she considers the possibility that it is simply the decades that have passed since she was last here that have made the house seem so unfamiliar. The main entrance, with its old oak door, shallow portico, and white columns, had since college reminded Dana of the boys' dorms at Penn where she and her friends from Bryn Mawr snuck in on weekends. But it now seems more like the front door to an abandoned asylum.

Here?, Philip asks as he slows the car near the bottom of the portico stairs. Dana is still staring up at the house, surprised to see that much of the glass above and alongside the door has splintered, the paint on the sills fissured and split. Philip tentatively asks where they are. *Edgeweather*, she says, more to herself than in response to the question, imagining what her great-great-grandfather would think to see the place looking so shabby and neglected. George Willing had built the house for his bride, Olivia, just after they married. From their portrait, which hung above the dining room fireplace, Dana had decided when she was twelve that the couple were horribly mismatched—an intelligent beauty from a lesser family and a wimpy rich kid. They had a son not long after they married and then the young husband left to fight in the Civil War. He died at the Battle of Hoke's Run, in Virginia. Of course he did, Dana thought when she first heard the story. Despite learning in high school that Hoke's Run was considered by historians more of a tactical blunder that led to terrible defeats weeks later, she'd heard her mother tell people that George Willing had died in the first battle of the Civil War. *A battle the Union won*, she'd noted in the same proud tone she used when describing the house's grandeur—the six columns that lined the river side of the house, the too-large ballroom, the ceiling which was the house's greatest extravagance, a loose replica of one designed by Robert Adam that George's mother had seen in an English country house and described to her son as the most beautiful in the world. It was an enormous production of meticulous plasterwork, detailed with ribbons, urns, and rosettes decorating ovals and octagons painted in pastel pink and green and blue. Many of the ovals and roundels framed paintings—all classical depictions of wedding celebrations.

The ballroom furniture and mirrors were either original Chippendale pieces designed by Adam or the closest possible approximation. The four large oval mirrors had been salvaged from a destroyed castle in Wales and repaired in London before being carried by boat to Connecticut. These were apparently a point of dispute between the architect and George, who insisted they appear at each end of the ballroom, on either side of the great fireplaces. George, of course, won. But to Dana's eye, the house lost. Highly ornamented with carved swags and festoons, the mirrors had always struck Dana, like the rest of the room where they hung and indeed the whole house, as gilded evidence of an insecure husband's fears of inadequacy. Even its name, Edgeweather, seemed off to her—a straining, willful amalgam of the names of more celebrated houses.

And still it stands, she thinks, looking at it now, both annoyed and relieved. Filled with most of the same furniture and decorations, covered in sheets, in rooms darkened by closed interior shutters and drawn curtains. All of it, along with the house in Palm Beach, the apartment in New York and nearly two centuries of cautiously invested family windfalls, became Dana's when her mother died in the mid-eighties. She sold everything but Edgeweather, which she had not visited since she was thirty-six years old. Real estate agents and even the wife of a famous Wall Street billionaire had reached out to Dana to see if she were interested in selling. As easy as it was to get rid of everything else, it had surprised her to realize that she couldn't let go of the old house. It still did.

Edgeweather's only resident now was a local named Kenny who occupied the apartment where the Lopezes had once lived. He kept the pipes from freezing in the winter, the lawn mowed in the summer, and hauled away the giant pines when they collapsed across the driveway. Or at least this is what his emails, that Marcella printed up and placed on Dana's desk once a month, described. Eyeing the roofline where it meets the top of the nearest column, it occurs to Dana that Kenny could have made everything up and for all she knew turned the place into a casino, which, as she imagines the locals getting drunk and spinning roulette wheels in the ridiculous ballroom, only the smallest, pettiest part of her is bothered by. The part that hates being taken for a fool, or worse, being left out. But mainly the idea amuses her, especially when she imagines how her mother would react. The possibilities so engross Dana that when Philip turns the car engine off and politely excuses himself to find somewhere to go to the bathroom, she does not notice. When he returns, she snaps out of her trance and tells him to drive the car around to the side of the house that faces the river. He hesitates. *Don't worry about the lawn*, she says and as the words leave her an old caution enters, slows her breath. Joe Lopez, whose dominion included the grounds around the house, spent many hours seeding, mowing, and weeding the lawn. Dana had seen him explode more than a few times when service trucks backed up onto the grass or when Lupita played there. She once saw him yank her so hard by the arm it looked like it would come right off of her body. Lupita had been holding one of Dana's bicycles in the middle of the back lawn, eyes closed and counting because Jackie and Dana had told her that once she reached one hundred she should come find them. They never planned on being found. The point was to ditch Lupita, run to Jackie's, and play in her bedroom where she could not find them. Dana remembers telling herself, and Jackie, that her mother was strict about her not playing with the children of people who worked for them. And she was. But she also remembers calling out to Lupita to ask her to play hide and seek, rolling the bicycle toward her and instructing her to hold on to it while they hid. What surprises her now is that there had been so little motive involved, the cruel impulse so fleeting and arbitrary, so strangely impersonal. She can't remember if she felt guilty or upset when she watched Joe Lopez drag his daughter back to the garage, but she remembers being struck by how totally compliant Lupita was, how silent.

On the lawn? Are you sure it's ok? Philip asks nervously, as if he, too, knew the wrath of Edgeweather's former, now long-dead, caretaker.

Yes, she says plainly, trying to stifle her need to use the bathroom by focusing on the house as Philip steers the car onto the grass. From this angle, parts of the house match her memory—the six preposterously large white columns still evoking the Antebellum South; the slate roof the same high cold lid it always was—

but the effect is altogether different, less convincing. Mainly, she has the impression, which she'd never had before, that the house does not belong where it is. That it's no longer in harmony with the woods, river, and hills around it, and as a result appears less inevitable. And it was that inevitability, its hulking permanence—seeming to have forever been right where it was—which had always been its power.

Late morning sun flames every window it faces. At first the light animates the house with what looks like life, an amused shimmer that could almost be mistaken for a warm welcome. But Dana knows that even before the sun inches past three o'clock and begins to hide behind the hills, the friendly glow will vanish and the house will return to its most enduring air: indifference.

Dana gets out of the car and walks several tentative steps toward the river. Unlike the house, which seems altogether less than she remembered, the river appears wider and more robust. She closes her eyes and listens to the sound of rushing water. She imagines where it goes after it passes Edgeweather, along Undermountain Road, down past Cornwall and Kent toward one of those terrible lakes choked with vacation houses and motorboats. How she knows about these lakes she cannot remember, but she shakes the vision of oil-slicked water and sunburned families and opens her eyes.

She walks to the rocky edge of the lawn where there had once been a small beach made from bags of sand Dana's mother had Joe haul from a delivery truck parked in the driveway. The beach is long gone and in its place a chaos of river rubble—sticks and beer cans, a sun-bleached grocery store circular, half-buried rocks. She and Jackie spent so many evenings here, obsessively curating collections of river stones, sorting them by color and shape, pretending they were rare jewels from a fairy's treasure. They'd embellished an old story Dana's grandmother had liked to tell them about an enchanted family who lived in the woods called the Knees who'd cast a spell that disguised their jewels as stones and hid them in the river for safekeeping. Dana cannot remember the origins of the treasure, nor how it had come to the Knees for protection. Neither can she remember what had happened to all those stones—if they'd stored them each year between summers or thrown them back into the river—only that she and Jackie had been committed to the project and it went on for years.

A smooth fist-sized rock bisected by a dull vein of quartz lies at her feet and she stoops to pick it up. It fits her palm perfectly, chilling her hand as she folds her fingers around its dark gray surface. She imagines her old friend stubbornly hiding behind her metal blinds. She wonders if she's opened her front door yet, discovered what she'd left there.

Dana squeezes the rock in her hand. It feels good to hold something sturdy and real and from the natural world. With her free hand she rubs a spot of dirt from the quartz vein but it still does not shine. The failed effort makes her both long for and pity the two girls who used to toil at the river's edge and make up stories about fairies and enchanted treasure. She turns back to the house, looks up at the wide pediment atop the columns. Here, on the third floor of the house, is where she and Jackie spent the most time. It was what Jackie referred to as the "normal" part of the house, because the floors were covered in simple carpets and decorated with soft couches and chairs with modern fabrics. The white-carpeted, periwinkle-curtained room they'd decorated and then slept in most Saturday nights looked like one they might see on a television show set in a middle-class suburb. There were no delicate antiques to tiptoe around as there were on the first two floors, including in Dana's bedroom which had a canopy bed that her mother claimed had been the bed of George Washington's daughter. *Who died of epilepsy*, her grandmother liked to add. Dana's parents never went up to the normal part of the house.

Dana eyes the crescent window above the middle column. A memory of being shoved hard against the glass there begins to surface, but before she allows herself to remember more she notices tiny bits of dead vine still clinging to the painted wood beneath the window sash. And then, finally, she sees what is not there. The ivy. The entire house had been stripped clean of its old garment, vines and leaves that once swarmed the gutters and windows, frocked the brick with green in summer and red in fall. How had she not noticed right away?

Of course it looked out of place. Of course it seemed less sure of itself. *It's naked!*, she blurts out loudly and pictures an old Park Avenue matron stripped, hosed down, and sent into The Colony Club at tea time. Dana looks more closely at the house and sees many of the bricks are cracked and loose, chunks of mortar fallen to the lawn. She starts to laugh. The sound she makes is triumphant, cruel. She sees the house but at the same time she sees her mother without hair or jewelry or makeup. A vain woman without armor, three stories high. More than two hundred years old, powerless to hide her age or obscure her wrinkles, all the old tricks taken away or no longer effective.

She is breathless, cackling, and it feels exactly right. She has come back for the first time in more than thirty years to stand before this house that is hers but not home—all the brick and glass and wood that a smitten rich kid could assemble in the middle of the nineteenth century—and with the same contempt it had shown everyone who had ever looked at it, she laughs, with such abandon and force that Philip approaches to see if she is all right. She waves him off without being able to make words but catches his eye and points to the house as if its disgrace were obvious. *Look*, she finally manages, and when he gazes on the place with palpable awe she turns her back on him. His reverence momentarily breaks the spell and she begins to breathe normally. She crosses the lawn and climbs the steps to the long wide terrace behind the columns. In the summers when she was young, there had been white canvas awnings that stretched over wicker sofas and chairs covered with green cushions and arranged around glass-topped tables set with fresh cut flowers. Now there is nothing but paint peeling from the moldings, the columns, and the steps. She sees a thick curl jutting out from the center left column and, slowly, she pulls the long sheet back and down until it reaches the column's base. She yanks it free and drops it at her feet. She thinks of Joe Lopez again, almost wishes he was still alive to see how Edge-weather had decayed on her watch.

She stifles a wicked giggle as she steps off the terrace and heads toward the side of the house furthest away from the car. She rounds the last column where a library had been added in the 1920s. It was built in the same late Georgian style of the main house and invisible on the approach from the road, but Dana's mother always thought it looked ridiculous. Her complaint was that its proportions were wrong, *suburban* was her exact word.

It is here, in the middle of the short glass hallway that connects the house to the library, where she sees the paint. Red letters, outlined in black, covering dozens of small glass panes and the white wood that frames them. The paint streaks beyond the glass windows onto the old brick where the hallway meets the house. Dana stops walking. She remembers her mother in the hospital during her last weeks, Maria Lopez painting her nails with red polish that looked garish against the white sheets and bed-clothes, the top of the heart monitor lined with tubes of lipstick and powder. It was a scene so ghoulish and macabre, so far from resembling any recollection involving her mother in her prime, it had, to Maria's horror, caused Dana to laugh. She is laughing now, though not from the memory of her mother, but in response to the riot of spray-painted profanity. From the other side of the house it sounds like choking and Philip comes running.

When Dana sees him appear, she doubles over with what began as laughter but devolves to a soundless panting. She gestures at the vandalism behind her. But Philip does not look where she points, and it is not the graffiti that spells "ASSHOLES" that is responsible for the alarmed look on his face.

Ma'am . . . I . . .

Yet again he is spoiling her fun, but she cannot quite form the words to ask what is wrong. Dana follows his gaze which returns reluctantly somewhere in front of and below her. When she sees what is there she stops laughing. The entire crotch and front of her brown suede pants are dark, soaked through with the reason she had left Jackie's driveway. In the abrupt vertigo of shock and embarrassment, she stumbles backward, her left heel lands hard on the toe-end of her right boot and in steadying herself she completely loses the thread of where she is, what is happening, who is standing in front of her. Overwhelmed, she squeezes her eyes shut, crosses her arms against her chest, and stands very still.

After a minute, Dana looks up and sees Philip, the shiny black car parked in the grass behind him, and as if she'd vacated her body and suddenly returned, she remembers where she is and how she got here. Philip . . . Jackie . . . Wells. She turns to the house. *Edgeweather*, she mumbles, recalling her laughter just moments before. Her other heretofore immobilized senses follow and suddenly she's aware of the wet suede chilling miserably against her thighs, the faint but specific and awful smell there reaching her nose. She does not look back at the paint-splattered windows behind her, but she feels acutely that the house has done this to her, ingeniously retaliated for her heckling contempt. She starts moving toward the car. She keeps her face down as she passes Philip since the only thing that could make the situation worse would be to see the pitying look on his face again. He calls to her from behind, *Ma'am, I . . . should we see if someone is home to help?*

She stops abruptly. She doesn't need help, she asserts childishly to herself, fleeing to the car now feeling like a declaration of failure. A cloud that had briefly obscured the sun moves on and light blazes again from every window. Even splattered with graffiti, the house suddenly looks pleased with itself, spectacular. Freshly provoked, Dana tightens her fists and in her right hand rediscovers the stone she had picked up before. Its cool surface, its weight, and the hard quartz crystals her fingers press into give it the feel of a divine weapon.

It is only luck, not strategy or accuracy, that sends the rock into the crescent window above the terrace. If it had landed where she'd aimed, it would have hit the center ballroom window between the columns. But Dana hasn't thrown anything more than a towel or a crumpled receipt since she was a teenaged girl and so her hand unclenches long before her arm has completed its movement and the rock flies up instead of straight, but with enough momentum to shatter the surface it hits. The bright, cracking sound on impact and the after-clatter of glass falling to the porch steps below is glorious. That she has inadvertently smashed Edgeweather's highest window is victory enough to restore Dana's equilibrium, and with it the welcome feeling that she is once again strong and in control.

Unlock the house, Philip, she says, looking directly at him now. *Or do I have to break more glass to get inside?*

Lupita

Everyone is old now, or dead. This is what Lupita thinks on the sixth ring, the one that lets her know that the person on the other end won't pick up, that the silence between them will go on a little while longer. She'd waited a week to listen to the second voice-mail, careful this time not to erase it. *If this is Lupita Lopez, please call me. This is your niece, Cristina. Ada's daughter. She . . . I found your number by accident months ago . . . My boss . . . I wouldn't bother you but . . . I'd rather we speak than just leave messages. It's important. Please call me.*

Lupita lowers the phone away from her ear and holds it in her lap under the kitchen table where she sits. It is after eleven in New York and she figures Cristina is probably already asleep. For Lupita, it's barely early evening, but she's already heated up and eaten what was left of the lasagna she'd made for last week's dinner with Jay, the neighbor she cooks for and eats with every Sunday night, a ritual that began more than a decade earlier after his wife Echo died of cancer diagnosed too late to treat. Whatever Lupita cooked—roasted chicken and potato salad, rice with ham and pineapple and peas, casseroles with hamburger meat and pasta—she always made enough so that when they split the leftovers they'd both have something in the fridge to eat through the week. Beyond this, there was little more to her diet than the yogurt she ate in the morning with her coffee, and the protein bars she bought by the box at the Harvest Market in Hanalei. It's Saturday, and she's already been to the Safeway in Lihue for

53

tomorrow's meal, a whole ham, half-price with the coupon she'd clipped from the weekly circular that shows up in her mailbox every Friday.

She'd finished her shopping after dropping the family from LA off at the airport. They were as they had been a week ago, but looser, less exhausted. The father still a soft touch with his daughters, handsome; the mother expensively dressed, kind; and the two girls languid as they dawdled and moaned. The family was beautiful, but even more so now with the dark, gold glamour of a week in the sun.

What Lupita had not seen seven days ago, in the center of the older girl's face, were two red, raised scars extending between the top of her upper lip and the bottom of her nostrils. At first she thought the girl had been cut or hurt during her vacation. But she then saw more clearly that it was a cleft palate, something Mary and the other girls at Wells Center School once would have called a harelip. It had obviously been treated but had left what looked like a permanent disfigurement. Lupita couldn't understand how she'd missed it a week ago. Perhaps because the girl had kept her head down at the baggage terminal after they'd landed, and later, as she'd slept on the ride to the hotel, only her forehead and hair were visible through the rearview mirror. Not seeing that particular buckle and fold of skin below her nose now seemed impossible given how profoundly it reshaped the girl's face. Lupita did her best not to stare. As she turned the key in the ignition, she felt simultaneously relieved and ashamed of that relief that the universe hadn't given with both hands to this girl, at least not in the way she'd first presumed; but she felt protective, too, imagining the taunts and averted glances she must have endured. She regretted her initial stingy thoughts as she peeked in the rearview mirror at the teenager who now sat straight-backed and awake next to her younger sister, as if she sensed Lupita's surveillance. She remembered how the girl's father whistled a week ago, his gentle tugging, *Wake up, Sleeping Beauty* . . . and she could feel a pinch of envy return. She watched now as the girl helped her younger sister with the seat belt, gently pushing the five-year-old's meddling hands away from the strap as she pulled it across her chest and found the buckle. The young one huffed and puffed impatiently through it all, resisting the help much as her older sister had resisted her father the week before when he roused her from sleep.

The age difference between the two girls appeared roughly the same as the one between Lupita and Ada, and with their long dark hair and light brown skin, the girls in the back seat of her van appeared like better-dressed, more polished actors playing a scene from her childhood. Ada taking care, fussing, Lupita pushing her away. She couldn't help but picture Ada with a similar disfigurement. She imagined it on her own face and considered how it would have shaped who she was, what it might have prevented, if anything.

She calls the number Cristina left on the voicemail again, but this time lets it ring a seventh, an eighth, a ninth time. She hangs up and calls again, letting it ring until she pushes the off button on the phone and reluctantly places it on the table next to her. She withdraws her hand and as she does notices the wreckage of dark spots swarming there. Wrinkled and sun-stained, her hand appears to her more like a claw or a talon. She tries to remember what the beautiful mother from LA's hands looked like and wonders if she makes her daughters clip and file their finger and toenails every week. Did she pay extra attention to her older daughter, to the parts of her body she could control?

Lupita tries to picture her hands and skin as they once were, when she came to Kauai, but she can only see what is in front of her. She rests her bare forearms along the tops of her legs and spreads her palms across her thighs. She surveys the many spots, pocks, wrinkles, scars, broken blood vessels and veins, and after a while the weathered chaos begins to look deliberate, like a set of meticulously arranged markers, or a map, showing her exactly where she's been.

Jackie

Dana's car is long gone by the time Jackie leaves her bedroom. It must be at least eleven and she's still in her nightgown. She has not yet eaten and feels increasingly light-headed as she makes her way down the hallway toward the front door. After only a few steps into the foyer, she loses her balance and stumbles to the floor. It happens so fast that when she opens her eyes she knows she's missed both the part that caused the fall and the fall itself. This has not happened before but it is the very thing Amy predicts when she makes her increasingly frequent cases for selling the house and moving to Noble Horizons.

As she waits for a sharp pain to flare from some part of her body, Jackie squeezes her eyes shut, and though it is not her habit, she prays. *Please God. Nothing broken. Please.* She shifts her hips. Still no pain. She cautiously wriggles her left toes and then her whole foot. She does the same with her right foot and no pain follows. She flutters her fingers and moves her hands and forearms and again, nothing. She remembers her ribs, and to test these she rolls in tiny increments from the left side of her body to the right, breathing deeply as she goes. Eventually, she is flat on her back with both legs bent at the knee, arms folded across her chest. After one more deep, deliberate inhale, she extends her legs along the floor, exhales, and without a wrinkle of pain, is convinced she has—for now at least—eluded her daughter's prophecies.

Still woozy, she remembers the reason why she is still not showered and dressed and fed. Who else could upend a morning so completely? Wreak havoc and speed away in a car leaving a mess behind? She inhales deeply again and holds it. She closes her eyes and sees a flash of yellow—a retreating bird, a jaundiced owl, a thief, wings flapping, stolen carnage in its mouth, flying away as fast as it can. Jackie releases her breath and shakes her resting head, upset, drowsy. The pine floor beneath her feels cool and reassuring against her head and back and bottom. Her eyelids droop, and as she drifts to a half-sleep, she wonders if Dana will return.

An owl. This is what Floyd comes up with in the twenty-six steps it takes him to cross from the barn to the driver's side window of her mother's wagon. Jackie knows how many steps he takes because she's counted each one. She counts when she needs to calm down and think clearly. Mostly during tests at school or before birthday parties with the other kids in her class. She counts what is in front of her. Braids, trees, balloons, stars, shoes. Footsteps.

One. Two. Three. Four. Five.

Six. What was he looking at?

Seven. A cow?

Eight. A person?

Nine.

Ten. Is he blushing?

Eleven.

Twelve. The only other time he's blushed is when we kissed.

Thirteen. Fourteen.

Fifteen. Maybe he's sick, flushed with fever.

Sixteen. Seventeen. Eighteen.

Nineteen.

Twenty. Is that the sound of a car starting?

Twenty-one. Twenty-two.

Twenty-three. Why is his shirt untucked?

Twenty-four.

Twenty-five. *Jackie, hi. Look at you. You, um, you came all the way out here on your own?*

Twenty-six. *Oh hey, uh, you wouldn't believe what I just saw . . .*

Twenty-six. *A huge owl. You'd never believe it. Big as a dog and fast as anything. Swooped down on one of the field rabbits . . . snatched it right there behind the barn. Came out of nowhere. Poor little guy never saw it coming.*

Twenty-six. *He must have heard your car pull in because it took off with the rabbit in its beak. Flew up over those pine trees to godknowswhere.*

Jackie hears the sound of tires skidding. Loud, frantic, nearby. She looks past Floyd, beyond the barn, and sees a flash of yellow streaking through the trees.

She turns the key and cuts the engine of her mother's wagon, something she hasn't thought to do until now. The engine ticks as it cools and Floyd leans in. A vision surfaces and before she dismisses it as impossible, she pictures Dana speeding home on Route 7 in her yellow Mercedes, too fast, grinding the gears when she turns onto Undermountain Road just as she's done every time she's driven since the night of her sixteenth birthday when Mr. Lopez sat in the passenger seat and tried to instruct her how to work the clutch, gas pedals, and gear shift.

Not possible, Jackie thinks again, trying not to look at Floyd. She sees the field stretching out behind the barn and imagines an owl circling—slowly, patiently, above them all—spotting the oblivious rabbit, eyeing its prey as it twitches in broad daylight, soaring to a stall and then plummeting with lethal precision. But as she imagines the predator flapping away with its kill dangling from its beak, she can't help but sense something wrong with the scenario. She checks the clock on the dashboard and sees that it's almost eight-thirty. The sun has been shining since six. *Owls*, she remembers her third grade teacher, Mrs. Fenn, declaring with some excitement as she held up a book with a photograph of a white owl with yellow eyes perched on a snowy branch. *Owls*, she continued, *are nocturnal. Which means they sleep during the day, and they hunt at night.*

Jackie looks up into Floyd's eyes and forces a smile. She tries to ignore his untucked shirt, his mussed hair, and the perspiration beading on his flushed forehead. Before she speaks, she squeezes her eyes shut, hard, and keeps them closed longer than is polite, long enough to locate a previously untapped superpower, one that will allow her, when she opens them, to see exactly and only what she wants.

Dana

She had no idea what to expect entering Edgeweather for the first time in over thirty years, but it was not the smell of coffee. Philip fiddled for a few seconds with the key she'd given him before turning around nervously to tell her that the door was not locked. She motioned for him to step aside and pushed open the old oak slab. Dana remembered her father explaining to Jackie once how the door had come from an Elizabethan castle in Sussex, England. She remembered, too, how he'd walked away from her after Jackie asked why anyone would bother transporting a door from so far away when they could have just built a new one. Dana's father was more amused by Dana's country friendship than her mother was, but he had his limits.

When she steps into the entryway and gets her first whiff, she tries to remember how many times she'd considered installing a security system here. Once in a while, even as she ignored the place, it had occurred to her that she should probably take care to keep it from getting robbed or ruined, but whenever she thought about looking into an alarm she quickly became agitated and changed her mind. It was as if the house was asking for her attention, and her response was always to turn her back.

And here it was, unlocked, open to the world, smelling like a diner. Philip had suggested calling the police before going in, but Dana was still feeling bold from smashing the window outside, so she waved him off and stepped into the foyer. The sweatpants Philip fortunately kept in his gym bag and had lent to her folded and gathered at the top of her boots, the rest hung from the tightly knotted cord she'd tied at her waist and covered with her sweater. She'd left her urine-drenched suede pants and panties on the ground behind the house where she'd changed. She was too embarrassed to bring them back to the car.

As she breathes in the unmistakable smell of coffee, she can't help but feel a dark spark of satisfaction that her mother would have been livid to find the house invaded and reeking of a beverage she thought common. *Coffee is for dockworkers*, she'd remark privately if someone in the apartment or at Edgeweather had asked for it, but in the moment, she'd always, very politely, offer tea.

No tea today, Mother, she mumbles and paces the foyer. She calls out into the unlit house less as a property owner to a trespasser and more as a co-conspirator would to another. *Hello? Hello there? Yoohoo.* She delights in the swish of Philip's sweatpants knowing how vehemently her mother would have disapproved of them, too.

At first, she can't remember how to find the kitchen. It had always been Maria Lopez's domain and as a child and even later, it was a place she hardly ever visited. In the hall off the entryway, she pulls open a door to reveal a shallow closet jammed with heavily taped boxes. She makes her way to the dining room, passes under and ignores the portrait of Edgeweather's original owners, and then tries another door. This one swings freely and opens into the brightly lit kitchen where she sees a short, plump, white-haired woman, dressed in a gray turtleneck hanging over purple sweatpants with a black woolen ski hat on her head. She is standing next to the kitchen sink with her arms tightly crossed. Her whole body is shaking. A steaming mug of coffee sits on the counter beside her a few inches from a large coffee maker that looks like a museum piece of midcentury plastic out of which Dana sees what she thinks is a brown stained paper towel that's been used as a filter. The woman does not move and her knees are bent slightly as if she's about to run or pounce, but the look on her face shows clearly that she's too startled to go anywhere.

And you are? Dana breaks the silence.

I'm, um, Kenny . . .

Funny, you don't look like a Kenny, Dana snaps.

The woman cannot speak. She is shaking so violently that Dana worries she'll collapse or have a stroke. She tells the woman to sit, and when she doesn't move, Dana drags a chair to where she is standing, places her hands on her shoulders and gently pushes her down. The woman does not resist but the shaking gets worse after she's seated. Dana considers briefly whether she has Parkinson's disease or some other nerve-related affliction. She picks up the mug from the counter and hands it to her.

Have a sip and get your wits about you, Dana says, stepping away to give her space. *And Philip, go find Kenny. If he's not in the house, look above the garage. Something tells me the door to the apartment there is not locked either.*

Philip, who has remained silent beside the kitchen door, nods and wanders out toward the foyer. Dana hears him call Kenny's name, again and again, the sound echoing more dimly as he ascends each flight of stairs, and louder again as he descends and heads out through the hall to the library. Before she hears the front door slam she wonders what he saw upstairs, if everything was covered in sheets and boxed up as it was supposed to be, or exactly as it had been left in the eighties before her parents died.

Turning her attention back to the woman sitting in the center of the kitchen, Dana strains for a gentler tone so as not to send her into an irreversible fit. *Ok, it's just us. My name is Dana Goss and this is my house. Can you explain please who you are and why you are here?*

The woman clenches her jaw and eventually sputters in a girlish voice, *Kenny, he said it was . . . that you were . . . that it'd be fine for . . .*

Dana struggles unsuccessfully to remain calm.

That I was what? Happy to have a stranger padding around my house drinking coffee?

The woman opens her mouth to speak, but before she does they both hear the door in the foyer shut and what sounds like more than one pair of footsteps heading toward the kitchen.

She'd always imagined Kenny to be a young man in his twenties. This must have been how old he was when Joe Lopez left Edgeweather to live with Ada and her family in Queens, a few years after Dana's mother died. *Kenny's a good kid. You can trust him,* Joe had said at the time, so she never bothered to meet him. If he was good enough for Joe, the house would be fine. Whatever else Joe Lopez was, he was fiercely protective of Edgeweather. Dana's only contact with Kenny was a system of faxes and, later, emails that went to Dana and her bookkeeper in which he gave updates on needed house repairs. He'd never missed a month in more than thirty years. Still, for as long as the arrangement had been in place, Dana is surprised to see a tall, silver-haired man enter the room with Philip. At first she thinks it must be Kenny's father but that thought is dispelled when he puts his arm around the woman. *It's ok, Mom. Why don't you go and pack up your things. We'll move Becky out of her room and she can bunk with Kendra for the time being.* Dana is speechless as the woman waddles to the sink, rinses her mug, and wedges it into the right front pocket of her sweatpants. *I'm assuming the mug is yours,* Dana says, breaking the silence. With more confidence than before, she speaks, but as she does she looks at her son instead of Dana, *Yes, sir, I . . . oh, I mean ma'am, Miss Goss. Brought it with me.*

From where? Dana asks, the agitation from their prior exchange returning. The woman shuffles toward the door to the dining room in her sweatpants, upsettingly similar to the pair Dana is wearing, but better fitting. *Nowhere you'd know.* Dana is startled by her cheek, but as she watches her leave she's less angry than she is curious to know how old the woman is, how close she is to her own age.

Kenny crosses the kitchen toward Dana with one of his arms stretched out, as if to shake her hand. And for reasons she cannot fathom, he is smiling. *It's wonderful to finally meet you, Miss Goss. I . . . It's just been so long and I think I'd given up hope of your ever coming back to Edgeweather.*

That's obvious, she replies with more warmth than she intends.

When Kenny's explanation of his mother's hardships—the second husband who died an alcoholic death leaving behind only debts, her back surgeries, etc.—goes on longer than a minute, Dana interrupts him. *I'm so sorry to hear all this, but what does this have to do with me? I assume by now you know you are fired.*

Fired? Kenny is cleary confused, but not thrown. *But Miss Goss you're the one who suggested she stay here. She's been up in that room since you offered it to her a year and a half ago.*

Dana wishes he would stop talking but she hasn't been able to process what he's just said quickly enough to find and speak the words that will shut him up.

Is it the graffiti on the windows out back that you're upset about? It only happened in January . . . I was waiting for the weather to warm a bit before tackling the clean up. I'll get on it tomorrow since you're here. I've got the paint remover and the razor blades . . . the combination worked the last few times the local kids got artistic with spray paint on the house. You should see what they did to the pool at the Kinsey place. Ripped off the winter cover and splattered nearly every inch of the gunite. Bunch of us gave Sam Dolinsky a hand scrubbing and scraping it off. I figure we got off easy.

What keeps Dana from exploding is not the fact that Kenny seems utterly calm and handsome in his jeans and red flannel shirt, it's that he believes what he is saying. And as she watches his stubbled jawline carry on about the graffiti outside, she realizes that what he said about her being the one to suggest his mother move in upstairs is true. Marcella had come to her with a printed email, incredulous that Kenny had the audacity to suggest that his mother move in with him above the garage. Marcella loved this sort of moment. Another person in Dana's employ crossing a line and in the crosshairs of potential consequences. Dana remembers vaguely how Marcella suggested they look for someone else, find an established estate management company to take over the house and grounds. Abruptly, and with painful clarity, she remembers the words she spoke in response. *Tell Kenny she should live in the main house. Pick any room she likes on the third floor. And please do it now.* Marcella's face turned to stone and Dana raised her hand to silence her from objecting. *Now. And don't mention it again.* In the eighteen months since that moment with Marcella, no one mentioned the woman living at Edgeweather. And because they did not, Dana simply forgot.

I thought . . . Kenny has finally run out of words and is standing almost exactly where his mother had been when Dana entered the kitchen earlier. She motions for Philip to follow her out to the foyer. She does not look him in the eye as she whispers at him. *This situation has gotten out of hand, so please go and apologize to Kenny and tell him I've had a long day and have not been well. His mother needs to leave the house tonight because I will be staying here, but once I leave tomorrow she's welcome to return. It's not a sustainable situation but we'll figure that out later. Hurry, get them out of here. I'll wait in the library.*

Philip squints at Dana as if she is speaking a foreign language. She steps away before he has a chance to respond. As she crosses the foyer and considers what has just transpired, it shocks her to recognize that a moment of spite toward Marcella would result in a stranger, an old woman she'd never met, living in Edgeweather for so long. *Forgetful god*, the chastising, grandiose words surface from some book or film she can't remember as she passes the paint-splattered panes of the breezeway. The letters spelling "ASSHOLES" in black and red viewed from behind look menacing, their intended aggression visible to her now and not the least bit funny, as they had been before. When she reaches the library, she looks for a light switch but at first finds none. There are two leather couches facing each other, on either side of which sit large table lamps; only one, she discovers, has a working light bulb. After twisting it on and finding the light casting on the two stories of unopened books depressing, she quickly turns it off and sits down on one of the couches.

Forgetful god, she kneads the words as she lets her body go slack against the stiff leather cushion. She spreads her fingers on the dry grain, rests her head against the hard arm, and as she falls asleep tries to remember where she could have possibly come across such a phrase.

Lupita

When she gets up from the kitchen table to go to her bedroom, she leaves her phone behind. She clears away an old pair of Crocs and a short pile of towels from the top of the cedar trunk at the end of her bed. She hasn't opened the old wood box in a long time and she can hear wood splinter along the hinges as she pushes the lid back until it rests against the end of the mattress. It takes her a few minutes but she eventually finds what she's looking for.

The doll has seen better days. She's kept it in the trunk since it surfaced a few years back in a rare purging of junk from the basement. Poor packing hadn't protected it from mice, sharp edges, even a leak from an uncapped pen. It was never a finely made or lifelike thing. Nor was it ever a toy. It was an object born of missing and for a short time mattered so much that she prayed to it every night and morning. It took almost a month to make, though it was little more than a dried corn husk, a dozen or so finger-length pieces of burlap string, a gym sock, a fistful of brown yarn, and a wooden spoon. Even after so many years, and with all the rips and stains and nibbled edges, it still had magic. Not the intended, hoped-for magic when it was made, but a quieter kind that could only be recognized now, far away from where it came from.

Lupita lifts the doll from the towel it has been wrapped in. She runs her thumb along the dark brown braids, reties the red-and-white checkered fabric bows at each end, and arranges them in front of the doll's stiff arms made from a single lilac branch that is now visible beneath the dried husk that had deteriorated under the tightly knotted jute. As she would smooth wrinkles on her own blouse, she strokes her fingertips across the front of the brittle garment, a poor replica of a simple spring dress once worn by the girl the doll was modeled after. She gently flicks a smudge of dirt from the hem and sends a small cloud of dust particles floating out and up around the doll's face. She picks the tiny specks that fall along the hairline and notices the strict part down the middle of the narrow head made of sock and spoon, the braids so tight they have not come loose in more than half a century. She runs her fingers over the husks, the yarn, the dingy gray cloth where the mouth should be. Lupita wonders what the doll would say if she could speak, how she would answer the thousands of prayers she'd whispered to her. Involuntarily, like an air bubble popping to the water's surface after a long, slow ascent, her sister's name sounds from the back of her throat, *Ada*.

When they were young and in Florida, before moving to New York and Connecticut, Ada was the closest thing Lupita had to a best friend. Their father worked long hours on a crew that built roads, and their mother cleaned houses and babysat in the evenings, so the two girls were often on their own after school and on the weekends. In the first year, they spent most of their time in the apartment—making forts out of sofa cushions, dressing up in their mother's blouses and pretending to be everything from police officers to princesses. They listened to the radio and tried to make sense of and mimic the English-speaking DJs and sing Elvis Presley songs. Occasionally, they'd venture outside to blow bubbles with water and dish soap, using the small plastic wands they'd kept from the pink bottles with colored bubble solution their father had given them when they'd first arrived. There were other children in the apartment complex where they first lived, but they were mainly from Cuba, and while they didn't pick on Ada and Lupita, they kept to themselves and communicated clearly with rolled eyes and turned backs that they didn't want to have anything to do with them.

Lupita was four and Ada was eleven when they came from Mexico with their mother. Their father's first job in Florida had been on a farm that grew ferns people potted and put in their houses. As her mother had described it, he and his friend were part of a program that allowed Mexicans to work in America without being citizens. They had a contract with the fern farmer and lived in a camp with other Mexican workers. When Lupita was older and had asked why their family had not left Mexico together, her mother responded by saying that there were no children allowed then, and that the camp where he'd lived had been like a jail. Later, when he started building roads and making a little more money, enough to rent a small apartment and pay for their journey to Florida, they joined him. Before then, they lived with their grandmother in the same three-room concrete house in Catemaco her mother had grown up in. It sat between other houses that looked exactly like it in a crowded neighborhood between a freshwater lake and the Gulf of Mexico.

Lupita's memories of her grandmother are spotty and impossible to fully distinguish from her sister's. It was Ada who'd told her she'd been a *partera*, a midwife, and a *curandera*, a healer, but when Lupita lived with her she did not know why people came to their door at all hours and waited for her to grab her large brown bag and come with them. She would sometimes be gone for days and then reappear, exhausted, and sleep late, sometimes all day. When she wasn't assisting in childbirth she sat in a chair in front of the house and people came to her with their problems. She sometimes prayed with them, often with her hands on their head or face or body, other times she chanted or sang and made them tea. Lupita remembers her grandmother's hands as large and rough, with long warm fingers, and when she was curled in her lap, they stroked her forehead, her cheek, and brushed the hair away from her eyes.

Lupita has no memory of saying goodbye to her grandmother when she was four years old, but she thinks she remembers the sound her grandmother made. It's not attached to an image of her face or her tears, or where she was standing or sitting, just the sound itself—a high, ragged keening she knows is the saddest, most suffering sound she's ever heard. She and Ada and her mother took a bus later that day from Catemaco to Reynosa but she does not remember it. What she remembers is her mother squeezing her hand so hard it hurt and whispering sharply at her to stay silent as a man she did not know picked her up and carried her over water. She remembers darkness and not being able to tell which way was up or down. The memory ends with the sound of water swooshing between legs, and the feeling of something terrible about to happen. She has never remembered what followed—crossing the Rio Grande in a small raft, walking and being carried in the dark through fields and along back roads to the bus station in McAllen, Texas, and waiting there until morning to take the bus to San Antonio, Houston, out through Louisiana, across the Florida panhandle, and finally down to Belle Glade, Florida, where their father was waiting. Because Ada had told her, she knew that this was how they came to the United States; that this is what happened, and that these were the places they'd passed through. Her mother never spoke about that night, the river, or the bus rides the next day, and Lupita understood without being told why that she was not supposed to bring it up.

Though the journey to Florida is mostly blank, Lupita remembers being frightened by almost everything after they arrived. First and foremost, by her father, who'd left Mexico when she was one and a half, whom her mother and grandmother and Ada talked about all the time, but whom she had no memory of. Until then, she'd only lived with women and she wasn't used to having a man around. The swift change in atmosphere, and in her mother's mood, when her father came home after work confused and terrified her.

The apartment her father had rented them was on the first floor of a three-story apartment complex. Lupita had never lived anywhere but her grandmother's house, had never slept even one night in a building that had a second floor, so the voices and footfalls above sounded to her like wild animals, or monsters. Ada comforted her with stories of their grandmother, and where they came from. Catemaco, she explained, was where witches and sorcerers gathered. Lupita loved hearing her describe how their grandmother was a good witch who brought babies into the world, healed the sick, and how, before they left home, she protected them with a powerful spell that would for all their lives keep them from harm.

Many years later, Lupita would look online and research the town she'd come from to find out that Catemaco actually had been a famous hub of withcraft, a place where many Mexicans, Americans and Europeans traveled to be healed or have curses placed on enemies. Of course there was nothing about her grandmother in any of the articles—she didn't expect there to be—but she was still disappointed.

Lupita never tired of Ada's stories about their grandmother. She had little more than a few vivid but fleeting impressions, so she badgered Ada to share what she remembered which she was mostly willing to do, unlike their mother who would order Lupita to take out the trash or hang laundry at the mere mention of her mother. *She will never stop missing her*, Ada told her. Their grandmother didn't have a phone and she wasn't much of a writer, so beyond a handful of signed generic birthday and holiday cards, their contact was scant. Still, Lupita believed that her protective incantation would keep them safe. She clung to that belief through the five years they were in Belle Glade, living in two apartments, three shared houses, and occasionally motels in between. She clung to it when she started kindergarten and didn't know more than a few words in English, and through the next two years of learning the language that came more easily to her than it did to Ada and her parents. But she clung hardest at nine years old when her mother told her that their family would be moving to New York City.

When Lupita was older she would understand the story better, how one of the men her father worked with knew the caretaker of an estate owned by a wealthy family who spent part of their winters in Palm Beach. The caretaker needed help removing trees that had fallen on the property during a storm and had asked his friend to recruit a few capable men to help. When Lupita's father heard about the job, he swiftly volunteered. The caretaker, a man Lupita would come to know as Miguel Esparza, was impressed by how hard and well he worked and called on him from time to time over the years when there were larger jobs to do. In the few months out of the year that the estate owners were in Palm Beach, Lupita's mother was hired to help with meals and cleaning. This is when she got to know Mrs. Goss who, she'd told her daughters, took a quick shine to her. She'd even bragged that Mrs. Goss already preferred her to Miguel Esparza's lazy wife, Frida. Two winters later, Lupita overheard her mother speaking very quickly and with obvious excitement to Ada. She was telling her that Mrs. Goss needed a caretaker for their country house up north and a housekeeper for their apartment in Manhattan. Less than a month after that, her mother sat her down on their couch to tell her they were moving.

When Lupita asked her mother if there was room for all

of them in the Gosses' apartment, she explained, as if such an arrangement were perfectly normal, that she and Ada would be the ones to live and work in the city and that Lupita would live with her father in the countryside where he'd be the caretaker of the family's large house. She described an apartment above the garage there big enough for all of them and she promised they'd be together every weekend, on holidays and in the summers. Lupita was immediately seized with panic at the prospect of being separated from Ada and her mother, whom she'd never spent a night apart from. She pleaded with her mother to change her mind, but she explained that the job was a godsend, that the family would be sponsoring not only hers and her father's green cards but Ada's and Lupita's as well, and that if things worked out, and they stayed with the family long enough, they would help them all become permanent citizens. For this reason alone, she said, they had no choice. At nine years old, Lupita only had a vague idea about the meaning of green cards and citizenship but she knew they were important and especially to families like theirs who'd come to the United States from Mexico.

In the months before they left Florida, Lupita noticed her mother becoming more energetic, less somber and exhausted, which had been her usual way. In that short period of time she was almost cheerful, which made knowing they'd soon be living apart even more painful. Her mother tried to make her understand how wonderful their new future would be. She'd made it clear that the security of being sponsored was by far the most important, but to this she added that growing up in a small, safe town, with nice houses and good schools, was far better than anything a big city like New York or swampy Belle Glade could offer; and, most practically, how working for the Gosses meant they would not have to pay rent anywhere and therefore be able to save up for Lupita's college education.

Going to college was something Lupita's mother had often talked about, and in the first few years in Florida, she told both girls that they needed to work hard at school in order to go to college and get good jobs. But after a few years of Ada struggling with English and getting poor grades, their mother stopped encouraging her and shifted her focus to Lupita, who she frequently reminded was the family's best chance. For what specifically she never said but it was clear that it meant graduating somehow into a life that did not involve cleaning bathrooms and babysitting other people's children.

The year before they moved to New York, Ada dropped out of high school. At the time, Lupita saw her as the lucky one, the one who didn't have to go to school, and even luckier once they moved to New York, where she didn't have to live with their volatile father, but instead got to stay with their mother in a beautiful apartment in New York City. But Ada didn't act like she felt lucky. After she quit school and started working with her mother cleaning houses, she became distant and impatient with Lupita; and in the weeks before they left Florida she stopped speaking to her altogether and when she did it was only to huff at her to shut up or stop singing or get out of the way.

On the drive north to New York, Lupita tried to connect with her sister by asking her to imagine with her what the Gosses' apartment and house would look like, but Ada wouldn't engage. Lupita persisted by asking her questions about the family who she'd worked for a few times with their mother in Palm Beach. Lupita was especially interested in anything there was to find out about their daughter who was, her mother had told her, only a year older than she was. But Ada cut her questions short, *They're rich and they have dirty dishes. You're the only one in this family who won't have to wash them.*

On the day they arrived at Edgeweather, Lupita begged Ada

to convince their mother to let her come with them to New York City. She responded by grabbing her small shoulders and shaking her violently, something she'd never done before. She said through tears that she never wanted to hear her complain again because everything she and their parents had done, and were doing—being apart for years, moving to Florida, getting work in New York and Connecticut, making beds, building roads, mowing lawns, babysitting, cleaning houses—*all of it* was for her. *This is not for me, do you understand? Not for them, either. None of it. This is for you.* Her sister looked like an angry stranger, and nothing had ever frightened Lupita as much, or made her feel as lonely. And so she ran—across the empty road, past the stables and fenced fields, and into the darkest woods she'd ever seen. With each hard footfall she felt her grandmother's magic weaken.

Three months later, when her grandmother died, it felt to Lupita like God was punishing her family. Her father explained that no one would be able to attend the funeral. That it would be years before they would be able to travel back to Mexico, if ever. Lupita remembered the night they'd left; her mother's tight hand and desperate whisper. She tried to picture Ada, and the stranger who carried her, but the strongest memory she had was of her mother's fear, and her own. She felt that same fear return when her father told her she would never see her grandmother again. Her family had already been divided, but it suddenly felt newly exposed. With her grandmother no longer in the world, Lupita believed they were now truly on their own.

The idea for the doll came to her from a dream she thought might also be a real memory of her grandmother. In the dream, she's holding a doll. When Lupita asked her about it, her grandmother explained that after having had two sons she'd wanted a baby girl, but worried she might be too old. She believed the best way forward was to show God what it was she wanted, and so she made the doll. With it, she prayed every morning and night, and eventually her prayers were answered. *Tu madre vino a nosotros.*

Soon after Lupita and her father moved in above the garage at Edgeweather, she set about making a doll that looked like Ada. She took dark brown yarn from an old wool scarf she found hanging from a hook in the garage. She stowed it under her bed and unraveled it at night after her father went to sleep. It was lighter than Ada's hair, but it was the best she could do. She stole the wooden spoon from the kitchen she and her father shared and scoured the boxes and closets in the garage for the rest. Before the end of summer, her doll was complete. Her mother would have wrinkled her nose at the uneven hem of the dress, but would have approved of the hair, which was thick and even and pulled into two perfect braids. It was as close to a replica of her sister as she could make. It reminded her of the nights they slept side by side on floors and pullout couches and old mattresses as they moved from place to place in Florida. Ada, more than her mother, soothed Lupita when she woke in the night from a bad dream. After Lupita described what had tormented her, usually a scenario involving a giant bird plucking her from the sky or an unseen ocean creature pulling her to the bottom of the sea, Ada would hold her hand and tell her it was safe to go back to sleep. *Los monstruos no son reales*, she would say, more a straight reporting of the fact than a tender coddling. Still, in those first months above the garage in Wells, Lupita wanted nothing more than to wake up and find Ada next to her, to hear her sure, sturdy voice reminding her that what she had dreamed was not real and that nothing in the world could harm her.

As her grandmother had done, she made a replica of what she wanted most. She showed it to God each morning and night and told him her heart's desire: for Ada to come back. Not just from

New York where she was living, but as the sister she'd known before, the one who made her feel safe.

It's long past midnight now and Lupita has swept the small brick terrace that surrounds the fire pit behind her house. Normally, the fire pit is alive with jasmine, plumeria, hibiscus and mint marigold, along with succulents arranged in ceramic pots and teak boxes. But tonight, she's hauled away the small jungle of leaves and buds and curling vines and filled the pit with sticks and driftwood she's gathered from the beach and stacked on top of cardboard boxes ripped into small panels, egg cartons she'd saved for recycling, and dozens of crumpled paper shopping bags. To make sure it burns, she soaks it all in lighter fluid.

The doll is tucked under her arm when she drops the lit match onto the flammable pile. She watches the fire catch—first the slick of fluid, immediately followed by the paper and cardboard, then the sticks and twigs, and from those the flames lick and twist upward into the windy night. She throws on thicker branches and boards and soon the fire crackles and roars and the air around the pit shimmers. It looks like a dragon's mouth spewing an old hate. Startled, she steps back. She reminds herself where she is and when—home, her backyard, now—and lets the heat on her face and arms calm her. She remembers the doll. She passes it from one hand to the other, pinches its sloppy hem between her thumb and ring finger, and leans closer to the fire. She dangles her failed magic above the flames, and then does the one and only thing she's ever done perfectly. She lets go.

Part Two

Hap

His father sings in his sleep. Mostly jingles from the forties—
Brylcreem, Schlitz beer, Camel cigarettes. *How mild, how mild,
how mild can a cigarette be? Smoke Camels and see.* His voice is radio
smooth, soothing, at least two octaves higher than his regular
speaking voice, and sounds young, despite his seventy-nine years.
In between the jingles, the same old Bing Crosby song, "Swinging
on a Star." *Carry moonbeams home in a jar . . .*

After four days sitting at his father's bedside, Hap only now
notices that the tissue-thin hospital gown bunching around his
neck is covered in snowflakes. Small and blue and perfectly spaced
a quarter inch or so from each other against worn, gray cotton,
their whimsy in this decidedly non-whimsical hospital room like a
knock-knock joke slipped into a eulogy.

How many people have worn this gown, Hap wonders. And
how often did those sitting bedside wince when they realized their
loved ones were covered in snowflakes? Maybe for some it was a
comfort, something that lifted their mood, amused them even,
if only briefly. Possibly this was the point of the design: to sneak
light into a situation that had none. Is that what his father's sub-
conscious was doing now, returning to these old songs?

Hap had been aware, dimly, from a story he'd overheard Alice,
his mother, tell when he was a kid, that his father sang advertising
jingles on the radio in college for pocket money. But that's all he
knew—it never occurred to Hap to find out more. It was the same
with his father's job as a photographer with a news agency. He

knew little more than that it required him to travel to Asia, Africa, and the Middle East. Another murky half-fact that speckled what little he knew of his father's life, most of which—like singing in college—now sparked more questions than answers. Four days after Hap's father had fallen down the lobby staircase at the Hotel Bethlehem, surfacing from more than twenty-four unconscious hours, not recognizing his son or knowing his own name, Hap knew his chance for answers had likely passed.

His father mumble-hums the Bing Crosby again. The words are now marbles in his mouth, impossible to decipher, but his pitch is still perfect, the sound carefree, bright, from a long-ago time in his father's life when the future was more vivid and mattered more than the present. When he still had a future, Hap thinks bitterly, standing up and away from the bed, the idea of a point in life where the future ceased—for his father, for him, for anyone—settling on him now, at forty-eight, like a slow, cold fog. He leans awkwardly against the wall next to the one small window in the room, a single pane with no handle or latch that looks over a narrow courtyard to another bank of small-windowed rooms.

Across the way, two floors below, a teenager curls in a window well, head down, arms up and tangled across his face; back and legs twisted into a pretzel that from two flights up looks cozy. Only a kid could bend his body into such a small space, Hap thinks. And only an oblivious, self-centered boy could find comfort here.

The exact type of medical calamity the boy is attending is out of view from where Hap stands, the only visible clues a short expanse of putty-colored linoleum floor, and what looks like a pile of coats on a gray metal chair, a perfect replica of the one Hap has been sitting in. He can't help but wonder who in this boy's life suffers just out of sight in the same bed his father lies in now, under the same water-stained dropped ceiling, between the same pale pink walls (besides the snowflakes, the only other flicker of whimsy in the place). The boy twists again but miraculously retains his leg and arm-knotted, torso-bent shape, like a snake in motion, coiled. A flash of resentment heats to an instant and sharp pain at Hap's temples. Is there anything more galling than the sight of a young man? More revolting than all that possibility possessed by a creature so completely ignorant of it? *Fuck no*, Hap answers his own questions, out loud and louder than he intends, looking away and back toward his father, who is silent now, his chest rising and falling mechanically with the thrum and wheeze of the oxygen machine wheeled alongside the bed. This here, *this* mess is the very opposite of the rubber-limbed nimrod below.

Young and dumb and full of cum, the crude phrase pops into his head uninvited, something he must have heard in a movie he'd seen on HBO, or, even more likely, something his childhood best friend Gene would have said in high school, or even now over dinner to provoke Hap's wife, Leah. As if they were both in the room now, huddled on either side of him looking out the window, Hap can hear Gene reduce the boy with this phrase, and in response he can hear Leah just as clearly, with false playfulness and palpable sarcasm in her voice: *Playing the part of Gene Grant this evening: Gene Grant!* But looking at the boy now, a simple pile of limbs and skin and solipsistic impulses, he can't help but see him as Gene would. A lucky little fucker.

Hap slumps into the window well. He squeezes his eyes shut and tries to silence his mind by picturing Leah and their newborn and still unnamed baby girl curled in his childhood bed at Alice's house less than a mile away. He has seen them only briefly in four days; the last time, yesterday afternoon in the hospital lobby for twenty minutes. Leah pleaded with Hap to come back to his mother's house and spend the night. *Hap, I can spell you here. I'll sit with your father, sleep in the chair next to him, while you get some rest and spend time with the baby.* When he said he couldn't, the angles of her face shifted from exhausted and compassionate to fully alert and impatient. She grabbed his wrists and as she spoke her voice pierced above the lobby noises and people nearby turned to see. Leah did not quiet her words. *You're missing it, Hap. She's been alive six days and you were around for exactly one and a half of them. Your father is unconscious, and it's terrible, but your daughter is awake—every three hours, around the clock, hungry and beautiful. Her first week is nearly over and you won't be able to go back to day two where you left off and experience it when you're ready. When it's done, it's done.*

The pain at his temples has spread to the top and back of his head. He holds his face in both hands. He thinks about the most recent names Leah has suggested—Kelly, Emma, Faith—all three from her family: aunt, sister, grandmother. He tries to remember his daughter's pink, bunched face to see if any of the names stick. But he can't. He'd spent so little time with her before he left abruptly. Since then he's seen and held her only twice, briefly. He tries to picture her again and fails. All he can remember is her jet-black tufts of hair, nothing like his or Leah's shades of blond.

He rubs his eyes out of frustration and what he sees instead of his daughter's face is his boss's a few months ago, reacting when he told her he was leaving *The Philadelphia Inquirer* to be a stay-at-home dad for a few years. Amused disbelief gave way to confusion and eventually landed on contempt. His boss was new, a forty-something former *New York Times* culture editor who'd taken a buyout and moved to Philly for the job. She and Hap barely knew each other, so it shouldn't have been a surprise that the conversation that followed was a short one amounting to asking Hap to pack up his office and surrender his building pass and bathroom key. Eighteen years at the *Inquirer* as a reporter and editor and a finger pointed to HR was his goodbye. His remaining friends at the paper—most were laid off or had left in the last decade of mergers and downsizing—organized a send-off in the bar at the Outback Steakhouse not far from the old department store building where the paper moved after its once-grand, long-occupied fortress had been sold. They shoved three tables together, wrapped a bottle of tequila with the sports page, and toasted to his early retirement. *Hope your wife doesn't get fired*, he'd heard as he put on his coat and said his goodbyes. He recognized the tipsy lisp of a young, recently hired online advertising guy: *It's not like editorial jobs for middle-aged white guys at newspapers are growing on trees.* Indeed. Leah's job as associate dean of interdisciplinary programs at Lehigh looked pretty secure but so had the newspaper business, which had steadily been constricting around him for the last fifteen or so years. Perhaps a college education of the four-year, liberal arts variety would soon be considered just as unnecessary as the morning paper.

Hap closes his eyes and starts to hum, an old trick his mother taught him to empty his mind when he was stressed. When he opens his eyes and looks down across the courtyard, the boy in the window is gone. Worry replaces bitterness and Hap squints to see who or what has called the kid away. But there is no information in what he sees: an unobstructed view of the floor, the metal chair, the shucked coats, a wedge of pink wall. No glimpse of the wrecked body causing the teenager to be in the hospital on a Tuesday morning; nothing to suggest who from his enviably young, dumb life was strung up with tubes pumping painkillers and antibiotics into their weary veins, dozing under a thin garment of snowflakes, singing songs for the last time.

Alice

She'd forgotten about babies. Not since her twenties, when Hap was an infant, had she experienced the immediate and finely tuned connection between a brand-new life and its mother. She hadn't remembered that like the most sensitive barometers, newborns gauge grades of absence and attention, fear and frustration, even in the most present parent, reacting instantly to the faintest disturbance; sometimes, happily, with coos and giggles, but much more frequently with fussing and volcanic screaming.

Her granddaughter, still unnamed at six days old, and still too new in the world for coos and giggles, has wailed almost nonstop since Hap and Leah brought her home from the hospital. Hap had been with them for a day and a morning before he left to meet Christopher at the hotel and never came back. And now Leah's disappearances keep getting longer. At first she would politely hand Alice the baby with apology and profuse thanks and then step outside to call Hap, usually without success, leaving messages and sending texts until she came storming back through the front door ten or fifteen minutes later. Now she doesn't bother to say she's heading out, just throws her coat on and either leaves the baby screaming in the bassinet or thrusts her into Alice's arms as if somehow she's to blame—not only for the child's upset, but for Hap's abandonment.

Today marks Leah's longest absence. She left after three and has been gone for more than two hours. No texts or messages of explanation, nor any promises to return. She's following her husband's example, claiming her own freedom in a time when she should be surrendering to the blunt truth that for now and the near future she has none. Meanwhile, their child screams— for milk, diaper changes, and constant, round-the-clock love, the warm skin of her mother's arm and hands and breasts. Alice walks the house patting her tiny back, bouncing gently, mimicking the snug safety of the womb she's just left. After completing yet another lap around the upstairs bedrooms and hall and beginning to descend the stairs, she feels, and not for the first time in the last few days, a creeping sense of history repeating itself, delivering a twisted karmic taunt. She wonders if this is the closing of a long, old loop or the beginning of a new one. Or perhaps a shadow from another time dancing on the wall to remind her what Mo always said: *There are no accidents, no chance encounters. Only the plan, unfolding as it was always meant to.*

So much of Alice's life seemed determined by happenstance and accident it was hard to accept the idea of a predetermined destiny. She found the suggestion insulting, as if she'd had nothing to do with any of it. Still, she knew how someone's arrival or exit could reroute your life. For Alice, Christopher's arrival and his exit had done just that.

He'd given her his seat on the bus. That's how it began. She was coming back from a job interview at Sarah Lawrence College and nearly missed the five-thirty Greyhound to Philadelphia. By the time she boarded the bus it was filled with commuters and holiday shoppers and many of the women, and some men, had loaded the seats next to them with department store bags packed with wrapped gifts. Most were turned toward the windows feigning sleep or simply scowling to discourage anyone from asking them to make room. There was nowhere to sit. And then a hand on the back of her arm and a friendly voice. *Here, Miss, take my seat.* It was such a simple act, one that from the distance of years seems kind, of course, but also perfectly ordinary. Still, it was the moment that brought Christopher Foster into her life. She can't remember exactly how she responded to him, if she spoke or gestured her appreciation, but she does remember the young man grabbing his small overnight bag from the floor in front of him and retreating to the back of the bus where, she would find out later, he'd persuaded an older gentleman—a talkative dressmaker from Chestnut Hill who made regular trips to the garment district in New York—to allow him to help move the bolts of fabric from the seat next to him to the rack above.

It does not surprise Alice to remember who sat next to Christopher but not who sat beside her. She can even recall the fabrics the dressmaker bought that day—dark paisley silk and ivory velvet—but has no memory of what she wore. It would have included a blazer of some kind—she'd always worn a blazer on job interviews—but whether it was the navy or the gray one, slacks or skirt, turtleneck or blouse, she has no idea. This was what frequently happened to her with Christopher. He told stories about his life in such a way that they eclipsed whatever else might have been competing for her attention; in them he animated his world so vividly and with such precision and intimacy, that it came to matter more to her than her own.

When the bus pulled into the Philadelphia station, Alice waited in her seat so she could thank him when he passed. As he made his way down the narrow aisle and came into view, she was caught off-guard by his looks. She'd only had a brief glimpse when he'd offered his seat; she was too harried from rushing and too desperate to find somewhere to sit down to get a good look at him. But she could see him now. With thick, fair hair and dark blue eyes, dressed in a white button-down shirt, brown corduroy slacks, and a short, half-zipped navy cotton jacket, he was the epitome of her idea, then, of a clean-cut, handsome young man. He looked like Ryan O'Neal in *Peyton Place*. As he approached, Alice forgot what she wanted to say to him. *Are you ok?* he asked and gently touched her arm for the second time that day.

Right away, they started dating. Christopher was working for *The Philadelphia Inquirer* on the city desk. Alice was completing her PhD at Penn, beginning to search for a teaching position at a university. For six months it was a whirlwind of meals in the immigrant neighborhoods of Philadelphia and weekend trips to New York where Christopher still kept his apartment from his undergraduate years at NYU and journalism school at Columbia. He introduced her to Japanese steak houses and off-the-grid soul food restaurants where people served biscuits and chicken on fold-up tables in their garages. He also took her to her first rally to protest the war in Vietnam. Alice had studied United States history with a focus on Pennsylvania and New York during the Civil War. She had been somewhat sequestered in the protected bubble of Bryn Mawr, though less so at Penn, and she didn't consider herself political. She followed the news and feared, as most people she knew did, an escalation of the conflict. After the Gulf of Tonkin attack the year before, she became especially worried for her cousins who were in their late teens and likely to get called up. But her relationship to events was distant compared to Christopher's friends, who were either conscientious objectors burning their draft cards or active in anti-war rallies and publications. Some had even been arrested. Christopher was against the war but did not burn his card. He said if he was drafted he would go, that he didn't believe in the war, but if he had to serve he would use it as an opportunity to photograph what was happening. When he first explained this to Alice, she thought he was unbelievably brave and more than a little naive. But the longer she knew him, the more she suspected it was the fear of retribution from his family that kept him from setting fire to that piece of paper. In the end, he never got called up. He was thirty-one by the time the first lottery was conducted in 1969 and the boys who went were mostly teenagers or in their early twenties.

Christopher was restless in the winter and spring of 1966. He was stringing at *The Inquirer* but itching to leave the East Coast and work where important things were happening. Alice had dated boys in school but none of them had ever cared about anything the way Christopher did. And until then she'd not been open to much more than the occasional date and had little interest in passionate men. She'd been focused on her studies and had worked babysitting and dining hall jobs to pay rent, buy food, clean her clothes, afford bus-fare—the day-to-day expenses not covered by the scholarships that had delivered her from Bethlehem, Pennsylvania. She kept in touch with her family but they still teased her for getting too smart for them, too big for her britches. The accusations, even in jest, bothered her, so Alice came home on weekends just frequently enough that her mother stopped sending postcards with notes on the back reporting that everyone wondered when she'd come home next.

Falling in love with Christopher—a project her family could understand and fully support without hesitation—gave her a pass not to see them so much. Christopher had a very different relationship to his family, but they, too, appeared relieved to see he'd finally begun to get serious about someone. According to his brother's wife, Ellen, whom Alice met only once, Christopher had not introduced a girl to the family since high school. At the time, it made sense to Alice that he kept his personal life discrete from his family whose politics and beliefs were at odds with his own. Both his parents were politically and socially conservative—his father an Eastern District federal judge in Philadelphia and his mother a housewife who spent most of her time involved in fund-raising efforts for the restoration of local landmarks as well as the private day school for girls she'd attended. Alice knew the school because many of her classmates from Bryn Mawr had gone there.

Christopher's two older brothers were both lawyers and married with children. All of the Fosters—parents, children and grandchildren—lived in big houses and worked and parented and socialized and went to school within the well-marked and rigidly observed boundaries of the Main Line. Christopher was the rebel but he'd only rebelled so far. He'd gone to school in New York but by agreement with his father, after completing Columbia Journalism School, and more than a year traveling in Europe and Africa, he took a job in Philadelphia. He'd been at *The Inquirer* just over two years when he and Alice met on the bus.

Christopher would later admit that in the week before he met Alice, he'd been rehearsing a speech he planned to give his parents, one that finally told them, among other things, that it was time for him to go where it mattered to report the truth of what was happening in the world, both in words and in photographs. Alice slowed the delivery of that speech down by eight months. But when he did finally make it—first to his parents and hours later to Alice—it was not about reporting the truth, it was about confessing his own: that he'd had male lovers since his freshman year at NYU and he needed to end their relationship because he could no longer lie to her, his parents, to anyone.

Alice sat still on the bench in the cafeteria at school and listened. In the seconds before she could speak, he filled the silence by lurching into a detailed account of how he'd explained who he was to his parents, and how they had rejected the news, actually disagreed with him! He was stunned, incredulous—but he was free. As she listened to him animate every appalling detail of their reaction, she recognized that he was, without malice, but with the solipsism of the self-righteous, recounting an exhilarating prison break to one of his unwitting jailers. He left no room for her to react. And she let him. She listened in horror as the future she'd only just begun to count on disappeared. Christoper's upset was big and urgent and consuming, and she was able to duck her own by joining his outrage with how his parents had negated him. Alice was mortified when he described his mother's reaction—*It's not true*, she'd corrected him, crossing her arms and silently daring her son to disagree; and enraged by his father's—*You've spent too much time in New York*, he'd declared, not for the first time, and then suggested that if he insisted on trying to embarrass the family, he should leave Philadelphia. *Let us know when you're ready to be reasonable*, Christopher mimicked his father's icy farewell. These words would turn out to be the last he spoke to his son.

A year later, Christopher called Alice to tell her that his father had died. By then, her own feelings—bickering siblings of grief and anger and resignation—had crowded into the space left by his absence. She felt badly for him, but it was from a new distance. *That's very sad news. Thanks for letting me know*, she'd said into the phone in her office, sounding colder than she'd intended. By then she had taken a tenure track teaching position at Lehigh University in Bethlehem. Before she met Christopher she'd imagined going farther away—Duke in North Carolina, Sarah Lawrence or Barnard in New York, the University of Michigan in Ann Arbor—but after their relationship ended, she retreated to the people and places she knew, the ones with few surprises, if any. She went home.

Hap

The food in the hospital cafeteria is how he had imagined food in the 1960s. Bright white bread, fluorescent orange cheese, casseroles with crusted toppings. The drink options, too, are from another era. Whole milk, Hawaiian Punch and grape Fanta on tap. Except for elementary school, Hap wonders if he's ever been anywhere that sold a glass of milk as a beverage. And Fanta, hadn't that gone the way of Tab in the late eighties? Clearly there were ample reserves of the stuff in Bethlehem, Pennsylvania.

The woman behind the counter is striking. Thick red hair, swirling and bound behind a clear nylon net; high cheekbones, bright blue eyes, and a very straight nose so perfectly proportioned and angular it looks, under the harsh fluorescent lights, as if it had been removed from a mannequin's face and grafted somehow onto hers. Hap reflexively compares all attractive people he sees to celebrities, and he can't help but think this woman is a dead ringer for Maureen O'Hara in *The Parent Trap*. Just like the food, he thinks, straight from the sixties. Her voice, however, is very clearly Now and unmistakably local.

Waddya want?

All business and obviously exhausted, the woman speaks as she stoops to pick something up from the floor behind the counter before flinging it into the trash can against the wall.

Lunch closes in a few minutes.

No lovely echo of mid-century Disney Studios here, only the sound of what Hap imagines is some combination or complete résumé of delinquent child support, credit card debt, online dating, and regret. And the accent is one hundred percent Bethlehem, PA. A hybrid mouth-swerve landing somewhere between the accent cousins of Philadelphia and Baltimore. In some mouths, like his mother's, the inflection is subtle and warm. In others, like his best friend Gene's, who still milked his up-from-the-bootstraps-scholarship-kid roots, the sound is plucky and endearing. Or at least it used to be. But in some, like this woman in clear plastic gloves, hairnet, and black jeans, it is, as his father said more than a few times, unlovely. She reminds Hap of his childhood. The hardscrabble and often fighting parents of many of his school friends, Gene's especially; even some of the teachers and coaches. Bethlehem was and still is mainly a town of the working middle class, an hour's car ride from Philly but a world away, with the unemployed poor and idle rich in disproportionate minorities on either end of the spectrum, the latter of course the least represented group in the Lehigh Valley.

Hap's family fell into the educated part of the working middle. His mother was a history professor at Lehigh University, a gothic swath of lawns and buildings for visiting privilege wedged in the hills above the once mighty Bethlehem Steel mills. The campus is less than a quarter mile from the rust skyline of smokestacks and blast furnaces that overwhelm the short length of the Lehigh River dividing the town center, but for the sons and daughters of steel workers the journey from the charred Oz on the valley floor to the turrets of Lehigh, or places like it, was daunting. By the time the last mills closed in the mid-nineties, after decades of layoffs and pay-cuts, crossing that distance had become close to impossible. Hap knew two exceptions: the first was Gene, from a family of unemployed alcoholics, a gifted student who tested high and performed higher. Valedictorian of Hap's class at Freedom High School, Gene got a full scholarship to the University of

Pennsylvania and then went to NYU Law School, after which he became the second black partner at an important Park Avenue firm specializing in mergers and acquisitions.

The other person Hap knew who'd risen from food stamps to graduate degrees was his mother. She was the daughter of a laid-off boilermaker who was the son of a welder from a family of blacksmiths and millwrights and bricklayers. Hap's mother's family could trace their employment at Bethlehem Steel all the way back to before the Civil War and the building of the first American railroads. Her father loved to brag that his father helped forge the gun turrets on the U.S.S. Pennsylvania. *Doesn't get more American than that*, he'd told Hap when he was a kid, more than once, between coughs that would become the lung cancer that killed him. Hap's mother would point out, usually on the way home from a visit with her family, that picketing the headquarters of Bethlehem Steel to protest for wage equality for women and minorities was just as, if not even more, American. And his grandmother, who'd been paid less than the men at the mill were being paid to lay bricks, had done just that. When Alice told this story she was always careful to leave out the part when her father found out, how he punched his wife in the head so hard she collapsed, was unconscious for several hours, and had vertigo on and off for the rest of her life. She shared this with Hap only once, when he was in high school, weeks after his grandmother's funeral. Alice had uncharacteristically drunk five glasses of wine at dinner and was, it seemed, trying to make sense of her mother's life. *She was tougher than she was brave*, she'd concluded, speaking more to herself than to Hap, and with a rare bitterness.

Hap's mother, Alice, whom he has called by name for as long as he can remember, was the first woman in her family to graduate from high school and the first in the family—man or woman—to go to college. She attended Bryn Mawr as an undergraduate on a full scholarship for daughters of Bethlehem Steel employees who showed exceptional promise, as determined by the widow of a former CFO, herself a Bryn Mawr alum. After four fully paid years at Bryn Mawr, Alice got her PhD at Penn and came home to Bethlehem, where she taught at Lehigh for almost forty years before retiring.

Hap's parents met in New York—*on a bus* both had answered, vaguely and unconvincingly, on several occasions when Hap asked. Their stories of what happened after were also identically incomplete. As they described it, soon after meeting they married and moved to England where Alice had been given a fellowship at Oxford. Hap was born there and, almost immediately after they returned to Bethlehem together, he was living with his mother alone in an apartment two blocks down the hill from Lehigh. What precipitated his parents' split was just as mysterious to Hap as was what brought them together. His assumption had always been that his father had married Alice after accidentally getting her pregnant and immediately realized that both she and the small city she lived in were too limiting. As Hap understood the story, his father left right after he was born, moved to New York to work for newspapers and soon after that began living abroad—Tblisi, Manila, Beirut, Jerusalem, Paris—where he worked as a news agency photographer.

Hap's childhood memories of his father were brief, but vivid, and mostly in restaurants. He was usually too spellbound to speak to the bright-eyed, unshaven man who materialized in faded jeans and white button-down shirts and told stories of being kidnapped, blindfolded, shot at, and starved. From as early on as he could remember, he could not imagine a more handsome, intelligent, exciting human being. These were their roles and they played them perfectly and with little variation: Dad dazzling with monologues that left little room for engagement or response, and son starstruck and mute, the perfect adoring audience. Alice never complicated the exchange with her opinions or sarcasm or any of her own history with the man. She dutifully drove Hap to a nearby restaurant, usually one she'd picked and made the reservation at, and with a polite nod from the car, handed him off for dinner. Two or three hours later, she'd pick him up, and on the drive home listen to all the wild and exotic stories he'd just heard.

Alice let Hap have his fantasy father and meanwhile, when he was eight, she married a man named Mo. It was Mo, not his glamorous father, who taught Hap how to play soccer and make model ships with miniature tools and balsa wood, to bake with almond flour and hemp milk and make cake frosting with cashews. Yet for all that, Hap saw him as a man he and his mother shared a house with and little more.

Mo died two years after Hap graduated from college. When his mother called to tell him, Hap felt very little. She explained that an employee had found Mo at the bakery door, collapsed from what the doctors at St. Luke's believed was a brain aneurysm. He listened to her get the words out and he worried for her, yes; was shocked, too, as Mo was vegan and in excellent shape for someone in his early forties, but he had no tears. Alice shed plenty and stayed in bed for three straight days while Hap did the best he could to help with the awful and rushed funeral arrangements until his mother's aunts and cousins—no strangers to calamity or its duties—moved in quickly and took over.

It wasn't until a few nights after the funeral, the night Hap returned home to the eastern shore of Maryland, that the finality of losing Mo pierced him. Hap had been working at a newspaper, living in a small rented house for more than a year and except for his college friend's parents who employed him, and the people who worked there, he knew no one. He remembers coming home that night, turning the lights on and seeing dirty dishes in the sink, a wooden bowl of rotting fruit swarming with tiny black flies, a mug of half-drunk coffee wedged between books on the shelf next to the couch, and not one message on his answering machine. He thought about the preceding days—the platters of cold cuts and breads brought in enormous aluminum trays by Alice's family; the stuffed grape leaves and kebabs Mo's two sisters cooked. One of Alice's many cousins brought trays of barbecued chicken and another two large bowls with meatballs covered in red sauce. Alice was vegan, so the ones who ate most of the leftovers were Hap and Mo's sisters, Yana and Una, who lived in Philadelphia. Hap had only met these women a half a dozen or so times and as a boy thought of them as strange, with their hijabs and clothes that looked like they were made of sheets. He knew Mo's family was Syrian but it wasn't until he died that Hap heard the full story of how he fled Syria at seventeen with his mother and sisters during the Six-Day War.

The afternoon of the funeral, Yana told Hap that their father had been, like Mo, a baker, and was killed by a stray bullet that flew through the window of his restaurant kitchen on the first day of the attacks by Israel on the Golan Heights. A call came from someone at the restaurant and without retrieving his body or finding out any more about what had happened, their mother dropped the phone, grabbed her jewelry, papers, and all the cash in the house, screamed for the children to put their shoes on, each fetch a blanket, and meet her at the door. They walked all the way to Jordan and eventually, after several difficult years in Amman, and with the help of a cousin in Philadelphia, made their way to the United States.

That night on the eastern shore, Hap remembered Yana describing Mo's life before he married Alice. She seemed detached from the events she detailed, as if they shaped a story she had long known every syllable to, but at the same time she seemed impatient, even angry, with Hap. When she finished speaking she stood up and scanned the living room, her eyes passing over but not landing on her children or sister or Alice. They returned to Hap, with what looked to him like pity. *It's important you should know how someone comes to your life. Now you know.*

Yana had left him sitting in the living room, unable to stand or speak. He felt like a stranger in the house he'd grown up in. He watched his cousins and uncles crowding the tables spread with lasagna and hummus and trays of cupcakes from Mo's bakery, but Hap didn't recognize his old life or the people in it anymore— even Alice, who for days had not asked him how he was doing or what was going on with his job. From the moment he arrived home in Bethlehem, it was clear she'd changed, even if everything in her house remained precisely as it had been. Mo's old Saab was still in the driveway, his blue canvas coat with brown plastic toggles remained ready on its peg by the door, as it had for years, and his many and mostly destroyed New Balance running shoes, which he'd never thrown out even when Alice bought him new pairs, lined the mudroom wall.

When Hap returned to Maryland a few nights later, he thought about the young man Yana described, the one who stole fruit for his mother and sisters from markets in Amman so they didn't have to spend the money they needed to travel to America, who worked seven days a week as a dishwasher to help with the rent his cousin insisted they pay; who never went to college, who became a baker, like his father, and married a single mother with a boy whom he would teach what he knew about sports and baking and kindness. He would be patient with him, always, even though the boy looked past him to the father who arrived on clouds of fairy dust once a year. He continued to be kind when the boy yammered on about how brave and important his father was, never once asking questions about or showing any interest in the one who carried him into the emergency room when he broke his elbow, made him pancakes or eggs or sometimes both before school, and chaperoned his class trip to Montreal when he was in the eighth grade. He'd loved the boy. But the boy hadn't noticed until he was gone.

That night in Maryland, Hap began to but could not cry. There were times like this when he was in elementary school, hungry, usually over-tired from having stayed up all night rough-housing with Gene, when something would happen—a favorite toy he'd break by accident, bedtime arriving suddenly and sooner than he expected—and he'd feel overwhelmed, furious with himself for having miscalculated, making a mistake that was not correct-able, and his whole body would tilt toward a big cry—his mouth wide, expecting the exorcism of sobs; his eyes and cheeks ready to be soaked by tears, the outside evidence of pain. So poised, and then nothing. Dry eyes and unbothered lungs. Fists of upset not thrown. Here it was happening again. Feeling sorry for and at the same time furious with himself, but with no outlet to express it. He was beginning to understand something that had never once occurred to him, until now: that he'd been spoiled. Yes, by a mother who was loving and kind and who saw to it that he had every educational opportunity; but his mother he thanked, in writ-ing and in person, at graduations and birthdays, and moments in between. His mother he interrogated about her family and col-lege years and how she met his father. His mother was a luxury he appreciated. But until now he'd had the unforgiveable luxury to take someone for granted who loved him unconditionally, gen-erously, and without claim. It was only in Mo's absence that Hap could begin to see him. The great claw of regret closed quickly that night and held him without mercy long after.

Hap's father never asked him about Mo. His lack of interest never struck Hap as strange or selfish. Not that he ever thought it through to completion, but if he'd been asked then he would have responded as if the answer were obvious: Mo wasn't that interesting and his father was, so why on earth would someone who traveled the world and regularly on the frontlines of pivotal events ask about a very nice but boring baker from Pennsylvania?

After Mo died, Hap, for the first time, began to question his relationship with the man he saw once a year but had always worshipped. Why only once a year? Why no sleepovers or trips or baseball games? Instead of asking his father directly, he began to avoid him. When his father sent him infrequent emails to make plans or try to schedule phone calls, Hap at first made excuses to evade seeing or speaking with him; eventually, he stopped responding. After Mo's death, it felt like a posthumous insult to carry on as they had. But it was only partly about Mo; as time passed Hap became less and less comfortable with the man he had his whole life insisted on calling Dad. When Hap was a boy and later when he was in college, Alice suggested he call him by his name, as Hap had always done with her, and with Mo, but he'd refused and kept on saying Dad, which, he sees now, helped convince him that in fact he had one.

Tired of making excuses, Hap eventually agreed to meet Christopher for dinner at a restaurant in Washington Heights to celebrate his thirty-ninth birthday, albeit one month and ten days late. At the end of a long and awkward meal, his father pointed out—with what appeared more like curiosity than pain—that it had been seven years since they'd shared a meal. At first it didn't seem accurate and before Hap responded he counted out the two times they'd seen each other since Mo died. He knew it had been more frequent when he was a kid but how much more? At first he could not recall and then remembered the rule: Father's Day or birthday, he'd have to pick one or the other so his father could plan ahead to be in Bethlehem in June or July, but never both. Had Hap lied to himself when he thought this was a fun game? Did his father snow him so completely all those years that he didn't see what was happening? And yet here he was, across another restaurant dinner table, calmly asking what was wrong. He looked at his father's thick silver hair and the wrinkles around his eyes, the evening stubble along his strong jawline. Abruptly, he recognized that less than three feet away from him sat a man he knew almost nothing about. The table, napkins, water glasses and food between them appeared like unconvincing props in an amateurish portrait of a father having dinner with his adult son. That this was their relationship after almost forty years of meals like the one they were having that night confirmed for Hap that he did not want to have another.

When he remembers that dinner now, he thinks it must have been the last time he was still young enough to make a decision based on the belief that there would always be time. There was his father, nearing seventy, trying to maintain the ultra-thin thread that had been their connection all these years. And in response, Hap ceased all contact. Until that point he'd managed to stay in touch, if erratically. Hap would send the occasional email, forward an article once or twice a year, photographs—of the lobby of The Jerusalem Hotel where he knew his father had stayed many times, of his first desk at *The Philadelphia Inquirer*. But from that night on, he let his father's calls go to voicemail, stopped replying to emails and notes, and nine more years passed without seeing him. The next time he would see him would be on the lobby floor of the Hotel Bethlehem.

His father had wanted to meet his granddaughter, that's what he'd written in his email. The word *granddaughter* seemed funny coming from this man he once idolized, and also like a lie considering he'd never met his wife, Leah. He had not been at their wedding two years before, not because he chose not to, but because Hap had forgotten to invite him. Alice never reminded him, nor mentioned his absence. But she did include him in a group email announcing the baby's birth the morning after she was born. Hap received an email from his father later that day stating that he was on his way from New York and would be staying at the Hotel Bethlehem. When Hap emailed back to say he'd check with Leah about timing, he didn't get a response, just a phone call at eleven the next morning saying he'd arrived.

Ya gotta go. The voice is a foghorn, loud and blunt.

Bethlehem's own Maureen O'Hara is clicking off lights and moving out beyond the counter that separates the cafeteria kitchen from the dining area.

We shut down between lunch and dinner.

Hap looks down at the cold, orange, breadcrumb-crusted macaroni and cheese on his plate and realizes he hasn't yet taken a bite.

Just a sec, he mumbles as he scarfs down a few forkfuls of the rubbery mess, which he swallows with a swig of room temperature milk.

Up Up Up she chants joylessly, both hands animating the directive. *Up Up Up.*

By the time Hap arrived at the hotel that morning, his father was lying at the bottom of the main staircase at the far end of the lobby. As he got closer he could smell what he imagined were soiled jeans. His father's white shirt had dark rings of perspiration expanding from his armpits and one of his brown loafers had come loose, exposing his foot, clad in a dark green sock, bent at the ankle, dangling. Hap walked slowly toward him and heard someone say he was breathing. He was surrounded by hotel employees and a very upset middle-aged woman screaming for someone to call an ambulance. She'd sat down on the lobby floor and put Hap's father's head in her lap. She was wiping his sweaty brow with a silk scarf that by the look of her disheveled hair had until moments before been on her head. The image reminded Hap of a pietà he'd seen in the Barnes Museum when he was in high school, before the collection moved to downtown Philadelphia. It was a pastel from a monastery in Italy somewhere and the entire wall had been removed and installed in the museum. *That's what money can do*, his teacher mumbled with reverence when the guide described where the image of the doting Madonna came from. *Move mountains, museums, monasteries, even. You name it.*

The woman, noticing Hap approach, looked up and scanned his face for answers.

Do you know this man?

Hap stared back at her, this stranger haloed in disheveled hair, with rouged cheeks damp with tears, his unconscious father in her lap.

Sir, I'm sorry, do you know him?

I . . . do . . . not, he said involuntarily, the unreal moment reducing him to the truth. He watched the makeshift Madonna stroke his father's silver hair with fingers loaded with rings that tapered to long nails shiny with pale pink polish. For the first time since Hap was a boy, he desperately wanted to know who this man was. Without realizing he was speaking, he looked into the woman's distraught face and asked, *Do you?*

Alice

There is no milk. The baby has not been fed and there is no pumped breast milk or formula to fill a bottle with. Alice has texted and called Leah dozens of times, but she does not respond. Despite a powerful reluctance to expose what's going on with Hap and Leah to her nosy family, she calls her older sister Kay and asks her to pick up formula from the store and bring it over as soon as possible. It's not ideal but it's better than nothing. The whole of the baby's pink and wrinkled body is now devoted to the single effort of screaming, her doll-tiny arms and legs shaking with each grunting wail like loosely attached appendages. They look as weak as Alice feels. She is almost seventy-three now, much older than the last time she did this. And unlike back then, this time she's on her own. With Hap, and even before Hap, there had been help. There had been Lee.

Alice first met Lee in the fall of her senior year in high school. She'd applied the prior spring to a scholarship that her principal, a tough but fair woman named Marilyn Benedict, knew about, *for a young woman who wants to go to Bryn Mawr* was how she described it and asked her to write an essay describing what she hoped to achieve by getting a liberal arts education at the elite women's college. Principal Benedict, herself a Bryn Mawr alum, wrote her a recommendation and sent her transcripts. At the end of September, she drove Alice in her Jeep to the Saucon Valley Country Club, a vast brick building that looked to Alice as big as her high school. When they pulled up, the woman whom Principal Benedict had instructed her to address as Mrs. Beach was standing to the left of the front entrance. She was elegant, dressed simply but expensively in a gray cashmere sweater set and navy silk skirt, and appeared nervous. Mrs. Beach was younger than Alice had imagined from the little she'd been told about her: that she was a widow without children whose husband had been high up at Bethlehem Steel.

Once inside, they sat next to each other in silence for a few difficult minutes on the sofa in a kind of waiting room just off the lobby entrance to the club. The poised woman seemed to expect Alice to initiate their conversation. *It's very nice to meet you*, she heard herself saying like an idiotic child would speak on a TV show. *Gee, Mister. Golly, Mam.* That sort of thing.

It's very nice to meet you, too, Mrs. Beach responded, with what sounded to Alice like disappointment which was distressing because she had by now determined that there was a lot riding on this meeting. Her parents had told her over the summer that as far as they were concerned there was no money for college. If she was so eager not to go to work after high school like everyone else, she should apply for scholarships and continue to save her babysitting money and maybe consider nursing school at St. Luke's. Nursing school was their idea of a college education and the far limit of what they could envision for their daughter who was not only a straight-A student and class secretary, but clear front-runner for valedictorian. Nursing school made sense to them because a good paying job waited on the other end. Liberal arts as a general concept did not go very far in Alice's family. *Liberal anything sounds like a waste of money to me*, her father had offered, more than once. Alice didn't know what she wanted but she knew that it wasn't in Bethlehem. She wanted a big change and without knowing why exactly she knew a place like Bryn Mawr—where Principal Benedict went to college, and, she'd read, Katharine Hepburn—looked like just such a place. Mrs. Beach could make it happen. Alice remembers the next sentences she spoke as if she'd just said them. *I'm aware that Bryn Mawr is a very competitive and expensive college. I've never received less than an A– on a paper or an exam and I don't intend to start now, especially if I'm given the once-in-a-lifetime opportunity to attend such a great school. I'm very nervous at the moment, but I'm not a nervous girl. I'm only nervous because I've never had such an important meeting with anyone. Mrs. Beach, I hope you don't mind me being direct. I just want you to know where I stand. I'm sure you've met lots of girls over the years and will probably meet many this year, too. But none of them will want what you have to offer more than I do, or be more deserving.*

She had no idea where it came from. She hadn't rehearsed or imagined what she might say. There was no situation she could compare this one to, so she'd gone in, she realized later, utterly unprepared. Still, the words came flying out, and Alice recognized right away how Mrs. Beach seemed to relax. She seemed as relieved as Alice felt, and when they exhaled at the same time, there was a brief amused moment of surprise. Mrs. Beach smiled and the barrier between them fell.

Please, Alice, call me Lee. And, no, I don't mind your being direct. I don't mind at all.

And so began a cordial, formal relationship that by the summer before Alice left for college, had become something more. At Bryn Mawr, Alice saw Lee for lunch or supper a few times each semester, by junior year she'd occasionally come home to Bethlehem and stay at Lee's farm in Allentown and not tell her family. And in between they spoke on the phone at least a few times a month. From the start, Lee helped Alice with more than tuition and dormitory fees. She helped her navigate the world of well-to-do girls from New York and Philadelphia and even made sure she had the right clothes and appropriate luggage to arrive with before the first fall semester. She took her shopping at Strawbridge's in Philadelphia several times a year and at Christmas to Lord & Taylor in New York. She lent her a double strand of pearls from Tiffany that her husband had given her as an anniversary present and when she graduated gave them to her as a gift along with a typewriter and a trip to London that she accompanied her on. They stayed at Claridge's and visited the Courtauld Institute and the National Portrait Gallery and wandered Hampstead Heath one afternoon until it became evening. By then, Alice knew she wanted to be an educator like her early mentor Marilyn Benedict, but at the university level, in the world where she'd felt happiest and most herself. Since her grandfather's stories of her family working for Bethlehem Steel and building ships for the Civil War, Alice was fascinated by how her gritty town figured into the larger story of the country, how it was once thriving and then not, and the historical forces responsible. As she approached the next phase of her education she chose American History and eventually the role that the Lehigh Valley and the steel industry played in the Civil War as the subject of her PhD.

There were no boys at Bryn Mawr and Alice did not make meeting them a priority. She was never the prettiest girl in a room. She was slim and, according to Lee, had enviable hands and an elegant neck; but she also once joked, lovingly, that if there were bets on who would become a college professor based on looks she'd be the clear winner every time. She wore cat-eyed glasses, had slightly protruding teeth, a gift from her mother, and wore her hair in a simple flip in the style of Mary Tyler Moore on her TV show, a variation of which she maintained into her seventies. No one had come along until Christopher and when he ended things it confirmed what she had suspected from the beginning: that not only was he too good to be true, but that she was also not the type of girl who got married.

A few days after Christopher had called to tell Alice about his father's death, he phoned again to say he was coming to Philadelphia for the funeral and suggested they have lunch. Alice was living at Lee's farm that year. She'd begun her job at Lehigh by then, teaching and working toward her doctorate, and was saving money on living expenses. It also made being alone—for both of them—easier. Lee had been sick with pneumonia over the summer and Alice wanted to stay close in case she needed anything after her maid left in the evening.

Christopher came to the farm and though only a little more than a year had passed since their breakup, there was something less boyish about him. He was more assured, and despite prevailing ideas about homosexuality that might have suggested the opposite, he was more manly. He'd grown up, whereas before he was still a starry-eyed boy with secrets and anger, playing a part. He still had the same gift for storytelling, and he took his time telling Alice about his father's funeral, how no one but his nephews, who were still children, greeted him warmly. His mother was ill and when he called to arrange a time to visit, his aunt told him she'd rather he didn't, that it would upset her. His oldest brother actually said what was on most of their minds: *You blew it. What did the lifestyle you chose have to do with any of us? You should have just left it alone, kept the family out of it.* Though hard to hear, it was not surprising, and made his decision to stay away easier. These were not his people, they'd made that clear. He told Alice that he felt no guilt or regret with his family. Only grief. The one regret he had, and the reason he asked to meet, was having misled her. He had used her, and the cover of their relationship, as a last ditch effort to avoid coming clean to himself and to his family, he realized now. He asked what he could do to make it up to her. She said she forgave him, even if his words felt more for his peace of mind than hers, and that there was nothing he could do for her. But as Christopher left he made a point to say that if she ever needed anything from him, *anything at all*, she should not hesitate to ask.

Hap

When he steps from the elevator and sees the two nurses standing outside the room, he knows his father is dead. The short, older nurse disappears through the doorway when she notices Hap coming toward them; the other one looks down as she folds her long skinny arms across her chest and nervously tucks her fists into her armpits. She hunches her shoulders and hugs herself, appears suddenly cold. Hap shivers, as if by suggestion, and slows to a halt between the elevator and his father's room. He has never been less sure what to do.

A plump, sunburned doctor who looks no more than twenty-five years old steps into the hallway. Hap has not seen him in the ICU before and for a moment considers the possibility that he's an imposter. As the young man approaches him, Hap's mind lurches for ways to discredit him. He lands on and quickly abandons the possibility that his performance is actually an elaborate initiation ritual at a Lehigh fraternity. Before he can come up with alternate theories, the guy speaks.

Hello, I'm Dr. Leventhal, I'm filling in for Dr. Baker who I know has been treating your father.

His voice, discordant with his college boy face, sounds like gravel and rock salt and is at least two octaves deeper than Hap's. It is oddly reassuring, despite its unlikely source. He says Hap's father's name out loud, kindly, as if he'd known about him for years. *Christopher. I understand Christopher Foster was your father.*

Was.

Once again, Hap senses this man might be lying and in fact has never seen his father. He scans his face but sees nothing but a shiny red forehead and an ingrown hair under his (also red) nose. But when he looks into his uncomplicated brown eyes he knows that what he's saying is true.

I'm so sorry, he went very quickly, he started hemorrhaging and went into cardiac arrest . . .

Went.

. . . something his doctors had been working very hard to prevent. But with what looked like a preexisting heart condition and high blood pressure, I'm afraid the odds were more stacked against him than we realized. I'm very sorry. One of the nurses tried to find you but it was too late.

Too late.

The doctor keeps speaking but his words are just sounds and Hap looks beyond him to the young nurse who hunches slightly, as if she's waiting for a bus on a cold night without proper clothing. The doctor stops talking and squeezes Hap's right shoulder. Like his voice, his grip is stronger than his physicality suggests. Hap knows he should thank him for doing his best but he says nothing. He knows he should start walking toward his father's room, but he won't move. Not yet. To say anything or step from where he stands would be to accept what has happened. By remaining silent, and precisely where he is, it stays unreal, before fact.

Sir? Are you ok? Can I get you a chair?

The young nurse has mobilized and is now inches away. Her hands are out from her armpits and very lightly touching his arm, the same one the doctor squeezed. She smells like the deodorant Leah uses. Again, he does not respond. She is asking questions, simple ones, but to answer would be like agreeing, or giving permission for his father's death. It is as if these hospital employees have come up with death as a thoughtful proposal and presented it as something they believe should happen now. And the only thing they need to make it so is Hap's approval.

The nurse says something more, pats Hap's arm and vanishes. Right away he misses her. He sniffs the air for her scent but there is no trace.

His phone vibrates with new texts—once and then again a few seconds later—but he does not remove it from the chest pocket of his shirt. He knows it's Leah. He hasn't been in touch with her since late morning. For reasons he only partly understands he cannot read her texts or pick up the phone and call her. He is off-shore from his life, which she is the center of, and he is powerless to come in.

The phone has stopped vibrating. An old woman on a stretcher, strung up with tubes and wires, is wheeled from the room next to his father's. A nurse glides her silently down the hallway and into the elevator. As she goes by, Hap recognizes the snowflaked gown tucked around her body; her emaciated and vein-tangled legs bent, one over the other, like a child's. He feels a flash of jealousy. Not of her age, or the condition that has placed her here, but of the care she is receiving. She is surrounded by soft things, unburdened of responsibilities, and wheeled with sure purpose by capable hands down pink hallways.

No one is whisking Hap away. The longer he remains where he stands, the more the sickening feeling he has in his chest becomes heavier, more solid. It shapes into something he knows he will always know: that he failed. His father only ever needed one thing from him and in this he'd failed him. As he sees it—all at once and with pitiless clarity—in forty-eight years as this man's son, he had one measly duty, one job that fell to him and no one else: to make sure he did not die alone. His father had wriggled out of Taliban captivity in Pakistan, survived plane crashes, bullet wounds, and a severe allergic reaction to a bee sting in the Adirondacks, but while his heart was exploding and he was taking his last breaths, frightened and alone and leaving this world, his son was two floors away eating macaroni and cheese and drinking a glass of milk. Of course it would be a child's meal, Hap thinks, because isn't that what he is? Not a man, but a selfish boy who'd turned his back on someone who'd required so little of him. As with Mo, there would be no second chance to get it right—not with his dying, not with his living. He would never again have another shot at being in that room when his father needed him, and there would be no making up for lost time.

Hap had been told he was lucky his whole life. By his mother, Mo, Gene, and Leah. But despite all the breaks, the good education, the loving kindness, his wife, his baby girl, his own good health, despite all these things he knows he should be grateful for, he feels not the least bit lucky. As he stands three doors away from the second dead father he neglected to know, the world has never felt so unfair.

Alice

The sun has set and it's been hours since Leah took off. The baby is wild with hunger. Kay turns up with bottles and formula and to Alice's great relief leaves the car running in the driveway as she hands off the pharmacy bag at the door. Of course she wants to come inside and meet her grand-niece and snap dozens of photos on her phone to instantly post on Facebook. But thankfully she respects the cue that for now the new mother and father aren't receiving company. She knows Alice well enough not to ask questions, so she waves goodbye and reminds her that she's only ten minutes down the hill if there's anything else needed. Kay will surely report trouble to their sisters and cousins, but for now all Alice cares about is feeding her granddaughter.

There you go, she whispers, as the baby finally fixes her mouth on the rubber nipple after fussing and refusing it for several long minutes. The house goes quiet, seems to settle around them. Alice gently pushes fine black wisps away from the pink, nearly translucent skin of her forehead. Only now does she register the hair. Hap's is dark blond to light brown depending on the time of year, Leah's is a shade lighter. Here, Alice thinks, here finally are the maternal genes pushing through. None of them showed up in Hap—not in skin tone, nor eye color nor hair. But here, a generation later, are eyes as piercing and hair as dark as Alice remembers his mother's.

* * *

114

Three weeks after she met Christopher to hear his amends, Lee's niece Dana called Lee from Bryn Mawr. Alice remembers Lee being unusually flustered and upset as she explained that a young woman who worked for Dana's family would be coming to the farm to stay for a while. Two days later, she turned up with Dana in a yellow Mercedes convertible.

Alice's first impression of Lupita was how young she was, how skittish and quiet. Despite all the effort that was being made for her, she spoke very few words and didn't seem to trust anyone. Lee gave the girl a choice between the former farm manager's cottage behind the barns, and a bedroom next to the one Alice stayed in on the second floor of the main house. Lupita chose the cottage.

After a few weeks, she relaxed a little, and as her belly grew, she became more responsive, certainly more polite, but she never opened up. She did not explain what had happened, or who the father was, only that she could not have the baby in Connecticut and that she could never go back there.

Dana's father was Lee's brother and Alice asked her when they were alone whether he should be called. *Oh no, that's the last thing we need, for George to find out that Dana and I are harboring his caretaker's daughter. He wouldn't understand and we'd have Lupita's parents—and very likely George—on our doorstep by morning.* Still, Alice knew Lee was worried whether or not they were doing the right thing. She pressed Dana several times for more details, but Dana ducked behind a performative yet unconvincing respect for Lupita's privacy. They would never know why she was so deeply involved, why she'd offered to help to the extent that she had.

Alice had known girls like Dana at Bryn Mawr. They were there because it was what was expected of them. They used the school as a waystation between ski trips and excursions to Europe and always gave the impression that beyond the campus there were big adult lives that they were already involved in. What set Dana apart was how brisk she was, how no-nonsense. She was a fast girl, a glamorous one, and she was not a girl looking for a husband. When she first turned up with Lupita she looked right through Alice. When she asked Alice to fix her a drink, Lee stepped in and did it herself. By the second day, after Lee purposefully included Alice in the discussions of what to do, Dana reluctantly began to treat her as an ally. It was obvious that Dana and Lupita had a tense relationship. Though they never exchanged adversarial words or raised their voices to one another in front of Lee and Alice, there was a current of anger between them. Both of them seemed to have a lot at stake.

After Lupita gave birth at St. Luke's, she held her baby once that Alice knew of and made it known that when the nurse took him away it would be the last time. The boy, another infant who would go without a name for his first weeks, wailed even louder than his daughter would forty-eight years later.

When Lupita and her son were discharged, she seemed desperate to sever her relationship to her child as soon as possible. She refused to leave the cottage and insisted that the baby stay in the main house. It must have been impossibly lonely and painful, Alice thought then and remembers now. She also remembers how Lee seemed to draw closer to Lupita after she gave birth, bringing a fresh nightgown and a soft cashmere blanket to the hospital room, directing the nurses to bring food and water. Lupita's situation had stirred in her a desire to take care, to mother—something Alice recognized from her own experience with Lee. Still, she was surprised to see her friend respond with such nurturing force, and Alice resisted the jealousy and possessiveness that it triggered.

The first night they were back, Lee explained that Lupita had not changed her mind about adoption as they'd all hoped, and as soon as the baby was settled, she'd be leaving. When Lee told Alice the boy would be taken to an orphanage in Philadelphia where a friend of hers was on the board, an unfamiliar but powerful instinct in her was provoked. Here was someone not wanted. A needy thing who had no power to protect himself. Alice was twenty-five years old and on her way to becoming a tenured history professor at Lehigh. After Christopher, men terrified her and now that she was living in Bethlehem again, she'd accepted the improbability of her marrying. And so, with the minor sadness of someone who is, at once, both settling for something other than what had been long imagined, and eyeing with pragmatic excitement a lucky alternative, Alice recognized that this unexpected baby boy was her best chance at becoming a mother.

When Alice spoke to Lee about what she had in mind, Lee seemed more relieved than surprised. *But before anything else happens, you need to speak to Lupita . . . it's her decision*, she said, and so Alice went to her cottage door that evening with tea bags stuffed with dried chamomile flowers.

Lupita was difficult to draw out, and so to fill the silence Alice spoke about her life—Bethlehem, Bryn Mawr, her family, Lee. She explained that she did not expect to marry but that she had a big family to rely on for help. Talk of family seemed to catch Lupita's interest and so Alice prattled a blue streak about her parents and sisters, aunts and uncles.

Two days later, when Alice visited the cottage again, Lupita met her on the porch. She said she would agree to what Alice had proposed, but only if she promised to never tell the boy where and whom he had come from. *You would be his mother and your family would be his family . . . He can't be a guest, or a trespasser . . . He should not be treated like someone from somewhere else.*

Alice agreed, but it took her weeks to appreciate fully what she'd committed to and what it would require to pull off. At first she thought that once she was raising the boy she could tell him whatever she wanted about his mother and how he'd been adopted. But when she considered this later she could not shake the memory of Lupita that day on the porch. She had been almost completely unresponsive and aloof in the weeks and days preceding the delivery, and all at once she became impassioned, fierce, insisting on what mattered to her, a primal force driving her from her silence. Alice would replay what she said that day for the rest of her life; remember her intensity, and her relief when Alice agreed to her terms, and then how she receded, almost immediately, the lifeblood that had surged and animated her moments before, gone. When Alice moved toward her, she flinched. She stammered something about being cold and needing to rest and quickly disappeared inside the cottage.

It was hard to know the girl then—she was traumatized, in flight from her family, everything and everyone she knew, giving up her child, unsure where she would live and how. It was as dramatic and important a circumstance as Alice had ever been involved in. But underneath it all there was something else, too, she and Lee both noticed a different energy emerge soon after it had been settled that Alice would adopt the baby. She seemed restless, if frightened—eager to begin her new life. They had the impression that the one she was leaving behind, for reasons that preceded her pregnancy, was one she'd long been ready to escape. Here Alice could identify with her. On paper Alice was a scholarship kid who went to college an hour away, only to return home to work a short walk from the house she grew up in; but she, too, had been desperate to leave the world she'd been born into. For less dire reasons, she suspected, but when she was Lupita's age, escaping Bethlehem and the limitations of the life her parents expected for her felt like the difference between life and death.

Lee's lawyer came to the farm later that day to talk through what was possible. He'd also brought a colleague who spoke with Lupita privately. When the lawyers left, Alice called Christopher. She now knew the one thing she wanted from him and when they spoke she was as direct as she had been with Lee at the Saucon Valley Country Club the first time they met. He hesitated after Alice finished. Responding first by explaining that when his mother died no one from his family was in touch about an inheritance or a will. He'd been cut out, which made the silence between them less complicated, but it meant that he couldn't support a child. Moreover, he'd been planning on leaving the country soon. He'd taken a job as a photographer for a news agency to go to places like Vietnam, Cambodia, and Jerusalem to record what people in the United States needed to see. Alice listened to him describe his plans to live oceans and time zones away and she felt an unexpected relief loosen her ribs and chest and shoulders. She had not held out hope after they broke up, but the half-life of her old dream of a future with him must have lingered in her unconscious, out of sight, yet lurking. She'd blushed earlier as she dialed his number and remembered him ascending the porch steps last fall. When she felt her heart gain weight and her chest tighten, she didn't link it to anything but the overall emotion of the situation. It shocked her now to realize she was still letting him go, accepting what was true. *The heart is a stubborn muscle*, Lee told her once when she showed her the love letters her husband had written to her from France when he was in the First World War. *Whenever I read these I still believe he's coming home to start our life.* Alice's feelings for Christopher were different, but still his leaving the country for a long time would help her finally move on, as would the boy, whom she named Hapworth, after Lee's husband. It seemed exactly the right thing to do. This happenstance of a son. Her Hap.

She told Christopher that the only thing she needed from him was a marriage certificate so they could both sign adoption papers, nothing more. Lee's lawyer said that being married was not a requirement for adoption, but Alice had made a promise to Lupita and she intended to keep it. She had her own family in mind, too, and how they'd need some toehold in a respectable story to make Hap's arrival something other than shameful. Christopher could have as much or as little involvement in the boy's life as he wanted. They would paper a divorce as soon as sufficient time passed and they could rely on the lawyer to guide them.

Christopher took a few days to think about it. By Monday of the following week he borrowed a car and drove from New York to meet Hap. *I suppose this is the closest I'll ever come to being a father*, he joked solemnly as he held the pudgy towheaded infant who wriggled and cried. In a week they were married at the Allentown courthouse by the justice of the peace, and less than a month after that, thanks to Lee's lawyers who were able to expedite the process, they signed the adoption papers. Lupita left with Dana the next morning, before anyone was awake. The only sign of them was Dana's briefcase sitting on the third stair in the front hallway. Why she'd left it and where she took Lupita, Alice never knew. But when Christopher left a few hours later, he carried the marriage license and the adoption papers, as well as a book he'd asked to borrow from the guest bedroom he'd slept in, in a briefcase with gold monogrammed initials that were not his own.

Alice then told the biggest lies of her life. The first was to the chair of the history department at Lehigh to say that she'd need to take an unexpected maternity leave for the rest of the spring semester. Thankfully, the chair was a man in his late seventies who made it clear he was not interested in hearing how one detects a pregnancy so late in the term and forestalled the explanation Alice had begun to make by interrupting to say there would need to be some last-minute shuffling, but it would be allowed, and congratulations. And then, her parents. She sat at their kitchen table and briskly reported that she'd been asked to step in for a Fellowship at Oxford University and she'd be back at the end of the summer. Someone had dropped out unexpectedly, it was very last-minute, very prestigious, and, oh and yes, she was four and a half months pregnant, yes of course it was Christopher's, he'd be coming with her, and she'd deliver the baby there. Of the many decisions she'd made since graduating from high school, this one was met by her family with more bewildered alarm than usual. But there had long been a barrier—a line drawn as her life became less knowable, especially if any aspect of her academic life was involved—that kept them from questioning even this development. After a thick silence, her mother's first question was, *What kind of hospitals do they have there?*

In August, when she "returned," she explained that she and Christopher had gotten married for Hap's sake but that the relationship had fallen apart in Oxford and they'd no longer be together. She'd hoped that the wallop of so much news would distract her mother and sisters from the fact that Hap was impossibly large for a month-old infant. In fact, his size was nothing but celebrated, by her father especially. *Now that's a boy*, he'd said with pride. Over time, Alice's family, either through subtext or by meaningful nods, communicated their respect that she'd gotten married to cover up her carelessness. Behind her back, she assumed they gossiped that she'd taken up with a playboy who had his fun and moved on. But the relative ease with which they accepted the situation surprised her. Right away they pitched in with hand-me-down clothes and advice, old strollers, and offers to babysit. It was clear they saw it as a single blemish on an otherwise lily-white, if aloof and unknowable, life. She wouldn't be the first daughter of Bethlehem to raise a son on her own, nor would she be the last. A few months later, with the help of Lee's lawyers, a new birth certificate was issued. With the date of birth changed to July 15, Alice and Christopher listed as mother and father, and the original birth certificate sealed, the past had been papered over as well as it could be.

At the beginning, it was Lee, of course, who helped the most. Because of the fiction of Oxford, Alice basically hid on the farm until the end of summer. In those first sequestered months after Lupita left, Alice and Lee would spell each other six hours on, six hours off and eventually Lee hired a nurse to cover her shifts. *I'm too old for this*, she told Alice one morning. *I told Dana I'd help her and so I have. But it's time for me to get some sleep again.*

Alice and Hap stayed at Lee's farm until he was ten months old. When they moved it was to the house she lives in now, a modest two-story Victorian she purchased with a ten-thousand-dollar down payment from Lee.

Six years later, Lee died. She came down with bronchitis, which worsened quickly to pneumonia, the third time she'd had it happen since Alice had known her. This time it didn't go away. Alice and Hap moved back to the farm that winter. Lee refused to go to St. Luke's, so Alice organized a schedule of nurses always to be on hand. Lee's brother was recovering from back surgery in Florida so he and his wife did not come to see her. Dana, who was living in London, called most mornings before Alice left the house to go to work and drop Hap off at school, but she did not come.

Alice held Lee's hand at the end, while a nurse stood by, monitoring her fluids and morphine. Before her breath became too labored and the morphine overwhelmed her consciousness, Lee tried to speak. *You came . . .* , she wheezed from flooded lungs, a faint suggestion of a smile wrinkling her dried lips.

A few weeks after she passed, Lee's lawyer, the same one who had organized the adoption, called Alice to let her know that Lee had left a trust in Hap's name that would pay for his college and any degree-seeking graduate studies he chose. If for whatever reason he decided not to further his education after high school, the trust would revert to the scholarship fund she'd created to grant young women from the public school systems in Bethlehem or Allentown a college education, one specifically to Bryn Mawr and another to any four-year college or university. For this, Alice was appointed sole administrator for as long as she was capable and she would also be responsible for appointing her successor so long as it was a woman. To Alice she left her jewelry, her clothing, and her books, as well as an account to draw funds from whenever she needed for whatever purpose she chose. The accountants would take care of inheritance taxes. There were no stipulations or protocols; in the will it said very specifically, *I trust her.* The rest of the estate—the farm and whatever investments existed, were to be liquidated and distributed to the trust, the scholarship fund, and the endowments at Bryn Mawr and Dartmouth, where her husband had gone to college. Alice was not told how much there was, but when she asked, Lee's lawyer told her that it did not matter. He handed her the blue plastic–covered checkbook, like any checkbook from any bank, and said simply, *There will always be enough.*

Alice often tried to imagine what Lupita's life became, where she ended up, whether or not she ever had another child. Mostly she thought of her when something occurred with Hap that seemed like something a mother would want to know. But when she'd been tempted to find her, to write or send a photograph or clipping, she remembered that morning on the cottage porch, how important it was to Lupita that the break between them be total. Still, when Hap's traveling soccer team won their division championship in sixth grade, Alice clipped the photograph of him scoring the winning goal in *The Morning Call* and put it inside a shoe box with pictures from most of his birthday parties and Christmas mornings. Over the years she added more clippings—the Honor Roll, various sports victories, a piece in the *Express* about his becoming a reporter for *The Philadelphia Inquirer*, both her parents' obituaries which listed Hap as a surviving grandson. In the pile there was also an issue of the Freedom High School newspaper that contained the article Hap wrote about Christopher and his job as a war photographer. These were not keepsakes for Hap or for her. Each one was something that at one point or other, Alice had the urge to send to Lupita. Of course she wanted her to know that life had turned out well for him, that he was a happy kid and a well-adjusted adult, but she recognized, too, that a part of her wanted Lupita to know that she'd kept her word. Alice was his mother and her family was his family; he was loved and he never doubted who he was or whether he belonged. The last item she put in the box was Hap's wedding announcement along with a copy of the program that listed the groomsmen and bridesmaids, families and speakers. Stroking the sleeping, jet-black tufted head of Lupita's granddaughter, Alice knew what the next would be: one small lock of hair. A trace of proof she wished she could share but was bound by a promise not to.

Hap

His father was a man who carried very little. In his windbreaker pocket was a debit card and an iPhone, and in the room at the Hotel Bethlehem there had been a change of underwear and socks, a thin billfold with a driver's license and a twenty-dollar bill, a toothbrush, a bottle of mixed pills and a pair of reading glasses. On the bus ride to Port Authority, Hap folded, held and arranged each item in different configurations on his lap. There was a set of keys, a small, thin one, for a mailbox, he imagined, two stainless steel Hillmans and a bronze Medeco. When he called Alice to tell her he was going to New York, to his father's apartment, to find an address book to begin contacting the people who needed to be contacted, she urged him to hold off going until he'd spent a few more days home with Leah and their daughter. *Stay a day, at least*, she said. *Leah needs you and not just to help and be with the baby, but she's starting to come apart, Hap. This can happen.* Hap heard her words, but instead of making him feel like he needed to rush home, it instigated a new sense of urgency to complete what he'd started, his father's death like an unavoidable rite of passage. Until he'd seen it through, he knew he could not be what Leah, or his daughter, needed. Hap told Alice he'd be back early the next day.

Less than three hours after getting off the phone with Alice, he is standing at the door of a fourth-floor walk-up apartment on Horatio Street.

Can I help you? A woman's voice calls up the dark stairwell. *Hello?*

125

Slow, shuffling footsteps follow. They sound like the noise that slippers make, not shoes.

Excuse me . . .

The shuffling stops for a moment.

Hello?, she chimes loudly.

The shuffling begins again and after a minute the slippers and the large woman they belong to ascend into view. Hap sees long gray hair first and then a very large red wool cardigan sweater awkwardly tied with a sash to contain what must have once been traffic-stopping breasts. Hap flinches as the woman plunks her last slippered foot above the final stair and the sloppy knot of her sash loosens further.

Excuse me. I've been calling out to you. It's a good thing I didn't need your help; otherwise I'd be in real trouble.

The woman is in her mid-seventies at the very least and speaks with a half-smile that is either from forced cheer or from pain or both. She has sharp cheekbones that tent folds of pale wrinkled skin which drape below her jawline.

Hello? It is now time for you to speak.

There is something so disarming about this woman, so direct and strange, so fearless, that Hap is momentarily speechless.

The woman begins again before he is able to form a response. *Shall I call the police and have them help us communicate? You and I aren't doing so very well on our own, are we?* She is still simultaneously smiling and wincing and her tone is breezy which makes what she is saying difficult to fully appreciate at first listen.

Hap stumbles through an explanation of how his father has lived here. That he'd died, yesterday, four days after falling down in the lobby of a hotel. A brain hemorrhage followed by a heart attack. He'd come to Pennsylvania to meet his granddaughter who was just born.

I'm here to collect his things, I guess, to see if I can find some kind of address book or computer file with names of friends and other family members to call.

The woman stares at Hap for a very long time. Her look is utterly blank, not probing or doubtful, just frozen, perfectly expressionless. She breaks her stare with a blink and her eyes complicate, appear pink at the edges, glisten in the dim light. Hap expects her to speak, but instead she turns back to the stairs she rose from and with one hand on the wall to steady her, she plops one foot down on the first step, and then the other.

What is your name?, she asks for the first time, her back to him.

Hap, he responds, his voice mysteriously scratching and breaking, like an adolescent.

No, she corrects him, the light in her voice wobbling. *What is your full name?*

Hap Foster. On my passport it says Hapworth.

Your parents . . . , the woman says doubtfully, wiping her eyes and drawing a deep breath.

I've known Christopher for more years than you've been alive. She descends another step and grabs the metal banister. Carefully, she turns around on the stair to face Hap. With her free hand, she points to the door where he stands. *He's had the apartment right there since he was at NYU, when my parents rented it to him. Not many men stay in a studio apartment for that long, but Christopher . . . your father, as you say . . . never minded.*

Both hands free now, she pulls her sweater more tightly around her and to Hap's great relief re-ties the sash. She speaks again, a mix of doubt and pity in her voice.

He's lived here since he was a boy and he never once mentioned a son.

She looks up at the ceiling and sighs as if facing a vast, costly renovation. Eventually she drops her gaze to Hap, and looks surprised to see him there. She draws a short breath and grunts as she exhales, sounding both defeated and in pain. With her free hand she signals for him to carry on trying to find the correct key. She then turns back to the stairs and starts back down again. Once she's disappeared from view, he hears her speak one last time, but this time softly, sincerely:

My dear, if you need anything, I'm in 1C, in the apartment exactly three floors below Christopher's.

Christopher. Never has his father's name sounded more like a stranger's.

So much of what his parents had told him never quite held up: their trite stories about meeting on a bus, their quickly dissolved marriage. But why had he not pressed either of them for more details before? Did he sense that the skimpy history they stuck to hid something he didn't want to know? For a few minutes, leaning into the door, the correct key now in the lock but unturned, Hap questions whether he should proceed any further. Wasn't there already plenty to confront without revealing more? Wincing, he turns the key in the lock and shoves the door open.

The first thing he sees is a brown leather briefcase sitting at the center of a threadbare rug like a loyal dog waiting for its owner to come home. Hap ignores it at first, scanning the four walls, one window, small sink and two-burner electric stovetop. There is a Murphy bed folded into the wall with wrinkled sheets drooping around the edges. This is not how he imagined his father living. As a kid, and after, the glamour of his exploits, the overall impression of his importance, and the nice restaurants where they met each year—all of it painted a very different picture. Hap shuts the door behind him and tries to make sense of what he sees. There are two framed photographs on the wall of children in what looks like India, standing waist-deep in water. In both images there are three boys and a girl laughing, eyes wide, transfixed by the figure snapping the photograph whose shadow falls over and around them in a long, exaggerated silhouette of a man. They seem oblivious to the Tetra Pak cartons and aluminum cans bobbing at their backs. They are, Hap recognizes, as he once was, transfixed. By the same man wearing a white shirt and worn jeans, with a Leica camera around his neck and other places in his eyes.

There is a teak and wicker lounge chair by the window with scuffed legs and low wide armrests. It is the only piece of furniture in the apartment besides a small table and two chairs next to the kitchenette. Hap sits down and allows his back and shoulders to relax into the forgiving weave. Somewhere in the building a Dolly Parton song is playing. It's faint but unmistakable and when it shifts to the part where Dolly is speaking and not singing Hap knows it's "Yellow Roses," an old favorite of his mother's. Hap runs his hands along the chair's worn armrests and strains to hear the lyrics, which come through the floorboards like a riddle from the other side, *You said goodbye like you said hello . . . with a single yellow rose.* The teak wood is soft against his skin. He runs his thumb along its dents and dark stains and tries to picture his father here, reading, listening to music, napping. He imagines a coffee mug resting alongside him and it occurs to him that for all the meals they shared he cannot remember if his father drank coffee or tea. He looks toward the sink and sees a drying rack with a brown ceramic mug but no coffee maker. On one of the two stovetop burners there is a newish silver kettle and so Hap decides it must be tea that his father drank in the spot where he sits now. Hap closes his eyes, exhausted by all that he does not know.

Another song rises like slow smoke from the apartment below. Rickie Lee Jones. He doesn't know the words but remembers Mo and his mother singing the song in the kitchen. He would have still been in high school, living at home. More than likely it was a weekend morning when they made almond flour pancakes topped with whipped cream Mo made from coconuts. He remembers wishing he made normal pancakes with Log Cabin syrup and not the hippie substitute like all the other weird hippie substitutes Mo had brainwashed his mother into loving. Hap remembers the song because it made no sense as Mo sang it and he was sure he had the lyrics wrong. *A weasel in a White Boy's School. We're all in a white Boy's School. Just like a weasel . . .*

What are you SAYING, he'd challenged Mo. *You're mangling the words. What does a weasel have to do with school?* And instead of answering, Mo smiled and sang and flipped his pancakes.

There is no wrong way to sing a song, his mother injected. *Even if you wrote the song yourself. There are ways that might more or less resemble the first time you sang it, or ways people might find easier to hear or understand. But there are no wrong ways.*

He remembers Mo watching his mother that morning. He looked like he was seeing her for the first time, like *she* looked at Hap when he gave her a story he'd written in school, or, when he was younger, handing her something he'd found on the street—an old, pale green, glass electricity conductor that once sat atop a telephone pole, an unwrapped bar of Ivory soap, an Oregon license plate. Even in high school, Hap could recognize love and here it was, brazen and unashamed and real.

Below him the song shifts to what sounds like Leonard Cohen—someone else Mo and his mother listened to. Hap still can't shake the memory of Mo's adoring gaze. He doesn't remember specifically wishing his father were with them that morning instead of Mo, but he knows he did so thousands of times. He also does not remember wishing that Mo would die that day, but now, in his dead father's tiny apartment, he knows that he did. He'd wished him dead—not because he'd hated him, but because even if he hadn't been responsible for his father leaving, Mo blocked the possibility of his return.

It surprises Hap to see himself so clearly now, and to recognize that he too had written a false story of his family. To Leah and to anyone else he would have said Mo was a great guy and good husband to his mother. And in the moment he would have meant what he said. Even after Mo died, when he first began to see how little he knew him, he still avoided some of the harder truths of their time together. In this friendly family there was a boy who wanted the man who shared a bed with his mother dead. Hap holds his head in his hands and, as he has done so many times in the last four days, squeezes his skull and rubs his palms across his eyes and face.

There is too much to know, he thinks, noting that his phone has not buzzed with a new text or voicemail in hours. He pictures Leah leaving his mother's house with their daughter, a cab outside waiting to take them to an airport to fly to her older sister's house in Naples, Florida. When he called from the mortuary to tell her he was leaving for New York, she hung up the phone. Leah was like this. Words, many of them—written and spoken and at every decibel level and pitch in voicemails and emails and texts—and then nothing. After a bad fight when she'd pull away, it would take weeks, sometimes months, to re-establish intimacy.

The first time he'd encountered her capacity to shut down was a few months after they'd started dating, the night he introduced her to Gene. Hap had recently transitioned from reporting to editing at the paper, and Leah was getting her PhD at Penn. He had the idea that by coming up to New York for the night to see a play, the dinner before would be short and Gene wouldn't drink too much. Leah had an alcoholic mother and though Hap didn't know all the particulars of what went on in her house when she was young, he knew it was bad enough for her to move in with her aunt and uncle her sophomore year of high school and live there until she went to college. Leah did not drink and Hap deliberately kept to one beer or glass of wine when they were together, but Gene was a five-vodkas-at-dinner kind of guy, on a slow night. The pressure Gene described being under at the law firm he'd started at sounded horrifying and in the last year Hap had seen him erupt into arguments with waiters and passersby after he'd had too much. For these reasons, Hap was not in a hurry for Leah to meet him. But most of his stories from growing up involved Gene, so Leah pressed. The day of, less than an hour before they left for the train to New York, Gene called to say he'd have to meet them for dinner after the play because something had come up at work. Hap was in the bathroom when the phone rang, so Leah took the call. By the time he'd come out she had already hung up, and Hap could see something had shifted. It was early on in their relationship and Hap did not yet understand how certain situations affected her, but from that brief phone call where Gene barked the new plan, without apology or salutation, he understood that it would not be easy between them, and as a result, not easy for him.

Gene turned up more than forty-five minutes late for dinner, already drunk and distracted. Nothing terrible happened, but it was painful. Leah barely spoke and Gene completely ignored her. Hap could see that it was not anger seething under her silence, it was something he hadn't yet seen. Fear. A kind of fight-or-flight stillness that didn't want to say the words that would escalate the potentially volatile situation into something unmanageable. When she went to the bathroom toward the end of the evening, Gene's only comment was sarcastic and dismissive, *Got yourself a fun one.* On the train ride home, Leah let the night speak for itself and didn't add to what was obviously a bad start.

Once it was clear Leah was in Hap's life for good, Gene toned down his bluster in her presence. Over time, she felt more comfortable around him, but was always cautious. *He is yours and so he is also mine, whether I like it or not, but let's not pretend to have the same experience of him,* she told Hap later, after they became engaged. He was grateful for her acceptance of his old friend, but by then, the combination of Gene's unabashed materialism and increasing dependence on alcohol made him less knowable, a friend in name and habit more than someone who could be counted on. Their infrequent calls and meals were occasions he no longer looked forward to, but tolerated. Gene was, as he had always been, his best friend, a status that seemed as fixed and infinite as family; but when they happened to be in each other's cities, or on holidays when they were both home in Bethlehem, their interactions started to feel less like old times and more like a hollow ritual of the friendship Hap had taken for granted all his life. At some point after college ended, but before that first evening meal with Leah, Gene had become something else for him; no longer playing any of the important roles he'd played since they were boys— trusted ally, fierce rival, finisher of sentences, co-creator of secret languages, relentless corruptor, conscience, confessor, penitent, defender, witness, brother. It meant that what played out when they got together was a thin pantomime of their old closeness, like a Revolutionary War re-enactment, with all the gestures and costumes and language of the era; theatrical time travel that lasted long enough to remember the sequence of events, the heroes and villains, the glories and losses, performed with faithful detail each time to make sure nothing was forgotten, or lost, but bearing only a surface resemblance to what it mimicked.

When he made plans with Gene, Hap instantly began to wrestle with whether he should come up with an excuse to cancel, and sometimes he did, which left him feeling guilty. But mostly he would show up to the Eagles game, or the steak house near Gene's office in Midtown, or the burger joint and bar at the bottom of the hill where they grew up and their mothers still lived. He'd go and he'd bear the obsessive talk of real estate, the impatience with waiters, the exaggerated stories of sexual conquest in unlikely places, and at some point swear to himself this was the last time. But inevitably some old story would crop up—the time they borrowed Mo's car when they were fourteen and drove it to a parking lot outside of town and couldn't find their way back; or the time they saw a woman get shot outside the Wawa in Easton after a soccer game. Gene was always better with the details—the silver Chevette that peeled away after the gunshots were fired, the pink v-neck sweater Mo was wearing when he and Hap's mother came to pick them up and how they couldn't stop giggling as she lectured them. Without these nights, Hap wondered where these details would go, whether or not the memories they belonged to would even last. After the boozy goodbyes, he was, more often than not, always glad he hadn't canceled, relieved to remember why someone he had nothing in common with anymore, whom he often didn't even like, still mattered so much. Gene was no longer an easy joy so much as a reminder of when he was one, which made their infrequent reunions as much a grounding as a grief.

Gene lives only a few blocks west of Christopher's apartment, but Hap has not considered calling him. There was too much to explain and he could already hear his old friend interrupting him, bullying the half-facts to ugly conclusions, reacting with energy that was not helpful. Even Gene would probably insist that he immediately return to Bethlehem to be with his wife and newborn daughter.

But Hap could not go back. He felt as if he'd been living in an elaborately painted mural that he'd taken for granted was the real world, and then his father fell down a flight of stairs and ripped it wide enough to see that in fact what was real had all along been on the other side. Having only caught a glimpse, he couldn't go home and be a father, or a husband, before knowing more. It would take a long time to gain Leah's forgiveness, but he could make it up to her. And to his daughter. But he couldn't make it up to Mo; nor could he make it up to the man who'd lived in this small apartment with little more than a good chair, a bed that folded into the wall, and a brown briefcase in the middle of the floor that looked like it had been left behind by someone who'd intended to bring it along, but had changed his mind at the last minute.

Alice

Hap's daughter is asleep with the bottle still in her mouth. Alice tugs the nipple away, gently, fearful the baby will register the absence and begin screaming. The door rattles open downstairs. At last, Leah. She starts to call out, to let her know they are upstairs, but stops before waking the baby. She can't believe she came so close to making such a stupid mistake after waiting all day for this rare quiet. She thinks she hears footsteps and as she listens for Leah, she remembers how Mo would come home from the bakery, take off his shoes, and in socked feet creep silently up the stairs to scare the daylights out of her as she got out of the shower, or sneak up behind her while she graded papers at her desk in their bedroom. She hated it and she loved it and when she was alone at home she'd often mistake the everyday creaking sounds of the old house shifting and settling for Mo's stealth attacks. For all her vigilance, he surprised her almost every time. It made sense. There was nothing expected about him. He was an anomaly, a fluke of elements colliding at the only moment they could to create the man she had loved.

In the spring of 1978, it fell to Alice to organize the retirement party for the chair of the history department at Lehigh, a somewhat paranoid hypochondriac who was allergic to, among other things, all dairy products. From one of the mothers at Hap's school, she'd heard about a man named Mo who made vegan desserts. A few weeks later, she met him at the bakery where he worked to go over the order. She'd brought Hap, who right away wanted every cupcake and cake in the display case. Mo was clearly Middle Eastern, probably not Israeli, she thought, with a name like Mo which she assumed was short for Mohammad. He appeared to be only a little older than most of the graduate students at Lehigh, and his clothing was cut to his body in a way that made his fitness apparent. A little vain, she thought, as she watched him ask Hap what he'd like to try. Hap asked for everything and Mo, exceedingly patient, fed him two then three cupcakes, which he took no more than a bite or two of and then enthusiastically requested another. Mo didn't seem to mind, and because Hap was being so polite with him, saying *thank you* each time he was handed a new treat—not his usual approach, even with strangers bearing pastries—she let him have bite after bite. *You're a good sport*, she'd said before they left, to which he responded by saying something that for days she wondered was flirtatious, maybe even suggestive. *I'll bet you are, too.*

Mo delivered the cake to the party himself. She'd called that morning to let him know that she could send a student to pick it up, but he insisted on driving it over. All afternoon, she found herself checking the parking lot through her office window, and was tickled to recognize him when he got out of the orange Saab hatchback and pulled the cake box from the back seat. He was in sweatpants, a singlet, and running shoes, and he seemed to bounce as he crossed from the parking lot to the sidewalk. Happy guy, she thought. As he came closer to the entrance, she could see with more detail his exposed shoulders, athletic arms, and tightly curled black chest hair poking above his shirt-line. She clapped her hands together and said, *Well ok!* By the time he got to her office door, she was smiling to herself because she could not remember having a silly crush on anyone since Christopher. Her life was work and Hap and sometimes family and she did not pine to have a boyfriend or husband the way many of the women she knew did. She did not want marriage, or company, even. What she occasionally thought about was sex. Not with anyone specific, just the act itself which she'd had very little of in her life. The one extended relationship she'd had, with Christopher, was exhilarating and intimate but it was not particularly sexual. She'd had nothing to compare it to at the time, so the long build-up to intercourse seemed perfectly normal. After three months had passed and they finally went through with it, Alice expected from then on that all sex happened quickly, in the dark, under the covers, and ended when the man climaxed, not the woman. She and Christopher shared many nights in bed together, but only had sex five or six times. As she didn't have any close friends her age to talk to about these things, she believed for a long time that what she and Christopher had was normal. Since then, she'd learned more and occasionally wished that she could just dial the phone and have sex delivered like she did pizza. But it didn't work like that, and a few awkward one-night stands with other history professors at out-of-town academic conferences were, for Alice, the closest she was able to get to the tidy efficiency of ordering sex when she wanted it.

One of the faculty secretaries escorted Mo, cake box in hand, into her office. *Where would you like this?*, he asked, his eyes catching the gentle mischief on Alice's face.

Oh, right here is fine, she said extending her hands and scanning his for a wedding ring, something she'd neglected to do when they'd first met. She didn't hide her excitement when she found only long unadorned fingers curled at the bottom of the pink box with the cake inside. *Yes!*, she blurted as if she'd found a long-lost and beloved book, one that she'd given up hope of ever finding. Alice took the cake.

Two years later, after she'd sorted out the divorce papers with

Christopher, Alice gave Mo a simple gold band and they had a ceremony between them at home, followed by a small vanilla wedding cake with lemon frosting that he'd made. *I'm with you*, she said, and neither of them needed any papers to prove it.

When Mo entered their lives, Hap was eight years old and unwelcoming. No cupcake in the world could bribe him, nor could any effort on either Alice's or Mo's part coax him from his wary distance. Their response was to let him come around on his own time. To Mo's credit, he never crowded Hap nor tried to assert a paternal role. By high school, the two of them got along fine but Hap wasn't as loving as Alice would have liked. If Mo had minded she might have pushed harder with Hap, but since he was polite and good-tempered for the most part, and his disinterest in Mo never reached a boiling point that required action, she decided to let things be. Even in junior high, Hap had his own life. He and Gene and the boys from the neighborhood left early and came home late and no one ended up in jail or hurt beyond a chipped tooth or smashed elbow. He got into college in Ohio and off he went. She didn't believe her role as a mother had a finish line—after all, here she was rocking his infant in her lap—but once he finished graduate school at Penn and started his career in newspapers, she began to relax. He'd survived his boyhood and young manhood and made his way to adulthood without calamity. At its root, this was the goal all along. To keep him safe and guide him into the world until he could take care of himself.

In her first weeks with Hap, Alice wondered if the connection she felt would sustain. If by not having carried him in her body, she would be missing some elemental bond needed to weather all the frustrating and despairing times ahead. Many nights, she stayed awake in their house and feared she would fail this boy who had dropped into her care from the sky. But as he grew from colicky baby to rambunctious toddler to chatty kid something like awe replaced those fears and instead of worrying about the years that lay ahead she began to wish them to stall. As Hap grew up, her appreciation for the miracle of his coming into her life became more acute. It was her greatest privilege to witness his very particular soul arrive in this world, watch his character and personality shape over years into the man he was now. He had been a kind and earnest child, an entitled boy unaware of his privilege; he was forgetful and selfish and not the least bit materialistic. He was a good, if imperfect, man and he was as unfettered and unharmed as she could have hoped.

For Hap, Christopher hung the moon. That he saw him only once or twice a year seemed only to magnify his allure. It did not bother Mo who surpassed Alice in hours logged at soccer and baseball games, ferrying Hap to and from friends' houses, shopping malls, and movies. He cooked every meal. Alice oversaw homework and bill paying and did all the laundry and housecleaning. It was nearly an even division of labor but Mo covered the day-to-day tasks like a parent even if he was never once called Dad.

Because it made the lie of his origins feel less pronounced, Alice insisted early on that Hap call her by her first name. His first word was *Mama*, which felt partly but not enough true, so she steered him away, and malleable toddler that he was, his second word was *Alice*. Even after Mo moved in, it was Alice and Alice only whom he came to for permission, approval, his plans, news of his first crush, his grievances at school. He behaved as if he lived with one parent who had a live-in boyfriend and it never changed. And Mo, perhaps because he was the only one besides Christopher, Lupita, and Dana who knew the truth, never complained. He'd roll his eyes occasionally or throw his hands up as Hap disregarded something he was saying or forgot to thank him as he rushed from the table after devouring a meal he'd spent an evening cooking. But he did not appear to suffer or chafe when Hap returned from his rare dinners with Christopher gushing with fantastic stories his father had told him.

Early on, Alice worried Mo would exact a tax for all that he tolerated. And in his way, he did. Not that it was overt, or ever so much so that she felt the need to discuss it with him, but there was a quiet, feather-gentle toll for his martyrdom. A stoic silence that figured into a million small decisions where his preference was given an unspoken priority over hers. Watching *60 Minutes* together instead of listening to the radio and reading, putting bags of lemon ginger tea in the teapot instead of chamomile, renting apartments on their short and infrequent vacations to Montreal and Washington, DC, instead of staying in hotels—these were small concessions she gradually came to accept as part of the unspoken contract between them. For his part, with Hap, Mo stayed present but never in charge. He told Alice once that because he was no hero to her son he could never let him down, which freed him to get on with what needed to be done without the pressure of disappointment. *Christopher, that's another story*, was the closest he ever came to criticizing the arrangement.

Christopher and Alice spoke on the phone before he'd visit with Hap. She never asked about his romantic life and she knew she'd hear his far-flung war stories secondhand in the car rides home after his meals with Hap, so she asked very little about his work. But they were always and only ever affectionate with each other and though they'd agreed to keep a distance between them, she felt love for him and would always be grateful he stepped up the one time she'd asked for his help. He never offered more, nor did she want more, but he gave Hap a sense of being connected to something special, in his boyhood especially, a fairy dust magic that got sprinkled once a year. Whatever complications loomed in the future, at the time they had seemed worth it. It was a strange configuration, but one that became comfortable. *As long as a song lasts*, Mo would quote from one of the poets he read. He meant there would one day be a reckoning, an unavoidable ending to the way things were.

She wonders where Hap is now, how much he has discovered. *Oh my boy*, she whispers to her sleeping granddaughter, imagining his agony. She wonders if he will ever forgive her. It's true, she'd lied to him his whole life. It seemed so harmless when he was an infant. But as the years of sustaining the charade piled up, decade into decade, and everyone got old, she watched how complicated and evolving Hap's relationships to Mo and Christopher became, how tortured he was. But there was nothing to do. It had been set in motion a lifetime ago and as Mo counseled many times, her job was to show up each day for her son, as she had, with love and intelligence and compassion. The outcome would be what it was and fretting about it or trying to manage it in advance would only succeed at undermining the present. *Just enjoy him, Alice. That's all there is to do.*

The smallest hand bats Alice's wrist. And dark blue eyes, open and alert, stare up into her face and hold her gaze. There will be so many faces, Alice thinks, and remembers the ones who mattered to her, the few who matter now, this one the newest of them all. So many faces to see and love and kiss and question. The weight of the girl's future life feels heavy in her arms. She whispers words she whispered to Hap when he was an infant, to herself as much as to him. They soothed her then as they do now, *It will all be ok, little one, it will all be ok.*

The only two checks she'd written from Lee's checkbook were both to the bank. The first was to pay off her parents' mortgages before they died. She told them that she'd saved the money and that it was a thank you for everything they'd given her. They did not argue, nor did they ever mention it again. The second check was to buy the bakery Mo had been working for. Shortly after he'd moved in with Alice and Hap, the brothers he worked for went bankrupt. The bakery was the only building they owned and it was being foreclosed on by the bank to pay off their debts, so Alice bought it and with Mo's savings he revamped the kitchen and expanded the business to include deliveries to restaurants and coffee shops in eastern Pennsylvania, New York, and New Jersey.

Valley Sweets thrived until the morning Mo died, twelve years later, as he was crossing the parking lot behind the bakery. An employee found him and called 911 but he was dead before the ambulance arrived. *It was an aneurysm*, the nurse at the hospital told her as if the information might make what happened less dreadful, *nothing preventable*.

Even now, there are places Alice brushes up against—the bench where Mo would lace his running shoes, their favorite seats at the back of the movie theater in town—where she feels him, his sweet soul, and she weeps as if he'd died that day. He wasn't too good to be true in the way that Christopher had been—he was truly the self he presented—but the life they had together, for the fourteen years that they had it, was beyond her greediest imagining. Would she have erased the whispered comments about his ethnicity? For Mo, yes, she would have spared him any discomfort. When this sort of ugliness occurred in the years when they were dating, before they lived together, Alice was furious. She would rise to confront the gas station attendant, the passerby at the mall, the teenager sitting next to them in a restaurant and Mo would calmly take her hand and shake his head. *Where I come from people died and continue to die because of retaliation. Don't retaliate now. Just love them and show them what love looks like. Maybe they've never seen it before.*

He showed Alice. Not just what love looked like, this she'd known from her family and from Lee and from Hap, but what strength and humility and commitment looked like. What a good man looked like. She missed him every hour of every day and she missed him now. The song did not last long enough.

Part Three

Jackie

With her back against the foyer floor, Jackie lies still and watches dust motes rise in slow motion around and above her. She'd drifted to sleep after falling, but has no idea for how long. By the angle of light beaming from the kitchen window, she figures it must be early afternoon.

She'd been awake for only a few minutes before Amy's knocking ended the silence. At first she thought Dana had come back, and reflexively, before she could manage her reaction, felt a mix of alarm and relief. She pictured her old friend standing on the other side of the door, restless in fitted suede pants, polished leather boots; her ringless fingers raking her short hair. But the more vividly she imagined the woman who had marched away from the house earlier and fled in her car, the less likely it seemed she'd changed course and returned.

And then she heard Amy's voice. Her rendition of *Mom*—an inextricable knot of scold and worry. When Rick was a little boy he would beg his mother to tell his sister to leave him alone. From the time he could talk he complained and cried and sometimes threw violent fits when, as he put it, Amy *bossed on* him. *She's bossing on me, Mommy! She won't stop bossing on me!* His face would often be splattered with tears as he pleaded to be understood. *She won't stop telling me what to do*, he'd say with as much desperation as he could muster.

Jackie finally understands what her son endured. She, too, has come to dread her daughter's voice which arrives in doubt-

147

ing tones over the phone, asking if Jackie has taken her pills, checked the thermostat, gone to the doctor's appointments she'd scheduled for her, called the insurance company to authorize her to follow up on her claims. These calls are almost as awful as her unannounced visits which began last summer and coincided with her complaining that the kid Jackie had hired to take care of the lawn was doing a shoddy job and taking advantage. From there her inventory of grievances could go anywhere—the shampoo Jackie used, the toxic fabric softener she bought, the window she left open, the gutters she's reminded her countless times to get cleaned, the type of milk in the refrigerator. *I thought we talked about this*, her most frequent refrain as she roots through the dresser drawers, closets, and medicine cabinets, throwing things out without asking. It's the same with the cupboards and freezer shelves she ransacks, weeding out unnecessary or unauthorized items that don't pass muster. The last time Amy was in the house she threw out a frozen pizza Jackie had bought at the grocery store. It's not that it looked especially good, but it seemed easy to make and something she could eat half of for dinner and the other half the next day for lunch. *I can't believe you'd buy this! Do you know what they put in these things? The salt alone will spike your blood pressure! I thought we talked about this.*

After Jackie retired from working as a secretary in the principal's office at Wells Center School, Amy became relentless. Jackie's first response was to stand her ground and let her daughter know that she could manage on her own, as she had since Floyd died. But Amy responded to any sign of resistance by overwhelming her with statistics and articles and anecdotal evidence. Didn't she know that by not complying she was only ensuring more work for Amy, who, with her own daughter moving home, her nursing job at the hospital, and second husband commuting to Danbury every day, was at the breaking point? *I'm just going to have to deal with it all later*, she snapped recently. Jackie was stunned at first not just by her daughter's insensitivity, but by her miscalculation. She was only sixty-eight, not ninety, she'd started to say, but then realized that ninety was only twenty-two years away, eighty only twelve, seventy, just two. After a while, Jackie's most frequent response to her daughter was silence. In less than two years, Amy had gained access to or had taken complete control of her bank accounts, medical information, retirement plans, insurance, everything; and in that time she managed to change it all. New bank, new leased car, new cable TV plan, new telephone provider, new primary care physician. New lawyer, too, to grant her power of attorney over everything medical and financial. *Rick will only make it worse*, she'd warned, when Jackie suggested they involve him. *Without Sandy doing the books at the restaurant, he'd have been out of business by the end of the first year. He's a mess.*

There was, at first, a part of Amy's bossiness that Jackie welcomed. She'd never minded the monthly onslaught of paperwork required to keep her family and her house going, but when Amy began meddling, Jackie thought it couldn't hurt to have another set of eyes on the bills. She regrets now that she failed to remember that when it came to helping, Amy only had two modes: not involved or complete control. And now it was too late and too complicated to undo. Buying groceries and dealing with the tradesmen and boys she hired to keep the house sound and presentable were Jackie's last remaining areas of autonomy, and these she would not surrender. Holding on, however, came with the high price of Amy's shock-and-awe tactics of relentless fault-finding, discrediting, and shaming of Jackie's choices and decisions. Amy was inexhaustible, despite the breaking point she often cited. Lately, Jackie flinched whenever she heard her daughter's voice.

Mom? Mom! What's going on? Why is the door bolted in the middle of the day and why are you not answering me?

Jackie wriggles her fingers and toes. Cautiously, she rolls to her side and maneuvers to a seated position. She's relieved to confirm again that nothing is broken or mangled.

I'm calling Rick and then I'm calling the cops and between us we will get this door down. Mom!

Amy is shouting at full volume. Jackie can't resist a smirk as her daughter sputters with rage. She knew withholding the key to the bolt lock on the front door had been a good decision. It just took a few years to appreciate exactly how good. In witnessing Amy's upset at having absolutely no control over the situation, she experiences a cool satisfaction, a welcome, if fleeting, justice. Still, she does not want her son or the cops summoned.

Calm down, Amy, she says. *I'm right here.*

You're WHAT? Excuse me? HELLO?

Here, Jackie repeats, but more softly now. Holding onto the doorknob for balance, she stands. Upright but still wobbly, she frees the bolt.

Hi dear, what's the matter? Jackie's limbs and back are stiff from lying on the floor and she holds onto the doorframe to steady herself.

You tell me, Amy says, irate, incredulous, yanking the door open the rest of the way. *How about we start with who Dana is. And then we can move on to why she left this at the door you refused to open.*

Propped against Amy's narrow hip and under her beige-fleeced arm, she is holding a brown leather briefcase. In her other hand, held high at the end of a stiff, straight arm, a scrap of torn paper—a page torn from a book, it seems, with a note scribbled in familiar handwriting:

Dear Jackie,

I'm sorry it's come to this. But I can no longer control what I never could. But I tried. I did try. Wrong as I might have been, it was for you. I was young. You were my friend.

I'll be at the house until tomorrow. It's time we talk.

Dana

Before she responds, Jackie grabs the briefcase and letter from her daughter's hands, and without breaking eye contact swings both behind her and lets them crash and flutter to the floor. And then she yells. It had been a long time—not since Rick was a boy knee-deep in mischief that left sofa cushions stained with red pen, or an entire peony bed a mess of petals, stems and upended bulbs. Yelling at Amy now feels good. Like a steaming hot shower blasting away layers of filth built up over years. Amy has never experienced her mother this way and in her shock she sits down on the stoop and listens.

Who are you to stand in front of my house and scold me? You are not the one in charge here. Go home and don't call me for a few days. And don't turn up here unannounced again! Jackie delivers these last words as she's turning away, and before Amy has an opportunity to respond, she slaps the door shut.

Jackie never yelled at Floyd. She only ever went silent the few times she might have, because she knew that nothing she said, no matter how forcefully, could return what she'd lost or change the past she would eventually make peace with. And if it wasn't exactly peace she'd made, it was a slow acceptance, arrived at over years.

Amy was only seven months old when Jackie kicked Floyd out

of the house. His parents let him come home and sleep in his old bedroom. In the first few months, when he or his sister or their mother came by, Jackie refused to let any of them in. When bills piled up she'd put them in an envelope and tape them to the door and write F L O Y D in black ink across the front. She never picked up the phone and since these were the years before she worked, so recently out of high school, she didn't yet have adult friends who called to check-in. Her mother came most mornings with groceries and helped her clean. Jackie ate toast and drank tea, dirtied few dishes, but her mother maintained that a house could never be too clean for a young child, so she wiped the counters and light switches and walls with Lysol and washed and washed again the baby's linens and clothes. When she was not cleaning and washing, she boiled glass jars and scrubbed and cut cucumbers, cauliflower, and beets from her garden and pickled them for winter. Since she was a kid, Jackie had never liked her mother's pickled vegetables, but Floyd loved them. Jar after jar, her mother filled the shelves in the hallway and in the closets next to the kitchen. Jackie understood she was not only expressing hope, but communicating clearly what she believed should happen next. This was as close as she came to giving her daughter advice on her marriage.

What Jackie never shared with her mother was that she had begun to seriously question whether or not her husband was even still necessary. That he might not be was a radical, perverse idea to her at first, but in the initial weeks after locking Floyd out of the house, she began to understand, with energizing clarity, that she in fact had everything she needed. Floyd had initially satisfied her girlhood aspirations to have a boyfriend and to be part of a couple. Once that had happened, he'd solved her curiosity and excitement about sex. In their first month together, she'd restricted their physical contact to kissing and light petting, but by October of her senior year she'd made it clear that he need not be so restrained. Soon they were having sex whenever they could, and by spring, she was pregnant. She'd only pretended to be surprised. Floyd was careless in general, even in this, and he never had rubbers. Jackie never made a fuss because without a plan for college and no real desire to work, she saw a baby as a way to speed up what she was impatient to have happen. A doctor in Torrington confirmed what was by late April clear to her. After they told their parents, a wedding was rushed, a house found, and Amy was born. Jackie spent no time contemplating any of it. What was there to think about? She was getting everything she wanted, only sooner than she'd planned.

So soon after marrying Floyd, it surprised her to recognize that life without him, or at least without his physical presence, could work. She'd need his financial support, but Jackie knew he wouldn't abandon his responsibilities. Floyd would never leave Wells, and with everyone in town watching, she knew he'd do what was expected. She figured he could pay bills from his parents' house, or wherever he ended up. She tried not to care where that might be, but she did, and so her task each day was not to act on or reveal the storm of contradictory feelings that raged behind the mask of her anger. Initially, her solution was not to engage with him at all. Doing so would only give Floyd an opportunity to explain himself, which meant he would either lie or expose the details of his betrayal, neither of which were bearable. And it might force an occasion where she would have to explain the severity of her reaction, something she was determined not to do. Of the available solutions, the one she wanted to avoid most was the truth.

Floyd was not allowed in the house for Amy's birthday or Christmas Eve. Jackie went home to her parents' and on Christmas morning he turned up with a box of poorly wrapped gifts and left them at the door. He didn't bother knocking. Her father described how he'd pulled his brown truck into the short driveway and walked the box to the stoop, turned around, and drove off. His gifts were arranged under the tree with the others and distributed by her father, one by one, after breakfast had been served and cleaned up, which had been her family's tradition. Here was the hardest moment so far—being handed her husband's gifts to her on Christmas morning by her father. She unwrapped each one—a navy blue scarf, a fruitcake made by his mother, and a Hummel figurine of an angel in a red robe with golden stars, holding a candle, singing— and was unable to stop the tears she'd held back since July.

After New Year's Day, she allowed him back in the house but insisted he sleep on a cot in the spare bedroom where they kept tools and Jackie's new sewing machine. Eventually, he bought a twin bed and dresser from a tag sale on the town green and for a while this was how they lived. Civil, in close proximity to each other, but no more intimate than respectful roommates might be. At first, Jackie refused to cook for or eat with him. She made sure she'd eaten a sandwich or a bowl of canned soup for dinner each night before Floyd came home. He never complained, simply grabbed a fork from the utensil drawer and opened a jar of pickled beets or cucumbers. Defensively, she imagined that in his choice of meal he was, night after night, sending her a message: *If you won't feed me, your mother will.* After five weeks, she began leaving him a plate of food—a sandwich and salad, mainly—between a folded napkin and silverware on the kitchen table. By summer that year, she would join him and make meals from recipes she'd clipped from magazines when they were first married—chicken à la king, orange and onion salad, chili casserole.

And then, almost a year after she'd changed the locks, Jackie was watering plants in the living room and through the bay window she noticed Floyd washing her car in the driveway. It was a hot June day and Amy sat a few feet away from him next to the bucket of suds and a big pink sponge. Floyd's white v-neck T-Shirt was soaked through and clung to his chest and back. Work on the farm and now painting houses and helping out on construction sites had kept him in the same shape he was in when they were in high school. Jackie watched his biceps flare as he moved the bucket to the front of the car and bent down to show Amy how to scrub the fender. He wasn't pressing very hard but she could see his back muscles tense and bunch through the thin, wet fabric. Jackie hadn't watched Floyd like this since before they were married. She tried to remember the last time they had made love. It was last June. The length of time shocked her. She didn't hate him anymore, but she also hadn't expected to feel anything more than tolerance and occasionally kindness toward him. Certainly not desire. Still, they rarely argued and, if they did, never in front of Amy. Without ever discussing it, they'd formed a kind of partnership in conveying to their daughter and other family members a perfectly normal marriage. And the truth was that separate bedrooms and the absence of sex became, for them, normal.

After Floyd moved back into the house, there were a few times, usually when he came home after a few beers with his buddies at the volunteer fire department, when he would let his hand linger on her shoulder or drop to her thigh. Jackie never made a fuss, she simply moved away and made it clear nothing had changed. And here they were. He'd stayed, acted as if he were a happily married man, made enough money to keep the lights on, food in the fridge and gas in two cars; and for her part, she kept a clean house, organized the shopping and the meals, and took care of their daughter. They were a team. And on a hot day in June, Floyd washed her car, made Amy laugh, and got his T-shirt wet. When he came into the house to take a shower, Jackie was waiting. That night he slept in her bedroom and never again on the twin bed in the room that less than a year later would become their son Rick's.

There were times when Jackie came close to telling Floyd about everything she went through the year before, the afternoon of July Fourth, and the long night after, but her instinct not to include him was strong, and once she was pregnant with Rick it felt like the universe correcting a terrible mistake, one that was best left concealed. Later, once Rick and Amy were in school full time, and she and Floyd had relaxed back into their marriage, she decided that when the right moment presented itself—despite the fury and grief the memory of that night still dusted up, even after so many years—she would talk to him about it, tell him what he did not know. But Amy and Rick graduated from high school, moved out, got married, had kids, and then, one after the other, moved back home. First it was Rick, at nineteen, with his pregnant wife, Sandy. They stayed until their son Liam was two. Less than two years later, Amy got divorced and turned up with her three-year-old daughter, Emily. They stayed for four years. When Amy and Emily moved in, Jackie was forty-eight years old; Floyd was forty-nine. They were middle-aged grandparents with a full house. The right moment never arrived.

A week after Floyd's fiftieth birthday, he drove to Millerton to pick up a drain pipe to attach to the gutter in the back of the house, something Jackie had needled him to do for weeks because the splatter was washing out the pachysandra bed she'd planted. It was an unusually warm, rainy Saturday afternoon in December and after procrastinating most of the day, he'd asked Jackie if she minded if the errand waited until Monday. But she insisted. She'd been doing laundry and cleaning with no help from Amy, who'd been studying for a nursing school test in her old bedroom, drinking cup after cup of coffee and leaving dirty plates and bowls on the counter and in the sink. Floyd had been watching basketball on TV as Emily sat on the couch next to him unspooling an entire roll of toilet paper. At four-thirty, after Jackie reminded him that the hardware store closed at five, Floyd pleaded with his eyes one more time to be left alone, but she was unmoved. She turned the knob on the TV off, grabbed the mess of toilet paper from Emily and told her to go to her mother's bedroom. Floyd grumbled as he put on his boots; the tires on his truck squealed as he pulled out of the driveway.

Less than an hour later, Gus Anderson, the local cop, Dirk Morey and two other guys from the firehouse stood at her front door in the drizzling rain. They told her Floyd's truck went off the road, down an embankment, and flipped into the side of a cement garage. He died instantly, they made sure to point out. As Dirk twisted the watch on his wrist and said they had no idea what caused him to crash through the guard rails, Jackie's mind raced through the possibilities—a deer, an oncoming car, a distraction that took his eye off the road just long enough to keep him from turning the wheel before the road curved? *Floyd is distracted easily*, she blurted, the wrong tense and the blame in her voice hanging in the air between them. She did not apologize or say another word, only closed the front door to the house and stood behind it with her hand on the knob, unable to move until Amy, with Emily on her hip, came out from her bedroom to ask why there were so many cars in the driveway.

Standing at the bay window now, Jackie watches Amy trudge to her car and leave. Adrenaline from losing her temper has her heart racing and her fists still clenched. As Amy's Subaru turns on to Hospital Hill Road and disappears, Jackie slumps against the window ledge. With a jolt, she remembers what Dana deposited at her doorstep—the leather briefcase and letter she'd grabbed from Amy's hands and tossed onto the foyer floor. She scans the brown lawn outside for something to distract her, but her eye lands on nothing. The briefcase sits behind her like a bomb.

Dana

The rigid, leather-covered cushion beneath her is Dana's first sign that she's not in her bed in the city. She opens her eyes, but is unable to see in the lightless room. Her mind is blank. She has no idea where she is waking, what time of day it is. She's experienced this temporary erasure before and knows by now to wait until a thread of something she can follow into memory presents itself. The outline of enormous bookshelves, the silhouette of lamps and rolling mahogany ladders gradually surface from the dark like cryptic symbols to be decoded, but no memory of where she is or why comes to her. She strokes the parched leather with her left hand. Lightly. Slowly.

Marcella . . . At the top of the townhouse stairs. Her smug smile. The phone call yesterday, the boy, now a man, fury and helplessness in his voice. *Yes, I'll come*, she remembers saying, rushing a coat over her body, Marcella calling after her as she left to find a diner that was only six blocks away but no place she'd ever seen or been to.

She saw the leather briefcase before she noticed the man sitting next to it. It appeared at the end of the booth like a piece from a museum exhibit of her past. Not the whole past, she qualified to herself, just the worst part that created the blueprint for the rest. And what would the plaque beneath this exhibit say, she wondered, eyeing the dulled brown leather and too-thick handle she can still remember the feel of in her hands. *Good Intentions* would be the kindest words, Dana decided, *Guilt* the more precise, and then she remembered leaving the case at Lee's farm, telling her aunt to throw it out, give it to Christopher, she did not care.

She imagined the exhibits depicting what came before and what followed. The first was the most obvious: Jackie's young family standing in the front lawn of their house—Floyd looking beyond the camera, of course, Jackie seizing his shoulder with one hand, cradling an infant in the other. What would she call that one? *Family?* The last would be this scene, now, in the diner, meeting the man who was barely born the last time she saw him, swaddled and screaming as if on fire. All these years later he was on fire again, but this time with questions there were no good answers to. She would call this scene, *Reunion.*

Dana imagined the exhibits in between—many of them depicting people and places she'd never met or seen, but had glimpses of through private detectives she'd hired over the years. They'd sent her pictures which she kept in a plain white envelope in her desk drawer. They included ten or so of a boy who'd grown from a wiry, seemingly happy adolescent into the adult fellow she now gazed at across the diner. She remembered an image of him sitting on the hood of a car, wearing a blue winter coat and thick mittens, a Middle Eastern–looking man alongside him holding a big snow shovel. There was another photo of him in his forties having dinner with a pretty woman with short blonde hair who appeared at least ten years younger than him.

She remembered the other photos, mostly of Jackie through the years—getting into her car in the parking lot at Wells Center School, in her twenties; and later, not quite middle aged, retrieving the mail from the black metal mailbox at the end of her driveway, her mouth a tight line, an awful perm, all business; and the one where she's in a peach-colored dress on the day of her son's wedding, sitting next to Floyd at a table covered in a paper table-cloth, both of them looking like most of the people Dana had ever seen in that town—limited and uncurious, tired.

She remembers another photograph of Jackie, alone, her hand resting on the metal railing outside a church entrance. It was taken the day of Floyd's funeral. Her expression is blank, unreadable. Dana had studied the photograph more than a few times over the years, and was never able to locate what she saw there. What she didn't see was a helpless widow. In the absence of obvious emotion, Dana believed she recognized something of Jackie's pragmatic grit from their childhood, her particular brand of self-reliance. It didn't go exactly as Jackie had wanted, Dana knew, but she had married the man she'd decided was the one for her, had his two children, buried him, lived and worked and mothered in the town she never intended to leave. Almost fifty, she was a widow with married children, a grandmother already, approaching life alone.

By comparison, Dana's twenties, thirties and even forties felt like a long summer between years in college, a protracted time to wallow outside the parameters of ordinary and ordered life. While Jackie was becoming the dependable secretary, good mother, and sturdy widow, Dana had affairs with men and women and cycled through people and money in successive locations, but after three or four years anywhere, after the possibilities had been exhausted and the place and its people were no longer novel or amusing, an affair or intrigue of some kind buoyed her away, toward some new piece of real estate that needed an overhaul and a small army at her command to do it, a fresh reservoir of oxygen to burn.

The first place Dana went to after college was London where she stayed for seven of the fastest, most viscerally exhilarating and loneliest years of her life. When she left she packed her jewelry in a hatbox that she carried on the Concorde and left all the clothes and furniture and people behind her in a house she'd rented on Primrose Hill. She let the lease run out and trusted that all the baubles and bodies would find fine enough homes. She'd call that exhibit, *Oblivion*.

One woman would appear in several of the most important exhibits, but never in the foreground, never obvious. She would be off to the side, sufficiently out of sight to avoid stirring suspicion, but present enough to ruin everything. There was only one photograph of her in the envelope in Dana's desk. It showed the woman as she looked sixteen years ago, aged but still exquisite. Every time Dana looks at this photograph her first vexed thought is always the same: that of all people this was the woman most likely to be the exception to her grandmother's rule, that unlike Dana or anyone else she knew, she was able to have, without choosing, both her face *and* her ass. Even now, her cheekbones sliced the air around her like weapons; her severe hair, silver and thick and knotted behind her head in a bun so tight it looked like blown glass. She is seated in the driver's seat of a parked minivan under a breezeway at a tropical resort. Her head is down, her eyes focused on something in her lap. She could be counting money or reading an email or a text on a phone. Dana has examined this photograph countless times, always looking for some hint of what she was thinking, how she might feel, what her life was like. But whatever she sees on this woman's face is only ever what anyone saw there: what they wanted to see. Because whatever true feeling she had—elation or anger or anything in between—was something she did not show. Dana never found what she was looking for in that photo, which suggested to her that time's only visible effect on this woman was the color of her hair and the texture of her skin, both still pleasing. There was only one word that would accurately name this exhibit: *Lupita*.

The man in the booth looked up and saw Dana across the

room. He put the briefcase on the table in front of him, moved to the seat's edge, and stood up. The gesture surprised her and at first she guessed it was made out of respect: like a peasant acknowledging the presence of a royal, she thought, more amused than flattered. But something about the stiffness of his hands at his sides let her know it was only the courtesy of a younger man responding to the sight of an older woman. She signaled with her hand for him to sit down but did not cross the room. She knew when she did it would close a circle long in the making, and no doubt open several new ones.

Finally, she approached the booth. She extended her hand to his, like an author meeting a character in a novel she'd written when she was young. *Hello*, he said, looking up, his face blank. He had nothing of his mother's coloring or complexion. But this she knew from the photographs. *Hello*, he said again, more warmly. Something about the rise of his eyebrows, the drop of his Adam's apple, the bunching of skin below his hairline—for a split second she had a memory of her father when she was young. He would have been in his forties, as Hap was now. It had been a long time since she'd thought of her father as anything but old and sick. She looked into Hap's face again to see what sparked the memory but saw nothing but a stranger. One who looked lost, but kind, two words no one who knew her father would have ever used to describe him.

Looking at Hap more closely she saw that unlike his parents who never had a chance to become much more than their adolescent impulses, he'd grown into an educated, civilized, attractive man. She allowed herself, for no longer than the time it took to let go of his hand and sit down in the booth across from him, a flash of pride. She reminded herself that she was not his mother, that she did not birth or raise him. Other women, unintentionally or because they volunteered, had been responsible for those roles.

Still, she reminded herself, if not for her he would not be. This meeting was nothing she ever foresaw nor would have asked for, but seated before a consequence of her time on earth she was relieved to see that he had exceeded even her most optimistic imagining. *Hello*, she finally said in return. *It's good to see you again.*

Jackie

The dip in the driveway of her parents' old house as she turns off Undermountain Road scrapes the muffler just as it has her whole life. She steers her car to the right of the garage and slows to a stop in the space between the garbage bin and the woods, exactly where she'd parked in high school and after, when she came to visit with Amy and Rick, and thirteen years ago when she came to take away the last boxes of her parents' belongings after they died. No one has lived here since, so she's not worried about trespassing. Still, being back feels strange, and the dark house and moonlit lawn have the eerie wrongness of a nightmare.

It was Dana who bought Jackie's parents' house from her even though the lawyer representing the buyer said it was an investment group from the city. The name of the company on the closing papers—Calliope Holdings, LLC—gave her away. Calliope was the queen of the fairies she and Dana had told stories about when they were children. Her survival, and the whole fairy world's survival, they'd believed, depended on at least one of the jewels she'd disguised as a river stone being discovered before the end of each summer. It was visible only in the light of a setting sun and could only be seen by a girl.

It wasn't until Jackie sat down in the realtor's office to sign the closing papers that she saw the name of the buyer and when she did she recoiled as if she'd seen a ghost. She asked for another day to decide and seriously considered not going through with the sale. But she still owed money on her second mortgage and looking ahead, between her social security and 401k, there was very little room for unexpected expenses. Rick and Amy were barely able to keep it together financially, so she couldn't count on them to take care of her. The next morning she added one hundred thousand dollars to the figure they'd agreed on and drove to the real estate agent's office in Wells and told her to call the lawyer. With the proceeds from the house, Jackie was able to pay off her debts and put enough away to stop worrying whether or not she'd be able to retire. Her only regret was that Dana had gotten what she'd wanted.

The moon is three-quarters full and the dirt road between her old house and Edgeweather has a dull glow that she remembers from summer nights staying out late with Dana, sneaking along the tree line and pretending not to hear Ada and Maria's calls for them to come home. Jackie was a girl who did her homework, brushed her teeth before bed, and followed the rules. But with Dana, in those years between eight and seventeen, she allowed herself, on occasion, to be defiant. The rebellions were little more than staying out past dark, but over time each little transgression helped Jackie understand that she had choices and that she could assert her will, selectively, and not only was it possible that there wouldn't be repercussions, but that she might end up getting something she wanted. It was all a matter of deciding on what to want.

She remembers the night she decided she wanted Floyd. It was her Junior Prom and Floyd had come with his sister, Hannah, which was a little strange, but certainly not as strange as Jackie's date, Dana. Since the prior fall, Dana pressured Jackie to take her. *We don't have these kinds of things at my school*, she'd explained. *There are formals, sort of, but they're boring and stiff and no one, not one person, not ever, has fun.* Jackie knew she was exaggerating to get her way. And a part of her liked that Dana was trying so hard. *We can shop for dresses in the city and make a weekend out of it. Whatever we do we can't let my mother talk us into letting her creepy dressmaker design something. We'll look like old biddies from her horrible club.* Jackie agreed, knowing that Dana would hound her non-stop until she finally gave in. *Brilliant!*, she'd screamed over the phone from the city when Jackie told her she'd talked to the teachers in charge of the prom who said it was ok to bring her. *This is going to be such a gas, Jack. I promise.*

A few weeks after Dana came back from winter break in Florida, Jackie met her in the city to shop for dresses. Maria drove them to various stores in midtown while they sang "We Can Work It Out" by the Beatles over and over, deploying the lyrics in all situations—traffic jams, a broken escalator at Saks, a dropped ice cream cone on the sidewalk at Rockefeller Center. Eventually they made their way to Bonwit's and spent the entire afternoon there. Dana even persuaded a sales assistant to go out and buy them ham and cheese sandwiches, pickles, and cupcakes for lunch. Seeing Dana in her element, where the rules and interpersonal dynamics were pre-determined—as in the lobby of her apartment building where porters and doormen and elevator attendants moved in deferential ballet around her family—incited both a smug pride that her friend occupied a high, rare place in the pecking order of a spectacularly intimidating city such as New York, but also provided a bracing glimpse at the vast distance between their circumstances. The difference between Dana's family and her own was never forgotten, but in Wells, which was Jackie's home turf, it receded enough not to be felt. In the city, though, there was talk of clubs and schools and towns in Florida and Maine and Antigua that Jackie had never heard of. *Bryn Mawr or Barnard? And please don't say Vassar,* was how a friend of Dana's mother's greeted them in the elevator at Bergdorf's. The presumption of one or the other, the warning of the third. It was a language Jackie didn't understand and Dana's response, *Bryn Mawr, I'm afraid. My Aunt Lee would never forgive me otherwise*, was a reminder that in less than two years their lives would change radically.

As Jackie saw it, Dana merely had to relax into a plan, allow each door to be opened for her and simply pass through at the given time. Jackie had allowed herself to ignore real plan-making, but in New York, where every inch had been built according to a meticulous blueprint, and inhabited by people who appeared to leave nothing to chance, Jackie couldn't ignore her future any longer. She'd given lip service to applying to the University of Connecticut but she never planned on going through with it. Her parents didn't press, in fact displayed little interest in her plans after high school, and so collaborated in an unspoken denial of the fact that she had eighteen months until graduation and no plans after.

After trying on dozens of dresses, viciously critiquing each one, they finally found two they loved and charged both to Dana's mother's house account. *She'll never notice, I promise*, Dana assured Jackie in the dressing room. It wasn't Mrs. Goss Jackie was worried about, it was her own mother who would be livid that Jackie took advantage of the situation, which is how she would put it. But take advantage she did and how could she not, she reasoned, after putting on the lemon cream chiffon dress that was a thousand times more beautiful than any of the ones she'd clipped from magazines over the last year. The Lemon Cream Dream, as she and Dana referred to it, had elegant cap sleeves and small white flowers embroidered along the bodice and hemline that hit a few inches below the knee. It *was* a dream, the dreamiest dress she'd ever seen, even if Dana thought it looked a little old-fashioned.

Dana, on the other hand, picked out a sleeveless black silk cocktail-length number with what looked like crystals embroidered at the neckline and waistband. It had little knife pleats, a wired ruffle hem, and a dusty gray taffeta underdress with a silver zipper in the back. They called her dress The Razzle Dazzle which made them laugh every time they said it.

Jackie's mother insisted she write a check for the dress and give it to Dana's family. The price tag had been more than seventy dollars, as much as or more than, her mother claimed, some of the furniture in their house. Jackie knew Dana would rip up the check and never give it to her parents, so even though her mother's hand actually shook while signing her name, she didn't worry.

The dresses took a few weeks to get tailored and Dana brought them with her from the city in March. Prom was in May and in the weeks leading up to it they tried on and paraded around in their dresses every chance they could. The last time was the weekend before and Dana argued they needed to practice several dances fully dressed and in the shoes they intended to wear. Jackie said she hadn't planned on dancing much but Dana begged her to watch *American Bandstand* with her on Saturday afternoon and practice all the latest dances so they wouldn't make fools of themselves. Jackie reluctantly agreed, and they were able to approximate less coordinated versions of what the teenagers on the TV show did. For the slow dance, Dana insisted on leading as the 45 of their favorite song, "Yesterday," played on the record player. Jackie did her best to follow, though repeatedly she felt Dana's arm pull too tight around her waist. *Loosen up, ok?*, she asked once but when Dana pulled her closer, something kept her from speaking up again. A rare, awkward seriousness settled between them as they stepped in time with the bittersweet melody of the song, and for a moment she felt both the hot illogic of being trapped along with Dana's sudden vulnerability. She wanted to pull away but she worried the consequences would be too hurtful. When the song finally ended Dana suggested they go at it again, to work out the kinks, but Jackie begged off, improvising sloppily that she had an essay to finish for her English class, that she'd left the books back at her house and should go. By Dana's quiet reaction to the sharp change of plans, Jackie suspected she'd been caught. Still, she quickly changed in the bathroom across the hall, carefully returned her dress to its box and with a cheerful promise to call later, she carried it home. Neither mentioned the dancing practice on the phone that night when it was Dana who called, not Jackie, nor was it ever brought up again.

The Saturday night of the prom Joe Lopez drove Jackie and Dana in the Gosses' Town Car. It seemed strange to Jackie to have him chaperoning but since Dana's parents would be in the city for a wedding, her father had insisted.

The night of the prom, Dana picked Jackie up at her house like it was an actual date. Joe pulled the car up and she marched formally to the door with a pale pink orchid corsage wrapped in cellophane and a white ribbon. Jackie noticed her parents squirm when Dana leaned in uncomfortably close to her chest as she slid the flowered bracelet onto her wrist. She remembers how Dana handled the gesture with a solemn reverence; Jackie knew, or at least she believed she knew, that her seriousness was a performance to provoke exactly the reaction it did.

At the Mohawk Ski Lodge, where the prom was held, Dana stood out. Her black dress fit so perfectly on her body that the other girls—in pink, green or baby blue floor-length get-ups many of their mothers sewed from Simplicity patterns—looked childish by comparison. Her brown hair was in an updo, and wrapped in a silk scarf, *like Audrey Hepburn in Charade,* Jackie's mother had noted earlier. When Dana walked through the front entrance of the lodge, into Housatonic Valley Regional High's Spring 1967 Junior Prom, no one knew quite how to react. Her mother was right, Jackie thought, she looked like a movie star. Some stared as she took her time unwinding her long silver scarf and folding it into the small black bag slung over one of her shoulders. Jackie stood to the side and watched Dana have her fun.

Jackie was so engrossed in the little spectacle, she didn't notice she'd slowly backed up against a short set of stairs that descended to a door that opened onto one of the porches outside. As she was already falling backward, she imagined broken bones, a trip to the hospital, and Dana furious that her evening had been ruined. But before that could happen, a jolt of arms and hands at her back, under her legs, and the piney smell of aftershave.

Whoa, the night just got started. You might want to slow down, she heard as she was actually being carried, fully carried by another person, to the bottom of the steps. She was aloft for less than a few seconds but when her kitten heels returned to the floor she felt an instant regret, like eating the last spoonful of the most perfect ice cream sundae, when the exact sensation of its magic was gone. She turned around, still within the circumference of where the boy's arms could reach, to see who had saved her. She was neither disappointed nor surprised to see Floyd Howland, a boy who had always been in the class ahead of her, at Wells Center and at Housatonic. In elementary school, Floyd was never the brightest boy, nor the one people noticed first, but after high school began he shot up six or seven inches and was now easily one of the tallest boys in the school. Jackie had always liked him, even had a crush on him in the eighth grade, but Dana had been the only person she'd told. Since then, their paths hardly ever crossed.

You ok?, Floyd asked, leaning down in his rented tuxedo and Brilliantined hair slicked to prom perfection. This, she knew it right then, was what she wanted. She didn't delude herself into thinking that the feeling was mutual, not then, not that night, but if Dana had taught her anything, it was that with clarity of purpose and enough perseverance, anything was possible.

Walking along the moonlit road, Jackie tries to locate what exactly she wants now, why she's followed Dana here after succeeding at staying away for so long. Up ahead and through the trees she can see a scattering of lights. It galls her that all of Undermountain Road is now Dana's; even more so that she'd been complicit in making it so. What was this place now but an untraveled road with a few empty houses no one entered, let alone lived in. Not a child for miles, she thinks, as if someone had whispered the words into her ear.

As she approaches the driveway, she hesitates. After all, the contents of the briefcase Dana left on her doorstep make no sense. Marriage and divorce papers for people she's never heard of. Legal documents articulating the adoption of a child she does not know. On the pages, only Lupita's and Dana's names are familiar to her; the date—April 15, 1970—is not a date she has any particular association with; and the address of the law firm, Young and Berube, is in Bethlehem, Pennsylvania, nowhere she has ever been or considered. But there is one stray scrap of blue paper, a piece of old hotel stationery ripped in half, with the name *Floyd* written in black ink next to the telephone number Jackie has had since she and Floyd rented the house on Hospital Hill Road the summer after she'd graduated from high school. Why his name and their number would be mixed in with the birth and adoption documentation of a boy named Hapworth Foster, a boy with two birthdays apparently—March 10, 1970, and July 10 of the same year—she has no idea. But along with the strange note Dana had inexplicably written on the torn-off title page of a book titled *The History of the Moravian Church*, it was enough to get her to put a coat on over the nightgown she woke up in that morning, drive over Wells Mountain, and trudge up the steps of a house she'd sworn a long time ago to never again enter.

Dana

It was love. It had never occurred to her before. Her great-great-grandfather loved his wife and would do anything for her. That she did not love him back did not deter him. Nor did it keep him from spending a fortune on this gigantic house and everything in it. Dana sits at the dining room table, a large round walnut antique at the center of a red-and-cream silk rug under a high plaster ceiling. After Philip had found her in the library to tell her he was leaving for the motel down the road, and that he would be back in the morning to take her to the city, she'd made her way to the dining room, avoiding the parts of the house she hadn't yet entered. Enough memories had been stirred and she'd had enough surprises.

There were twelve chairs around the table, but Dana had never seen them all occupied. It had usually been just the three of them—her father with his back to the window that overlooked the lawn and the river, Dana and her mother seated to his left and right respectively. Across the room from where they sat stood a fireplace between two small alcoves. And above the fireplace, the painting of her great-great-grandfather George Willing, with the object of his adoration, Olivia.

Running her hand over the dark wood now, Dana realizes that Jackie never sat at this table. Not once. She hadn't noticed when they were young because eating upstairs was a great relief from having to tolerate the boring and often tense silences of her parents and the tyranny of table manners they required. How did her parents get to be the age she is now without recognizing how awful they were? How outdated and idiotic their snobbery and prejudices? Her anger boils quickly and is so familiar a feeling it's almost a comfort to indulge it.

Dana looks up at the painting again and regards her great-great-grandfather, whom until now she'd mostly ignored in favor of his delicate, nineteen-year-old wife with light red hair and green-gold eyes. Through childhood and adolescence, Dana studied Olivia Willing's painted image, scoured the clippings of wedding announcements, obituaries, and photographs her father kept in the library with the family memorabilia. But most of what she knew about Olivia came from her Aunt Lee. During a visit the summer before she'd started at Bryn Mawr, the subject of Olivia came up. They hadn't spoken about her in a long time, but Dana, close then to the age Olivia had been when she married George, found herself wondering again about her great-great-grandmother, surely the most beautiful and notorious member of the family. Lee seemed to share a reluctant appreciation of her, despite the choices she'd made. *Apparently my grandfather despised her and didn't like his mother's name to be mentioned, so whatever I know comes from my grandmother's fascination. No wonder, Olivia left her six-year-old son behind to live with her sister in Paris. Before the Civil War had even ended! It really is astonishing. You have to remember, though, she was young and newly rich and her husband had just died. But it's true, she left her son to be raised by a governess until he went to boarding school. Of course the woman he ended up marrying would be curious about a mother-in-law capable of such decisions.*

When Dana came back to New York that summer she asked her grandmother what she remembered. *Your great-great-grandmother was not much of a mother, this of course we know, but we do owe her. Whatever beauty you or your father or any of the Willings or Gosses who came after had or have, all of it surely comes from her. Until she showed up, I don't think our people were much to look at. She never came back to Edgeweather after she left. She never remarried, either, though I think she lived quite a life abroad. An expensive one! It's a good thing Father went into banking otherwise who knows how we'd have all ended up.* Despite her grandmother's spotty and ungenerous assessment, Dana still wanted very badly to align with the copper-haired, fine-featured Olivia. Beyond her surface, there was something about her choice to leave her young son behind in the middle of a war, to live in Paris, choices that would be unthinkable now but must have been even more so back then. Whether it was because she was selfish or strong-willed or unstable, she did something shocking, and in that Dana could find a hero.

In the dining room, looking at the painting now, she sees her own resemblance to her great-great-grandfather. The heavy eyelids, the brown-black eyes, the slightly exaggerated distance between them, the intensity. He was, as she has always been, whip-thin. In his dark eyes she recognizes a quality she possessed, for a while, at least. Not just arrogance rooted in privilege, the rush of boundless possibility when coming into money and freedom young, as she had, but a vulnerability, too, a contradictory awareness of money's limits known only to those who had as much as they did. When George Willing met Olivia Henshaw, he surely spotted the coast of that limit, and in every minute that followed he must have been determined to win her.

Dana knew they'd met in Newport, where his parents had a summer cottage and her father was rector at the Episcopalian church. She tried to picture the fair-haired sons of robber barons who must have courted her, how mightily they must have competed for her attention. But few were as wealthy as good old George's family who had, almost a century before, turned a shipbuilding company in colonial Rhode Island into a real estate fortune. And even fewer would have been as willing or as able to lure her with the promise of a wedding gift as significant as Edgeweather. She suspected there was no length to which he wouldn't go. He probably went to war because he thought it was something that would at last earn him her respect, if not her love. But it never could. The painting didn't lie. It was clear to Dana, even across a century and a half, that the woman had no interest in him beyond what he could buy or build for her and though he may have known it then, it never stopped him from trying to prove himself worthy. One glance at his narrow shoulders and delicate hands, there could be no doubt in anyone's mind that George Willing was not meant for the battlefield. If his wife had loved him she would have never let him go. And surely with senators and governors and a fortune at their disposal his family could have easily cut a respectable path for him away from the front lines. But to Hoke's Run, Virginia, he went. With a rank beyond his experience and a coffin waiting. He lasted less than one full day.

Until now, Dana only ever had contempt for her great-great-grandfather; she'd judged him for the wedding cake house he built and all the extravagances he filled it with. But as she sits in the dusty consequence of his obsession, it surprises her to feel a shift. Yes, he was a pampered fool. An only child, a needy showoff. But he was also determined, and he acted sincerely, spent his late youth and early adulthood single-mindedly attempting to win the love of a woman who was at best indifferent to him and at worst disdainful. He went to war and died for her, Dana decides. The more she thinks about it the more it makes sense. He'd won her hand with jewels and the promise of a great house. They had a son in the first year. The war with the South was on and likely he could feel her tolerance for him was fading. So he went to war and he never saw her again. Was his wife relieved? Embarrassed? Or was she exultant? Did she feel the heavy tax on the wealth and position she'd secured lift forever?

A car door slams outside. Dana barely hears it. She looks up at George's flimsy frame and dark eyes and recognizes something else there. Why it makes her feel strangely relieved she does not know. He was led by his heart, she thinks defensively, made a spectacle of his love, sacrificed everything, and when he died he had no regrets. She scans Olivia's pale features. Even from where she sits she can appreciate how delicately painted and life-like Olivia's slender neck and décolletage are. What a pair, Dana thinks and sees the once-upon-a-time Willings as both doomed and oddly heroic. Two children of a new country born with assets and liabilities—one money, the other beauty—and in not so original an equation, they each used what they had like weapons and bagged big game. She looks at them standing side by side, the river behind them. Olivia's hands are folded tidily below the high-cinched waist of her gown, George's left hand on her far shoulder, his right on the one that seems to pull away from him. He is holding her not like a trophy or a possession or even the way Dana has seen most husbands touch their wives with affection. He is holding her like someone who must. Someone who accepts his wife, forgives her—for despising him, even—who would fight for her, whose fate is bound to hers beyond the point of choice. He loves her. When that might have happened no one will ever know, but by the time this painting was created (according to her grandmother soon after they'd married), he was already determined to do whatever it took to be in her company, make her happy, and win her love.

Good for you, George, Dana whispers, apologizing in her way for having had only contempt for him until now. *You got what you wanted, even if it didn't last very long.* She thought of her parents' marriage. When she was old enough to begin to see them as people, more than only stern punctuation to her heavily scheduled hours, she saw them as disappointed colleagues who were stuck together. Her mother's nervousness didn't help, nor did the erratic medications her psychiatrist prescribed which would make her sleepy and detached one week and frantically making plans she'd soon abandon the next. Her father stayed cordial, for the most part, and aloof, perpetually annoyed. There were never displays of affection, and few words between them outside the necessary sentences required to schedule and coordinate their day-to-day movements. Her father had a low threshold for more and if too many questions were asked, or too many anecdotes from the day were told at dinner, for example, he had a way of raising his hand slowly and successfully shutting down whatever was being said. That ordinary hand—open-palmed, un-calloused, and smooth, with long fingers and meticulously trimmed nails— never hit anything except the dinner table on rare occasion, nor had it harmed her, nor anyone else that she knew of, but she knew that it could. His open palm had the promise of a fist. It was nothing she'd ever said out loud or shared with anyone, not even Jackie, but it was something she knew. And by her mother's unblinking and swift compliance, she recognized that she did, too.

Dana slowly pushes her chair back from the dining room table and begins to stand, considering for the first time since she arrived where she will sleep. Before she is fully upright, she hears a sound at the front door. Less a knock and more a pounding, which stops soon after it starts. The silence that follows is broken by the creak of a door and a voice that pierces air, time, and Dana's equilibrium. She falls back into the chair with a thud the moment the words hit her ears: *Dana, get out here. It's Jackie.*

Jackie

The foyer is empty and immediately familiar. The space never looked to Jackie like the first room of a house so much as how she imagined the lobby of a fancy hotel. She almost turns back but before she can, Dana appears, her manner like a rattled hostess receiving an expected, but late, guest. She leans against the white molding that frames the entryway and smiles, as if trying to pretend that seeing Jackie face-to-face for the first time since they were nineteen, standing in Edgeweather's foyer in a pink flannel nightgown, navy wool car coat, and knee-length black rubber boots, carrying a brown briefcase, was perfectly natural.

Without moving from where she stands, or shifting her stance, Dana starts to speak.

Jackie, I . . .

Before she can finish her sentence, Jackie interrupts, pointing her finger in front of her.

Stop it. I didn't come here to catch up or hear any stories. Just tell me what you're up to. Jackie's tone is direct, controlled. She drops her finger, puts both hands back on the briefcase and takes a few steps toward Dana before setting it down on the foyer floor between them. They are less than a few feet away from each other now and up close Jackie is shocked to see how much Dana resembles her mother when they were young. The same lines fanning from her eyes, crossing at abrupt angles between her brows. The same wide, thin shoulders that seemed always to be tilting slightly back, even when she was seated, as if they held carefully tucked wings.

It occurs to Jackie that she and Dana are now both significantly older than their parents had been when they were growing up. She knows this should not surprise her, but still it erases whatever else she had intended to say. Mute, she stands a few yards away from Dana, who seems to be cataloging every detail of her slapdash outfit. For only a fleeting second, Jackie regrets not getting dressed properly before rushing over.

For a while, the two women simply stare at each other and say nothing. Forty-nine years, Jackie thinks. The silence between them was older than Rick and more than twice as long as the time they'd actively been in each other's lives. Arms crossed, Jackie fidgets her middle finger over her left elbow, feels the wrinkled skin there sagging like buckled fabric, the joint and bone jutting beneath, brittle as twigs.

Dana speaks first. *Can I get you something to drink?*

Jackie regains some of her composure and manages to restate what she'd said a few minutes before. *Stop it. Stop fooling around. What are you up to?*

Dana steps from the wall. *Ok. Ok, then. Let's have it out. But not here.* She stoops to collect the briefcase from the foyer floor, turns her back to Jackie and heads toward the stairs. Jackie doesn't budge. Not before Dana is more than halfway up the first flight does Jackie unfold her arms and begin to cross toward the bottom stair.

Remember the Knees? Dana calls out behind her as she clears the landing. *Do you remember how they could make something that was one way appear to be another? Rocks into jewels and all that. You did that, too.*

Jackie stops on the fifth stair and steadies herself on the dark railing before looking up at Dana who's still speaking. Before tonight, she hadn't thought of the fairy people who lived in the forest along the river in a long time, how obsessed she and Dana were with finding the treasure they'd hidden in the water. They'd both taken it so seriously, and never once suggested to the other that it was anything but real.

Dana continues speaking as she climbs the stairs. She faces forward but her head tips back, up, and just slightly to the right.

You were so determined not to see Floyd clearly. But then I made it much worse. I know that I did. At the time I thought what I was doing was right—ok that's not quite true. But you do have a part in all this. You can't pretend that you don't. I'm done taking the blame for everyone . . . And I'm tired of your not knowing.

Jackie knows she needs to leave. She cannot stay and hear Dana accuse her of further wrongdoings and take more potshots at Floyd. Jackie turns to go, but as she does notices the chandelier hanging from the ceiling above the landing. It's a small contraption of crystal and undusted metal—light splitting and fracturing through its dangling ornaments which at first look like brilliant, many-fractaled crystals, but up close are pear-shaped, and plain. Six of them hang evenly above a clear, fist-sized crystal finial, which as a child, as now, made her think of a small cannonball. Jackie has a sudden desire to reach up and rip the useless bauble from its chain and hurl it at Dana, watch it clip the side of her head and send her careening down the stairs.

Follow me, Dana shouts from the top step, interrupting Jackie's reverie. *It's time you saw the rocks as they were.*

Dana

The gray carpet is too clean. No dust motes or mouse droppings, no stains or ruin. In fact it looks like it has been vacuumed recently. In decades, Dana thinks, no one had visited Edgeweather— certainly no children or nannies who were the only ones who ever came up to the third floor—so it makes no sense to her that it should be so tidy and clean. She glances toward the hall where the Saturday night bedroom she and Jackie decorated had been. After she'd graduated from college, her mother mentioned casually on a phone call that she'd needed the room for storage and had what she called *the bedroom set* moved into the apartment where Joe Lopez was still living. Dana cannot remember how she responded to her mother, but she remembers feeling punched. She wonders now if those beds are still above the garage and filled with Kenny's children. Or possibly grandchildren, given his age. She softens at the thought until she notices the very large television in the main room and remembers Kenny's terrified mother from the kitchen. This is where the woman has been living and clearly long enough that she's assembled an entertainment center where there used to be a simple RCA set with rabbit ears and slow moving drifts of static. Odd, she calculates quickly, how Kenny's mother could afford this fancy unit and not enough to rent an apartment. A swift flame of righteous anger lights, and not only does Dana feel vindicated for being upset in the kitchen earlier, she completely forgets who is standing only a few feet behind her, having just followed her up the stairs.

Before she turns around, Jackie begins. *Don't speak Floyd's name again. You of all people have no right to make judgments about anyone, especially him. And to me?* Jackie starts to say more, but Dana interrupts.

You know nothing. The words spring from her throat before she's considered them, but they don't surprise her. They are the words she's been silently thinking since Jackie stormed into her house in nightgown and coat looking like someone who'd wandered out of a nursing home. Without intending them to be, they are the simplest, plainest explanation for why they are here, speaking for the first time since they were nineteen years old, why Jackie is red-faced and furious in a room where they'd spent thousands of easy, joyful hours together.

With her back still to Jackie, Dana eyes the far end of the room, where a hallway starts. She pushes against a memory, but standing so near the place it was created makes it difficult to suppress. Agitated, she squints to see if she can find the knob on the first door, but nothing beyond the first few inches of floor and wall are visible. *You know nothing,* she repeats, now rebuking her younger, more foolish self, and naming the old weight of another secret. She looks into the hallway again to find the knob on the door she now feels desperate to locate. Her pulse hurries. Behind her, the sound of Jackie's footfalls down the stairs. But she is sixteen again, unable to follow.

For the first time, she would have the house to herself. She'd realized this before the portrait photographer she'd escaped Jackie's prom with had even started his truck. It was a Saturday night and Dana's parents were in the city at a wedding. The original plan had been for Joe Lopez to take the girls back to Jackie's house no later than midnight, but sneaking out of the ski lodge early meant no one would be looking for her for at least a few hours. As Dana's father had ordered, Joe was waiting in the parking lot until the dance ended, and Jackie was too busy chasing Floyd to notice.

His name was Ben, though it hadn't occurred to Dana to ask until moments before she marched him through Edgeweather's front door and bee-lined for the pantry cupboard where the alcohol was kept. *You live here?*, he'd asked for the second time. She started to answer but hesitated. *My parents work for the owners and they're not around*, she said, resorting to a new game of role-playing since her public high school prom fantasy hadn't played out as she'd expected. *We live above the garage*, she lied, as she poured more whiskey into the flask she'd swiped from her father's fishing vest earlier—more as a prop initially than as a means to get loaded—and headed for the stairs. *Jesus*, he yelled, louder than she thought him capable of, a new energy in his voice as he looked up at the high ceilings and down the hall to the foyer, *these cats are loaded. What the hell.*

What Dana knew about Ben was what he'd told her in the car: that he'd dropped out of his junior year at UConn the year before and was scraping money together to go to San Francisco by photographing weddings and proms and christenings. His aunt was the gym teacher at the high school and she'd been the one who'd arranged for him to take photographs at the prom. He'd mentioned no less than four times that she was going to be furious that he'd left before finishing the job. Photography had been a hobby, he'd explained as he drove, his right hand moving from the steering wheel to her shoulder, then to the top of her knee, which he squeezed and stroked as if it were perfectly natural.

Dana had been kissed by a few boys in school and most recently by the pimply son of one of her parents' friends in Palm Beach who'd taken her sailing over the Christmas holiday. She hadn't been attracted to him but she wanted to practice kissing with her tongue so she didn't seem like a novice when the time came with someone she liked. Jackie was shocked that she'd kiss someone she didn't think was handsome, but for Dana it was a practical matter. Ben's hand on her knee felt like those pimply kisses, like something to endure in order to get what she needed; in this case it was deliverance from the prom where Jackie had ditched her to orbit as near as she could to Floyd.

Dana didn't understand why Jackie was working so hard. She'd never looked prettier—the dress was a little corny but at least it fit well, unlike the rainbow of baggy pastel sacks the other girls had on. As she ignored Ben's voice and hand, Dana wondered if Jackie's fawning over Floyd's sister had managed to draw his attention by now. She hoped not. It stung to remember how the evening had begun, arriving at Jackie's, entering the living room and finding her holding up an old shawl of her mother's, sarcastically asking if she should wear it. When she winked at Dana it was obvious she'd walked into a disagreement and that Dana's role now was to say, emphatically, no, which she did and in a tone she instantly regretted as Jackie's mother winced and collected the shawl in her arms and carried it back to where it came from. Later, when Dana slipped onto Jackie's wrist the corsage she'd asked Joe Lopez to collect from the flower shop, she felt a mixture of self-consciousness and giddy surprise that the evening was unfolding as she'd imagined. The idea of going with Jackie to her prom was at first more of a dare, a proposition born of a whim when Jackie mentioned the event months before. The night was clearly a big deal at Housatonic Valley Regional High School, and important to Jackie, and the more Dana heard about it the more she didn't want to be left out. So she needled and pushed and eventually Jackie agreed.

After all that, she'd left the prom early. As Ben's small truck rattled farther away from the dance, and his hand moved like a greedy leech across her knee, Dana worried she'd overreacted, and that bringing a stranger back to Edgeweather was a mistake. He was handsome in an *Easy Rider* kind of way with his ponytail and leather wrist band, and he'd been flirtatious with and focused on her when Jackie hadn't been. The more whiskey she drank from her father's flask, the less worried she became. She'd dismiss him when she was ready, but not yet.

From the moment she and Jackie stepped up to Ben's makeshift studio at the far end of the ski lodge, he was alert and smitten. The girls put on a show as he focused his lens and snapped picture after picture, Dana flinging her arm around Jackie, sitting her on her lap, even kissing her on the cheek. As she pushed the envelope further and further, Jackie, who was game at first, seemed distracted and quickly cooled. Before Dana was ready to stop, Jackie wriggled away claiming she was hungry. This is when they parted, Jackie heading straight to the table where she'd insisted they sit, across from Floyd, who'd stopped her from falling earlier, and his sister, Hannah, whom Jackie had never once before mentioned but all of a sudden treated like a best friend. *He lifted me like I didn't weigh anything!*, she'd gushed to her. *He's much taller than when we were in elementary school together.*

Dana had heard and seen enough. The evening they'd planned and shopped for and been excited about for months had been ruined. She'd watched Jackie make a fool of herself, and for a boy who barely noticed her. *Let's go*, Dana told Ben, though she didn't know his name at that point; and just as she expected he would, despite the line of six couples who would never get their portraits taken, he packed up his cameras, lights, and backdrop, and out they went.

She took him to the third floor because there were no family pictures there and also she didn't want him in her bedroom.

From the second they'd cleared the top of the stairs, his attitude shifted. She hadn't yet turned the light on when he came from behind and had his hands on her—one on her chest and the other trying to shove aside the gray taffeta under the skirt of her dress. The shift in dynamic was so abrupt she thought at first he was joking. *Hey, cut it out*, she snapped, as though she were still in control. But he persisted and soon there was no cloth or ruffle between his hand and her skin. *Stop it!*, she screamed, still registering the physical barrier that had been breached. She pushed him away but he grabbed her arm. *Oh no*, he instructed. The cold expectation in his voice sobered her and she realized now that she'd steered herself into a horrible trap. The house was empty. Joe Lopez and probably Jackie, too, still thought she was at the prom.

Hey, relax, what's the big hurry, she stalled, trying to reclaim some trace of friendliness between them, but he pulled her toward him, roughly, and told her to shut up. By this point she'd taken her shoes off and while she knew she couldn't get past him to the stairs, she could, if she got free, run down the hall to one of the rooms there and possibly lock herself in. As she got closer to him, his hand relaxed slightly and she slid free, sprinted ahead and grabbed a door handle. When she yanked it open, a shock of moonlight blinded her. She maneuvered behind the door to shut it, and as she did recognized the room as one used for storage, the one with a crescent window, which that night framed and refracted the bright light of a full moon. When she heard footsteps behind her in the hall she rushed to lock the door, but it was too late. Ben pulled it back so hard she almost fell, but she was able to let go, scramble to her feet and run into the room. As she neared the window, she pictured herself jumping through the glass onto the roof, but before considering whether this was actually an option, Ben's hands reached her. As if he'd read her mind he slammed her into the window, the glass and wood buckled behind her but did not break. *Now YOU cut it out!*, he hollered and pushed her harder against the window, the bottom sill pinching against the back of her leg. With one hand on her throat, he started pulling and tugging at her dress with the other, and when he finally found the zipper he yanked it so hard the fabric ripped. The sound sharpened Dana's panic and she surged with clenched fists and began bashing the side of his head with all her strength. She would never know if it was surprise or genuine pain, but Ben let go long enough for her to run past him, into the hall, and down to her bedroom on the second floor where she forced her shaking hands to lock the door. When she heard him descend the stairs looking for her, she called out until he came to her door. As he shook the knob and began hitting the door, she tried to summon a tone she'd heard her mother use with people when something went wrong and there were no maids or doormen or drivers to step in, most recently at the baggage claim at the Palm Beach airport when the suitcase with her jewelry briefly went missing. *Unacceptable*, she'd interrupted the Pan Am employee as he politely explained the efforts being made, and then dismissed him as if she owned the airline, *You need to find it*. Summoning her mother's authority, Dana spoke with as little desperation as she could. *I have a phone in here*, she lied, *and I've called the police who are on their way now. And you should know this: My name is Dana Goss and my family owns this house and is close friends with the governor of the state of Connecticut*, another lie, *and I promise you that if you don't leave this second you will spend the rest of your life in jail*. After a short silence, she heard his shoe scuff near the door; then the sound of him running erratically down the hall and stairs followed not long after by the dim growl of his truck starting outside.

Because she knew they'd blame her, Dana hesitated to tell her parents about the attack. At dinner with them in the city the next evening, she struggled to find a way to begin, but as Ada was clearing the first course, she accidentally knocked a bowl of soup that splattered onto Mr. Goss's trousers. When Ada nervously apologized and moved to retrieve the bowl, he smacked her hand away and coldly told her she was done for the night and to leave. Her father then turned to Dana and told her she was grounded from evening plans with her friends in the city until further notice since she'd clearly evaded Joe Lopez the night before. He said he didn't want to know what she'd gotten up to but knew that the excuse that Jackie had given Joe at the end of the night about Dana feeling ill and accepting a ride from one of the teachers made no sense.

In the days that followed, there were times she came close to telling Jackie, mostly in the pauses between her obsessive Floyd-focused reports of the rest of the evening. But Dana was so deeply shaken by her own drunken behavior at the prom, and the murky and frightening feelings that seemed to drive it, she held back. She decided she'd answer honestly when Jackie got around to asking about her night, about Ben. That she would never ask hadn't occurred to her. When they spoke on the phone the next day, Jackie teased Dana about running out of the prom early with an older boy and told her she'd covered her tracks with Joe Lopez, but she did not ask where they'd gone or what had happened.

Weeks passed and Jackie never mentioned it again; not a word of curiosity or concern about the stranger her best friend and prom date left with that night. Through the end of the school year and into the summer, Dana's impulse to tell Jackie persisted. Despite her building resentment, she believed they should talk about it, put the night in its place as they had so many lesser upsets since they were children. It became a kind of test to see how long it would take her friend to bring it up. But Jackie was not interested, her silence had made that clear. Still, for a long time, it felt important to Dana that she know. And then it didn't.

Part Four

Floyd

He'd left the diapers and the jug of iced tea in the backseat. Jackie didn't seem to mind staying behind while he walked back to the car. Amy was asleep beside her on the blanket they'd spread out at the far end of the second field at Hatch Pond where they could see the fireworks but be away from the drunken shenanigans closer to the parking lot. Families like the Moreys hauled in kegs of beer and took over the brick barbecue pits in the first field by the entrance and many of them stayed through the night until morning. They would also bring an arsenal of illegal and very loud firecrackers. Amy was seven months old and still breast feeding, so the last thing Jackie wanted was to be near the families who used the Fourth of July as an excuse to get rowdier and more intoxicated than usual.

Celebrating the holiday at Hatch Pond mattered to Jackie because it was where she and Floyd had their first kiss. *Right out there, at the end of the dock*, she'd reminded him when they pulled into the parking lot. He did not need reminding. For most of their first year together, before Amy was born, he'd gone over that night hundreds of times, wishing he'd done it differently.

His sister Hannah had invited her entire high school class to her sixteenth birthday party at the farm and at the end of the evening, Jackie needed a ride home. Something had happened with her father's car, his mother had explained, after informing Floyd that he'd be driving her home. Soon after they got in his truck, Jackie suggested they make a quick stop at Hatch Pond.

The moon was full, she'd said, and above the lake it must be quite a sight. Yes, he'd agreed. Of course. He was tipsy that night. Tommy Hall had smuggled a bottle of his mother's vodka out of the house and had come over to kill time in the cow barn while Floyd did the afternoon milking. The two boys spent the evening drinking the vodka out of Mason jars mixed with chunks of frozen orange juice Floyd sneaked from the basement freezer. It was long past dark when Tommy left and by then Hannah's party was breaking up. When Floyd came through the kitchen door, his mother, without turning around from the sink, said *Floyd, Jackie here needs a ride home*. Half an hour later, the two of them stood at the end of the dock looking at the moon in excruciating silence. Floyd was woozy from having been up at five-thirty in the morning with the cows, drinking with Tommy, and listening to him talk about having sex with his girlfriend, Dorinda. Dorinda was a little heavy but had huge breasts and the guys in school loved to joke with Tommy about how they felt and ask him if he'd milked her yet that day. They teased him because they were jealous. Tommy was one of the only guys their age who they knew was having sex on a regular basis. And Tommy was a talker.

Every time he ran through the events of that evening, Floyd always ended up blaming what happened with Jackie on Dorinda's tits and Tommy's bragging about what she let him do with them and to her. Why else would he have pretended to look at the moon when he was actually sizing up Jackie's pretty decent-sized breasts and wondering if she would make out with him and let him touch them. Why else would he have become so determined to put his hands all over a girl he'd never given a second thought to. He remembered her from the prom a few months back, catching her as she fell and thinking she might be sauced, then believing his guess was right when he saw her with the drunk girl getting their picture taken together. That night, and a few days later, he did picture the two girls naked, but the appeal was not Jackie, not specifically. Or maybe part of it was, because that night on the dock he all but stood on tippy-toes to see down the scalloped neckline of her thin white, button-down sweater in order to get an eyeful while simultaneously scheming how he might get a handful, too. Why else would he have kissed her?

He regretted it the moment it happened. The way she held onto him, the instant seriousness. The starry-eyed look on her face and the growing expectations he saw there extinguished the low flame lit by vodka and Tommy's bragging. And yet by the time he'd dropped her off at home that night, they'd made a plan to spend the Fourth of July together.

Maybe he had agreed to see her again because he knew that eventually she would let him touch her breasts and probably anywhere else he wanted, too. At seventeen, access and compliance eclipsed almost everything, even looks. And it's not that she wasn't pretty, she was. But she looked like so many other girls in Wells. She even resembled a much younger version of his mother. The same straight light brown hair, the same small plain face with upturned nose and hazel eyes. She was nice, too, if—he sensed it even then—a bit judgmental, a little strict. Maybe none of these little annoyances would have bothered him if he'd kissed her a month sooner. He'd wondered this often in the first year with Jackie. Would she have mattered to him from the start if he hadn't encountered someone else only three Saturdays before?

The girl was pushing a grocery cart outside of Trotta's grocery in Millerton. She seemed roughly his age and had long black hair tied in a thick, loose ponytail. It was the end of the day and the waning light cast dim sparks from the chrome on the cars in the parking lot. The purple and red sky marbled in the windshields and the glass doors at Trotta's and the parking lot felt as if it had been transported to a beach town, like the kind in the movies Hannah loved, with Frankie Avalon and Annette Funicello. The girl looked a little bit like Annette Funicello, but more intense. The loose strands from her gathered hair fell across her face, caught the last rays of sun, and wriggled in the wind like lit, electric fibers. He didn't know her name or where she was from, and yet he couldn't shake the sense that he'd seen her around. He couldn't stop staring.

Floyd had come with his father on an errand to pick up bolts of fencing wire at the hardware store. His mother had asked them to stop by Trotta's on the way and bring home paper towels and soap. As usual, his father sent him into the store while he stayed in the truck with his black thermos of bourbon, the one he kept in the glove compartment. Floyd knew to move quickly so his father didn't get completely sauced before they got back on the road, but even the prospect of being yelled at while his father sped through stop signs and swerved drunkenly into oncoming traffic couldn't budge him from his spot. Powerless, he watched the girl push the full shopping cart across the lot toward a car where an older woman stood waiting. The woman, he recognized her from somewhere. It took him a few seconds before he remembered—Mrs. Lopez. She attended church with his mother. His father didn't care about church so Floyd wasn't expected to go regularly, but at Christmas and Easter he had no choice. Lupita. The girl's name was Lupita. He remembered her from elementary school. Two grades below him at Wells Center, one of Hannah's few friends then. Her family worked for the family that owned Edgeweather way out on the Cornwall side of town. He hadn't seen her since she was in the sixth or seventh grade and he dimly remembered Hannah saying she'd gone to St. Margaret's in Amenia instead of Housatonic.

Hi, he called out. *Lupita, right?* She looked up and they stood a few yards from each other under the darkening sky, but he couldn't think of what else to say to her. He'd never felt anything but lust or indifference or annoyance for a girl before. He'd not been friends with any and beyond a few quick pecks playing spin-the-bottle in eighth grade before high school started, he'd never touched one. His response now was more than lust, though it was definitely that, too. But there was something about her face. It was friendly, in a strange way very familiar to him, but at the same time it was serious, intimidating. She looked at him now as if she knew something about him that he did not. That's the only way he could describe it to himself later as he tried to make sense of his reaction to her.

Lupita didn't respond to his clunky greeting, nor did he figure out what else to say. They stared at each other while her mother loaded the groceries from the cart to the car until Floyd's father got out of the truck and started hollering. *What the hell, boy.*

Lupita was in the car and out of the lot by the time he answered. All he could think to say was, *I think her name is Lupita.*

I don't care what her name is, son, that one's not for you. Floyd could smell the bourbon coming from his pores. He had shoveled cow and chicken shit his whole life but to him there was nothing worse than the smell of dark alcohol reeking from his father's sweat glands. He winced as he let a whiff of the awful body brew invade his nose. His father clenched his fist and knocked him hard at the top of his hip where there was little skin, only joint and bone. Floyd's knees buckled. The blow was unmistakable punctuation to his father's pronouncement and also a clear signal to get in the store and fetch the groceries they'd come for.

From that afternoon on, Lupita was the only girl on his mind. She was the center of every fantasy—sexual, romantic, mundane. He imagined her naked—in the shower, on a beach, in his bedroom—and pictured every kind of imaginable sex with her.

He daydreamed about raising children with her on the farm, even imagined them grocery shopping. They'd exchanged no words, but by seeing her and by her holding his gaze for a few charged moments, she had become what he wanted most. That want was agitated and no doubt deepened by the hard fact that nothing could come of it. If his father had anything to do with it, Lupita Lopez was not and would never be allowed.

As Floyd reaches the end of the second field, he can't remember why he's going back to the car. It's not the first time he'd deliberately left something behind. In the two years he'd been with Jackie, he'd built up a mental catalog of needed items that justified hasty exits—wallet, a phone number for a job scribbled down on a matchbook, work gloves. Additionally, he'd developed a talent for conjuring impromptu tasks that unexpectedly needed completing—gas tanks to fill, borrowed tools that needed returning, garbage runs for his aunt. Long-planned or spontaneously concocted, his escape hatches allowed him to slip away with little warning anytime he wanted. Not that he had a plan when he did—mostly he drove his truck around town, occasionally stopping at Tommy Hall's apartment or his family's farm. He felt guilty for fibbing, but knowing that he could disappear for a while gave him a sense of control, something he'd lost since finding out that Jackie was pregnant a year and a half ago. The decisions that followed—getting married, renting the house, assuming financial responsibility for this sudden family—felt less like his own and more like orders given collectively by his family, Jackie's, and Jackie herself. As Tommy said the day of his wedding, *Son, you got bagged and tagged*.

So he sneaked away every once in a while, but never long enough to raise suspicion. And Jackie didn't seem to mind or suspect anything. This evening, after they'd laid out the blanket and unpacked the food and he'd made his excuse to return to the car, her response was typical. She held both hands above her eyes to ward off the sun blasting behind him and said, without disappointment or doubt, *Ok, we'll be right here.*

On his way to the parking lot, Floyd passes a large white shed where the town beach association kept an old lawnmower and life preservers that no one, not since Floyd was a kid, ever used. He steps around to the back where there is a mess of smashed Coca-Cola bottles, and a small, stuffed giraffe whose legs are covered by a child's T-Shirt dirtied with pine needles and sap. This was where he went when he pulled the ripcord the very first time. Two years ago to the day. He and Jackie had come to Hatch Pond with Tommy and Dorinda and a few other friends of his from school. He'd turned their Fourth of July date into a group activity to relieve some of the pressure and hopefully send a signal to Jackie that would adjust her expectations. Everyone brought beers and vodka and bags of potato chips. After his first beer he switched to ginger ale since the last time he'd been drinking around Jackie he'd ended up kissing her and making plans, and he had no intention of letting either happen again. She, however, had two beers and by the end of the second one was resting her right hand on the back of his T-Shirt, between his shoulder blades. He was just beginning to feel her fingers move in a slow, circular motion, when he saw Lupita. She was with her mother again, and an older man he assumed was her father, along with a few other people he didn't recognize. It would take almost an hour before she saw Floyd and when she did she laughed, the flash of her teeth a quick, bright comet. They locked eyes and with his head, as cautiously as he could, he motioned her toward the parking lot. Several excruciatingly long minutes later, she stood and began to navigate the obstacle course of coolers and portable grills surrounded by families sitting in lawn chairs and on old blankets. Floyd interrupted something Jackie was saying to excuse himself to go the bathroom. *It's that way*, Tommy shouted at him as he left in the opposite direction, but Floyd paid no attention. He watched Lupita circle to the woods side of the shed, out of sight, and he wasted no time following her there.

You have a girlfriend, she said plainly as he stepped toward her, oddly calm, as if she were stating any other obvious fact. He didn't say anything in response, not because he felt caught or conflicted, but because he was speechless. It was the first time he'd heard her voice. It was lower than he'd imagined, scratchier. Less girly but somehow still more feminine. He stared at her as if to confirm the encounter they'd had more than a month before was real. That *she* was real. Her hand began to wave him off and her head shook, indicating a second, and better, thought. *I have to get back*, she said as she attempted to move past him in the narrow gap between the shed and the bramble that preceded the woods. Awkwardly, he thrust his hand out to block her path and then yanked it back in the same movement, grazing her forearm. She didn't flinch, just looked directly into his eyes and laughed. Not a friendly laugh, a taunting one that had under its music a dare. He still could not find words, but he knew she would not stand there longer than a moment more, so he stepped toward her and kissed her on the mouth. Unlike with Jackie that night on the dock, this time he didn't miss. He landed his lips directly on hers and she kissed back with such force he stumbled backwards into the shed wall. He'd thought about kissing Lupita many times since he'd seen her in the parking lot at Trotta's, but he hadn't anticipated the instant desperation he felt when he finally did. Everything that he was discovering—her voice, her lips, the impossibly soft skin of her cheek, the smell of Juicy Fruit gum on her breath, her surprising strength—each registered like the very best that any of these things could ever be, but as he adored them for the first time, he felt them leaving, very likely for good. As he remembered his father's ugly words in the parking lot, he sensed her pulling away. *I should get back*, she stammered, suddenly looking nervous. Floyd felt that if he didn't do something quick he'd never see her again. Words, like miracles, came: *Come to the farm tomorrow morning . . . at seven, if you can. I know it's early, but I'll be done with the morning milking and no one will be around then. Pull into the road called "Crow's Path" and meet me there behind the big green barn. You can't miss it.* Lupita nodded her head. The plan was made, and she was gone.

At the car, Floyd realizes he still has Jackie's Kodak camera hanging from a leather strap around his neck. She'd asked him to buy her one so that she could document all of their daughter's firsts—today was Amy's first Fourth of July picnic. And now he remembers why he's come back to the car. Diapers and iced tea. He opens the trunk and grabs the bag and the jug and thinks about taking a swig, but decides against it. He turns to walk back to Jackie and Amy, but before he's taken a step, he sees the yellow Mercedes convertible, and next to it, waving, Dana Goss. *Hello there*, she shouts, her hand scooping the air, *I need your help*.

Lupita

The fire has burned down and sputtered out hours ago. The stars have left. Soon it will be morning. Lupita watches the jagged, inky silhouette of the hills over Princeville articulate, gradually, as light slowly makes its way west. She's watched this show thousands of times. She knows just how dark the sky will bruise from black to purple, how slowly it will brighten to a chalky pink before the sun appears, and she will sit in this grass, a few feet from where the sand begins outside her gate, until it does.

She'd driven the car before. Her father kept a set of keys on the hook next to the phone in case it needed to be moved or taken to the shop in Millerton for repair. She'd watched his driving closely for years, studied when he pressed the clutch and the accelerator and when he pulled and pushed the gear-shift. The prospect of having control over such a complicated, powerful machine fascinated her. She'd been waiting to practice in the yellow convertible since the day Dana's parents gave it to her for her sixteenth birthday. It galled Lupita that her father would spend time teaching Dana to drive but refused to give her even one lesson. Never mind, she'd decided when she could hear Dana grinding the gears the first few times she'd driven. She'd find a way. There were six times she was left alone at Edgeweather since Dana's birthday in March and each time, within a minute of her father's leaving, she'd snatched the extra set of keys, pulled open the garage door, and started the car. She never drove more than five miles an hour, mostly in loops, and always stayed in the parking area and driveway. She didn't dare go off the property because Jackie might see and if she did would surely call Dana in the city to rat her out. By July, Lupita had mastered shifting from neutral to first gear and backing out of the garage. Even though she drove at such slow speeds, nothing in her life until then had given her as much joy as being able to sit alone in that car and move it where and when she wanted. Still, she'd been getting restless to drive on the open road. When Floyd told her where to meet him the next day, she decided this was her chance, that she'd had enough practice. She knew there would be grave consequences when she returned. She knew, too, that Jackie had her sights set on Floyd, a fact that should have discouraged her from having any further contact with him, but instead was very likely part of why she needed to go.

Jackie had ignored Lupita since the third grade, treated her as the help the way Dana had. When Lupita went to the Catholic high school in Amenia, Jackie warmed to her slightly—said hello if she saw her at Hatch Pond or the movie house in Millerton—but never more than that. It was clear to Lupita that Jackie had no use for her and she understood by then that having something you wanted from someone was the basis for most human interaction. Now that Lupita had a few friends, not wildly close ones, but girls who were happy to have her around, Jackie became less important.

And then came Floyd. Wide-eyed and stuttering in the Trotta's parking lot, smitten and risky behind the shed at the beach, Jackie waiting for him just a short walk away, on a picnic blanket with their friends. Boys and men had made passes at Lupita since she was thirteen, but none of them fell apart so completely as Floyd did in her presence. His desire was contagious. Where his ended and her own began she couldn't quite locate. Possibly it was in his awed gaze, or in an old and unresolved resentment she had toward Jackie, or more simply it was in her visceral response to his handsome face, strong body, and unruly brown hair. She did not know, and like the consequences that surely awaited her, she did not care. She would drive to Floyd's farm that morning and meet him behind the barn.

It was before six in the morning when she crept down the stairs that led to the driveway from the apartment above the garage. Since the eighth grade, Lupita had never seen Dana outside her house before 10 a.m. so she wasn't worried about her. Nor was she worried about her mother who slept as late as 9:30 on weekends. It was her father, usually awake before dawn to begin his morning routine, who was the reason she held her breath and moved as silently as she possibly could. Normally he'd already be up, lighting his pipe in the driveway, walking the property, inspecting the big house and regulating the heat or air conditioning depending on the time of year. But on Saturday nights and holidays he allowed himself more than a few beers and always slept late the next day.

Lupita was a scholar of her father's sleeping and eating and drinking patterns, all of which determined his moods: sentimental and tender, like the night before at Hatch Pond when he puffed on his pipe and spoke about his first year in Florida living six guys to a room and working fourteen-hour shifts at the fern farm in Ocala, how much he missed his family then; or quick-tempered and violent, as he was less than a week ago when her mother discovered she'd left her wallet at the grocery store. Without a word he grabbed a jar of olives and threw it across the kitchen at her where it cracked against her hip and she screamed and fell to the floor. Minutes later Lupita pulled the wallet from one of the grocery bags where her mother had forgotten she'd placed it. She held it up to her father brazenly, waved it with purpose and tossed it on the counter, to which he responded by storming across the kitchen to the hallway that led to his bedroom and slamming the door shut. By then Lupita's mother was standing again, continuing to unpack the groceries. Lupita no longer got mad at her for not reacting, for staying with a man who ran so hot and cold, who hurt her. By then she understood why her mother had tolerated, even thrived, living apart from him five days out of seven for most of the year. But what she could never understand, or forgive, was how, knowing what her husband was capable of, she could step aside and let her daughter be the one to bear the brunt of his anger. Lupita had insisted her mother show her the bruise, and when she pushed her slacks down along her thigh, it was already purple and yellow and the size of a dessert plate. She imagined most daughters would weep to see their mother this way, scream at their father, or even call the police. But Lupita softly traced the edges of the bruise with her forefinger before packing a towel with ice and handing it to her mother. *You should keep your wallet in your purse*, she said with her back turned as she left the kitchen and retreated to her bedroom.

The car purred from first to second on Undermountain Road and whined as it hit thirty-five miles per hour—the fastest she could imagine driving—on Route 7, after which she shifted to fourth gear and the sound flattened again. Accelerating was simpler than slowing down, easier to assemble speed than control it, which was why Lupita missed the turn onto Crow's Path the first time, barreling down Ticknor Road. The enormous green barn at Floyd's farm flashed outside the driver's side window and soon it was behind her. Her watch read 6:50 a.m. by the time she'd managed the car off Ticknor and up the narrow dirt road. High grass scraped and dragged along the undercarriage of the low slung Mercedes. That the morning might leave the car damaged had not occurred to her until now, just as she missed first gear and pushed the black knob forward to the loud sound of grinding metal. Finally, the car shuddered to a halt behind the barn and as soon as it did, Floyd appeared by the driver's side door, laughing gently but clearly nervous. He had a thermos in his hand and even before saying hello he held it up and said, *I made you some tea.* He proceeded to unscrew the silver metal top. Floyd's sweet bumbling put Lupita at ease and she remembered the power balance. *Oh, no thanks. I don't drink tea.* Floyd seemed not to know how to react. He just stood there with the thermos in one hand and the top sloshing with hot liquid in the other. It was as if someone had insisted to Floyd that tea was the one thing Lupita would be pleased to be greeted with so early in the morning, and the cogs of his logic seized when confronted with her rejection.

Lupita was surprised by how dressed up he was. He'd told her last night that he'd be finished milking the cows before seven, and the bright blue button-down shirt that looked as if it had been ironed, or new, did not seem like a garment someone working in a barn milking cows would wear. As with the tea, the shirt made him appear like a little boy desperate to please. In response, Lupita felt both drawn to and cruel toward him. *Are you going to help me out of this car?*, she asked a bit impatiently, but again dizzy with anticipation about what would happen next. Floyd opened the driver's side door and Lupita slid out and stood before him in the dusty road. *Hi*, she said, holding his gaze. *Hi*, he repeated back, stepping toward her and looking down into her face. As it had happened the night before, behind the shed at Hatch Pond, Floyd's body asserted a confidence his words could not. He placed both hands on the tops of Lupita's narrow shoulders, stooped down slightly, and kissed her. Less desperately than last night's rushed moment, and for much longer. At first Lupita remained passive as his lips moved against her own, but as his body inched closer to hers, his chest tilted above her and his large hands stroked her shoulders and upper arms, she felt her breathing meet his, her body sway and bend to the particular rhythm of his hands and lips and tongue. A sudden humidity enveloped them and her cotton blouse began to stick to her back and chest. All at once, everything she registered was new—hard, eager kisses; calloused hands grazing her thighs and chest; the dense, sturdy flesh of his back and arms under her fingers. What she experienced in the tumult of sensations was nothing she'd felt before: desired, excited, and at the same time safe. When she decided to go through with what would surely be the most transgressive morning of her life, feeling safe was not on her list of expectations. But this was how she felt. Before Floyd unhooked her bra and took off his shirt, she understood this was a place she would live in forever if she could. She would think back on this hour with him all the rest of her life and remember it as the happiest, most exquisitely perfect, and the most misleading.

They were tangled over the reclined front passenger seat when Lupita noticed the time on her watch reading just after eight o'clock. She'd planned to be back no later than eight-fifteen, which was the latest she could imagine her father sleeping. She buckled with panic, her hands flying to find her shirt and bra. *I have to go. I have to go right now.* Floyd scrambled with his shirt and buttoned his jeans, which were still very much on, and Lupita did the same. Floyd jumped from the car and Lupita maneuvered over the gearshift to the driver's seat as she buttoned her blouse. They did not say goodbye, but as Floyd walked backwards, up the grassy incline and across the short expanse between Crow's Path and the back of the green barn, he held her gaze the entire way. When he stopped and watched her, everything in the air and on the ground around and between them progressed in an adjusted speed, slower than normal, faster than stopped. A fly or a bee—

Lupita could not tell which—buzzed around Floyd's head but it did not break his stare or puncture the trance that held him.

And then something did. He did not wave goodbye or gesture that he had to go, his body simply shook for a moment, a spasm of panic that was barely perceptible from where Lupita sat. Had he remembered something? Did someone call his name? He'd gazed at her as if nothing else in the world existed until the moment he looked away, turned his back to her, and walked beyond the green barn and around front to the driveway. Shaken by the sudden change, Lupita struggled to put the car in reverse and eventually managed to back up onto Ticknor Road. After grinding the gears a few times, she tore down the road as fast as she could handle in the little yellow car she'd stolen less than two hours earlier.

Dana was standing with Lupita's parents in front of the garage when she returned. Before anyone else could speak, and before Lupita could even get out of the car, Dana blurted, *Oh my God forgive me Lupita, I just remembered I'd asked you to test the brakes on the car. Here, let's go for a spin and show me what you discovered. Everyone, please forgive my silly brain. I must have had too much wine last night at the Independence Day celebration. What a dodo bird you must think I am.* She looked like a creature from another planet standing at least six inches above the Lopezes in heeled black leather boots, wearing a sleek red-and-orange striped long-sleeved jersey and tight, very white, pants. *We won't be long!*, she half-chuckled, her contrition wearing off, as she yanked open the passenger door and jumped in the car, which was still running. Lupita already had the gear stick positioned in reverse and her feet were poised on the clutch and the gas. The car was moving before Dana shut the door.

Jackie

She has left Dana on the third floor of the house, crossed the driveway and started back to her car when she thinks she sees a light on in the horse stable. It's late, and the wind coming off the river is damp and cold. Her lower legs are covered by rain boots, but her nightgown and coat do not protect her from the biting air. Instead of turning left on Undermountain Road and returning to her car, she crosses right toward the long, low stone building where the horses had been kept.

There had always been at least four or five stallions traded or bred, but never ridden by anyone but the stable hands. Still, she and Dana both loved spending time in the barns and had dedicated many hours to brushing manes and assigning all manner of motive and personality to the animals. Jackie can't remember many of the specific horses, but there was a blue-black Arabian she adored that Dana claimed as hers. This was in the eighth grade, and she remembers Dana pulling rank after a brief scuffle when the horse arrived and they both swooned over its luminous coat and astonishing eyelashes. His name was Brandenberg or Bamburger or something odd and stuffy and Dana right away named him Calliope, after the Queen of the Knees. It was an old joke between them, Dana insisting on the wrong gender for a horse, but Jackie didn't think it was funny this time and insisted on changing it to a boy's name. Dana dug in and got angry and eventually told Jackie to shut up, and reminded her that she didn't go around *her* house trying to name *her* animals. *I don't have any ani-*

mals, Jackie responded flatly and walked home, furious and hurt. Dana never apologized but the next day announced that the horse would be called Cassian. *Happy now?*, she'd asked, not looking for an answer. Jackie would come to the stables during the week and pet Cassian's snout and marvel as he exhaled plumes of steam when the air was cold. Occasionally she would bring books to read for homework and as with anyone who worked at Edgeweather, the couple who ran the stable always greeted Jackie warmly and let her do as she pleased. She was Dana's best friend, a status that afforded her access to the grounds when the Goss family wasn't around, which was most of the time.

The dirt road that leads to the stables is lit by a three-quarter moon. As Jackie fiddles with the gate that blocks the road between two stone walls, it shocks her how familiar the metal feels in her hands, how intuitive and unthinking her movements—pulling the bolt free, sliding back the latch, lifting the gate up before she pulls. She steps in off the road and leaves the gate open. Shadows from the gnarled locust trees that line the road ink the field and Jackie looks up to the moon that makes them. It has a wild, cold look to it—silver and white and streaked with high, thin clouds. She looks to the stables, but at this angle can see no light on. Why she is drawn there, now, she does not know. It's as if on this property, she is a child again—following Dana to the third floor of the big house, crossing the road to the stables. She hasn't forgotten that there has been no contact between them for more than four decades, nor the reasons why. She also hasn't forgotten that minutes ago Dana shouted crazy and hateful things about Floyd. But she is here, after a long time away, and the place was—she could feel it—pulling at her with its old magic.

She remembers hollering at Amy earlier in the day, how good it felt, how long overdue. And yet when given a chance she did not raise her voice to Dana. She was unfriendly and curt but she did not unleash what she'd stored up for so long. Instead she cowered on the stairs while Dana bad-mouthed Floyd and flaunted but did not disclose her secrets. Jackie knew better than anyone Floyd's strengths and his weaknesses. Dana had no right to speak to her about him—it was just another desperate attempt to claim him by boasting about knowing more and better. And yet she stood mute when Dana told her that she knew nothing—her only response was to walk away. Jackie's fists clench at the missed opportunity, but the anger is so old and elemental in her, she senses that if she hadn't left the house she might have lost control.

The reason she had never confronted Dana was simple: she knew she could never trust her again. After the initial shock of her betrayal, Jackie began to understand that there was nothing that obligated her to Dana. She was bound to Floyd—by a child, by property, by law, by the church—but with Dana what between them was binding? Nothing. For all of its celebrated virtues and value, its showy posturing and promises of endurance, she saw friendship as little more than a willed thing, a made mist that looked like matter between two people, intention not just its bond but its substance. And intention, she knew, was the flimsiest stuff of the world, with no weight, no properties, no shape, and yet the only thing all friendships require at their beginning. No lawyer or judge, mediator or priest needed. Not to make it, nor to unmake it, which requires even less. To end a friendship, it just takes someone willing to throw it away.

When Jackie looks back on her childhood, her friendship with Dana appears almost like a building—as solid as Edgeweather, or the hospital where she was born; as important as Christmas, or high school. She'd never once considered how perishable it was. Most of the time it felt as dependable as her parents, something she took for granted during the week when Dana was in the city, or in Palm Beach at Christmas, and even when her own attention shifted to Floyd. She was falling in love and getting pregnant and married, but Jackie never feared Dana would vanish, that she wouldn't always be around in one way or another. She was someone she allowed herself to treat as less important because she was so important, because she was presumed. It was a mistake she never again made—not with Dana, not with Floyd, not with anyone.

At the gate, Jackie is shivering, unsure where to go. She looks down toward the stable and remembers the first time she'd gone in, the summer between her second and third grades the day after Mr. Goss walked up their driveway. Jackie's mother was unloading groceries from the station wagon and her father was at work. It was a broiling hot day and Jackie was standing in the shadows of the garage to keep cool. There was something slightly tense about the exchange and all that Jackie can remember is her mother suddenly calling out her name, and saying *Jackie, my daughter Jackie is here. Jackie! We have company!* And the man who described himself as their neighbor inviting her to visit the stables and see the horses. He even suggested nine o'clock the next morning to which he made a point to Jackie's mother that she could bring her husband. They could all come.

Jackie was thrilled. She'd already ventured onto the lawns at Edgeweather dozens of times by then, had peeked into the windows of the stable when it looked like no one was around. And now she was going inside. At first her mother said no one would be going to the stables the next day but Jackie pestered and begged and convinced her father to take her in the morning. Her mother refused to go and only agreed to let her father take her by making him swear not to leave her side the entire time.

Careful not to stumble, Jackie moves away from the gate and

makes her way down the dirt road toward the stable door. Something shines off one of the windows and her heart lurches for a moment. What did she expect to find here? When she looks again she realizes it's not a lamp or light, as she'd thought earlier, just the reflection of the moon on one of the panes. She feels foolish but relieved no one is there. It doesn't look like anyone's been in or around the building in a long time. Weeds and saplings have grown up along the thick walls; vines appear around the windows, stealthily disrupting the mortar, slate shingles and copper drains. Still, the stable door is for the most part clear. She steps up to it and puts her right hand on the cool wood.

This is where she and her father came that morning, where she saw Dana for the first time. Pushy and loud and surrounded by two farm hands, her father, and another man whom she would later know as Joe Lopez. Dana was wearing an aqua blue ankle-length wool coat with navy velvet cuffs and collar, and below the collar and down the front, there were six gold buttons in two rows of three. It was the most beautiful piece of clothing Jackie had ever seen, and against the dark slacks and shirts of the men, and the general brown of the barn, she seemed like a character who'd stepped out of a color movie, like Dorothy in *The Wizard of Oz*. After the fathers introduced themselves, Dana approached Jackie and said, with deadpan seriousness, *I'm Dana, but you can call me Dana*. Clearly a joke she thought was funny, she repeated twice more before Jackie snapped, *I heard you, your name is Dana*. Jackie's father dropped a soft but firm hand on her shoulder, a clear signal to be more friendly. Dana then proceeded to show off the horses. *Come along*, she bossed, gently, *let me show you*. She held out her hand and Jackie said as politely as she could *No thanks*, but walked toward her and looked ahead to the stalls to indicate she was game for the tour, just not holding hands.

Unfazed, Dana began pointing and describing this gelding and that mare; who was fast, who was crazy, and then she approached a stall door behind which stood an enormous black stallion, an Arabian Jackie would later know commanded stud fees more than her father made in a year. Dana pointed to the horse, which by now had turned around and provided an ample view of his reproductive anatomy, and said, *This is Cindy. She's one of the sweetest. Isn't she beautiful?* Jackie looked at the two stable hands, Joe Lopez, and at her father but everyone was smiling and staying silent. Dana seemed to be waiting to see if Jackie would go along with her shenanigans or challenge them. She chose the latter: *What's wrong with you? Look at his privates.* Dana didn't respond, did not look at the horse's privates. Instead she smiled like someone who'd waited her whole life to hear a very particular and secret password, held out her hand again, and said, *C'mon, I'll show you the saddles.* And this time, after only a brief moment of hesitation, Jackie took her hand.

Instead of opening the stable door, Jackie turns back to the road. Without knowing what she'd been looking for here, she'd found what she needed: something to remind her what started it all. Some clue, beyond proximity and boredom—which obviously played important roles—to what bonded her to Dana for so long. Before she reaches its wide oval driveway, she can see Edgeweather through the trees, lit like a department store. Every window alive with light. Jackie instinctively thinks of the electric bill and can hear Floyd teasing her for being so thrifty when she'd switch off lamps and radios and fans in the few rooms in their house. Remembering the lightness between them that came later, after Rick was born, triggers not only a fresh protectiveness and a rekindled anger toward Dana, but also an unwanted thud of doubt. Despite everything she believed she knew, and all that had happened in response to that belief—Floyd sleeping in the spare room for half a year, terminating her friendship with Dana—could she have possibly gotten it wrong? Dana's taunting her about knowing nothing, about there being more to the story, had, with the onslaught of memories of simpler times at Edgeweather, loosened her tightly held conviction. As had the briefcase—filled with documents she could not make sense of, covered with names and places she didn't recognize. It was a dreadful, dizzying feeling to be both furious and unsure. There was no remedy but to go toward its source, so for the second time in almost forty-nine years, she crosses the driveway to Edgeweather's front door. But this time she will not go inside, not be drawn into and confused by the rooms where she and Dana were young together. With fists, she knocks.

Lupita

Lupita's phone, which she'd put in the chest pocket of her denim shirt, buzzed a few hours ago. She knew it would. It had been early evening in New York when Cristina tried again to reach her. By the sound of her jumpy greeting—*Hi! Oh! Oh my gosh*—it was clear she hadn't expected Lupita to pick up. And then she explained why she'd been trying to reach her. She wanted to let her know what Lupita had guessed already but had not been ready to hear—Ada was dead. She'd passed away in hospice the day before Cristina's first phone call over a week ago. She'd called to let her know about the plans for the funeral, which was quick and small and had now already happened. She also wanted to tell her that Ada went peacefully, without a struggle, and that the Catholic priest from her church came and was able to perform last rites while she was conscious. She was woozy, Cristina said, but managed to ask the priest to bless her family, and had named Lupita, specifically—*my sister*, she'd insisted several times—along with her own husband, Mateo, who'd died years before. Near the end, she mumbled something about a house, about her father, too, Cristina thought, but she was making little sense and soon the morphine swept her into sleep and she was gone.

Before Lupita could respond, Cristina said she wanted to explain how she had her phone number: *I work for Dana Goss.* Lupita had not heard Dana's name spoken out loud since she was eighteen years old. The strangest sensation, like erratic currents of electricity racing from the back of her head, across her chest, and down through her spine and legs. She did not want to hear more but she could not make her mouth and throat say the words.

Cristina spoke quickly, nervously, as if she might get hung up on at any moment.

I shouldn't say, but a few years ago I saw your name on a file sticking out from a pile of papers on Dana's desk and I couldn't help but look. I was so thrilled to see your name! There was an old photo of you in your van. I'd only ever seen a few pictures from the family albums my mother kept from her childhood. Your parents . . . I . . . I wrote down the telephone number on the side of your van but never dared call it until now. I don't . . . whenever I tried to talk about you with my mother she . . . I'm sorry . . . I realize this is all at once . . . and you don't even know me . . .

Lupita finally broke through her immobilized state and interrupted Cristina to thank her for letting her know about Ada. She didn't know what else to say so she asked her niece if she needed anything. *A phone call?*, she answered apologetically. *In a few weeks, maybe? To get to know each other . . .* Lupita promised she'd call, but doubted she would.

Lupita stands up from the place on her lawn where she's been sitting and leaves her phone in the grass. She turns back to the charred fire pit and pictures her sister on her deathbed, mumbling about the past. She imagines her cloudy eyes, her dried skin and cracked lips; her voice, desperate under the drugs to be absolved. It was not their father she was trying to say something about. It was not him.

As a very young girl, Lupita developed a muscle that allowed her to shut her mind to what she could not bear. It was a skill she began using before she had words to describe what she needed to erase. In Florida, before moving to Wells, it was her father's hands gripping her mother's arm, his gray-socked foot kicking a bag of groceries that had been left on the floor, flour exploding onto his bare leg, milk spraying across the hallway floor onto the wall; in Wells it was a thousand twists of her skin between his thumb and pointer finger, countless shoves and smacks, slammed doors and thrown objects. She could bear these by learning how to move on from them, as they happened, even, shove them under her awareness, stored but not remembered, away but not gone, influencing everything but never taking credit. Lupita expected Ada had done the same, though for different reasons. At her end, morphine and fear of what waited on the other side must have loosened what had lurked unsaid for most of her adult life. And out it came. Unintelligible to anyone but Lupita. Lupita tried to imagine the consequences of her sister's last words making sense to anyone; how many lives upended, if any, now that so much time had passed and so many people had died. Whatever the answer, here was a reason to celebrate Ada's death, she recognizes, with unexpected relief. Everyone was finally safe from the truth.

Beyond the gate, Lupita steps slowly across the cold sand toward the low breaking surf. She lets the water and foam run over her feet and ring her ankles, the sand dissolving under her feet with the reach and retreat of each wave. The electric current unleashed by Cristina's words still streaks along her spine and up along her brow and crown. It is neither unpleasant nor pleasant, but as it moves through her it heightens her senses. She turns back to shore and can see the cedar shake roofing that needs replacing, has needed replacing for more than a decade. As it is, she barely keeps pace with the gas, electric, and property tax bills. Still, after thirty years and three refinanced mortgages, the place is hers. She owns it. She knows she could sell the house now for more than a million dollars, which amuses her. *I'm a millionaire but I can't afford to fix my roof*, she has joked with friends. But Lupita will never sell.

This is the one place in the world where she is not an employee, not a tenant, not a guest. There are no rules and no authority above her here. It is hers and she will do what she needs to do to keep it. She will do what she needs to do to stay safe.

There were very few times before coming to Kauai, and for years after, when Lupita felt safe. But by the time she was in high school she at least felt like she could spot danger. Mainly from her father whose violent eruptions increased as his marriage deteriorated and his children needed him less and less. She knows he must be dead by now, and when she thinks of him it is not with fear or fury anymore. She thinks how lonely his life must have been, how few skills he had to interact with the people he loved or to navigate a world where he was, if not invisible, translucent enough that people looked through him. It's not that he was despised or feared as Lupita knew many Mexicans were in the other parts of the United States, it was that he was not considered. The Goss family relied on him but they did not care to know him. The men he hired to work at Edgeweather were grateful for the jobs; but as he got older he became bossier, pestering and second-guessing them more frequently. It hurt her to think of him as someone who was either ignored or tolerated. Lupita understood some of what he must have felt. She was invisible to most of the tourists who came here—in a hurry to get to their hotels or rented condos, running late and reluctant to make their flights when they left. She was a necessary interaction for most of the people she encountered each day, not a desired or chosen one. This, too, she had made peace with, long ago, but it is only lately that she can see between her life and her father's a sameness. The tears that fall now are not only for Ada, they are also for the man she lived alongside more than any other person. She made more meals for him than her mother ever did, washed his clothes and hid the marks and scars and bruises he left on her. He did not know any better, nor did she.

She settles down at the edge of the foamy sea, leans back and nudges her elbows into the damp sand. With each wave, the tide creeps, crosses her feet, skims her shins and wrists, and pools around her. The night before with no sleep, the rising water, the confirmation of Ada's death from her niece, who works for Dana Goss of all people—Lupita can feel the disrupting force of each of these things release a web of long-constricted tendons and muscles and initiate the slow uncoiling of an old, tough knot. Her teeth chatter, lightly, the only sound she can hear above the noise of water breaking. She pictures faint sparks falling from her mouth. The salt spray stings her eyes and she imagines it as holy water, washing her clean, wiping away old stains. But she knows that nothing can clean her, not even an ocean of holy water. And nothing can prevent her from remembering what she had been gifted until now to bury, if not forget. It has begun and she has lost the will to stop it.

You're welcome, Dana had said once they had pulled out of the driveway and tore down Undermountain Road like bank robbers fleeing a scene. She spoke through a thick plume of cigarette smoke that whipped and vanished in the air outside the convertible. Lupita knew right away that Dana expected something in return for covering for her, so instead of replying, which she knew wouldn't impact what would be asked, she just focused on the road, felt again the new thrill of driving the car at high speed.

The striped jersey Dana was wearing was one Lupita remembered sneaking into Dana's bedroom at Edgeweather and trying on. It had been tight in the shoulders but hugged her chest in a way that made her appear more developed than she was. It achieved the same effect on Dana. Lupita knew every stitch and pleat of Dana's wardrobe. She was certain she'd worn her clothes more often and with more care and appreciation than Dana ever had, even though there were many pieces that were uncomfortably snug or altogether too small.

Lupita had been trying on Dana's clothes since she was twelve years old, after her father left her alone at home for the first time while he ran errands. That day and most every time after, when he drove off she'd race to his bedroom and look out the window to see his truck's brake lights flare before he pulled out from the driveway onto the road. And then she flew—from the window, down the hall, to the kitchen where her father kept the Edgeweather keys on a hook next to the phone. From there she rushed down the steps, across the drive, to the service entrance of the big house. There were two keys for that door—one that looked like an antique, black and heavy and cold in her hands, and the other shiny, copper-colored, and new. Lupita's hands shook every time she twisted them in their locks to free the door. The first time, she stayed downstairs. She'd been inside Edgeweather each Christmas to help with the tree, but never beyond the foyer, and her father never let anyone inside when the Gosses were in the city. This was the first time she'd seen the ballroom with its giant fireplaces and long bank of tall windows festooned with curtains that appeared to be made from gold. And above it all loomed the dizzying plaster ceiling organized in a pattern of circles and ovals that held small paintings like the kind she'd seen in the Wadsworth Atheneum in Hartford on her seventh-grade school trip; these were surrounded by geometric shapes that framed dusty pale green and pink panels bound by gold borders. The details of the paintings were too small to see clearly, but they looked like party scenes, festively attired people gathered before backdrops of mountains and trees. From two of the circles hung magnificent crystal chandeliers, each nearly the size of the tractor her father mowed the lawn with. It did not seem possible that a room like this one could be as near as a short run from the garage where she lived. In it she felt small and foolish, and even more so when she imagined the beauty and displayed wealth the windows and mirrors had reflected for a century.

On later visits, she hardly ever returned to the ballroom, but instead lingered on the second floor where the family bedrooms were located. Mostly, she scoured Dana's closet, systematically trying on every sock, nightgown, sweater, dress, coat, and undergarment she could find. Lupita's own wardrobe consisted of simple wool dresses and plaid skirts her mother bought on sale at Korvette's on Thirty-Fourth Street in the city and hand-me-down blouses and sweaters from Ada.

But the first time, on that first visit, Lupita lay down on Dana's bed wearing a white cotton training bra and sky blue silk panties, both of which she'd discovered in one of the dresser drawers. Under the white lace canopy, she stifled a nervous laugh. She'd never before experienced such a potent collision of the physical and emotional. Trespassing into rooms she'd lived next door to for years but had only imagined, the first-ever feeling of an undergarment on her flat chest, the smooth surface of silk against her skin—all of it was shot through with a tactile wonder.

Later, after she'd smoothed the bedspread, folded and put away the clothes she'd tried on, and returned home, she would struggle to remember each individual detail and moment, but everything merged into one intoxicating jumble. The closest things she could compare it to were her childhood recollections of her grandmother, which came to her as an amalgam of sensory impressions—the close, warm safety of being held in her lap, the roughness of her hands. But unlike the memory of her grandmother, which had always soothed her, especially after first moving to Florida, the one of stealing into Edgeweather was exciting, irresistible. And though Lupita never again encountered precisely the same charged euphoria of her first visit to Dana's room, it was a place she returned to whenever she could, dozens of times between the ages of twelve and eighteen.

The sound of burning paper and tobacco crackled in Lupita's ear as Dana lit another cigarette. A quick blast of smoke momentarily stunk the air before dissipating behind her as she pressed her foot harder on the gas pedal.

Look, Dana said with artificial dismay, *I thought I'd do you a favor back there but if it's too much to carry on a conversation let alone a simple thank you, never mind.*

Thank you, Lupita said mechanically, imagining what Floyd was doing at that moment, what or who had startled him as she was leaving less than an hour ago. She wondered what Dana knew of him. She figured Jackie would have surely gushed nonstop to her. As if reading her mind Dana said, *I saw you with Floyd last night.* Lupita's heart seized and she could feel the steering wheel in her hands dampen under her palms. She chose not to reply. *Pretty gutsy to creep behind an outbuilding with him in front of the entire town.* Her legs, even in cotton shorts, got hot, and she felt her feet become slick in her sandals. *I know some fast girls in New York, but they can't put anything past you. Tell me, was Floyd the reason you stole my car this morning? I can't imagine any other reason why a racy girl who just the night before was seen sleazing in the shadows with someone else's boyfriend would steal a car.* If there was any choice in the matter remaining, Dana eliminated it by putting all of her cards on the table. *Spill it. Or I'll tell Jackie what I saw last night and what I imagined must have happened this morning. And then I'll tell your father.*

By the time they returned to Edgeweather, Lupita had told her everything from seeing Floyd for the first time in the parking lot at Trotta's, to driving away from the green barn that morning. She didn't mean to disclose so much, but once she started to describe how they met and what happened after, Dana became ravenous for every detail. With her leverage, she clearly felt emboldened to probe with abandon. *Was your bra off or on? Who touched whom first? Did he take off his belt? Did he touch you below the waist?* She was especially curious if he ever mentioned Jackie. Even though Lupita had answered no the first time she asked, Dana couldn't let it go. At every turn or knuckle in the story she'd inject some version of *And what did he have to say about Jackie?*

Lupita was exhausted by the time they got home. She'd undergone a pitiless and mortifying interrogation while still trying to focus on driving, doing things with the car she'd never done before—using her turn signal, heeding traffic lights, turning left at a four-way intersection in Goshen.

Once the car was parked in front of the garage, but before they'd exited, Dana's voice softened. *Lupita, your secrets are safe with me. Including this morning. Just stick to our story. I'd asked you to take the car for a spin to test the brakes. I know it sounds ridiculous and when you look in the mirror in a few minutes you'll wonder how on earth they will ever believe you, but if I back it up what can they possibly do? Just don't complicate it. Keep it simple and nothing will happen, I promise.*

Dana paused to pull a pack of Benson & Hedges and a silver lighter from the glove compartment. Lupita watched her closely as she located each item, eager for any clue that would begin to explain what was motivating her. But Dana's face and movements revealed nothing as she poised her cigarette before the flame. After a short silence, she spoke again, but defensively, as if Lupita had challenged her.

Can't I simply help out a friend? We've known each other most of our lives, haven't we? And besides, it's not my place to tell Jackie what her boyfriend has been up to—it would destroy her. And given what you've told me, it sounds like he is well on his way to greener pastures. As far as I'm concerned, she never needs to know any of this.

Lupita knew Dana was not being straight with her, but had no idea what she wanted. She was just as unknowable to her as she had been when they were kids. As politely as she could, she said, *Thank you, Dana*, and exited the car and turned to ascend the stairs where she knew her parents would be waiting. She could feel Dana's eyes on her as she reached the door to the apartment, but she didn't turn around. She had her father to face now, a more urgent and formidable authority than the spoiled, meddling rich girl sitting in the driveway behind her. Still, she was glad to have her ludicrous but unchallengeable story of testing the brakes in her back pocket as she opened the door. One thing she was sure her father would not do was question a Goss, even the youngest of them. The only authority higher than God was the person who not only had sponsored his family's green cards and their citizenship but who signed his paycheck in a tight, tiny black ink row of letters all held in the somewhat flamboyant looping lasso of the first letter of his last name, George P. Goss. He would never, under any circumstances, threaten his standing with him.

Her parents were waiting at the kitchen table when she entered the kitchen. *Is it true? Miss Dana asked you to drive her car?* When she answered her mother by nodding, she saw in her mother's face that she knew she was lying. Her father put his hands out but would not look his daughter in the eye. Lupita handed him the key. *Next time you tell me*, he muttered as he slipped the ring on the hook by the phone and trudged out the door, which he closed meekly behind him. Watching her father constricted by the slapdash fabrication of his employer's daughter was worse than whatever punishment his fists could deliver. For all that had happened that day, but mainly this, she began to sob.

When her mother crossed the room, Lupita mistook her intention and for the first time in a long while, she relaxed her shoulders to accept her comforting arms. What she received instead was a hard slap across the face. Because she had been so ill-prepared for it she lost her balance and fell back on the kitchen floor. Her mother left her there, cradling her stinging cheek with both hands. When she went to inspect it later she saw in the bathroom mirror what Dana and both her parents would have all seen but she had not. Not the red cheek, swollen and angry from her mother's slap, but the grotesque arrangement of six red and purple welts, roughly the size of a nickel each, staining her neck in a slow swoop from below her right ear, down her neck, across her clavicle and above the top of her right breast. She had seen them before on older girls—the boys at Catholic school called them *bad girl badges*—but never up close like this. They must have been below her sight line in the rearview mirror of Dana's car.

She could not fathom what her parents now believed about her. She didn't care what Dana believed, but how could she have interrogated her over the last few hours and not mention what would have been apparent from fifty feet away? Not a word about it until moments ago, *when you look in the mirror in a few minutes you'll wonder how on earth they will ever believe you.* The humiliation and treachery were too much to comprehend and so she looked in the mirror at each bruise, each place where Floyd's mouth sucked her skin so hard the blood vessels broke and splintered into welts. She remembered his lips, his devotion in those perfect minutes together, his unbreakable focus on her. She pictured him turning away, disappearing behind the barn. And then her father's face, her mother's bruised hip, her own shoulder, which bloomed in purple and red only a month ago when he punched her after dropping and smashing a box of light bulbs outside the hardware store. Her father and Floyd could not be more different, she thought at first, and then as she opened her eyes and traced the

hickeys lightly with her pointer finger, she thought again. Whatever their differences might be, they were alike in one, now obvious way: they were both men who left her bruised.

It would be ten months before she saw Floyd again—at a distance, and briefly—after a late season baseball game at Housatonic,
where he'd graduated from high school the year before. Lupita
had agreed to go with a friend from St. Margaret's who had a
crush on one of the players. After the game, Judy vanished with
the boy promising she'd be right back, but by the time the bleachers had emptied out and most everyone had driven home, she
still hadn't returned. Lupita saw an open door to the school and
decided to wander the halls and see the place she would have gone
to high school if her parents hadn't insisted on St. Margaret's. She
wondered, and not for the first time, if going to the public high
school would have changed things between her and Floyd. She
indulged the fantasy of going steady, which she knew was ridiculous, but she couldn't help but imagine him waiting for her to get
out of class to go to lunch together, holding hands as they entered
the cafeteria. She passed through a long hall lined on either side
with gray metal lockers and wondered which one had been his.
She roamed until she began to worry that Judy might return to
the bleachers by the baseball field and assume she'd taken a ride
home with someone else. She turned back to retrace her steps.
And there, crossing directly in front of where she was standing,
carrying a stack of rough wooden boards in his arms, was Floyd.
Behind him another boy carried two pitchforks and a shovel.

Hi Lupita, the bored nasal voice came from her right side and
in her peripheral vision she instantly recognized Hannah.

What are you doing here?

She'd only turned her head an inch before returning her gaze
to where Floyd had been, but he and the other boy had already
disappeared down the hall. Lupita could have choked the life

right from Hannah. *Baseball game*, she managed, *I came with my friend who's dating someone here*.

Hannah's eyes widened as she pounced with questions, *DATING SOMEONE HERE? WHO? WHAT FRIEND?* Hannah was not subtle, not as a kid in elementary school and not as a high school junior.

Judy Micetti, she goes to my school, and I can't remember who. Lupita knew that Judy was at that very moment with Derek Werntz but she was not about to tell Hannah.

Oh. Ok. I gotta go. Floyd and my boyfriend Mark are helping me carry a bunch of stuff from home that we're going to use to make decorations for prom. The theme this year is town and country and we found a bunch of old tools and barn boards from the farm to represent the country side of things.

She was turning to leave but stopped to convey news she had clearly shared so many times the sentences rolled out like badly acted lines in a school play. *Did you hear that Jackie is getting married to my brother? I think she's pregnant because there's a big rush to make it official as soon as possible. Can you believe it? What a disaster that'll be.*

Each word was a bullet. And every one made Lupita angrier. She wasn't sure who she was angriest at, Hannah, Floyd, or Jackie. *Jackie*. It was Hannah who headed for the exit door outside but it was Jackie she pictured, smug and pregnant. Though they lived next door to each other, in the three years since Lupita started at St. Margaret's they only occasionally crossed paths, and if they did it was on the weekends at the movies in Millerton or passing each other in cars on Undermountain Road. And since the day at the barn with Floyd she'd successfully avoided Jackie. Lupita didn't trust that Dana never said anything to her about what had happened the night of the Fourth and the morning after, and she had no interest in finding out. She did not, however, feel guilty. She was devastated that Floyd never came and found her in the weeks following their morning at the barn. The way he touched and held her had made it seem that no one could have mattered more to him. But clearly someone did, and that someone was Jackie. Lupita had started dozens of letters to him, but she didn't know what to say. I love you? I want you to hold me again? The truth was that she had no idea who he was, just that the time she spent in Dana's car with him was the most powerful experience of her life and she loved everything about it. As emotionally and physically charged as her attraction was, it did not seem a strong enough case for risking a letter. And besides, her schedule was unforgiving and her father drove her back and forth from school every day so there weren't many opportunities to rendezvous.

Still, she was gutted by what Hannah had told her. The next few times she sneaked into Edgeweather, she rifled through Dana's desk and coat pockets for letters from Jackie, notes or a diary of any kind that mentioned Floyd. She never found anything. Just cigarettes, flasks of alcohol, and a birthday card from Jackie that had a flip note scribbled, it appeared, in a hurry. *Happy Birthday, Old Pal. Love, Jackie.*

The girls at St. Margaret's did not know Floyd or Jackie, or anyone in Wells. They were from families—many of them Italian and Greek—in the nearby towns over the New York State border. Most of the girls had been at St. Margaret's together since the fifth grade, so when Lupita arrived in ninth she'd braced for a reprise of the rough treatment she'd received when she'd started at Wells Center School.

On her first day at St. Margaret's, three girls approached her outside her assigned homeroom and Lupita could feel her body begin to tense the way it had in the third grade. The girls were cousins, Mia, Amanda and Anna, whose family had come from Puerto Rico when they were young and they were eager to meet someone else whose first language was Spanish. It surprised

Lupita how proud of their roots they were, and their language. In the first weeks at St. Margaret's, it made her nervous when they addressed her in Spanish at school, but over time their ease relaxed her and the three of them took her under their wing. Amanda and Mia were both seniors and graduated at the end of Lupita's freshman year, but Anna was a junior and around one more year before she was gone. By then, Lupita had made friends in her own class, but she missed the easy sistership she had with the Torregrosa girls who each fled to New York City to school and jobs after high school.

Lupita did well at St. Margaret's and received a full scholarship to Albertus Magnus College for women in New Haven, Connecticut. Her plan, worked out with her parents over many months, was to work at Edgeweather over the summer after graduation, help her mother clean, do laundry, and whatever else was needed, and leave for school in late August. She had originally wanted to go to school in California, to San Francisco in particular, but her father refused. Nothing farther than two hours by car was the rule and it had to be Catholic and it had to be women only. Albertus Magnus was the only school she applied to.

By the spring of her senior year in high school Floyd was married, the father of a baby girl, and living in town with Jackie. He existed for Lupita as an idea, a tormenting figment of shapeshifting teenage desire. From the few hastily concluded encounters she'd had with him, she'd built a charged, private hiding place. When she relived these moments she slowed them down, added words that had not been spoken, gestures and actions that had not occurred; she continued on past the point where they'd ended. Occasionally she fully invented scenarios—sexual and otherwise—but the ones she returned to and embellished the most were the ones that had happened.

By the end of her senior year, Lupita hadn't been in Dana's

bedroom in more than three months. Her opportunities were limited partly by full days at school, part-time jobs on the weekends, and hanging out with friends, but the chief obstacle was her father, who was almost always home. He didn't have friends, and most of his contact with others was limited to the workmen he hired to do at Edgeweather what he could not—restoring damaged antiques, electrical wiring, pumping the septic system. He was tough on most of them, and occasionally disrespectful. It embarrassed Lupita to witness.

There were no other Mexican families in the area and though her father had never said so, she was certain he strictly limited his interactions to those he employed because these were the only relationships he felt secure in. Unlike Lupita who spoke with no accent or inflection, his accent was pronounced; and though his English had improved since they lived in Florida, it was still choppy. Her mother's was too, Ada's far less so, but they had friends in New York. Mexican women they saw in the evenings and on the weekends when they stayed in the city. Lupita did not know these women but had heard her mother and Ada gossip about them and their families.

The weekend before Memorial Day was the first time since Christmas that Lupita's mother and Ada were both at Edgeweather. Holidays at Edgeweather, and the weeks leading up to them, were the times Lupita could expect to see Ada. More and more, because the Goss family came less frequently on the weekends, it was becoming the same with her mother. The Gosses went to Palm Beach for Easter every year, and until Memorial Day weekend tended to stay in the city on weekends. The early weeks of May involved an unusual amount of cleaning as well as her mother driving trunks of warm weather clothes from the city to be hung in closets and folded in drawers. This year, Ada and her mother came up on Friday evening and planned a ham dinner for Sunday after church. Ada had been acting moody and curt since they arrived, but Lupita didn't pay much attention. For years, she'd responded to her more as she would an eccentric aunt than a sister. They hadn't lived under the same roof, eaten their daily meals together, or been involved in each other's lives since they lived in Florida. When Lupita asked Ada how she was, her responses indicated that a sisterly chat was not forthcoming. *Nothing new* or *Same as yesterday* was the most she could expect. And occasionally, Ada would pretend she didn't hear and simply walk away.

On Sunday morning, knowing Edgeweather was empty and her parents and Ada would be attending church together, Lupita told her mother she had a sour stomach and a terrible headache. Lupita rarely complained of being sick, so she knew she'd be believed. Once her family left, she raced out of the garage apartment and across the lawn. She didn't bother putting clothes on, just pulled her bathrobe on over her pajamas and ran as fast as she could to the big house.

After unlocking the service entrance door, she noticed a quality about the house that felt different. She hesitated in the hall just off the door for a few minutes before going further in. She listened and smelled and waited but there was nothing she could identify, so she proceeded into the kitchen, out through the dining room and into the main foyer of the house. Again, a fleeting sense of something wrong, but she figured it had been so long since she'd been there, and also it was spring, so there would surely be some change reflected in the house. She went straight for Dana's room. Though she knew no one was around, Lupita still trod gently on the stairs, her boots barely registering a sound as she pressed lightly with each step up the center staircase; at the wide landing where two cantilevered flights rose and turned from each side, she did not stop, just stealthily proceeded up to the left, and into the hall toward Dana's bedroom. It was the most remote on the second floor, sitting above the ballroom and kitchen and facing out to the river between the fifth and last column. Lupita would be required to help with the beds and laundry this summer so she knew she'd be in and out of this room plenty of times before she left for Albertus Magnus in the fall, but with only five weeks left before graduating from high school and summer officially beginning she sensed this might be the last time she'd be here alone.

Instead of rummaging through Dana's closet right away, she went to the bathroom where she'd never spent much time. There must have been at least twenty towels throughout the room. The brightest white, piled in plush stacks on gray marble shelves, or hung from glass dowels fastened at each end to shiny metal mounts. The hardware in the room, along with the faucets and exposed pipes on and around the sink and bathtub, gleamed like the silver dining service Lupita's mother would transport from the big house in a wheelbarrow a few times a year and spend weekends polishing while she listened to her beloved Amalia Mendoza on the radio. It had never occurred to Lupita to run a bath before, but the light from the window warming the colorless luxury of the room made it irresistible. In a row of what looked like glass apothecary jars on the shelf between the bathtub and sink, she found bath salts that smelled like roses and lavender and with a small wooden scoop she poured two generous helpings into the steaming water. When the bath was full she shucked her boots and pajamas and bathrobe and hid them behind the tub. She did not want her eye to land on anything from the world above the garage she'd just left. She only wanted the uninterrupted fantasy that Edgeweather occasionally provided, and as this was very likely her last time, she wanted it to be special.

It took more than a few minutes to gradually lower herself

into the fragrant water and acclimate to the heat. Once there she watched the late morning light glint off the metal and warm the marble surfaces. Though she felt tired, she resisted closing her eyes because she did not want to miss a moment or a single detail. She was a girl in a bathtub, soaking in a high, far room and no one knew.

Dana

After all these years, that old nerve—of being left—still spasms when touched. Her reunion with Jackie had lasted less than a few minutes. Of course it would end abruptly because of something she'd said about Floyd. It still bewilders her that a boy, of all things, would have driven them apart. And Floyd, a weakling for all his brawn—a pawn who shouldn't have been so easily played. If he'd had any strength of character he wouldn't have followed when she called.

Hey, there, she'd said, after waving to him across the Hatch Pond parking lot. *Hi*. She told him they were headed up the hill to Peter Beldon's cabin where there was a campfire and a good view of the fireworks and asked if he could help. They'd over-prepared, she explained, and could use an extra set of hands. He began to shake his head and take a step back, so she hastily added. *We'll give you a six pack of beer for your trouble. And you'll know people. Lupita . . . she's up there already. You remember Lupita, right?*

Dana had seen her father fly-fish on the Housatonic and always wondered how he knew when to pull the rod to set the hook and what that moment felt like. Now she knew. *C'mon, it'll just take a minute*, she could feel the barbed metal graze the inside of Floyd's cheek. *I'm sure Lupita would be happy to see a familiar face up there, even if for just a minute. She's surrounded by college boys, the worst.* A moment of silence followed, she let the line unspool a few feet, made room for the image she'd just conjured to linger until Floyd said, *I guess I could lend a hand. Just need to make it quick as Jackie and the baby are back at the blanket.* Hook set, she scanned the small trunk of her convertible for something to hand him. The only things she had in the car was her useless briefcase, where she'd stashed the remaining money she'd withdrawn from her trust, a few blankets, and a canvas laundry bag filled with bottles of alcohol she'd taken from the pantry at Edgeweather. She didn't want to leave the briefcase at the house, which would reignite her mother who'd already expressed her disapproval and conveyed her father's disappointment that she'd abandoned the summer job at the bank. *I knew you'd only last a few days*, she'd said after the taxi driver from the city dropped her off at Edgeweather. The words stung because Dana hadn't at all planned to walk out on the internship so much as arrange to take a few days off. She wanted to come up for the fireworks Thursday night, take a long weekend, and go back to the city Monday. She was going to talk to her father about it after she'd made plans with Jackie. But Jackie, once again, was not picking up. She'd tried for three days in a row with no luck before she finally got her on the phone. She held back her agitation and attempted to sound disinterested when she asked what she was planning on doing for the Fourth of July. She'd barely spoken the words when Jackie interrupted to say *Thanks, Dana, I'm afraid we've made plans. Floyd and Amy and I are having a family-only picnic at the pond. It's Amy's first Fourth and even though she'll sleep through most of it, we wanted to make a day of it, start a tradition. It's important to Floyd.*

If it hadn't taken five calls over three days to get her on the phone. If she'd used any other phrase besides *family-only*. If Dana hadn't known for almost two years by then that Floyd had fooled around with Lupita, was very possibly still fooling around with her. If none of these things were true, or had not happened, Dana could possibly have let it go and simply changed the topic, carried on with the charade of friendship they'd been playing out since their last years in high school, said goodbye and moved on. But instead she quickly excused herself, lied that someone at the bank was calling her, and without waiting for Jackie's response hung up. She then remembered that Peter Beldon had invited her to a cookout at his family's summer cabin in the woods above Hatch Pond. It hadn't occurred to her to go until that moment and, before thinking it through, she picked up the phone and called the phone number at Edgeweather. It rang a few times before she heard the words, *Goss residence, Lupita speaking*.

A day later, she was standing in the parking lot of the town beach at Hatch Pond where somehow she knew she would cross paths with Floyd.

Here, she'd said to him, all business now, the plea in her voice gone. With the two blankets and the clinking sack of booze she gestured toward Floyd who nodded and took them both in hand as the clunky brown camera around his neck knocked against his sweat-stained blue T-shirt. Her hands free now, and nothing else from her car to carry, she pivoted toward Peter Beldon's station wagon and grabbed a few towels from the front seat to perpetuate the flimsy pretense that Floyd's help was needed. Nervously, she eyed the nearby field for Jackie and her swaddled infant before she shouted, *To the cabin!* Like a dog, Floyd followed.

A door slams downstairs and before she reacts, Dana hesitates. *What am I doing?* She asks herself seriously, because for a moment, like so many over the last year—a phone conversation she's knee-deep in, a card she is writing, a shopping list she's going over with Marcella—she has no idea what is happening, who or what she's seeing or doing. She sits down on the top step and rushes through a list of what she knows to bring her back to the present—Wells, Edgeweather—but nothing of what has just happened and why she is where she is returns.

Wind blows against the house and the old beams holding the place together creak loudly above Dana's head. She's never had a day with so many disorienting moments. The wind picks up, its whistle through the eaves and attic more ominous than when she and Jackie spent nights up here, scaring each other with ghost stories. *Jackie*, the name pierces her reverie. She remembers their climb up the stairs from the foyer, Jackie's quick exit. She imagines her outside now, bundled in her thin wool coat and nightgown, making her way in all that dark.

Lupita

The seawater has risen, crept imperceptibly above the tops of her thighs. With each new wave a low, fast swell swarms her torso and splashes her neck, the force for a moment lifting her body, pushing her limbs up and back, nudging her a few inches further into deeper water. She grips the sand as she would bunch sheets in her fist but it is only a pantomime of holding on. She is nothing to the sea, no match for its power; the sand its shifty accomplice, changing shape beneath and around her as the water rushes in, vanishing as it retreats. The undertow has graduated stealthily from a gentle, caressing invitation to a rough command. But she does not stand. She does not leave. A rogue wave overwhelms gravity and she is up and tumbling in the hurly-burly chaos of foam and ocean, her palms and heels flexing to brush the grainy bottom, but there is nothing.

After the bath, Lupita pulled a large white towel from the nearest stack, patted and rubbed her skin until it no longer dripped on the black and white tile floor. She drained the tub and wiped away any pooling evidence of her time there, folded the towel carefully, as her mother had shown her and Ada a thousand times, and placed it at the bottom of the stack.

Without clothes on, she passed through Dana's bedroom into one of the two long, walk-in closets where a low, wide dresser stood. She opened the middle drawer and noticed that most of what was there was completely new. Dana's panties, bras and slips had always been delicate and fancy, mostly cotton with occasional silk pieces here and there. But everything she saw in the drawer now had a layer of detailing and ornament the others never had. Stitched bows and satin ribbons, buds folded from silk.

Her mother did not gossip with her about the Goss family, Dana in particular, but Lupita knew she thought Dana was wild and spoiled, especially in her last few years of high school. Dana had completed a year at a women's college, like Albertus Magnus, but not Catholic and certainly much more expensive. Lupita imagined her life there and wondered who or what had provoked the update to this little-seen part of her wardrobe. She pulled out what looked like a camisole and held it up to the light, but as she did her eye landed on something hanging from the back of the door. She could not make out its design, only that stitched upon it was an unusual amount of embroidery. When she saw the draping sash and the ripple of hem a foot from the closet floor, she realized it was a robe. Gold and red and brown stitches vivid against creamy silk draped from the hook like a glamorous waterfall. Lupita barely folded the camisole before she returned it to its place and shut the drawer. She turned back to the robe like a spellbound moth ignoring the currents of heat radiating from a porch light. Still naked, she pulled the garment from its hook and felt its weight, which was much heavier than she anticipated. She cradled the material in her arms and walked it back to Dana's bed, laid it gently, front down, on the white coverlet, smoothed its folds and spread the enormous arms out as wide as they would reach. Lupita stepped back from the bed to take in what she saw there—a golden dragon on an ivory cloud detailed with red and brown, its tail and wings and torso twisted in flight, his face in three-quarter profile turned defiantly and with warning to whoever dared approach. The creature's wings flared out onto the sleeves, its tail curled down a few centimeters above the hem and back up above the waist. She approached the bed and lowered her hand to feel the stitching. It must have taken miles of thread, shiny and fine, she imagined, to create the small area upon the tail where her middle and pointer finger stroked. She couldn't help but wonder: How many hands made this one thing? How many years did it take them? She remembered something her father said about the roads in Florida, that it took hundreds of men like him and more than a year to build a stretch of road that took only a few minutes to drive. She pulled the robe at one edge and folded the dragon side down onto the bed to see the front which was mostly a sky of cream punctuated by seven very faint silhouettes of clouds stitched in silver and black thread and scattered elegantly down the chest and just below the waist. Such a gentle, unassuming first impression this made, she thought, considering what it fronted.

She put it on. It had the heft of a long winter coat, but once her arms had slipped through the wide sleeves, and the collar had settled on her neck and shoulders, the weight was magically distributed to make the garment feel much lighter. She closed the front and tied the cream silk sash and stepped to the mirror above Dana's vanity table. What she saw disappointed her: a childish girl playing with something finer than she was. Like she had in the ballroom downstairs when she had sneaked into the house for the first time, years ago, she felt shamed by the finer world the robe represented. Her thick dark hair, still in the loose bun she'd stuck it in when she woke up this morning, was lopsided with stray hairs flying at all angles on top and still damp along her neck from the bath. She reached behind her head and pulled the hair from its rubber band and let it fall down her back and around her shoulders. She grabbed Dana's cheap plastic brush, the same kind she and her mother used at home, and began to tame the tangles and smooth the unruly strays. She twisted away from the mirror while she brushed her hair so that when she turned around she might have a new experience of her reflection. An ordinary girl, transformed in the dragon's grip into a sophisticated beauty. Finally, she looked, and indeed something had changed. Not unrecognizably, but by enough degrees that she felt the sting of shame from before lighten, if not vanish. She wished Floyd could have seen her this way. It was the vision of her she would have picked for him to carry into his boring life with Jackie.

She remembered the morning with Floyd behind the barn, the leather seats rubbing her thighs, his hands, his determined mouth. She glided back toward the bed and rolled up onto the coverlet and under the lace canopy she had rested and fantasized under alone so many times. She lay back on the pillow and remembered again when she saw Floyd in the parking lot at Trotta's, handsome and strong, dumbstruck by the sight of her. She remembered him behind the shed, terrified and awkward and then, physically, so sure. She let her hands touch the silk, loosen the sash, and trace the hem along the front, up toward her chest to the hollow of her clavicle, which she pressed lightly and circled with her thumb. Wrapped in silk under the fine white tent of Dana's bed, she felt for a few seconds what she came here to feel: far away. Free and alone, floating above the eggshells she walked on at home. This was the last time, but she knew that once she left Wells she'd no longer need this secret place or the escape it made possible. In a few months, she'd be gone. When she came back to see her family it would be only when she could not avoid it and for as briefly as possible.

She understood that she would very likely never see Floyd again. Surely never kiss or touch him. Hard truths she'd accepted after Hannah told her he was marrying Jackie. It was, she recognized months after, a relief. If she'd ended up entangled with a farm boy from Wells like Floyd she would never leave. And a life here was not what she wanted. With these thoughts, the faraway feeling dwindled and the transporting reverie she'd expected, on her favorite spot, in her secret place, turned out instead to be a goodbye. To Dana's room, Edgeweather, Floyd—the stubborn hope for him and the more enduring erotic idea of him. He was no longer what she desired, in the world or in Dana's room.

Lupita looked up and noticed a small cobweb in the near corner of the canopy. Fine white threads spun into what looked like a stretched cotton ball wedged between the top of the dark post and the wedding cake white lace draped on either side. Just another trespasser, she thought, and felt a sudden and overwhelming desire to leave. Impatiently, she began to wriggle out of the robe. She sat up, slid her arms out from the sleeves and let the collar slip from her shoulders and down her back. Free of the robe, she faced the mirror above the vanity. Who she saw reflected there, above her left shoulder, leaning against the inside frame of the bedroom door, stopped her breath.

Since she was nine years old, she'd known him as Mr. Goss. Arms crossed, head tilted slightly to the right, wearing a version of what she'd always seen him wear: twill trousers and an unbuttoned, thin gray cardigan over a navy polo shirt. After a few frozen seconds during which neither moved or made a sound, Lupita's body sprung to life and constricted into a ball, her hands flung across her chest, her legs quickly bent up toward her belly. *Good morning*, he said gravely, putting his hand on the doorknob, slowly beginning to pull. She grabbed for the robe to cover herself, but he abandoned the open door and rushed the bed, leaned over and ripped the garment from her hands. In a panic she lunged for it again, too late, and as she did she slipped from her precarious pose and tipped over on her side, exposed momentarily before she returned her hands to her chest and pulled her knees tightly together. As she flailed on the bed to regain her composure and hide her body, he stood still and watched her, crumpled the robe, fist over fist. He swayed slightly. She wondered if he was drunk. She'd only ever met him in passing and always with her family. She tried to remember if his voice was slurred when he spoke moments before. But his voice was the voice of newscasters and congressmen, priests and presidents. She had no reference point for drunkenness besides her father and the kids at school who poured alcohol they'd stolen from their parents into bottles of Coca-Cola at football games, and none of them would be as composed as he was if they were drunk. Mostly she'd seen Mr. Goss from a distance, walking from the car to the house, or crossing the lawn to the river with fishing gear. He was like Cardinal Rutolo whom the priests and nuns at St. Margaret's referred to all the time, someone whose whims and decisions governed nearly every facet of their day-to-day lives at school, but who visited only once or twice a year, and was rarely ever seen.

She began to inch off the bed with the idea that she could escape to the bathroom behind her, lock the door and put on her clothes, but before she had stretched her foot to the floor, he circled the end of the bed, grabbed the wood post and flung himself with accelerated momentum around to where she was attempting to descend. He stopped to her left, and without permission put his hand on her shoulder. Shame of her nakedness and fear of consequence for being discovered in his daughter's room had driven her panic until now, but as his clean, manicured hands squeezed the flesh just below her shoulder, much harder than he appeared to her capable of, her panic flared total and primal. As in a nightmare, she shook but could not move; was terrified but unable to speak or scream. Mr. Goss stepped directly in front of where she was crouched on both knees; his right hand reached for her other arm, skimmed the skin from her shoulder to her elbow, and moved quickly to the top of her thigh. When he spoke to her it was without anger or urgency, emotion of any identifiable kind; there was nothing but his voice, direct and plain. *Stay right where you are. We are going to have a talk.*

She is underwater, the place where the land goes and the compass breaks and everything before ceases to be; there is only a weightless, somersaulting now. She reaches for sand but there is nothing but the water and the white. She tries to lengthen her body, find the angle that will involve it again with gravity, but the undertow and the opposing hurl of collapsing waves yank and bend her until she eventually goes limp. She is drowning. In time, the sea calms, slackens its grip and allows her to surface for air, re-orient with the elements and locate where she is within them. Her eyes scan frantically to find the horizon, to locate anything familiar. Above her a lace sky, and on the ocean floor below, a dragon glares from a wrecked carcass. Across the room, Lupita sees a familiar figure in the doorway. *Abuelita*, she whispers with desperate wonder, *tú has venido. Ita, ayúdame.* She'd prayed to her and she is here. She will be safe now, healed in her grandmother's embrace. She blinks to see more clearly and sees her grandmother's hair is dark and fastened in a tidy bun, not the long, silver strands she remembers spilling down around her shoulders, the hair she remembers pulling on as a child, that spilled through her small hands. And her arms are smooth and thin, not plump and wrinkled and draping with soft folds. These are not the arms that once held her. They are, she recognizes now, her sister's. The woman in a yellow church dress, with a small white handbag clutched against her chest, is Ada. She's so close. Lupita calls to her, but in her throat there is no voice, no sound; her eyes meet her sister's and in them she screams for help. Ada does not move from where she stands, but she holds her gaze. Her eyes, so much like their father's, are a rope to grasp, a new hope that this can be stopped, survived, will not change her, will ruin nothing, and when it ends she will still be the same girl who minutes ago reveled in warm, calm water that smelled like lavender and roses. But the eyes that hold hers let go, they look away in a head that shakes from side to side with judgment and disgust; the rope goes slack in her hands, her sister turns away. She goes under.

Later, after Mr. Goss abruptly and without words leaves the room, Lupita surfaces. She is frantic to cover herself, but as she does feels like it is someone else, not her, hurrying on the pajamas, bathrobe and boots she shucked so carelessly only an hour before. That girl is someone she does not yet know. A girl who is stunned and alone, who has been made new but feels ancient. A girl who runs.

Dana

Time had taken plenty—energy, beauty, sex, family, certainty, friends, the future—but until she saw Jackie step under the portico light and knock on Edgeweather's old oak door, it hadn't occurred to Dana that something might be returned.

When Jackie fled from the third floor, Dana didn't follow or call after her. The reunion, all that it brought back, and its swift end, were more than she could process into actions. She was disoriented, confused, and so she stayed still until she wasn't and then made her way down to the foyer and out into the driveway. At first, since there was no car parked in front of the house, Dana had assumed Jackie had already driven home. But she hadn't heard a car door slam or an engine rev. She scanned the dark lawn toward the river and then back across the driveway until a glimmer of pink caught her eye. When she looked closer she could see the fabric of Jackie's nightgown dangling below her dark coat as she moved along the road toward the stables.

Dana crossed the lawn to the stone wall, where she could see Jackie unlatch the gate and start down the short dirt drive. She knew what her old friend was remembering and wondered what exactly had stayed with her after all these years. The fidgety horses? The hovering adults? The light rain that morning? The trick she'd tried to play on her, calling the stallion a mare? They were little girls then, with big feelings and small, uncomplicated lives. Now they were two women in their late sixties, one shivering in nightclothes next to an unlit, empty stable, and the other, stooped along a stone wall, in borrowed sweatpants, spying on her. It was so grim and ridiculous Dana nearly laughed out loud as she moved to a place between the trees where she could see more clearly. Still and pale in the dimly lit night, Jackie appeared like a scarcely remembered figment from an unsettling dream.

Dana wondered what would happen next. Would she go to the river? Walk back down the road to the house she grew up in? It occurred to her that Jackie did not have the keys anymore and she wondered where Kenny kept them. Her body tensed in anticipation, as if bird watching or spotting wildlife on safari in Africa. She crouched behind the wall when Jackie stepped away from the stable, and then rose slowly to watch her approach the gate again. *Where will you go now*, she muttered to herself. As Jackie retraced her path along the road and stepped back into the driveway, Dana didn't expect her to return to the house. Jackie had never been one to change her mind. As a kid, she didn't waver from vanilla ice cream; in high school she stayed loyal to the Beach Boys, tolerated the Beatles and refused to listen to Bob Dylan and the Rolling Stones; and the only boy she ever wanted was Floyd. Standing in the shadows along the house, Dana could not remember an instance when Jackie had revisited a decision or judgment she'd made. She didn't ascribe her intractability to strong character or good judgment so much as titanium stubbornness and deep-rooted pride, which made her pounding on the door she'd just stormed out of so unlikely. But here she was.

Dana made her way to the side of the house, careful to stay in shadow. She edged along the brick wall outside the study where, long ago, her father had made his phone calls, read and signed the stacks of papers he'd carried in his briefcase from the city. She was never allowed in that room. Even in college and in the few years after, before they'd all stopped visiting, it was the one place at Edgeweather, besides her parents' bathroom, that remained off-limits. Not just to her, but to everyone. *A man needs a sanctuary*, is what he'd say. Her grandmother told her that when he was young her son always made forts and secret hideaways in the woods. *Drove his sister crazy, poor Lee was always searching for him. He liked to disappear, that one.*

Dana remembers her father occasionally leaving the city on business without warning. He'd vanish from the apartment for a few days and when she asked her mother where he was she'd only receive silence in response. As she got older, it stopped occurring to her to ask. But when she was young, she followed her father's movements closely and when he was in his study at Edgeweather, she'd stand with her ear pressed to the closed pocket doors and listen when he was on the phone. She could never quite make out what he said, his words warped into sounds that made no sense, a low-toned foreign language. He only caught her once. She hadn't heard the approach of his footsteps before the doors suddenly slid back and he was there. Tonight, as she crept around the corner to the front of the house and saw Jackie at the door, Dana felt the urge to rush the portico and holler *WHAT ON EARTH*, the same words her father spat in disgusted surprise before he pulled the study doors shut and returned to whatever he'd been doing. But she resisted the impulse to ambush and settled against the house, careful not to cross into the light beaming from the windows.

Jackie has been at the door for more than a few minutes, knocking—three times, fast, a pause, then twice, harder, and on and on. Dana watches and once again has no idea where she is or what she is seeing. She panics and begins to tell herself what she knows: she is outside, in the dark, a woman is knocking. She recognizes the entrance to the house, Jackie, old and in bed clothes. She remembers that Philip drove her from the city today. The rest follows but the reason she is here stays murky. She knows she'd hoped to accomplish something by turning up at Jackie's house with the briefcase filled with copies of adoption papers and, for no reason she was aware of, a history of the Moravians of eastern Pennsylvania. Had her aunt put the book in there? Her lawyers? The man she met at the diner yesterday? And then she remembers: Hap, Lupita, Floyd, and all the rest of it, straight back to her dialing the number at Edgeweather from her father's bank the day before the Fourth of July, a lifetime ago.

As if it had just happened, Dana now remembers every word she and Lupita said to each other on that phone call, how the vague idea to complicate Jackie's perfect picnic inked to life before she'd thought it through. She hadn't considered what actually might happen. She'd had no plan, only a reactive instinct set in motion before reason or conscience could divert her: to go where she was not welcome, with Lupita.

And then she waved. She can feel how her arm rose when she saw Floyd standing by the station wagon; how her hand jumped to life in a phony greeting, her fingers falling quickly in line and fluttering forward and back as she called him over. If only she'd left it by her side, turned her back on Jackie's husband and left him alone. What would everyone's life look like now? She can't help but wonder how much differently her own would have turned out. Would she and Jackie be close? Would they even be in each other's lives? There was no knowing, but she remembers the night she lost what remaining hope she still had for reconciliation. It was after that dreadful summer had ended, after she'd returned to Bryn Mawr for her sophomore year. She'd just come back to her dorm after dinner when she saw a note taped to her door.

The words were written in light blue pencil on a folded piece of white paper. *URGENT—call Lupita 203-364-1679*. Dana ripped the taped paper from her door. It had been almost two months since she'd seen Lupita and she'd tried not to think about her, or anything else that reminded her of the Fourth of July. It jolted her to see her name here, at school, where Wells and everyone in it seemed like they didn't exist.

Dana crumpled and unfolded the phone message while she waited in line behind two girls to use the hall phone. It was the first Sunday night after the summer holiday and most of the girls were already calling their boyfriends or parents. Dana kept wondering why Lupita had called her, what on earth could be so urgent. Not only did she resent her for the intrusion, but for stirring up memories of the summer, which became more vivid with each passing second. When at last it was her turn to use the phone, she dialed the number she recognized as the one for the telephone in the apartment above the garage where Lupita still lived with her father. Her mother Maria would be in the city with her parents until they left for the winter in Palm Beach where, since July, Lupita's sister Ada now worked. According to Dana's mother, who'd reported the news as if she'd arranged it herself, Ada was already dating the caretaker's son, Mateo.

The phone rang once before Lupita picked up.

Dana, is that you?

Dana grimaced in silence before she agreed to be identified. *Ok, so it's me. What do you want.*

I'm in trouble, she said in a voice Dana did not recognize as Lupita's. Since they were children, Lupita had always seemed gloomy and serious, a bit of a pain occasionally when she silently hovered at the edge of and spied on whatever she and Jackie were doing. Later, in the few times she'd been in her company after high school, Lupita remained aloof and silent, proud. Not least when she caught her stealing her car to meet Floyd two years ago. But she was not aloof or proud now. *I didn't know who to call.*

The telephone connection was not clear and what Lupita said sounded to Dana like, *I don't know why you call.*

Why am I calling you? You left a message asking me to! The question is why on earth are you calling me, Lupita? How could I possibly help you? I'm at school. How did you even find my number here anyway?

Lupita spoke calmly now, her old steel returning. She told Dana she was pregnant with Floyd's child, that they'd been together on the Fourth. She let Dana register the news before adding: *In the woods behind the cabin, exactly where you told him I would be.*

Jackie stops knocking and comes down the portico steps to the side of the house, less than two car lengths away from where Dana is standing. She approaches the window nearest the front door and begins to bang against the glass. Closer now, and more harshly lit, her hair appears thinner than before, a dull silver pulled behind her head in a black plastic clip like the one Dana has seen Marcella wear to keep the strands out of her eyes when she vacuums. She notices a slightly exaggerated curve in Jackie's upper spine, how it pushes her neck and head forward just enough to remind her of the osteoporosis chart in her doctor's office in the city.

Jackie looks weathered, but hearty, her arm seems inexhaustible banging against the glass. Dana pictures her when she was young. Trim, by country standards, and plain. Her style was simple, neat, and in her looks and physicality she'd always reminded Dana of Judy Garland. Appealing, healthy, in the realm of pretty. In manner she was earthy, unfussy and blunt, the qualities that first seemed so attractive; the same ones that Dana would later register as insensitive and curt. She remembers Jackie's cool dismissal when she'd asked what her plans were for the Fourth of July. The quick, clear line she'd drawn between Dana and her family, how she discarded her, after years of friendship, for a farm boy. When she considers Floyd now, she sees a dumb country lug easily manipulated by women. In this way, he was no worse than many men she'd known. Still, when they were teenagers, he seemed the poorest choice. A two-timing sneak who did not care for, let alone love, Jackie. After Dana saw Lupita and Floyd sneak behind the shed at Hatch Pond and bullied a confession from her the next day, she hesitated before telling her friend. By their last years in high school, there was a felt but unnamed distance widening between them—Dana's planning for college and Jackie's tunnel vision on Floyd made their usual midweek calls less frequent—and when they did speak or see each other on the weekends, neither wanted to hear about what mattered most to the other. Spilling dreadful news about Floyd would only make things worse between them, and Dana understood Jackie well enough to know that she'd treat the information—and very likely its messenger—as an unwanted obstacle in the clear path she'd set to gaining her heart's desire. So Dana said nothing and Jackie got what she wanted.

Long before July Fourth, there were times when Dana was tempted to puncture Jackie's illusions about Floyd, usually after listening to her brag about how well-liked he was, or something having to do with the farm he hoped to run someday; but as high school ended and Jackie got pregnant and married and settled into the little house in town, what she knew about Floyd and Lupita felt less and less important and more like gossip. For all Dana knew, what was between them had ended the morning behind the barn. It wasn't until she'd unexpectedly heard Lupita's voice answer the phone at Edgeweather that she felt the need to find out. A day later, she waved, called out to Floyd, and he followed her up the hill.

It never occurred to Dana that Jackie might think that she was the one Floyd betrayed her with. But according to Floyd, who'd called Dana the next day to say that Jackie had thrown him out, this is exactly what she thought. *She thinks I took off with you, that you and I . . .* he'd sputtered before Dana slammed the phone down and ran to her car. She drove to Jackie's as fast as she could, knocked on the door, circled the house, called for her. Jackie's refusal to engage felt like her dismissal days before. As mortified as Dana was by the fallout of her mischief, Jackie's clear message—that Dana was disposable—cut deeper. The longer she remained outside Jackie's house, the angrier and more resentful she became, and eventually she left.

Almost forty-nine years would pass before she showed up again at Jackie's door to tell her what she'd failed to the first time. Had she been protecting or punishing? For years, she almost believed the story she told herself: that she'd tried to save her friend from a philandering husband and paid a high price for it. But time and the occasional therapist chipped away at that tale and eventually she accepted the uglier truth of what drove her.

The consequences were more difficult to make peace with. She'd kept track of Jackie and Lupita, and even Hap, through the photographs the private detectives sent, but she was never exactly sure what she'd hoped to find in those images. Evidence that what she'd done had disrupted the dreary fates of those involved and re-routed them to better lives? This never arrived. What she saw, year after year, were glimpses of the people she'd nearly destroyed, piecing their lives back together in time to get old.

After she left Hap in the diner, she was sure she needed to tell Jackie everything, as soon as possible, before he bee-lined to Wells and appeared at her door with bits and pieces of the story, but not the truth. When Dana came home she told Marcella to have a car ready by seven the next morning. This was yesterday, but it felt like years had passed.

And here was Jackie, only a few yards away, and Dana still

did not know what to say. Another impulsive plan to protect her friend falling apart just as she recognized she was only seeking something for herself. Beating Hap to Jackie's door gave Dana a second chance at what she'd missed the first time. To be understood, if not forgiven. Why else would she have taken her up to the third floor of Edgeweather tonight? She'd kept so many secrets from Jackie for so long, beginning with the night of the prom. Not just what happened after, but what she'd felt before. Feelings too frightening to express shoved into elaborate fantasies she'd willed to life—a beautiful shared bedroom in the attic of her house, insisting on being Jackie's prom date, even buying her dress. There was too much to say. And to try would upend too much. If Jackie hadn't forgiven Floyd, she had at least made peace with what she believed he'd done. Given the damage she'd already caused, Dana knew she didn't deserve to be absolved, or understood. The best she could hope for now was to spare Jackie another loss.

Dana had convinced Hap to give her back her briefcase and all the documents inside. She almost felt sorry for him that all it took was a promise to return the originals once she'd made copies for herself. At first, she wasn't clear why she wanted all of it out of his hands—it was more of an urgent feeling than a reason—but in the hours that followed their meeting, she recognized that if she did end up telling Jackie anything, she might need some kind of proof. And it didn't escape her that if Hap somehow reached her first, without the contents of the briefcase he'd have little more than a wild story. In exchange she told him everything she knew of how he came to be, and when he asked who and where everyone who was still alive was, she wrote down Jackie and Lupita's names and the names of the towns they lived in on an old florist's card she'd fished from her wallet. She told him that the choice to contact his birth mother and the family of his father was, of course, his, but that he should be aware that there would be agony for everyone involved, that these were people who'd long since moved on with their lives. She didn't know if this were true of Lupita, only what she'd seen in photographs. But she'd survived. And that was something.

Dana notices the banging has stopped just as Jackie sees her. Without realizing it, she has shuffled and readjusted her place against the brick and inadvertently progressed, in fractions of inches, out from the shadow to where she stands now, half-lit under the pitiless floodlights.

Me first, Jackie says as they make eye contact. Dana braces for a half-century of rage and judgment, but when Jackie speaks, it is softly and not the high ragged holler she expects. She gestures to the house, the grounds, the woods. *Despite all this*, she says, more bewildered than angry. *You wanted what I had. And you took it. Or at least you tried to.*

Dana steps closer, fully lit now. *You're right*, she says without defense or qualification, *That's what I came to say. Whatever else is true, and whatever else I might say to explain, you're right and I'm sorry. I don't have any explanation other than . . .* She pauses, clears her throat, and as she does recognizes that though she'd come back to Wells with much more to tell Jackie, what she is saying now is the part that is hers alone, and true: *I was jealous. And angry. I loved you . . . more than you knew, I think . . . and you . . . you had this life beginning. I didn't belong in it anymore. I was wrong. I didn't think any of it through.*

Jackie appears disappointed. She shakes her head and mutters something unintelligible while she refastens her coat, which had come loose banging her fist against the window. She crosses her arms at her chest and narrows her eyes as if she's identified a double meaning or trap in Dana's words. She draws a breath before speaking again. Her voice is exhausted, final.

It was a long time ago . . . and none of it matters. We were friends and then we weren't. I may not know everything . . . but I know that I wasn't the one responsible. You may have all the details and secrets to share now, but I wasn't interested in them then and I'm not interested now. Keep your briefcase and your papers. They have nothing to do with me. It's been . . . Jackie pauses, looks up at the house and out across the lawn. She does not meet Dana's eye again as she turns to leave. *I'm sorry you came all this way.*

As Jackie starts toward the driveway, Dana remembers the first time her friend told her about Floyd. It was years before he'd ever noticed her, when Jackie was in eighth grade and he was a freshman in high school. He was the older brother of a girl in her class, *the perfect boy,* was the phrase she used. She'd never spoken to him, but she'd decided he was perfect. Her conviction was as clear and unyielding then as the line she drew to keep Dana away from the life she'd begin with him later, as clear as the line she was drawing now. Dana can feel the sting of once again being put in her place, banished; but as Jackie walks away, she sees her shoulders hunch and shiver, her hands knot together to stay warm. Disarmed, Dana calls out, *Can I at least walk you to your car?* Jackie does not respond as she keeps walking.

No more words, no more anything. I just want . . . It's late and cold and . . . I don't want you to be out there . . . alone . . . No one should . . . As Dana's last words leave her mouth, Jackie reaches the place where the driveway meets the road. She stops, appears to bend slightly at the waist, but does not turn around. Lit from behind by the house and on either side by half a dozen or so floodlights arranged in the trees and along the stonewall, she looks momentarily confused, and tired, and Dana begins to move toward her. But before she takes a full step, Jackie straightens from her slouch, pulls the collar of her coat up toward her neck, and for the last time, she leaves.

Dana watches the bright, empty driveway like the last person in a movie theater who stays long after the final credit has rolled to the top of the screen and the music has ended. Crickets saw the night air and for the first time since she came outside she can hear the river's low murmur at the bottom of the lawn. She hears something else there, too, but cannot place it. A high chirp, a quick whistle. She looks away from the house, in the direction of the sound, but there is only the lit grass, the edge of the woodline. She hears the sound again, but now it's behind her. Jackie, she thinks, her blood racing. The whistle a signal of willingness, a peace offering. Dana spins around, certain for a few seconds she will see her old friend, but there is no one there, just the bright and empty driveway. The floodlights before and behind her seem to glow brighter.

Turn them off, she screams, edging back to the house. She starts to call Marcella but quickly remembers where she is. She shouts for Philip, but no one comes. Then Kenny. Again, nothing. Just the sounds of frogs and crickets and rushing water. She'll turn the lights off herself, she decides as she raises her boot to ascend the portico stairs, but before her heel touches down she realizes that she has no idea where any of the switches are. Her hands begin to shake and she stills them by holding onto the paint-flaked railing. She ransacks her memory but dozens of houses and apartments flash before her, hundreds of light switches and lamps, driveways and entrance halls. She glides down, slowly, almost imperceptibly, until she is fully seated on the bottom stair. Momentarily she has no idea where she is or why her hands, off the railing now, are tight at her sides, clenched into fists. And then she remembers. The switches. She needs to find the light switches. Their discovery the only escape. If she knew where they were, if she only knew, she'd flick each one off, one-by-one, kill every light inside and outside the house. She'd plunge the whole goddamned place into darkness.

Floyd

He hadn't planned on being gone long. Just enough time to catch a glimpse of Lupita and get back to Jackie and Amy, while there was still enough light to get down the hill. Before the fireworks that they would watch from their blanket began. This is what he believed was achievable when he walked up the path from the parking lot with someone he barely knew, someone who'd never before been friendly. His impression of Dana until now was that she had no interest in him, nor in anyone else from Wells who wasn't Jackie. Today, she'd greeted him warmly, waved, and called him toward her with an encouraging smile.

But it's dark now, and he's alone and on the ground. Slowly, he stands. Brushes off the pine needles from his jeans and as he does he yawns. A primal flexing of a set of tiny, little-used muscles that extend from the back of his throat, behind his ears, down his neck and out through arms and chest. The unexpected spasm possesses and passes through him in an instant, like a fast, unexpected wave overwhelming a small boat, or an exorcism. He turns away from the dark cabin, its blue door closed. Voices rattle the windows. Someone shouts and he begins to walk, avoiding the wobbly rocks that form a circle around the smoldering campfire. Above him the stars dot a dim constellation, scarce lights from the highest ceiling. There is no moon and the trailhead is not visible at the edge of the clearing. His head pounds. Had he been drinking? Did he fall and hit his head? He rubs his face and neck and blinks his eyes to see. Down the hill the sound of a giant boulder

259

dropped from a great height is followed by a quick, faraway whistle. Then another. And another. It's only when a few stray green and red lights shoot above the treetops does he remember what day it is. Where has he been? Why is it dark? He has no answers, yet he's sure he must keep moving. He steps more quickly across the clearing, and above him the sky brightens with Christmas tree colors—red and gold and green and white—the suddenly loud world clapping him on and whistling him forward. The lawn ends and he hears the pop and click of a lesser burst behind him. He turns and sees the cabin lit momentarily from within. There are no lamps on but with each electric pop a small explosion of silver light guts the place, reveals for a split-second the skeleton of openings—windows and door and cracks along the roofline. He does not understand what he sees or hears there but knows he must turn his back to it. The pounding in his head amplifies as the frequency of detonating fireworks accelerates to such a level that it sounds like a house burning, beams and boards popping as sap and air explode, the structure they make collapsing.

He approaches where he thinks the trail begins but sees only trees and bramble. Above him a tinsel sky, behind him murky strangeness, and in between a slowly emerging memory. He lurches into the woods, where he stumbles over roots and stumps, scrapes his hands on sharp bark as he falls. He scrambles to his feet and searches the dark for something familiar—car lights below, the edge of the trail—anything that will lead him back to what he hopes is still home.

Jackie

The walk from Edgeweather to the house she grew up in is still one she can make in the dark. As the lights of the big house recede behind her, Jackie wonders how many Friday nights she watched this road from her living room window, waiting for the Gosses' black Town Car to appear from the city. She'd leave her green knapsack packed with toothbrush, nightgown and changes of underwear next to the front door and when the car passed by, she'd throw it over her shoulder, call out to her parents who were by then in bed, and run out into the night to see her best friend. On most weekends, she wouldn't return home until Sunday evening. On the slow walks back she'd sing the latest song they'd blared on the record player in their third floor bedroom, singing along, again and again, until they knew all the words. The one she remembers now is "The Lion Sleeps Tonight," a song she hasn't thought of in a long time but seems appropriate as she walks in the dark wood. Softly, she sings the opening lyrics, *In the jungle, the mighty jungle* . . . which distracts her from the unsettling memory of Dana's stumbling from the shadows alongside the house minutes before. Jackie was thrown by how desperate she appeared, how vulnerable. And by her remorseful words, the only ones she'd spoken to her today that sounded true. What throws her most now is how sorry she feels for Dana and realizes that if she had simply come to her with an apology that did not attempt to justify her actions or indict anyone else, she would have had very little armor to reject it. Instead, she delivered a briefcase full of riddles and an ominous note to her doorstep and, later, in the first minutes of their reunion, disparaged Floyd and told her that she both knew nothing and was responsible for everything. She can't help but feel foolish to still be surprised, even disappointed, that after all these years, Dana was exactly who she'd always been. Someone who wanted what was not hers, and who, if given the chance, would take or destroy everything that mattered.

Standing next to her old mailbox, Jackie squints to see the only other house she's ever lived in, the house that was now Dana's. But there is only the murky suggestion of a roofline above lifeless and empty space. Her eyes land on nothing. She steps in the direction of her car, and as she does feels an old heaviness return. It weighs on her shoulders and back, presses against her chest. She remembers it arriving the week after Floyd died, and again after each of her parents died; and once, long before—the very first time—when it felt like the end of everything. By now she knows there is nothing she can do to keep it from coming—it will show up, settle in, and stay for as long as it needs to. But in time, gradually, its pressure will lighten, and as with every person and every experience that had come before, some part of it would always be with her.

To the car from the picnic blanket and back should take no more than ten minutes. Ten minutes each way, Jackie figures, one or two minutes to pull out the bag of diapers and jug of iced tea from the trunk. It's possible he ran into someone. Probably Tommy Hall and his cronies from the volunteer fire department. They loved to keep Floyd away from Jackie as long as possible, always pushing him to have a few beers after they'd finished work in the afternoons. Or it could be his sister Hannah or the cousins she ran around with. Everyone in Wells came to Hatch Pond for the

Fourth. The only people she knew wouldn't be here now were her parents, who never came. They were shy and avoided the big town gatherings like this. You'd never run into them at the pancake breakfasts and spaghetti dinners to raise money for the volunteer fire department, or find them sitting in the bleachers at a football game at the high school. She pictured them at home now, watching the evening news, frowning at the coverage of the gathered masses camped out all day along the East River in New York City to get a good view of the fireworks.

She knew where her parents were, but not Floyd. After calculating time to the car and back, running into family or friends from high school, even adding in time to relieve himself in the outhouse or the woods, the longest explainable amount of time she can come up with is an hour. It's been almost two.

They'd arrived after six o'clock for a picnic dinner she had spent yesterday afternoon and this morning preparing. The cooler Floyd carried was filled with beer for him, ginger ale for Jackie, and jars of strained applesauce and pears for Amy. Jackie didn't normally drink much, but she was being especially vigilant now that she was pregnant again. She hadn't told Floyd yet because she wanted to be certain and her appointment with the doctor was still a week away. But she knows. All the signs are there. Her breasts were extremely sensitive again for the first time since she was pregnant with Amy and for the last three weeks she'd teetered on the brink of vomiting every day. She is teetering now. The wind has shifted and seems to be blowing directly from the picnic area at the end of the first field. The smell of grilled meats mingling with the sulfur smoke of cheap firecrackers pushes her over the edge and she vomits less than a foot from where Amy sleeps. She's mortified and as she wipes her face she scans the field to see if anyone has seen. Jackie had insisted they sit at the far edge of the field, so Amy could sleep in the shade, and to be as far away as possible from the noisy families swarming the barbecue pits. There are a few scattered couples and one family more than half the length of the field away, so she's hopeful no one saw. She then worries Floyd will see the mess when he comes back and start asking questions, maybe even guess that she's pregnant, so she stands and rubs it into the grass with her tennis shoe, and to make sure there is no trace, she removes everything from the blanket— the cooler, the food, her bags, Amy—and tugs the blanket back far enough to cover up the damp grass. She then carefully reassembles the picnic as it was, and waits.

It is after eight when she slowly begins to pack Amy's bottle and blue rattle into a bag. She carries the Tupperware with watermelon, the cherry pie, and the basket with the rest of the food and utensils and plates and napkins and puts them all in a neat pile in the grass. She folds the blanket and tucks it under the arm she's using to hold Amy. In her other arm she carries the bag that holds Amy's things. She leaves the cooler behind.

The sun is behind the treetops by the time she makes her way to the end of the parking lot where Floyd parked. The sky is every shade of blue, darkening toward black. She is nearly to the car when she sees the yellow convertible. Next to it, on the ground, is the pink diaper bag.

For the second time that day, she vomits. She's eaten very little since breakfast, none of which has stayed down, so with Amy still in her arms she heaves toward the cracked asphalt but nothing comes out. She wretches violently and begins to panic that in the absence of food in her belly she will vomit the child just beginning to grow inside her. She knows this is ludicrous, but the more powerfully her abdomen and esophagus contract the more convinced she becomes. She forces herself to stand. She steadies as her body calms and she wipes with her free hand the drizzle of bile that has spilled down her lip and chin. Amy is crying now and yet she can't stop staring at the yellow car. Her eyes jump from the wheel well to the license plate to the diaper bag to the jug of tea. None of these things belong together; they are so at odds with her sense of order and place that she drops to one knee fearful she will lose her balance. Amy is squirming in her arm, her screams furious. She has not had her diaper changed in over an hour, and the consequences are now joining the nearby smells that upset Jackie's stomach earlier. She grabs the bag on the ground next to her and struggles to stand.

On the drive home, Jackie remembers the morning years ago at Floyd's family's farm—his blue shirt, the yellow car she'd convinced herself was not Dana's flashing onto the road behind the green barn.

Of course she'd wanted to conquer Floyd. He was something money couldn't buy and he was Jackie's. As children, Dana hadn't been competitive but she was possessive. She didn't want to hear about other girls in Wells. At any age she'd known her, Dana managed to always steer what they talked about back to their childhood games—the music they loved and memorized, the TV shows they watched religiously, the Knees, the river stones, the adventures they had in the woods. When they were together she wanted only to be in their world. Anything outside it threatened her. Jackie had noticed all this but it wasn't clear to her until the night of her prom. The evening had been a disaster. Dana wanted to dance, but only with Jackie. She wanted to have their portrait taken together and she made a spectacle of it. She ignored everyone at their table and if asked a question answered loudly and dramatically and only faced Jackie as she did so. Eventually she hijacked the photographer, who drove her home.

After the prom, Jackie cooled toward Dana and avoided her in the weeks that followed. When school let out for the summer Dana came up from the city and the two of them fell into their old routines—lying out on the back patio lounges listening to the radio, watching TV on the third floor at Edgeweather. They watched whatever was on, mostly reruns, because it was the summer. Jackie liked *That Girl* and *The Flying Nun*, which Dana put up with but thought both Marlo Thomas and Sally Field were corny idiots. They both loved *The Ed Sullivan Show* and *Peyton Place*, though they were devastated when Mia Farrow didn't come back in the third season. Since they didn't have friends in common, the girls talked about celebrities as if they went to school with them. They had wildly different and conflicting opinions about them all—Dana worshipped Joel Grey, Jackie thought he was creepy; Jackie loved Paul McCartney, Dana dismissed him as a fake and by their junior year was bored of the Beatles altogether and only had ears for the Rolling Stones, a band Jackie thought was trashy. And so on.

Squabbles marked their friendship from the beginning so the first noticeable shift in the summer of 1966, between their junior and senior years in high school, was that they gradually became polite with each other. After years of arguing passionately over disputes as trivial as whether Marlon Brando or James Garner had the best chin or which was more refreshing, iced tea or lemonade, they gave up trying to convince or prove anything to the other. They also became more secretive. When Jackie told Dana about Floyd kissing her for the first time, Dana rolled her eyes. After that, Jackie barely mentioned him and Dana didn't ask.

The summer after they graduated from high school, Dana came to Jackie's wedding in a black suit and brought an antique umbrella stand that Jackie was sure she'd last seen under a mirror in the foyer at Edgeweather. She'd fashioned a white silk scarf into a sloppy bow, tied it to one of its spindles and put it on top of the table where the presents were piled, and shouted in an English accent, *For your brollies, mum.* Jackie recognized the scarf right away as one Dana had worn constantly her sophomore year. At the small reception Dana kept to herself but after the cake was cut, she managed a barbed apology as she made her exit, *If the nuptials weren't planned at such breakneck speed I might have had a little more time to consider what to get you.*

Driving home from Hatch Pond, Jackie remembers something Floyd's sister, Hannah, said to her after she'd found out they'd gotten engaged. She and Floyd were standing by his truck in the driveway at the farm. A friend had dropped her off, and as she stumbled from the car, clearly drunk, she steadied long enough to look Jackie directly in the eyes and slur, *You don't fool around, do you? Locked it all down before the stupid lug had a chance to think about it. Seems like yesterday you needed a ride home from my birthday party. Dainty!*

She'd dismissed the outburst as the drunken ramblings of a protective sister. Now she considered her words more seriously. She *had* moved fast, let herself get pregnant, and encouraged Floyd to consider marriage the only possible option given the circumstances. She also chose to dismiss the strange morning at the farm along with dozens of moments when she saw his head turn and his eyes follow girls at school, or at the town beach. This was what men were like, she'd said to herself. Her father notwithstanding, she knew by then that men were susceptible in ways that women were not once they'd chosen who they wanted to be with. It was, she believed, before women had chosen, when they were still assessing their options, when they were most dangerous, and she was becoming aware that more and more women were choosing to delay making a choice. Some were rejecting making a choice at all, simply wallowing in their options, indefinitely. Jackie knew perfectly well that many of Dana's friends, like Dana herself, were in this last lethal category.

Jackie parks the car in front of the garage, gathers Amy, and leaves the picnic food and blankets and dishes in the trunk. Amy is limp in her arms as she crosses the driveway and climbs the front steps to the house. Once inside, she switches the porch light off after she shuts the door behind her. He can trip on the steps, she thinks, break his neck for all I care. But after two steps into the hallway, she stops and turns back. She stands with Amy in her arms until she begins to sway gently with exhaustion. She is now a wife who wishes her husband to break his neck on the outside stairs. Of everything that's happened that day, this is what instigates tears: the transformation of something she wanted so badly—a happy marriage, a loving husband, a family—into something hateful. There is nothing Floyd can say that will make it right between them, but she is not prepared to be that woman. Before she turns back toward the hallway to put Amy to sleep, she reaches her hand out and flips the switch. She may not want to share a bed with or speak a civil word to Floyd for a long time, but tonight she will leave the light on.

After she puts Amy in her crib, Jackie retreats to her bedroom. It's the first night she will sleep alone since she and Floyd rented the house. She switches the lamp next to her side of the bed and walks slowly toward the bathroom. At the sink, she goes through the motions of brushing her teeth, wiping her face with a cool washcloth, and changing into her nightgown.

In bed, she twists the lamp switch off and right away notices she's left the window that faces the front yard open, the shades up. She begins to wriggle out from the sheets and the light cotton blanket to get out of bed and close them, but something catches her eye and she stops. The leaves on the elm tree outside flutter up and down in the breeze, catching the porch light like a school of fish blazing as they bank through an underwater sunbeam. She cannot make sense of what she is seeing and for a few seconds remains spellbound, still. As Jackie's eyes gradually adjust to the dark she begins to identify the gnarled trunk, the old low boughs rising at steep angles into the moonless night. She remembers the tree's age and in her mind caresses the number like a child would clutch a beloved stuffed animal, or how when she was a kid she rubbed her twenty-five cent allowance between her thumb and pointer finger until the coin and her hand were both damp with sweat.

An abrupt wind blasts and the leaves flap up again to expose their silver bellies. Faint, faraway thunder rumbles like logs rolling from a pile. Jackie fixes her eyes again on the tree's thick haunches. Older than anyone living, she reminds herself, waiting for the appearance of lightning or the sound of louder thunder. Older than every house in Wells. Every tree, too. Older than Dana and Floyd combined. Older than airplanes and phones and television and cars. Older than Edgeweather. Older than the Fourth of July.

Jackie shuts her eyes and scooches down into the middle of the bed, her body now completely covered by the sheet and blanket. Outside, she hears the muffled crack of an exploding firework. A small animal skitters across the roof. Jackie's stomach, still sour from vomiting before, rumbles and whines. Just empty, she thinks defensively, as if someone had suggested something more serious.

Another firework goes off. Minutes later, another. Eventually, the erratic bursts—explosions she is sure she can feel rattle the house, despite the four and a half miles to Hatch Pond—are followed by a rat-a-tat-tat sequence of fast pops that sound like mortar fire. The blasts accelerate and are soon punctuated by louder, more significant explosions. The finale, she remembers, closing her eyes, the part of the night that had always been for her the whole point. She imagines women and children sprawled across the first and second lawns, on blankets, in aluminum folding chairs covered with strips of brightly colored nylon; men mingling in the parking lots, drinking and smoking and mumbling imperceptibly; couples squeezing into each other, looking out over the water from the end of the wobbly dock. She sees them from above, as if she is seeing them all for the last time. Their heads lift, their faces turn toward her, and when she recognizes no one she unleashes her pyrotechnic fury. So many explosions at once, so fast upon the next they become one explosion, one sound, one angry point in the sky for everyone to see and feel as it rips the air with hate. Let them look. All of them. Both of them. Dana. Let her watch as she explodes in the sky. Let the fiery matter that Jackie once was rain down on her treacherous head, scorch her porcelain skin, singe her hair, destroy her duplicitous face.

Outside, the world goes quiet. Jackie pictures the people of Wells, their necks still stretched to the sky, their eyes hungry for more spectacle, their ears straining to be shocked. She can almost hear them groan with disappointment when nothing comes, feel them hesitate in the ordinary dark, reluctant to pack up their coolers, fold their blankets, stub out their cigarettes, finish their beers and return home. She clutches her pillow with both arms, bunches the thin cotton casing in her fists and pulls it from under her head, down below her chest, to her belly. She has not felt nauseous since she returned home, but now feels a sharp cramp radiating from her pelvis to her lower back. She has not eaten but she feels full, uncomfortably bloated; at the same time, she feels perspiration beading across her brow, down her temples and between her breasts. Hot now, her whole body dampening with sweat, she kicks off the sheet and blanket. The bloating sharpens into cramps that feel like knives stabbing into her abdomen, behind her hips and pelvis. They strike with alarming force and leave her immobile in a fevered heap, clutching her knees to her chest. Eventually, she rolls from the bed to her feet and makes her way down the hall to the kitchen phone. As if expecting the call, her mother picks up on the first ring.

Jackie returns to the bare bed and waits. She knows what will happen. Her mother will arrive, still in bedclothes and the same white bathrobe with pale blue piping she's worn in the summer months since Jackie was a girl. She will rummage in the hall closet for a hand towel, run it under cold water in the bathroom sink, and with it wipe the sweat from Jackie's face and neck and arms and legs before covering her with a thin nylon windbreaker and guiding her out the front door to her car. Because the hospital is less than a three-minute drive down the hill, neither she nor Jackie will hesitate to leave Amy in her crib where she'll sleep at least another four hours. The attending ER doctor will tell them what she already knows; that the life that had only recently started to grow inside her is gone. And eventually, if there hadn't been any yet, there would be blood. Her mother will agree to tell no one, not even Jackie's father, though she will tell him the moment she gets home. He will never, not even once, let on that he knows. In the morning, Jackie will call Scott at the hardware store in town to come and change the locks on the garage, front, and back doors. This will be the only part Floyd will find out about. And Dana will no longer exist. The two of them will know the consequences but only half their crimes. *None of your business*, Jackie will answer every time either one of them, or anyone, demands an explanation for her severity. Dana will insist on an explanation just the one time; and Floyd for weeks will holler and plead and write a note in black magic marker on the back of a brown Trotta's grocery bag and slip it under the locked front door, *What have I done*, it will say in enormous letters without question mark or punctuation.

All this will happen, but before it does she must wait for her mother to come, lie jackknifed and writhing on a bed she will no longer share.

The wind kicks up again and through the open window she hears the chatter of branches and the squall of ravished leaves. It roars on and on, a great whooshing sound, like static on a television set after the last broadcast, or the pounding surf she and Dana were afraid to swim in three summers ago in Rhode Island. She's never heard anything that sounded so powerful, or so lonely. Nearly everything she had counted on—Floyd, a second child, a happy marriage, even Dana—was now gone. Replaced with pain almost as excruciating as labor, but worse because of what it signaled, not a beginning, as with Amy, but the end.

Above the house, the night air moves between branches, hisses through the high, vast canopy that has swayed there for centuries. The hiss builds to a howl and in it Jackie thinks she can almost hear a voice, singing notes and words to a song she does not know. The sound is neither male nor female and it soars high and loud, escalates from voice to siren, and while it does the hairs on her arms and legs prickle to attention. At its apex, it overwhelms every other sound, inside the house and out, and then collapses to one high, thin, ragged note. It reminds Jackie of the crude flutes she and Dana used to make from paper when they were kids. All that was needed was a plain sheet ripped from a notebook, a pair of scissors and tape, and no matter how many times they made them, Jackie was always surprised that from such simple, everyday materials, music could happen.

Soon there is only the sound of wind-ruffed leaves. Again, she detects the traces of a voice, speaking this time, not singing, but as before, she cannot make out the words, nor determine the sort of message they make—a warning, a secret, an instruction of some kind. Eventually, the wind calms, the tree stills, and just as myste-riously as the voice began, it stops.

The night turns quiet again. Jackie rolls onto her back hoping to relieve the pressure on her abdomen, but the pain there only sharpens. She listens for sounds outside, but beyond the dreary commotion of crickets there are none. With compounding regret, she wonders what it was she was supposed to hear. Something important, she decides, dread rising as the plain beams of her mother's headlights sweep across the wall above her bed. Some-thing she needed to know.

Lupita

She's beyond the break. Shoved by invisible hands into the busy water past the reef's edge, toward open ocean. Saltwater burns her eyes and nose and throat and sloshes in her stomach despite her best efforts to keep it out. Across the low light of morning, she scans the shore for the hedge and roofline of her cottage but she's drifted too far out and down now, beyond Makahoa Point, which marks the end of Hanalei Beach. After the Point there are a half a dozen beaches and a few spits of sand between headlands, and then only jagged lava thorning the narrow shore along the Napaali Coast. She knows that to thrash against the pull here will do her in, so she points her exhausted body toward what looks like the widest stretch of sand and moves with a current she hopes will carry her there.

In her flight from the big house—out the service door, across the short lawn and driveway to the garage—Lupita tried to erase what had happened. With each hard slap of her boots against the grass and asphalt, she willed the hour and all in it away.

And then the next morning, Ada at her bedside, poking her awake, pinching her shoulder, the words *How could you* barely audible, more statement than question. *You were there?* Lupita asked, still disbelieving, then horrified for a flash that Ada had somehow been involved in what happened, another arrangement made for the Gosses. Ada's response—standing from her crouch, tears spilling from her eyes, repeating the same three words as she stepped away—made clear her involvement was no less or more than what it was. Which was worse, her sister believing she'd willingly lay on Dana's bed with Mr. Goss or her sister seeing what had actually happened and choosing not to help her. Either was too awful to accept. At the door, Ada paused, still looking toward Lupita but not meeting her eyes. It seemed as if she was about to say something; but just then their father shouted from the kitchen. And she was gone.

After Memorial Day weekend, Ada returned to the city and soon moved to Palm Beach to work in the Gosses' house there. Mr. Goss mostly stayed in the city until the end of summer, which was unusual, but his absences went without comment and no one seemed bothered. The one weekend when he did join his wife and daughter, Lupita stayed in bed and told her mother she had a headache and could not work in the big house. She didn't care whether or not she believed her, there was no force that could put her in that house with him. This was the last weekend in June. By then she'd not had her period for five weeks and for the three days prior she'd been struck with fits of debilitating vertigo and nausea. She knew she was pregnant. Even as she prayed to the Virgin and to her grandmother to tell her what to do, she took for granted they would turn their backs on her if she chose not to have the baby. From what her mother and Ada had told her, her grandmother had assisted with hundreds of births. In the instances when there was a stillbirth or a pregnancy she could not save, she would light candles and pray for the lost soul to find its way. Lupita could recall the sound but not the words of her prayers, an impression of her sadness. She imagined more than remembered her saying the same unforgiving words she'd heard her mother speak more than once, *Lo único peor que un niño muerto es aquel que es asesinado por su madre.*

In her last months at St. Margaret's, Lupita had disappeared into studying for her final exams and completing her term papers. With money she'd saved from birthday presents and money the Goss family had paid her over the years for helping at the big house, she bought a suitcase from the Sears catalog. A flame red plastic Samsonite with metal snaps. She gave her father the money, he wrote a check, and they sent the carefully filled-out order form in the mail. And then she waited—for the suitcase to arrive, to graduate from high school, for the end of the summer—without a plan, only fear that her stomach would bulge before she'd figured out what to do.

The morning before the Fourth of July, Dana called Edgeweather from New York. Lupita answered the phone in the manner her mother had instructed. *Goss residence, Lupita speaking.*

Oh, it's you. Dana sounded startled.

How can I help?, Lupita said, as politely as she could.

Ok. Right . . . well . . . Here you are. Perhaps . . . you just might . . . she sounded unsure, as if she was forming a plan on the fly.

Excuse me?

Dana reclaimed her authority. *It's last minute, I know, but I need to organize some food to bring to a pal's place tomorrow . . . it's just up the hill from the town beach and you can see the fireworks above the trees. Could you organize some deviled eggs and whatever else people eat on the Fourth of July?*

Lupita was silent as Dana continued with a proposal: *If you get going on all that today and pack up the car tomorrow, I'll then drive everything over.*

For the first time, the words Mr. Goss spoke to her that morning returned, *Let's help each other out. You're obviously curious.*

Lupita froze. She'd forgotten whom she was speaking to for

a moment and then when she remembered she couldn't make sense of what was being said.

Hello? Dana's voice poked from the receiver. *Lupita, what's going on? Are you there?*

And her father's returned. *Maybe we can solve this.*

Lupita?

She struggled to respond, *By organize . . . you mean . . .*

Excuse me? The play in Dana's voice was gone.

Lupita recovered, with forced civility. *What I mean . . . I didn't know if you meant for me to buy deviled eggs or make them. I can do either.*

The world having righted itself, Dana softened, *I'm sure what you make will be better than anything at the grocery store. I'll see you tomorrow. PLEASE don't let me down. And never mind about telling my mother. I'll find her.*

Lupita returned the phone to its cradle. She stood in the short hall off the foyer where an elegant half oval table held a heavy black phone and a small bowl of white peonies. She'd picked the flowers that morning from the long bed outside the library and with Q-tips, delicately rid each bloom of ants, something Ada had taught her to do last summer. Somewhere upstairs her mother was ironing sheets. In the library, Mrs. Goss listened to opera on the stereo system while she received a manicure and pedicure from the middle-aged woman who drove up from Kent once a week in the summer. The citrus smell of the peonies was strong. The aroma of bacon wafting from the kitchen mingled in the damp botanical air. Lupita's stomach swerved but the terror of having to explain a sudden mess kept it under control.

In the evening, after driving up from the city, Dana called the Lopezes' apartment to check in on progress. Before hanging up, she asked Lupita if she wouldn't mind coming with her the next day to lend a hand carrying things from the car, setting and cleaning up. *Who knows what we'll find up there*, she said, as if they'd gone on many such outings before, *but with two of us I'm sure we'll manage. Oh, and wear something festive. Maybe you'll even have fun.*

Dana had never before asked Lupita to do anything for or with her. As a girl, she would have been ecstatic to have been asked to do just about anything with Dana. But they weren't little girls anymore and this was obviously not an overture of friendship. It was work. Though usually when there were jobs to do at the big house she did not interact with Dana. All the directives came through Lupita's parents and, once in a while, Ada. Mrs. Goss was the one she saw the most, but only ever when she was stripping beds, folding laundry or doing light housework; for the most part she avoided Lupita, save to say a friendly but distant *Good morning* or *Oh, hello* if by chance they were caught in the same room alone together.

The next day, Lupita half-heartedly put a basket of food together. A jar of pickles, two bags of potato chips and a plate of deviled eggs. Dana found her in the kitchen to tell her to bring the car to the house at five-thirty and they'd go from there. It was almost one and she'd clearly just woken up. Lupita avoided looking at her, so at first she didn't notice the robe. She was slicing a boiled egg in half when she looked up and saw the cream-colored silk, the silver and black stitched clouds, the long sash. Dana was at that moment turning to leave and as she did the dragon came into view. *I know you know how to drive*, she teased coldly over her shoulder as she left, the serpent crouched upon her back, its mug glaring. This is when she cut herself. The small kitchen knife she was using sliced the pad of her right thumb, but she did not notice right away. By the time she looked down at what she was doing, the bowl filled with yolks she'd taken from the halved eggs was splattered in blood. After she'd bandaged her thumb, hastily made another batch of eggs, and cleaned up the kitchen, she walked the picnic basket out to the garage and shoved it in the back seat of Dana's convertible. It was already almost eighty-five degrees outside and there would be at least a few more hours before they drove to Hatch Pond, but Lupita didn't care if the eggs went bad.

Makahoa Point is behind her now and she's passed Wainiha Bay. As far as she has drifted from the long half-moon of Hanalei Beach, she's somehow managed to avoid sharks and jellyfish and stay near enough to shore that she's not been carried out to sea. But as close as she is—no more than a few hundred feet from the short beach after the bay and before the long underwater fortress of reefs—she is powerless to cross the distance. She can see cars fly past on the Kuhio Highway, but the ocean does not want to let her go. Outside the reef there will only be a few more shots to come in. Her vision begins to wobble and she feels sleepy, her eyelids heavy. The water continues to shove her further out and she resists the strong pull to shut her eyes, go limp and drift. She figures if she can stay alert long enough to clear the reef and slip from the current before it launches her past Ka'llio Point, she still has a chance.

A lanky southern girl named Louise dressed in what looked like pink tennis clothes was the first to complain about the spoiled eggs. *Who made these?*, she whined after spitting into a paper towel. Lupita said nothing. Peter Beldon, who'd organized the party, pretended not to hear. Dana, minutes after they'd reached the cabin, had vanished back down the steep path saying she'd left something behind in the car. There were only four other people there: Peter Beldon, Louise, Peter's roommate, Oscar, and another boy their age named Bart who piled sticks and fallen branches from the woods into a circle of stones arranged a short distance from the cabin.

There was no electricity or running water, but Peter had shown them an old water pump at the wood line. Inside, there were kerosene lanterns for light, and blankets in case it got cold after dark. He'd bragged that his family, in one form or another, had owned the place since his great-great-grand-something was one of the first senators from Connecticut. Louise and Oscar followed Peter past the blue door into the cabin and Lupita ducked around the side of the building where she found a half-rotted wood swing strung with rope from a thick, almost perfectly horizontal limb of an old oak. She waited there for Dana to come back up the mountain and scold her, or give her the silent treatment at least, for the spoiled eggs. Since she and Dana began the half-hour climb up the hill from the town beach, she kept asking herself why she'd agreed to come, and why Dana had asked her in the first place. It didn't make sense, but very little did lately.

Lupita knew she would not attend Albertus Magnus in the fall but was pretending to her parents and to herself that she still was. On days when she didn't feel sick she would momentarily forget that she was pregnant and then, with a wave of nausea, remember. Her body had not yet begun to thicken and swell but she'd begun to feel strangely full even if she hadn't eaten anything. She also needed to go to the bathroom all of a sudden and many times a day. Her body was shifting rapidly in ways she could feel, sometimes acutely, but the changes were not yet noticeable to those around her. Freshman orientation started the week before Labor Day, so she calculated that she had until the middle of August to make a plan. In a late-night panic she considered returning to Catemaco to find relatives to take her in. She was sure she could cross the border legally now since less than three years before, she and her family had finally gone to Hartford to stand in a library where they'd pledged an oath to the United States with twenty or so other people, none of whom looked like they were from Mexico. They all left with certificates of naturalization which their father kept in a photo album on the dresser in his bedroom. Still, with the freedom to now return, something she'd wanted to do for so long after they first came to Florida and even after they'd moved to work for the Gosses, she had no way of getting there. She had no car, nothing close to the amount of money needed for a bus or plane ticket. Even if she could somehow get down there, she knew her relatives would call her parents. She had $16 left from the money she'd saved, no options, no one to confide in or ask for help, and here she was at a picnic in the woods with rich college kids. People like Dana, who would never know, not for one freezing cold second of their quilted lives, what it was like to be as cornered and alone as she was now.

In the car on the way to the pond, they barely spoke. When Dana turned onto Route 7 from Undermountain Road, she reminded Lupita for the second time that day of their drive two years ago. *The last time we were in the car together, you were the one driving. Don't you remember?* She chose not to answer, hoping Dana might take the hint and stop talking. Which she did, until they were getting out of the car at Hatch Pond. She'd eyed Lupita from top to toe, taking her in with sudden and exacting scrutiny: her two thick ponytails, her green shorts, and the yellow and orange checkered blouse with thin white spaghetti straps, the only thing in her closet that could meet Dana's *festive* standards. *Good*, she'd declared, her eyes then quickly moving on, sweeping the parking lot and near field.

Lupita saw Floyd before he found her. He came around the side of the cabin looking precisely as he had the last time she'd seen him. Strong, kind, untroubled and young. There was something particular about his loping gait, the proportions of his limbs and torso and his tidy but still roughed hair. He was, as he had been before, beautiful. He was also clearly in a hurry and nervous, scanning up and down along the wood line and then back again. He even glanced up, into the trees, as if who or what he was looking for could be found there. Wearing a light blue T-Shirt and old jeans, he looked like a boy still in high school. No one had ever seemed so far away.

When Floyd spotted her, she knew she should leave. Nothing good could come from talking to him now. But it was too late. He waved hello and started to jog toward her. As much as she knew she should run as fast and as far away as she could from him, she felt a desperate urge to tell him everything. But she thought of Jackie, and the daughter she'd given birth to soon after they'd married. She reminded herself that she had no place in Floyd's life, that they did not know each other beyond a few childish kisses. But she was trapped, and here was the one person with whom she'd willingly shared a secret. *Hi*, he said, as he approached, his jog slowing. *You ok?*, his face shifting from excitement to concern.

She didn't know how to answer without saying too much, the potential consequences were too great. Not for herself or even for Jackie and her daughter, but for her parents, and Ada.

Hey, you all right? I'm going to have to leave in a minute—I agreed to help Dana bring some things up the hill—she told me you were here . . . I wanted . . . well . . . I just thought I'd . . .

She wondered if Floyd had just spoken more words to her than he had the night two years ago at the bottom of this very hill and the morning after. They'd barely spoken at his farm. She had no idea what to say now.

Can I show you something?, he asked, filling the silence. *It will only take a minute.* She nodded and stood and he motioned her to the wood line. *We used to come up here all the time in high school*, he explained, sounding nostalgic and pointing to a well-trod deer run that appeared between blueberry bushes. *Drinking beers and killing time. I only got a minute but you should see it . . . I'll bet none of these knuckleheads you're hanging around with today have any idea what's back here. C'mon.* As Lupita stepped over a fallen branch and wobbled momentarily, Floyd's hand gripped the bare skin above her elbow to help steady her. She startled violently, as if electrocuted, her arms flying up and over her chest. At the moment his hand made contact she grunted a high frightened sound that she'd only ever heard come from her throat once before. She was shaking, her heart slammed hard and she could feel sweat beading down her body. After a few seconds, her panic dissipated, and she was mortified. *I'm sorry*, she managed. Floyd looked more surprised than Lupita and seemed to be trying to understand what had just happened, *Ok . . . ok now . . . didn't mean to scare you . . . Just wanted to help you there . . . let's go have a quick look and I'll get going.* He stepped past her on the path, put five or so feet of distance between them before pressing ahead through the forest of birch trees.

Lupita tried to still her shaking hands and slow her breathing, but it was useless. More and more over the last weeks, her body was operating on its own, against her will. She focused on the back of Floyd's T-shirt, the perspiration wetting the space between his shoulder blades and behind his armpits. She watched him brush against a dead branch and knock it to the ground. As her body slowly calmed, she wished they would never stop walking, continue on to Vermont, to Canada, clear to the other side of the world. Even as she imagined this she realized how childish the fantasy was, how it didn't include the baby that would be born, the one she knew she would not love, even if Floyd promised to. Again, she wanted to tell him. If anyone would be willing to help her, it was him. And what were the odds, of all the times they could have met again in the two years since they last spoke, that he would appear now, in the least likely company, at her most des-

perate moment. Her courage swarmed. He was here. She started
to speak as they crossed into a clearing. *I need to . . .*

Here we are!, Floyd announced, interrupting her, stopping
sharply when he realized what he'd done. *Hey, I'm sorry . . . I didn't
hear . . . And anyway, this is it. That's all I wanted to say.* If his face was
flushed before, it was on fire now, slick with sweat. As he wiped
his left hand across his forehead and down his drenched neck, she
noticed his wedding ring for the first time, its metal sparking in
the late-day light.

I didn't . . . it was nothing, she sputtered, and looked past him to
the reason he'd brought her here.

The ledge they stood on dropped off sharply behind Floyd
and left an unobstructed view. He motioned her forward, out to
the edge, below which were the woods they'd hiked through earlier, and past the woods, the town beach. Lupita stepped closer
and could see down to the pavilion, the white shed between the
fire-pits and the parking lot, and the short dock that stretched
into the algaed water. They were close enough to see people
spread out on blankets and gathered around the coolers, but far
enough away to make it impossible to see who they were. Lupita
wondered which one was Jackie.

On the other side of the pond, a low hill with white clapboard
houses dotted with shuttered windows and chimneys rose toward
three church steeples, a clock tower and a flagpole that appeared
above the tree line. Lupita had never seen the town from a distance like this and at first she didn't recognize it. It looked so
tidy and contained, as if each building and landmark had been
compressed into a painting. If she hadn't lived there for most of
her life she'd have thought it looked like the perfect town, a place
where nothing bad could happen.

Pretty cool, huh?, Floyd said, as if trying to convince her that
where they'd grown up, and not just the view, was better than it

was. Lupita looked down toward the beach and the people she would not miss. The blond and freckled children of Wells who'd let her know when she came from Florida nine years ago that she didn't belong. Floyd had not seen her then, just as he hadn't seen her in the years after, even though they'd gone to the same elementary school. She was invisible to him until she was someone who could be kissed behind sheds and barns. And here they were, she began to recognize, alone again, in the woods, out of sight.

I need to get back, Lupita blurted abruptly and turned to locate the path they'd taken. Before he could respond, she rushed from where they stood, her body once again taking control, carrying her away as fast as it could into the woods.

She's missed her chance at shore. Shot past the beaches between Kolokolo, Kepuhi and Ha'ena Points and for as far as she can see there is blinding whitewash breaking over the reefs that stretch without interruption to the far end of Maniniholo Bay. As long as there is a reef between her and the beach, there is no chance of making it in without being shredded on the coral. Water swells and slaps at her from all sides. She needs to make it to the other side of Ka'ilio Point, past long sandy Ke'e Beach which she's sure is barricaded by reef. After Ke'e there is no approachable land until Hanakapi'ai where, she remembers, there is a waterfall coming off the steep cliffs at the back of a small beach. She'd been there a dozen times after hiking down off the Kalalau trail. She knows the approach to shore from the water there is clear because all that separates the beach from open ocean is sand and a lethal riptide notorious for dragging haole tourists to their deaths.

* * *

She did not see Floyd again until after she'd joined Peter and the others around the fire. *We were starting to get worried*, Peter said seriously and with what sounded like genuine concern. Oscar cleared a place on the log next to him, and Lupita, not knowing what else to do or where to go, took a seat. She wondered but did not ask where Dana was. The four friends resumed their talk of concerts and vacations and the draft they'd taken care to avoid. Floyd appeared a few minutes later, looking confused and serious. He approached where Lupita was seated, and brushed past Oscar whose face and neck and arms were flame red with a rash he'd just described defensively to the group was caused by an allergic reaction to the cheap vodka Peter was using for the drinks. Floyd accidently grazed his shoulder, which caused the boy to lurch abruptly, fumble his drink and spill it across Lupita's shoulders and down the front of her blouse. Everyone around the fire froze until Floyd stooped protectively toward Lupita which prompted Oscar to shove him off and bark, *What the hell do you think you're doing?*

Suddenly, they were brawling. Shoving and grunting and throwing punches, which mostly did not land. Peter and Bart shot up and each grabbed one of Floyd's arms to pull him off Oscar whose face was red not only with rash now, but with blood from his nose. Floyd wriggled free and was grappling with Peter when Bart grabbed the camera strap from behind him and began to pull tightly. His grip on the strap was firm and though Floyd at one point spun him on his back to shake him loose it only managed to expel his energy and before long he collapsed. Lupita screamed and ran toward the men but by that point Floyd was unconscious. *What did you do?*, she hollered as Bart pulled the camera from around his neck and put it on the ground. *Relax, I'm in medical school*, he said as he felt Floyd's neck and wrist and guided his head toward a place on the pine-needled ground. *He'll be fine. Just going to be asleep a little while. Is he a friend of yours? Swell chap.*

Lupita backed away from where Floyd lay and sat down against the cabin. From there, she could see his chest rise and fall and so she knew he was alive, like Bart said. The blue door then burst open and Dana rushed at Peter, demanding he explain what had happened. Lupita watched as she raised her arm and stabbed a finger at him, the sun's last light dancing on her bracelets and watch, the rest of her in shadow. She remembered the silk dragon, its haughty shine as it scowled from Dana's back just a few hours before. The day that followed flashed in the twitching fire: the steep climb up the hill, Dana's excusing herself as soon as they arrived, Floyd appearing behind the cabin, as if on cue, asking if she was ok, her violent reaction when he touched her, the view from the ledge, and now Dana, emerging from the cabin. *Wear something festive*, she'd instructed on the phone last night, and this morning teased again about their car ride two years ago, the one when she insisted on knowing every detail of every minute she'd spent with Floyd. He'd mentioned that Dana had asked him to help carry things up the hill, but Lupita knew that by then there was nothing left in the car she couldn't have easily carried on her own.

As she watched Dana interrogate Peter and snap at Bart to stop interrupting her, something flashed in her peripheral vision. Past the others, toward the trailhead, she saw Peter's girlfriend, Louise. She was moving slowly and from her neck hung Floyd's camera. At first it looked like she was fleeing the scene, but when she stopped and fiddled with the lens, and then raised the Kodak to her eye, it was clear she wanted to record it. She pointed the black and silver device toward Floyd's collapsed body, past the fire, to the cabin. Lupita tipped her face to the ground and pretended to disappear. *Thief*, she mouthed, as the shutter clicked.

Soon after, Dana convinced Lupita to come inside the cabin to clean off her blouse. They dabbed the cotton with damp towels and as Lupita stood to go outside again she was seized by a wave of nausea. She retreated to one of the bedrooms to lie down until it passed and without intending to, she fell asleep. At some point later, she woke to find everyone inside the cabin, drinking and carrying on. When she didn't see Floyd, she rushed outside, but there was no sign of him. When she asked the others, they had no idea when or where he'd gone. She couldn't believe he'd been left alone—unconscious, in the dark, no one bothering to check on him. She paced the perimeter of the clearing looking for any sign and insisted that Peter and the others look, too. No one budged.

Enraged, Lupita gathered their picnic gear and shot toward the trailhead. *He's already home, safe and sound*, Dana called as she hurried behind her into the woods, sounding shaky despite her forced cheer and attempt to regain authority. Slowly, they made their way down the hill—Dana shining a flashlight, Lupita carrying a wicker basket clunky with soiled plates and napkins and good silver from the kitchen at Edgeweather. And with it, Floyd's Kodak.

It would take Lupita more than three years to develop the film in Floyd's camera. When she did she was relieved there were no photographs of Jackie or their daughter. It must have been a new roll that Floyd or Jackie had put in the camera expressly to photograph their July Fourth picnic. Most of the photographs were blurry and poorly lit images of Peter and the others drinking and horsing around inside the cabin. There was only one that Lupita didn't immediately throw away. In it, the late-day light obscured Peter, Bart, and Dana's faces as they stood to the left of the campfire, arguing. On the other side of the fire lay Floyd, with close-cropped hair, wearing a light blue short-sleeved

T-shirt and jeans. His thick arms limp at his sides, his hands still clenched. There was something wrong about the angle of his torso in relation to the rest of his body, the way his head and face flopped onto the pine-needled ground. Behind him stood the log cabin with its red metal roof and dark blue door, half-open. Against the cabin, Lupita crouched, her face buried in her arms, crossed above her knees—one hand, the one with a bandaged thumb, held her elbow, the other at her shoulder, grabbed the exposed flesh there as tightly as Floyd squeezed his fingers into white-knuckled fists.

Lupita looked at the photograph only a few times before ripping it to pieces. It evoked too potent a mix of conflicting feelings to keep around. Besides the life she lived in Kauai, it was the only physical evidence she had of that strange night born of Dana's mischief—a night that had inadvertently given her what she needed most at that time: a way out.

Lupita waited as long as she could before calling Dana at school. A girl she'd overheard in the bathroom at St. Margaret's said that it was common knowledge that it took at least six weeks to know that you were pregnant. For Lupita, it had taken four, but she knew that when she called Dana there could be no room for doubt. She didn't know how Dana could help, or even if she would, but if there was any chance at all, Lupita knew that she needed to be believed. She was.

When Dana drove her to the airport in Philadelphia from Lee's farm, she'd asked her where she wanted to go. *Kauai* was Lupita's answer. She didn't know anything about the place beyond what she'd once heard one of the nuns at St. Margaret's say: that it was the farthest place one could go and still be in the United States. After Dana bought her ticket at the TWA counter, it took three flights and two days to get to Lihue Airport. This was the first time Lupita had flown. When she felt the engines move the plane with increasing force down the runway and shove it into the sky, she experienced her first moment of relief since the morning in Dana's bedroom before Mr. Goss appeared. She knew the boy was safe now, with someone who could love him; and she was beyond her family's reach, untouched by their judgment and punishments. She'd left them a note the morning Dana drove her to Lee's farm in Pennsylvania. It was on a piece of spiral bound notebook paper from school, folded in half and left on the kitchen table. There was nothing she could say to make it right, so she wrote, *Thank you for everything you've done for me. I am sorry. Love, Lupita.*

On the plane, she imagined the physical distance widening between her and the life she was leaving—Wells, her family, St. Margaret's, her college scholarship, Edgeweather, Floyd. She pushed the button on her armrest and tilted her seat back, the rattling fuselage, the velocity, the miracle of breaking from the earth's surface—all of it together like a long-awaited narcotic flooding her veins. She had no idea what lay ahead, and for the first time in nine months, she did not care.

When she arrived in Lihue, she had seven thousand dollars in cash tucked behind the lining of her suitcase. Before she'd left for the airport, Lee had come to her door and handed her a pale pink cosmetics bag with a copper-colored zipper. *This should get you started, wherever you go. My advice is to get a job immediately and stay away from men for a while. When you know where you want to be, use the money to help buy yourself a place to live. Somewhere that is yours, no one else's, and that you can afford without too much struggle.*

When Lupita came to the farm, she had at first avoided Lee. She was Mr. Goss's sister, and she feared she'd call him and he'd turn up without warning. Nothing frightened her more. Not even her father. Each night on the farm, she checked and double-checked that the front and back doors, and the windows, of the small cottage she slept in were locked. She trusted no one, especially Lee. The lengths to which she'd gone to make her comfortable, and the adoption she'd arranged, Lupita dismissed initially as pressure from her niece and, later, as actions she was taking on behalf of her friend, Alice, to make sure she had a child. But when Lee came to her cottage the morning Dana drove her to the airport, there was something in her tone of voice and in the way she looked at her that suggested that she somehow knew the truth of how she'd become pregnant. It made no sense, but looking into Lee's face for just a few quick moments before she left, she'd felt like someone had recognized her.

Lupita did not have the words to thank her that day, but she found them eleven years later, after she'd secured a mortgage for the cottage on Weke Road with a combination of what Lee had given her and money she'd saved. She mailed a photograph of the house she'd taken with a Polaroid camera. On the back she wrote, *Dear Mrs. Beach, I did what you told me to do. Thank you.*

She also followed Lee's advice about work, getting jobs cleaning rooms at hotels initially, and after a while driving a taxi at night, too. Eventually, she bought her own car and left cleaning behind. At the time, there weren't many women driving taxis on the island and the hotel manager she'd been working for, a kind old pothead whose wife had been friendly to Lupita in her first year on the island, frequently cautioned her that it wasn't a safe line of work for a young woman. But in a car, driving, even on the job, was where Lupita was happiest, where she felt most in control. When she quit her job, he and his wife made her supper and promised to give out her card and send her work from the hotel, which they did, and after a slow start, she built up a steady business.

She was almost forty when a woman she'd cleaned with at the hotel asked her for a job. She was leaving her husband and needed extra money to afford an apartment. No one had ever asked Lupita for help before and though her first instinct was to say no, she remembered Lee, and Alice, even Dana, and how she was able to leave Wells and start a new life. So she helped the woman get her taxi driver's license and she leased another van. Over time, she hired more women—some she knew from around the island and others who'd heard she had jobs—and by the time she turned fifty-five she had seven vans, a garage, and a dispatcher.

As the taxi service grew, Lupita gradually became friends with a few of the women who worked for her. Some she let stay in the other bedroom in her cottage if they needed a place, others she lent money to and encouraged to go to school. When she turned sixty, a group of them—many who'd moved on to other jobs and marriages, and some who still worked for her—took her to dinner to celebrate. One of the women who'd driven for her for more than twenty-five years, whose daughter had recently started working for Lupita as a part-time dispatcher, gave a toast. She thanked Lupita for being *a good boss, a great friend, and the mother many of us needed*.

As for men, she kept to herself in the first jarring months, too frightened to speak to anyone before or after work. But she was new and young on the island, and she'd attracted a number of guys who were willing to keep her company and show her around. By the end of her first year, she began to get to know a few of them. Mostly they were employees at the hotel she worked in, a mix of local boys and men, runaways and transplants who worked as porters and lifeguards and assistant managers. Later, when she began to drive a taxi, they were mechanics and drivers and dispatchers. These were the people she knew, the ones she'd meet up with at the local restaurants and backyard barbecues. It was the quieter ones she gravitated toward. The guys who hadn't been overtly flirtatious, who didn't make passes right away. They were the ones she would occasionally develop feelings for, who seemed to sense exactly the right moment to make a move, and often she would not deflect. What happened after tended to follow a pattern: a cold shoulder, a friendly but distant wave or nod across parking lots and hotel lobbies, and then presumptuous late-night phone calls from bars. It surprised and hurt her the first few times, but then she calculated that these losses—familiar acquaintances and colleagues, not exactly friends—were ones she was willing to accept in exchange for an occasional connection that involved both affection and physical desire. This went on for years. But her energy for these encounters depleted and she became less willing to forfeit the relationships in order to have them. As a result, by her sixties she'd gathered a considerable group of men her age and younger who called her for her opinion on mechanical problems, advice with their girlfriends or wives, and whom she could reach out to for help, if needed. These were not intimates so much as friendly comrades who, over time, treated Lupita as one of the guys and not the token female they may have once been biding their time to have sex with.

The diminished frequency of late-night calls from bars also coincided with Lupita's attending evening classes at Kauai Community College in Lihue. After having her old transcripts from St. Margaret's faxed to the admissions office, she took her first class, statistics, the only one that worked with her schedule, in the fall of her forty-first year. The other students in the evening classes were mostly younger, but they had kids and jobs and some of them she knew from the hotels and the airport, and a few of them were women who worked for her.

After completing her associate's degree in Liberal Arts, which was the highest degree given at the college, she enrolled again, this time taking classes toward an associate's in Hawaiian Studies. These were the classes that excited her the most. It embarrassed her to realize she'd been living in Hawaii for more than three decades without knowing much about its language, ecology or history. Its history especially. She was upset by the conflicting accounts—many she found outside the curriculum—of the overthrow of the Hawaiian Kingdom in the late 1800s by a couple of American businessmen. She became fixated on Queen Liliuokalani and the circumstances of her arrest and abdication, as well as her failed attempts to recapture what had been taken. As Lupita learned more, she began to understand the resentments and outrage she'd seen and heard in Kauai through the years. Her new awareness coincided with what seemed like a surge of local fury around that history, agitated by a century-late official apology by the US government to native Hawaiians. She went to some of the rallies and town halls to understand better and even lend a voice. Because of the color of her hair and skin, some people assumed she was at least part native Hawaiian, but instead of making her feel welcome, she felt like an imposter, so she chose to root quietly from the sidelines.

When she received her second degree, Lupita framed it and put it on her kitchen wall next to the first. It was not the bachelor's degree she would have had at Albertus Magnus, but when she saw the two degrees hanging together she felt that something she'd lost had been reclaimed. She was sixty-two years old then, nearly the age she imagined Lee Beach would have been when Lupita had stayed on her farm. She knew that there was no possibility Lee was still alive, but it didn't stop her from wishing that there was some way she could know she'd graduated from college. Alice, too, who would appreciate what it meant to do something no one in her family had done before. But Lupita would never initiate contact with her. She would not risk disrupting the life of the boy who was now a man, and who was not hers.

* * *

The ocean has dulled to gray under the shadow of storm clouds. Above Lupita, they have streaked from mist, twisted and bloomed in the late-morning sun, gathered at the headlands and crowded the sky. After hours of treading water, floating, and pushing her arms through ragged half-strokes, she has come back through a break in the reef without cuts. She is safe in the shallows but can only see the smudge of open ocean, not the shore behind her that is only a few kicks and a tumble in the breaking waves away. Her lips are blistered and dry, her eyes on fire. Her arms drift down, her body bobs, and a wave curls above her, tucks her into the crook of its swirl and drags her under as it collapses. She plunges, rolls, is thrown. Her oldest memory of water returns, a stranger's legs swoosh through a current beneath her, and from somewhere in the terrible dark her mother whispers to stay silent.

Sand is the last thing she expects, but suddenly it's everywhere. Damp and granular in her fists, needling her shoulders, roughing her heels. A gentle wave slaps against the back of her neck like polite congratulations. She attempts to lift her torso, but when another, more forceful wave shoves her from behind, her elbows buckle and she topples forward. She panics in water that is only a few inches deep, her knees and legs scraping against broken shells and branches twined with seaweed. The water retreats and for the first time in hours her body is not submerged. She claws the grainy shore, brings it to her face to make sure it is real.

Lupita tries to stand but before she is up the world swerves and she drops back down on all fours, closes her eyes and does not move. Gradually, she crawls from damp to dry beach until she's stopped by the hard mass of a fallen tree. Here, she collapses, rolls onto her back and stretches her arms and legs as wide as they will reach. She inhales, deeply, and smells the air around her—briny and damp, musky with life and rot. She looks up into the dark, chalky sky and sees what she thinks are sea birds circling there, as if in slow motion. Gradually, on legs she can scarcely feel, she tries again to stand. A surge of blood rushes to her head and she stumbles, her joints flare with new pain. She steadies, and with eyes still stinging with the sea's salt, she registers the blurry world: the short beach, the dense copse of trees at its edge, the dark sky above it all. Rain taps her head and face, speckles her arms and hands. She does not know this beach, but she knows there is a path to the road somewhere. The tourists have found everything, invaded every untouched corner of the island by now, and this place is too perfect to be left alone. She cannot see the evidence but she knows it's there; the garbage she's seen wash ashore more and more with each decade: the soggy, sun-bleached cigarette carton, the half-full bottle of shampoo, the fouled diaper, the jagged glass from smashed beer bottles that will be swept out by the tide, destined to someday wash ashore, far from here, smoothed by time and ocean into something unrecognizable, beautiful.

Her legs bend under her, the movement of the ocean still lingering. She sits down on the sand, her back against what she can now recognize is an old Kiawe tree. She notices its massive root system exposed, dangling and coiled like an underground crown ripped to the surface by insurgent forces. Safe now, she grows drowsy. She can feel all the major and minor muscles in her back and shoulders begin to loosen. Waves hit the shore, hard, again and again, the sound she hears from her own bed at night, but closer. Against the dead tree she sleeps.

Hap

He's been standing under the Departures Board for close to an hour. After walking to Union Square from the diner near Dana's, he rode the 4 train to Grand Central without knowing what would come next. In his right hand he holds the card she slid across the table before leaving. It's white on one side and mint green on the other, Alice's least favorite color. *I can't stop you from seeing these people, but you shouldn't,* Dana had advised, but in pencil she still wrote down on each side what she said she would: names, towns. After she left, Hap looked, briefly.

When he got off the subway, it occurred to him to take Metro North to Wassaic and find a taxi to drive him the rest of the way to Wells. He could find his half-sister and brother, meet their mother, hike the trail to the cabin above the lake where Dana told him he'd been conceived. He could retrace the steps that led to his existence, bear the news to those who still did not know. He could do these things—part of him feels he must—but to what end? Does he want to dislodge people he's never met from their lives? Does he have a responsibility to? And what after? Find the woman who did not want him?

Going home seems as impossible now as it did six days ago when he rode in the ambulance with his father from the Hotel Bethlehem to the emergency room at St. Luke's. His cell phone died yesterday, but before it did one of Leah's many texts, which had collapsed in less than two days from fury to despair, described

297

exactly how he felt: *I don't know who you are right now. And I did not choose to do this alone. You are ruining everything*.

He flicks the edge of the card a few times and drags the pad of his thumb across its flat surface. If he takes the long journey to the place written there, he will find the woman who carried him in her body and brought him to the world. How many times did she hold him? Once? None? Had he ever felt the warmth and swarm of her? The home of her. Did that memory linger some-where, buried under everyone and everything that came after? He'd never know.

So much discovered in so few days, yet he's never felt so acutely aware of his ignorance. The mural had come down, but only to reveal another less complete, but more complicated one; one that would surely fall, too, and be discredited or trivialized by the one that came after. And on and on. Life appeared no more than a long, bleak unraveling, a stripping away of layers, like the skins of an onion, one by one, peeled back to expose what? The truth? Did it always end in nothing? Was there only a space the layers folded around that held no meaning beyond the years it took to arrive there?

In the briefcase, there had been papers gathered in folders he'd shuffled through quickly at first, wary of what he might see. There were the marriage and divorce papers between Alice and his father. And there were names he did not know—Lupita Ange-les Lopez, Dana Isabel Goss. But as he looked more closely at what looked like adoption papers, he recognized his own, and below it, next to his parents' signatures, the date April 15, 1970, almost three months before he was born. Another set of his papers listed his birthday as March 10. His head spun and his eyes shut and for a long time he sat on the floor of his father's apartment and willed his mind to go completely blank.

Eventually, he'd forced himself to look through the rest of the papers. A bulging green folder with "Dana Goss" written near the top held a strange assortment: a still-glossy Sotheby's catalog for an auction titled "Property from the Estate of George and Annabelle Goss" which featured pages of early American furniture, paintings and jewelry; and six three-by-five index cards covered with addresses, one after another—London, Santa Barbara, Paris, La Jolla, Chicago—each written in different shades of black and blue ink but all in his father's crisp, rigorously clear handwriting. Every one was crossed out but the last one, in New York City, on West Eleventh Street. The next morning, he'd dialed the number written neatly below the zip code from a payphone at a diner on Sixth Avenue.

This makes no sense, he'd said, again and again, sitting across from the woman who had turned up less than fifteen minutes after he'd called. He watched her elegant fingers balled into fists, one upon the other, pressing into the tabletop as if she were holding a small pepper grinder. The one on the bottom moved slowly inward, toward her body, and the one on top remained fixed, applying what looked like great pressure. The papers were spread out on the table between them, the opened briefcase beside her on the booth seat. She told him to be quiet. That he needed to listen. And that once she'd finished, he needed to move on. That none of what she had to tell him could possibly matter to him now.

Hap passes the card between his fingers like a magician and looks up at the terminal ceiling. How had he not seen it when he first arrived? The enormous dome painted aqua blue and on it in gold a long cloud of stars bisected by the symbols of the zodiac. The raised club and winged horse remind him of Mo, and the tarot cards he used to read to his mother and their friends. He kept them wrapped in a gauzy red fabric in his sock drawer and would become suddenly serious when he'd ask the person he was reading for to shuffle the deck, cut it in half, and pick the cards he'd then arrange with mathematical precision on the kitchen table. Occasionally, Mo offered to read Hap's cards, but he declined every time. When the tarot came out, Hap steered clear and scoffed at the silliness of reading the future in arbitrary symbols. He wonders now if he'd agreed, even once, what the cards might have said. Would they have told him that most of what he thought he knew was not true? That he'd been raised on lies, and that he'd live more than half his life before finding out? If he'd heard these things then, would he have believed them? Surely not.

What he did know, with biting clarity, was that not only had he lacked the attention to notice the many clues scattered before him since he was a boy, but he'd been so relentlessly uncurious and absent of imagination that it never occurred to him to ask the people around him the most basic questions. Who are you? Where do you come from? What matters to you? Some journalist he turned out to be. No wonder it had been so easy to leave the newspaper.

He searches the vast ceiling for a crab, the symbol of his birth sign, Leah told him on their second or third date. He already knew more than he wanted to about the zodiac. Mo talked about it often, read horoscopes from the paper, used the excuse of Mercury in Retrograde to explain lost bills, missing keys, and sent packages that never arrived. As well, an old girlfriend had given Hap a slim book as a gift one Christmas when he was in high school called *Cancer*. He'd read it, but he never told her. And he pretended to Leah that he was hearing for the first time that he was very empathetic, likely to be moody, hypersensitive, and someone who tended to isolate from others. He hadn't identified with any of it. Why hadn't he told her the truth, Hap wonders now. Something about Mo's mystical side, more than a decade after his death, must have still embarrassed him, the same way his nut milks and meditations always had. But also it surprised Hap that Leah was so interested in such things. She was such a type A academic, her star at Penn clearly on the rise. Most likely he just wanted to hear a younger woman he was attracted to but hadn't yet kissed explain why he was the way he was. It was hard to remember what it was like having such a crush on her, to be so intimidated and flattered and hopeful. But even that night, he remembers, after she told him that he was probably a big dreamer but sloppy with details, he couldn't help but think that most of it was just a racket. Crystals, psychics, astrology—stories hung like shiny ornaments from the stars, the sun, the moon, sweeping across the sky with needy believers chasing behind who took them for truths. There is nothing we won't pin a story to, Hap thinks, his eyes following the gathered stars of the Milky Way to a ram, a bull, a fish. Still, he can't help but wonder which sign of the zodiac he belongs to now.

He'd been told on a field trip once that the night sky depicted here was reversed, not the view from the earth as we see it, but the one that appears to God when he looks down on it all from above. *The other side of the sky*, he remembers someone saying—in his class then, or maybe later—and the words spark an image of the entire universe captured in a snow globe, swirling and observable, like a toy an arm's length away. The idea momentarily relaxes him. All the mystery and complication in one small, held space. He tries to imagine his life this way, his forty-eight years in the palm of his hand, and as he does he can't help but be appalled by the boy, young man and adult who carried on, solipsistic and oblivious, for so many years. He'd gotten it wrong with Mo, with Christopher, whoever he was; and he was getting it wrong right now, with Alice and Leah and his daughter. One week ago he walked into St. Luke's to become a father only to return two days later to lose one. And he's been stumbling ever since. To where? An enormous gold room filled with no one he knows, standing under a painted sky that only God can see.

Hap feels the card wedged between his middle and ring finger. He bends it there until its surfaces give way to a crease. With his other hand he pinches it tightly and folds it again, pressing with force each corner to keep it from opening. He pulls his wallet from his jeans and begins to tuck the folded card in the empty gap behind the place where he keeps his driver's license, credit cards, and expired IDs. All the cards that up until now have told him who he is and was. Student, reporter, Lafayette Bank customer, Planet Fitness member, resident of Pennsylvania. Before he closes the wallet, he hesitates. Putting the card here makes the information written on it feel real, official. He pulls the card out, closes his fist around it.

At the center of the terminal, the clock with four round, bright faces shows the long hand at twelve and the short hand leaving six. Hap feels his heart accelerate. He thinks of his daughter and counts back the days that have passed since she was born. Does she still not have a name, or has Leah made the decision without him? He lets himself imagine how angry and bewildered his wife must feel and as he does the extremity of his failure pierces. He starts fumbling for the cell phone in his back pocket but remembers the dead battery. He's not even certain she and his daughter are still where he left them, with Alice.

Alice. Had he thanked her yet for inviting him and his family to live in her house, for helping with the baby? He didn't think so. Alice was nearly seventy-three. Mo was forty-one—seven years younger than Hap now—when he died. Alice, Mo, Christopher, Leah, his daughter, the regrets were piling higher by the second. He had messed up and missed so much.

Hap closes his wallet and shoves it in the front pocket of the jeans he's worn since the morning Leah went into labor. He sneezes, twice, in rapid succession. And then again, violently. He braces for another but it does not come. He closes his eyes and without planning to he holds his breath, Alice's old trick to prevent a relapse of hiccups. His nose itches and with his wrinkled sleeve he rubs harder and longer than he needs to, and behind his eyelids flash pinpricks of light. A drowsy wave crashes up and down his body and when it recedes he steadies himself against the wall. He closes his eyes again, feels the cool marble at his back and sinks to a seated position. Maybe he hadn't been misled. Perhaps the truth, the thing he'd been so desperate to pin down since he arrived in New York, was that his life was exactly how it had appeared. He opens his eyes and scans the room. From the floor, the terminal appears larger, more hectic with strangers pushing across their jagged trajectories. He remembers the hour, the time of day when most people leave work and rush home to their families. He looks up again at the painted sky. His wife needs him. His daughter does not know him. His mother is taking care of them both, now, just as she took care of him.

Hap stands away from the wall. Beyond the clock, at the top of a long inclining corridor, he sees an exit. As he moves toward it, his shoulders and arms get bumped and knocked and when he feels the folded card slip from his fingers he does not stop. The last light of the day blasts from the doors and overwhelms the particulars of the people crowded there. He sees their shadows spill and wriggle on the marble floor and he joins them. At the door, he feels the warm sun on his face. He will follow it west to the Port Authority bus station, and in that shabby terminal find the first bus home. Nothing has ever felt so simple, so clean and good and right. His hands are empty.

Lupita

She dreams. It's the same dream she's started hundreds of times since she came to the island. In it, she's alone, standing at the edge of a river, the one she grew up next to but never swam in, never toed into or explored. Dana and Jackie's realm, where Lupita watched them linger at twilight, spinning tales of hidden treasure and wood trolls as they pulled rocks from the water and held them up to the setting sun. She steps in and feels the icy water chill her heel and toes and grab at her ankle, but before she submerges her second foot, a voice booms from the wood-line, commanding her to stop. In an instant, she's away from the water, onto the lawn, running for what feels like her life. Here is where the dream has always ended.

But this time, when Lupita takes her first step into the river, the water is warm and there is no voice. She wades in, slowly, despite her fear. The water feels soft against her skin, soothing, and the deeper she goes, the more relaxed she becomes. A warm rain begins to fall and with it she notices the faint smell of roses and lavender.

She can see the big house—its old vines climbing the columns and walls, crossing the lifeless windows. The water begins to creep up the lawn and the rain falls harder. The river rises around her, caresses her neck and face. Lupita feels her feet leave the stony riverbed and soon she is floating. Huge swells surge from upriver and crash onto the lawn, but she is not swept away. Instead, she moves with ease in the current, treads in place as the waves become enormous. She watches them lap against the long porch, past the columns that flank the house, and rise quickly up the steps to the window ledges.

As she watches the water inch past the second floor windows and approach the roofline, she suddenly wants nothing more than to stand on top of the house before it's swallowed. With all her strength, she swims. The current is with her, and in what feels like only a few seconds, she approaches the chimney, the one she watched smoke curl from in the winter when she was young and wondered if Santa Claus would dive down on Christmas Eve even though the Gosses were in Florida. It mattered a great deal to her that he might make two visits to one family, that Dana could actually be given two sets of presents, have two stockings filled, receive two letters from Santa telling her she'd been a good girl that year. It seemed impossibly unfair.

Lupita grabs at the chimney. The brick feels like sand in her hands, flimsy and fast vanishing. She does her best to hold on and steady her feet, but she slips and wobbles on the slate roof as the water rises above her waist. Before she's submerged, she hoists herself up and straddles the edges of two of the six chimney pots. They are a tawny ceramic that darkens when wet and beneath her feet they look like drowning flesh. She watches the river invade and overwhelm them and she has no pity. The water rises, pulls her up and off, and soon there is no roof, no house, no trace of what was there. Around her there is nothing but raging water, foam and fury. Unafraid, she drifts.

The chop eventually calms, the rain ceases, and the water becomes crystal clear under a sky now brilliant with stars and a high, bright moon. Beneath her, Lupita sees what appears to be a vast ship taking shape and slowly rising toward the surface. When the deck meets her feet and the schooner is fully atop the water, the wind stirs, the great sails billow, and she feels the vessel begin to move. Quickly, it gains speed and explodes forward, catching air and streaking across the water like the flat stones she watched her father fling into the river when he didn't think anyone was watching. It was the only time she ever saw him do something that had no purpose but pleasure. And never for very long. Three or four rocks skipped toward the distant bank and then back to work, or home, mumbling imperceptibly as he went, pipe smoke curling behind him.

The ship moves fast toward far away, its sails are full, stretched to bursting. Below, for her, the river spills its secrets—rubies and sapphires, diamonds and emeralds—millions of them, catching the moonlight, glinting beneath the surface like underwater fireworks. Above the prow, Lupita grips the wooden railing with both hands. She has no plan, no destination; there is nothing she wants, not one thing she fears. Her body feels as light as paper.

The river widens. The ship surges forward. Soon there is only open ocean, limitless and welcoming. Waves curl and collapse on all sides, spraying her clothes, tickling her skin. She is a girl again, squinting into the wind and water, and someone is beside her.

Acknowledgments

Huge thanks to my editor, Wendy Sheanin, for showing up, again and again, with patience and rigor and enthusiasm. My publisher, Jen Bergstrom, who is as fun and kind as she is brilliant. Aimee Bell and Jackie Cantor at Scout for wise editorial counsel as well as encouragement. And Carolyn Reidy, who writes the best cards, among her many other superpowers. Ongoing gratitude to the indomitable and peerless Kimberly Burns, and to Lauren Truskowski and Sally Marvin. Paula Amendolara, Gary Urda, Tracy Nelson, Colin Shields in sales, and Abby Zidle, Anne Jaconette, Bianca Salvant, and Anabel Jimenez in marketing for working their respective magics. Lisa Litwack for going the distance on the jacket. Boundless gratitude to Sara Quaranta for so effortlessly directing traffic and to John Paul Jones for accommodating every last change. Robin Robertson at Cape for key notes at several crucial stages, and for ongoing faith. Marie-Pierre Gracedieu, Luiz Schwarcz, Otavio Marques da Costa, Anna Flotaker, and Beatrice Masini for continued belief and careful stewardship. Tracy Fisher, her team at WME and Claudia Ballard for evergreen excellence. For the true blue who read at various stages (some more than once): Lisa Story, Adam McLaughlin, Susannah Meadows, Pauls Toutonghi, Marion Duvert, Karen Kosztolnyik, Emma Sweeney, Jill Bialosky, Lena Dunham, Sarah Shun-lien Bynum, Kassie Evashevski, and Taylor Beck. Boundless gratitude to the team at TCA (present and past): Chris Clemans, Lilly Sandberg, Griffin Irvine, David Khambu, Raeden Richardson, and especially Simon

Toop for exacting but somehow always cheerful feedback, and for balancing all the many spinning plates on poles. Thanks to Diana Rico-Morales for a close read and critical insights, and to Carmen Hage-Vassallo for meticulous notes and suggestions. And to Cecilia Martinez-Gil, much gratitude for chiming in so selflessly in the final hour. As well to Julia G. Young for being so generous with your time and expertise on mid-century immigration from Mexico into the United States, and for pointing me in the direction of invaluable resources. And in every capacity, and for the very first green light, gratitude and love to Jennifer Rudolph Walsh. Lastly, and most importantly, to Van Scott, my partner in all things, without whom this book would not have been written.

THE END

OF THE

DAY

Bill Clegg

This reading group guide for *The End of The Day* includes an introduction, discussion questions, and ideas for enhancing your book club. The suggested questions are intended to help your reading group find new and interesting angles and topics for your discussion. We hope that these ideas will enrich your conversation and increase your enjoyment of the book.

Introduction

Following his acclaimed *New York Times* bestseller, *Did You Ever Have a Family*, Bill Clegg returns with a deeply moving, emotionally resonant second novel about the complicated bonds and breaking points of friendship, the corrosive forces of secrets, the heartbeat of longing, and the redemption found in forgiveness.

Many seemingly disconnected lives come together as half-century-old secrets begin to surface. It is in this moment that Bill Clegg reminds us how choices—to connect, to betray, to protect—become our legacy.

Topics and Questions for Discussion

1. *The End of the Day* is told through many different perspectives: Dana, Jackie, Lupita, Floyd, Alice, and Hap. Whose voice did you most identify with and why? Did your opinion of any of the characters change throughout the story?

2. When we first meet Dana, she is annoyed by her staff, most particularly by a woman named Marcella, whom she describes as patronizing. Do you think she is? Why do you think Marcella has to approach Dana in this way?

3. Edgeweather is described in many different ways throughout the book, both as a crumbling home with only one tenant and a grand estate. Discuss how the house mirrors the characters' own personal lives throughout the novel.

4. Jackie's mother says about Dana and her family that "Those people . . . they don't treat people the way we do" (pg. 20). Jackie shares this with Dana while mocking her mom, though she admits that it's partially true. What do you think Jackie's mother meant by that? Do you think she knew more information about the Goss family than she lets on?

5. Why do you think it took Hap until his father's death to realize that his family was hiding something? What do you think he did with all the information that Dana tells him?

6. Hap and Gene are childhood friends, who have grown apart. "No longer playing any of the important roles he'd played since they were boys—trusted ally, fierce rival, finisher of sentences, co-creator of secret languages, relentless corruptor, conscience, confessor, penitent, defender, witness, brother" (pg. 133). Why do you think Hap feels loyalty to continue to be friends with Gene? Compare the friendship between Hap and Gene with the friendship between Dana and Jackie.

7. Lupita finds freedom in the feeling of driving Dana's yellow convertible and even wearing Dana's clothes without her knowledge. What do you think Lupita found in this experience? How does her relationship change with Dana's possessions (the car, robe, and her room) throughout the book?

8. When Jackie is reflecting on why she didn't confront Dana when they were young, she considers the tenuousness of friendships. "No lawyer or judge, mediator or priest needed. Not to make it, nor to unmake it, which requires even less. To end a friendship, it just takes someone willing to throw it away" (pg. 211). What do you think of Jackie's perspective on friendship? Do you think Jackie and Dana would have remained friends if Floyd hadn't come between them?

9. When Jackie confronts Dana years later, Dana doesn't correct Jackie's belief that she slept with Floyd. Dana states, "You're right . . . I was jealous. And angry . . . I loved you . . ." (pg 256). Why do you think Dana doesn't mention Lupita?

10. Dana keeps Lupita's secret from Jackie. Why do you think Dana remained loyal to Lupita? Do you think she had an ulterior motive or was protecting her best friend? Why do you think Dana invited Lupita to her Fourth of July picnic?

11. Why do you think Clegg chose to end the story on Lupita's perspective? What do you think the ship that Lupita finally boards means? Who do you imagine is beside her?

12. The story weaves together characters from very different backgrounds whose lives overlap in various ways. What choices do you think unite characters who are otherwise very dissimilar? Which pairing of characters surprised you most?

Enhance Your Book Club

1. *The End of the Day* shows the many ways that families and friends' lives can intersect across generations. Create a family tree of the characters in the book. Which relationships do you think are strongest? Which fracture throughout the novel?

2. Lupita flees to Kauai where she finds she is able to rebuild her life far from New York. Why do you think Lupita is drawn to Hawaii in particular? What locations would members in your book club choose to live other than your current one?

3. Through the novel, character make choices (both seemingly small and large) that will affect the course of their lives. Assign each member of your book club a character (Dana, Jackie, Lupita, Floyd, Alice, and Hap) and have them identify what they think is the defining choice in their character's story. How did their character's choice impact the rest of the story?